William Barton Rogers, Emma Savage Rogers, William Thompson Sedgwick

Life and Letters of William Barton Rogers

Vol. I

William Barton Rogers, Emma Savage Rogers, William Thompson Sedgwick

Life and Letters of William Barton Rogers
Vol. I

ISBN/EAN: 9783744673938

Printed in Europe, USA, Canada, Australia, Japan

Cover: Foto ©Raphael Reischuk / pixelio.de

More available books at **www.hansebooks.com**

LIFE AND LETTERS

OF

WILLIAM BARTON ROGERS

EDITED BY HIS WIFE

**WITH THE ASSISTANCE
OF WILLIAM T. SEDGWICK**

IN TWO VOLUMES

VOLUME I

The Riverside Press

PREFACE.

THESE volumes have been prepared in the hope that Mr. Rogers's life, work and character as revealed in his letters, may be of some service to the cause of science and education, and especially to the officers, graduates and students of the Massachusetts Institute of Technology, to whom this Memoir is dedicated. Certain subjects, such as those dealing with educational and scientific matters or with the early history of the Institute, have accordingly been treated in more detail than would otherwise have seemed desirable.

No life of Mr. Rogers would be in any degree adequate which did not include much of the lives of his three brothers who, with similar tastes, and pursuits almost identical with his own, occupied so large a share of his thought and affection.

The materials at command have been voluminous, and we have had difficulty in making the necessary selections. Many of the letters given have been taken not from those actually sent, but from a first draft which was kept as a copy. Our aim has been to add to the letters only so much of editorial comment as should serve to make a connected history. The geological letters, as well as those on other scientific subjects, are given as showing the direction of Mr. Rogers's researches rather than the more correct conclusions to which these may have led.

We are indebted to many friends for permission to use letters; to others for aid in solving doubts and removing difficulties; and, for the careful preservation of documents, to Professor S. W. Holman, who has long had in contemplation the preparation of a history of the Massachusetts Institute of Technology.

CONTENTS.

CHAPTER I.

ANCESTRY.

CHAPTER II.

YOUTH AND EARLY MANHOOD.

1804–1828.

CHAPTER III.

PROFESSOR OF NATURAL PHILOSOPHY AND CHEMISTRY AT WIL-LIAM AND MARY COLLEGE.

1828–1835.

CHAPTER IV.

PROFESSOR OF NATURAL PHILOSOPHY IN THE UNIVERSITY AND
DIRECTOR OF THE GEOLOGICAL SURVEY OF VIRGINIA.

1835–1842.

CHAPTER V.

PROFESSOR OF NATURAL PHILOSOPHY AND FOR ONE YEAR CHAIR-
MAN OF THE FACULTY IN THE UNIVERSITY OF VIRGINIA.

1842–1846.

CHAPTER VI.

PROFESSOR OF NATURAL PHILOSOPHY AND FOR ONE YEAR CHAIR-
MAN OF THE FACULTY IN THE UNIVERSITY OF VIRGINIA (*continued*).

1846-1853.

CHAPTER VII.

FIRST YEARS IN BOSTON.

1853-1859.

APPENDIX.

LIST OF ILLUSTRATIONS.

LIFE AND LETTERS OF
WILLIAM BARTON ROGERS.

CHAPTER I.

ANCESTRY.

William Barton Rogers. — His Brothers. — His Father Patrick Kerr Rogers. — The Rogers Family in Ireland. — Emigration of Patrick Kerr Rogers to America. — His Life in Philadelphia. — His Marriage. — Removal to Baltimore. — Appointment to the Professorship of Natural Philosophy and Chemistry in William and Mary College. — His Death in 1828.

WILLIAM BARTON ROGERS was born in Philadelphia on the 7th of December, 1804. His father was Patrick Kerr Rogers, afterwards Professor of Natural Philosophy and Chemistry in William and Mary College at Williamsburg, Va. His mother was Hannah Blythe, who died in Williamsburg in 1820 and left four sons between the ages of seven and eighteen. Of these the eldest was James Blythe, and the second William Barton, the subject of this memoir. The third son was Henry Darwin, who owed his middle name to the esteem of his father for Erasmus Darwin, grandfather of the famous author of "The Origin of Species." The fourth son was Robert, who afterwards assumed the middle name of Empie out of regard for the Rev. Adam Empie, for several years President of William and Mary College.

These four sons of Patrick Kerr Rogers and Hannah Blythe all achieved distinction in science. They are often referred to as "the brothers Rogers." They were all Americans by birth and education, but their ancestry was a blending of Irish, Scotch and English. Their father came from the North of Ireland not far from Londonderry. He was born in 1776, the eldest son of Robert Rogers of Edergole.

" Robert Rogers, the fourth of the name in lineal descent, was born about the year 1753, and lived on the Edergole or Knockbrack estate, which he owned in fee, and held, on lease, acres of land adjoining. This estate lies between Omagh and Fintano, in Tyrone County, Ireland. Newtown Stewart, in the barony of Strabane, then a good market for cloth and yarn,[1] ten miles off, is the nearest town, and Londonderry, forty miles distant, the nearest city. The number of his tenants, or extent of acreage held by him, is not now known. His social grade in the community is not indicated by his estate alone. When the Presbyterian Church which he attended was reconstructed, he rebuilt and furnished anew the large central pew which he had inherited. He was disposed to favour what was then termed the New-Light doctrine, but tolerant enough to listen to the religious and political opinions ascribed to the French philosophers.

" In the small villages and rural districts of Ireland at that period — more than a hundred years ago — those whose wardrobe was limited to a single suit and an extra shirt or two (and they were largely in the majority there, as well as everywhere) determined social position in the community by the interval between the family wash-days. In their estimation, those whose wardrobe was extensive enough to have their washing done once a year constituted the ' great families,' and

[1] *Statistical Survey of the County of Tyrone for 1801-1802*, by John McEvoy. Dublin, 1802.

those who needed to have a family wash-day every six
months composed the second class in society. The
washing of the Rogers family was done but twice a
year by the house-women and tenants at the brook
which flows through the estate.

" In the winter of 1774–75, when twenty-one years
old, Robert Rogers married Sarah Kerr, of about the
same age, who, tradition avers, was sprightly, conspicuous in conversation, and ever ready to discuss and
advocate the New-Light doctrines of the Presbyterian
Church, of which she was a member. This marriage
had been delayed a year by her father, a recognized
' gentleman ' in the community, who insisted that
Robert Rogers must attain his majority before he
could lawfully make a marriage settlement of all his
lands upon the children of this union in equal shares,
and that without compliance with this stipulation his
assent would not be given.

" Robert Rogers was a well-to-do Irish gentleman, liberal in his views, hospitable, convivial and duly appre-
ciative of education and learning." [1]

He was himself the youngest son of Robert Rogers
of Edergole, who died about 1772. The last will of
the latter, dated June 14, 1769, is still extant, and
from this it appears that his eldest son was James;
his youngest, as already stated, Robert; and his
daughters, Elizabeth, Mary, Jean and Margaret.
His land fell to the two sons, Robert retaining one
portion, and James that part known as Knockbrack
and Sheep-hill. A document has been preserved
showing that on November 8, 1786, James leased
Knockbrack to his brother Robert for sixty-one years,

---

[1] *Memorial of the Brothers Rogers*, read before the American Philo-
sophical Society of Philadelphia, November 6, 1885. By W. S. W.
Ruschenberger, M. D. Dr. Ruschenberger obtained these facts from
Mr. Alexander Rogers of Baltimore, a cousin of W. B. Rogers.

at an annual rental of £24 7*s.* 6*d.* Concerning the
Rogers family, it is further stated

"that, prior to the year 1641, they preserved the
Bowling Green of Strabane and four townlands on
the left bank of the Fin (their title was lodged in the
castle of Strabane when burned by the O'Neils about
1642); that, in the troubles which afterwards ensued,
they went to Lanarkshire, in Scotland; that about
the year 1650 one brother, named William, returned
and settled at Edergole, near Ballinahatty. He is
known to have had four sons, namely, James, John,
William and Alexander. John had sons, John (who
got the family place at Edergole), William (who got
Scotch Drum and Lower Edergole) and Alexander."[1]

The life of Patrick Kerr Rogers, father of William
Barton Rogers, is full of interest.

"He was the firstborn, in 1776, of the twelve children of Robert Rogers and his wife Sarah Kerr. Four
of them died in infancy. The rudiments of Patrick's
education were received in a schoolhouse built upon
the estate. It is described as having had clay walls,
a thatched roof, clay seats covered with bits of carpet,
and as warmed by a turf fire. The teacher was a
lame rustic boy, whom his aunt, Margaret Rogers, a
lady of notable intelligence, had trained for the office.
His classical learning was acquired under the tuition
of an uncle, a clergyman. His mother died in 1790,
and his father married, in 1791, a second wife who
bore him three sons and two daughters.

"At the age when he should choose a profession he
found himself one of a numerous family of brothers
and sisters, and, though the eldest, without the right
of primogeniture in his father's estate. Entertaining

---

[1] Letter of Andrew Rogers, at Glenfern, to John Rogers at Glennock, Newtown Stewart, and by him forwarded to W. B. Rogers, at
Boston, September, 1858.

opinions not rigidly orthodox, he was unwilling to enter the clerical profession, though he had the example of two uncles. At the time, a commercial career seemed best, and he therefore entered a counting-house in Dublin. How long he lived there, or was thus employed, has not been ascertained. But about the time of the Irish Rebellion, which broke out in May, 1798, he contributed to Dublin newspapers articles hostile to the government which, his friends believed, were likely to cause his arrest." [1]

A kinsman, Alexander Rogers of Hill-head, having supplied the necessary means, he fled to Londonderry and sailed for America, arriving in Philadelphia, after a passage of eighty-four days, in August, 1798. At that time there were many Irish refugees in Philadelphia. Mr. Rogers evidently made his way rapidly, for only a few months afterwards we find him appointed as a tutor in the University of Pennsylvania.

In the winter of 1799 he was admitted to the Pennsylvania Hospital as a student of the eminent Drs. Benjamin Smith Barton and Benjamin Rush, and to certain medical lectures of the University of Pennsylvania by Drs. Shippen and Wistar. He attended also lectures on chemistry in 1799 and 1800 by Dr. James Woodhouse. During these years a warm friendship existed between him and his preceptor, Dr. Barton, to whom he dedicated his graduating thesis, and after whom he named his second son William Barton Rogers. While still in the medical school he was married, January 2, 1801, to Hannah Blythe, "an intelligent woman, a year older than himself, endowed with a cheerful and affectionate disposition."

" Patrick K. Rogers is described as a tall, erect

[1] Ruschenberger.

man, of grave deportment, having dark hair well
sprinkled with gray, and soft, sleepy eyes. He played
the violin and sang well, but never in company, or in
the presence of strangers, because such performance
or display seemed to him inconsistent with the dignity
of a gentleman.

"Hannah Blythe was the youngest daughter of
James Blythe, a native of Glasgow but a resident
of Londonderry, and his wife Bessie, a daughter of
James Bell, a mathematical-instrument maker and
an English citizen of Londonderry. James Blythe
was a publisher and stationer. He founded, in 1772,
the 'Londonderry Journal,' the first tri-weekly paper
printed in the North of Ireland. It became a daily,
and is still published. . . . The paper was printed
and issued from the house in which he lived. His
daughter, Mrs. Ramsay, who died in Baltimore at the
advanced age of ninety-two years, often mentioned,
among the reminiscences of her early childhood, the
gathering of a crowd reading a placard on the front
of their house, headed 'BLOODY NEWS FROM AMER-
ICA,' announcing the battle of Lexington, April, 1775.
She also stated that many Protestant citizens rejoiced
over this resistance of Americans to the British rule.

"James Blythe died in 1787, leaving a widow and
three daughters, Elizabeth, Mary Ann and Hannah.
The widow, Bessie Bell, who was an intelligent and
energetic woman, removed to Strabane, about fifteen
miles southward from Londonderry, took into partnership a foreman from the old establishment, and set
up and conducted a newspaper till she died in 1794.
The business was unprofitable. The daughters were
left without support. They promptly determined to
emigrate, embarked in a ship belonging to their
cousin, Adam Crampton, of Londonderry, and, after
a voyage of three months, arrived in Philadelphia.
They were received by their cousin, wife of Thomas
Moore, merchant, who had left Coleraine some time
before on account of his affiliation with the 'United

Irishmen.' These daughters are described as active, intelligent women, and being, like most ladies of that period, proficient in the use of the needle, with it supported themselves respectably and independently.

"In May, 1802, Mr. P. K. Rogers received the degree of Doctor of Medicine from the University of Pennsylvania. His thesis on *Liriodendron tulipifera* (the tulip-tree), in which he records the results of experimental observations of its chemical and therapeutic properties, was printed and is extant. A son, James Blythe, the eldest of the brothers Rogers, was born in Philadelphia, February 11, 1802. The city directory for 1802 states that P. K. Rogers, M. D., lived at No. 55 Lombard Street, implying that he had established a home for himself very soon after his marriage." [1]

In 1803 Robert Rogers, the father of Patrick and grandfather of William Barton Rogers, died, and Dr. P. K. Rogers, being the eldest son, returned in the same year to Ireland to adjust the family affairs. This duty occupied nearly a year, after which he returned to Philadelphia, bringing with him two of his younger brothers. Among his papers is a ticket to a medical course in the University of Pennsylvania, dated 1805, and bearing the name of Mr. Frederick Rogers. This may have been one of these brothers. Meanwhile his second son, William Barton Rogers, was born. At this time the family was living at 262 North Second Street, probably between Vine and Callow Hill streets, and the family fortunes were at a low ebb. Among Dr. P. K. Rogers's papers is a brief autobiographical statement which, unfortunately, is limited to this period of his life and the trying years which followed. The paper, which bears no date, and begins and ends

[1] Ruschenberger.

abruptly, was apparently written in Baltimore about 1817. It is as follows: —

"In the year 1803 I was engaged in full business in Philadelphia as a physician, and the products of my practice were more than equal to my current expenses. But I was encumbered with small debts to a considerable aggregate amount, perhaps three thousand dollars, gradually contracted during the first years of my professional and family establishment. My father dying in 1803, I thought it important to go to Ireland to adjust family affairs, and to obtain that share of property to which I was entitled. I was barely able to bring to Philadelphia, after an absence of almost a year, as much money as paid my debt. This agreeable business I performed promptly, and when done I had neither money nor an establishment.

"It being difficult in the medical profession to make a second beginning in the same place (and I was wedded to the place by a thousand attachments), I was never able afterwards to procure a share of business equal to the expenses of my family, however moderated. Other aids were sought to make good the deficiency, but they only served to involve me more rapidly in debt.

"A medical library appeared to be a thing wanted at the seat of medical learning. Some respectable booksellers advised me to undertake the enterprise as one not calculated to interrupt my professional exertions in any great degree. They were sanguine and liberal in aiding this establishment, and several thousand volumes were speedily arranged. The library was not supported, and in less than two years I begged to return the books as the only measure that would enable me to do them any degree of justice. Many of the works were more valuable than salable; all were said to be somewhat injured. Except about two hundred volumes, all were returned, and I allowed the booksellers damages. The library room, fixtures,

damages and contingent expenses left me in debt at least four thousand dollars.

"Previous to and during these transactions, I was engaged in giving lectures on the practice of medicine, in the winter season, yearly. On the death of Dr. Woodhouse, I applied for the chemical chair in the University of Pennsylvania, but I had not a sufficient number of patrons in the board of trustees. My scientific friends thought I had a claim more just and reasonable than that which is founded on family connections, and accordingly they urged me to relinquish the practical lectures, and prepare a full course on chemistry for a popular audience.[1] I complied. Apparatus, and the appropriation of much time to experiments for demonstration, involved me in more debt and undermined my practice. For some years I experienced the most pungent anxiety on account of my circumstances. Sensibility to reputation, and the dread of a species of disgrace attached to insolvent persons, prevented me from seeking relief in the humane and benevolent institutes of our country.

"Several of my creditors, interested for my happiness and the welfare of my family, advised me to remove to Baltimore or New York and resume the exercise of my profession, believing I would not be harassed, as the more importunate had already stripped me of effects. I was left without even the necessary accommodations for a house and family, as furniture and kitchen utensils.

"In Baltimore I have sought repose of mind and subsistence for my family. The latter I have found; the former has, during more than four years' residence in this city, been interrupted only by the importunities and suits of my Philadelphia creditors. I again feel the terrible condition of a debtor destitute of

---

[1] Perhaps the first series of popular lectures on chemistry given in this country, — certainly the first, or one of the first, to which ladies were admitted.

resources, while looked to by a numerous family for support.

"A considerable part of my debt was contracted with friends, — real friends, who never intended to coerce, much less distress me. Some of them are no more, and their descendants are not at liberty to act as the deceased would have done. Others have failed in trade, and their claims have passed into the hands of trustees for the benefit of their creditors. From either class of original creditors or their successors it is now impossible to obtain assent to a general release."

During these years three children were born, — a third son, Henry Darwin, August 1, 1808, and two daughters, both of whom died in infancy.

In 1808 the family lived at 205 Mulberry (now Arch) Street, Philadelphia. From 1809 to 1812 they lived at 13 South Ninth Street, where they remained until their removal to Baltimore. The fourth son, Robert, was born in Baltimore, March 29, 1813. A fifth son, Alexander, born May 4, 1815, died a few years later.

In 1810 Dr. Rogers published an outline of a course of lectures entitled "A Syllabus of a Course of Lectures on Natural Philosophy and Chemistry, with the Application of the Latter to Several of the Arts."

"It may not be improper for me to mention that between the years 1808 and 1811 I delivered several courses of lectures on chemistry and natural philosophy in Philadelphia, some of which were attended throughout (no doubt for amusement, or from courteous or friendly motives) by the director of the mint, Robert Patterson, and several of the professors of the University of Pennsylvania." [1]

---

[1] Letter of P. K. Rogers to Thomas Jefferson, May 21, 1819.

Dr. Rogers removed to Baltimore about the end of 1812.

"At first he lived at 15 Market Street, Fell's Point, where he had an apothecary's shop, and subsequently at 68 South Charles Street. He was elected physician of the Hibernian Society in 1816. The same year it was charged that 'Dr. P. K. Rogers, at Fell's Point, persists in the use of variolous matter in preference to vaccine, against the public remonstrance of Dr. James Smith.' [1] The controversy on this question carried on in the newspapers was detrimental to his professional business." [2]

It does not appear, however, that his opinions on vaccination did him lasting injury, for on June 7, 1819, he was elected by the Maryland Medico-Chirurgical Society their "orator" for the next year, 1820.

In the letter of May 21, 1819, to which reference has already been made, Dr. P. K. Rogers applied to Thomas Jefferson for a professorship in the newly established University of Virginia. He received from Mr. Jefferson the following reply : —

THOMAS JEFFERSON TO PATRICK KERR ROGERS.

MONTICELLO, June 23, 1819.

SIR, — Your favour of May 21 was received in due time. The Visitors of the University of Virginia had determined at their meeting in March that it was not expedient to divert any of its funds from building during the present year, but that propositions should be made, and an engagement entered into with Dr. Cooper, to undertake the Professorship of Natural Philosophy, Chemistry, and Mineralogy, as also that of

[1] *Medical Annals of Baltimore,* by John R. Quinan, M. D., 8vo, pp. 274, Baltimore, 1884.

[2] Ruschenberger.

Law, and to open these schools in April next. The
probable impracticability of providing buildings this
season for the other professorships induced them to
expect that another year would be necessary for that
object, and that a general opening of the University
would have to be postponed till 1821. It is now
visible that the slow progress of building will produce
the delay they apprehended. I am sorry, therefore,
that this state of things, and the anticipation of the
appointment of a professor to the school you desired,
leave no room for availing the University of the offer
of services you have been pleased to tender. Accept,
pray, the assurance of my great respect.

Th: Jefferson.

"In 1819 his qualifications and capacity to teach
were recognized, and he was elected Professor of Natural Philosophy and Chemistry in the ancient College
of William and Mary (founded at Williamsburg, Va.,
in 1692), in place of Dr. Robert Hare, resigned. Dr.
Rogers left Baltimore in October, 1819, and was soon
settled with his wife and boys in the Brafferton House,
on the college campus. He was earnest in his work.
He made all the apparatus required to illustrate his
lectures. In this making and mending he was habitually aided by his sons, who thus acquired unusual
facility in the use of tools for working wood and
metals."[1]

During the summer of 1820, after the close of the
session of the college on July 4, Mrs. Rogers was attacked with malarial fever and died. To avoid this
fever, which always prevailed in that locality during
the summer, Dr. Rogers usually left Williamsburg
as soon after the close of the term as practicable.
Eight years after the death of his wife, having come
northward for the college vacation, he was seized with

---

[1] Ruschenberger.

malarial fever and died, at Ellicott Mills, Md., August 1, 1828, in the fifty-second year of his age. The reverence and affection with which the brothers regarded their father and the influence of his somewhat remarkable and unique character are more fully illustrated by incidents dwelt upon in the next chapter. Of the life and character of their mother, who died before the sons had attained maturity, pleasant traditions alone remain.

CHAPTER II.

1804–1828.

The Family Life in Baltimore. — Education of the Brothers and their Graduation from William and Mary. — Their Early Correspondence. — William's Youthful Oration. — He assists his Father at the College. — Removal of the Brothers to Baltimore. — William and Henry open a School. — Their Lectures before the Maryland Institute. — Correspondence with their Father. — An Address by P. K. Rogers. — First Railroads in America. — Reminiscences of the Father by a Student of William and Mary.

LITTLE is known of the childhood or boyhood of William Barton Rogers or of his brothers. When Dr. P. K. Rogers left Philadelphia and removed to Baltimore in 1812, James, the eldest, was eleven, and the second son, William, only eight years old. The family life appears to have been a hard struggle with poverty and debt, and the boys had few luxuries. They enjoyed, however, the inestimable advantage of educated parents devoted to their welfare. The seven years of Baltimore life, as far as we know, passed without special incident. On some stray sheets of paper torn from an old ledger, William has given a glimpse of the family life of this period : —

"These pages formed part of an account book of my revered father, used by him while a practicing physician, and when his chief and favorite employment in the intervals of business was the instruction of James, Henry and myself. Henry was then too

young to be sent to school, — at least so my father
thought.   On this subject his views were peculiar, and
I have ever regarded them not only as benevolent but
wise.

"The same anxiety that led him to postpone mere
book instruction to the natural development of the
physical and intellectual powers in Henry's case
caused him to restrict our attendance on school, at a
later period, to half days.   So that, with the exception
of a short period during which James and myself
walked about two miles to Baltimore College [1] to receive instruction in Latin, we never spent any of our
afternoon hours in school.   Henry, I am sure, was
exempt during the whole of his schoolboy life from
attendance in the afternoon.

"It thus happened that our education was conducted
in great part at home, and by the daily personal attention of our kind and judicious father; and to this
cause I may justly ascribe the thoroughness of our
knowledge on all the subjects which we studied, though
in the apparent extent of our attainments we were by
no means in advance of our playmates trained in the
ordinary system of school drudgery, and confined to
their books for the greater part of the day."

It is related that music formed an entertainment
in the household, Dr. Rogers and his son Henry
playing the violin and William the flute.   The sons
also recalled in after years the intense boyish delight
of certain walks with their father into the suburbs
of Baltimore on Sunday afternoons, with the glass of
fresh milk drunk at some farm-house on the way.

While the family lived in Baltimore William was
for a time employed in the china warehouse of Mr. M.
F. Keyser.   Here it was that he acquired a skill and

---

[1] Probably Baltimore City College, the Public High School of
Baltimore.

dexterity in packing china, which he never lost.   In later years this accomplishment — for such, in his case, it really was — proved very useful in the packing of fragile fossils or other specimens.   In after years he once excited the admiration of his family by packing a thin glass tumbler side by side with a heavy iron implement so skillfully that the glass arrived at the end of a long journey uninjured.

The appointment of Dr. P. K. Rogers to a professorship in the College of William and Mary in 1819 was in many respects fortunate.   It formed an epoch in the family history, and promised to the anxious parent a relief from financial distress.   It offered to him also the welcome opportunity of educating his boys, who were now rapidly approaching manhood.

Dr. and Mrs. Rogers with their children removed from Baltimore to Williamsburg in October, 1819.   James, the eldest son, appears to have returned for a time to Baltimore, and to him William addressed the following letter which we give, unchanged, as it is the first of his letters which has been preserved.   It was written at the age of fifteen : —

WILLIAM TO JAMES.

WILLIAMSBURG, December 22, 1819.

DEAR JAMES, — I received your letter three days ago, and was glad to find that my second letter had met with a better fate than my first.   Along with yours I received one from our very eccentric friend S. S. ; he is at Rocky Mount in Franklin County, and, as he states, at the foot of the elevated Blue Ridge. The stile is such as might be expected from one who, with a few atoms of self-importance, possesses a world of good nature and affection.   It is forcible, warm,

and now and then too florid, but his letter is replete
with good sense, and displays an active mind as well
as a benevolent heart.   He is to have the superintendence of a farm, the property of one of his relations, and expects that his situation will be extremely
pleasant and quite independent. He seems very desirous of establishing a correspondence with me, and frequently mentions you, always with the most friendly
regard.   The classes remain stationary and decorous;
there has not been the least misbehaviour since the
opening of the session, but the courses progress in
the most orderly and agreeable manner.   It were fortunate if the students were as remarkable for their
talents as good nature, but it is not so ; with the
exception of about eight, there was perhaps never an
assemblage of young men so totally destitute of genius
and so miserably deficient in understanding.   Yesterday (as Mr. Hawes tells me) Dr. Smith [1] inquired
of a student what was the nature of a material substance, the answer was, "One which affects our senses
and exerts reason ! "   Father asked the same person
for a definition of a solid; after much hesitation, a
good deal of muttering, and abundance of broken
sentences, the gentleman answered with great philosophical gravity that it was " A — a — a body which
was solid."   The chemical class, however, advance as
well as could be expected, and will no doubt bear a
good examination ; there are a few members in particular who answer extremely well, among these stands
Robert Saunders.

Christmas is now fast approaching, when I suppose
the inhabitants will enter upon the same routine of
dissipation as is usual at this season.   For my part, I
intend to visit as little as decency will admit, and Mr.
Hawes has joined me in this determination.   Neither
of us have yet been to Dr. Coles's or Captain Tra-
vers's ; we took tea at Mr. Campbell's shortly after

[1] President of William and Mary College.

Mr. H. arrived, but have not been there since. We generally sit up until between eleven and twelve o'clock without inconvenience, and find the stillness of the hour to favour studies in astronomy. It is the most sublime as well as the most difficult of all the sciences ; it requires intense study and great application, but by the joint force of these its difficulties are soon overcome, and its utility and beauty become more strikingly manifest.

We are all extremely well, but anxiously anticipating your return, in hopes of which and of your health and happiness I am,

Your very affectionate Brother,

WILLIAM B. ROGERS.

P. S. — Robert Saunders intends writing to you shortly, his father wishing such a correspondence for his improvement. If he writes, Father says you must not neglect to return him a friendly answer, and, should you have leisure you had better not wait for a letter from him.

Father and the children all send their most affectionate love to you, as well as to our relations in Baltimore. I must now bid you good-night as it is near my bed-time. Answer this speedily.

W. B. R.

The following " Report of Standing " addressed to Dr. Rogers shows that James and William were in attendance at William and Mary during the session 1819–20. It has been reproduced as a contribution to the educational history of the period; and it need only be remarked that the term " Society " was used as a synonym for " Faculty." Ferdinand Campbell, whose signature appears upon this facsimile, was the Professor of Mathematics and a great favorite with the students of the college, who characterized him in the following rhyme : —

William and Mary College, Feb 23rd — 1820

AS those whose sons and wards are at a public seminary, must feel the greatest anxiety for their proficiency and their welfare, the Society have determined to send stated communications* one after each public examination, to the Parent or Guardian of every Young Gentleman pursuing his studies at this Institution.

In the opinions which the Society express, you may depend upon the greatest candour and impartiality, nor can they commit any mistake with regard to the acquirements of the Students, this being effectually precluded by the daily and semi-annual examinations. But although the Society omit no opportunity of informing themselves concerning the temper, character and habits of those over whom it is their duty to watch, yet it is obviously impossible for them to obtain in every instance, that accurate knowledge which is so desirable on these important subjects. Here therefore they are liable to err, and due allowances for this source of fallacy, accordingly are necessary. It is almost superfluous to add that the mistake, where there is one, will be generally on the favourable side. The error however it may be remarked must be slight, for it is deemed impracticable, for any young man to deviate widely and for any length of time, from the rules of propriety without being at least suspected, and even suspicions in an affair of such essential importance to the future welfare of a student, deserve the most serious consideration, and are accordingly stated. From this system, where Parents and Guardians have co-operated with the Professors, the most beneficial effects have already ensued; by means of it, irregularities and improprieties have been nipped in the bud, and that abundant harvest of vice and dissipation which might have followed, has been easily and of Your [son] James & & [Arm] the Society is happy to state, that they have been orderly, diligent, and attentive to their studies; and in Mathematics and Chemistry have made the most flattering improvement. In Philosophy likewise, their progress is creditable. ———

The Society think you had better inform your sons of the foregoing opinion. This information it would be well to accompany with those commendations which such conduct merits, the applause of those we love and esteem being perhaps the strongest incentive to virtue.

By order of the Society,

Ferdinand J Campbell Secretary

"Here comes old Ferdy,
With rectilinear walk,
His head full of diagrams,
His pockets full of chalk."

In the summer following the removal of the family
to Williamsburg, Mrs. Rogers was attacked by the
fever which prevailed in the malarial climate of Lower
Virginia and from which she died.   The death of
their mother was a heavy blow to the boys, but it
seems to have drawn their father into relations with
them closer, if possible, than before.

On the invitation of Colonel Robert Saunders, Dr.
Rogers and his boys left Williamsburg after the death
of Mrs. Rogers, and spent the rest of their vacation
in the house of their host at Short Pump, Va.   That
this was a wise step appears from the following passage
in a letter from Professor Campbell to Dr. Rogers:—

WILLIAMSBURG, October 7, 1820.

MY DEAR DOCTOR, . . . Although at the time
of your departure I supposed that your family would
have incurred no risk by remaining in Williamsburg,
I rejoice now that I did not advise you to stay, and
that you concluded on seeking the benefit of a change
of air.   For such has been the unhealthiness of this
place that scarcely any of the old inhabitants have
escaped from severe illness; and, to add to this misfor-
tune, the physician on whom all are disposed to rely
most (Dr. Galt) has likewise had a bilious attack,
which has deprived them of his services for three
weeks, and still continues to do so. . . .

I saw old Kitt[1] the other day; the only thing he
wanted was a little corn for the fowls, which I believe
he got.   We are mindful of you all every afternoon
when we view your abode, or see Henry's ducks, who
visit us every day.

[1] A family servant.

In the autumn of 1821 James left William and Mary College to study medicine at the University of Maryland, in Baltimore. A correspondence now began between the brothers, which was continued as long as they lived. The following is important as showing their early interest in science, and also as an estimate by his eldest son of the father's attainments : —

JAMES (19) TO WILLIAM (17).

BALTIMORE, November 9, 1821.

DEAR BROTHER, — In compliance with my promise of soon writing to you, I now sit down to write you a short letter, in which you may not calculate on anything new, except a new and in my opinion a rather singular opinion advanced by Dr. De Butts, which he delivered this evening, one which I think is wholly unsupported by any evidence. It is this, that no two bodies of heterogeneous character are presented to each other without thereby chemical union being produced ; for instance, a drop of water applied to a plate of glass adheres to it by virtue of chemical attraction, or affinity ; and that the different forces of this attraction are to be observed in all degrees, from the simple case I have mentioned to those in which the most powerful chemical attraction exerts its influence. In a word, what Father denominates " heterogeneous adhesion " is with him really a chemical union. I believe this opinion to be erroneous, inasmuch as there is in this case to be observed none of those changes which are said to be characteristic of chemical affinity. When you write me (which do soon) give me your opinion on this point. Dr. De Butts seems to have considerably improved as a lecturer since I last heard him, but yet he falls far short of Father. However, I think his lectures are sufficiently full for his class, for very few of the members of it that I know are capable of comprehending one half of what he says. I have often, while listening to the Doctor, wished the students could hear one of Father's lectures on the subject, for they as far surpass the Doctor's in point of correctness, science and elegance, as the meridian sun does the evening star in brilliancy. . . .

Two months later James writes again to William, who appears to have been ill, and gravely records his impressions of his brother Henry, — impressions which, especially in view of the eminence which the latter achieved, are interesting : —

JAMES TO WILLIAM.

BALTIMORE, January 10, 1822.

DEAR BROTHER, . . . You will please inform Henry that, as he has arrived at that age in which he might write a letter, nothing would give me more pleasure than to receive a letter from him, in which I shall expect him to tell me what he is studying, and how he comes on in his studies. I have, I think, perceived in Henry that constitution of mind which is admirably fitted for success in this world, and which, if properly cultivated, would manifest genius of no ordinary cast. . . .

James, having been graduated in medicine in 1822, immediately opened an office and formed a partnership for medical practice with a friend. But he was not successful. His letters contain repeated and urgent appeals to his father for money for his bare necessities. The following illustrates not only the struggles of a young physician, but also the prospects and the lines of medical practice at that period : —

JAMES TO WILLIAM.

BALTIMORE, May 7, 1822.

DEAR BROTHER, . . . My partner and myself have had an office open now for more than two weeks, and in all that time have had only three patients, and those not promising profit, — prospects which certainly are not very flattering; but we are told the city at present is very healthy, unusually so. We have patience, however, if we have not patients, and are on the lookout, and endeavouring to do the best we can.

The weather is becoming very warm, and a fair prospect presents itself for bilious fevers. Indeed, I am oppressed in my winter clothes, and have no light ones to change. I'll thank you if you will tell Father this, that he may afford me, if possible, means of procuring some, at least, by the first of June. There has been a good deal of sickness of late in uncle's[1] family. I bled no less than three of them within the last week, but they are all now nearly well. . . .

In May, 1822, an interesting event occurred in the delivery by William Barton Rogers, then only seventeen and a half years of age, of an oration at the celebration of the third " Virginiad," at Jamestown, Va. His friend, Robert Saunders, Jr., also made an oration, as appears from the following: —

JAMES TO WILLIAM.

May 30, 1822.

DEAR BROTHER, — Looking over one of the papers of yesterday, I observed a description of the celebration of the Virginiad at Jamestown, in a letter addressed by a gentleman who was present to one of the Norfolk editors. He mentioned that two orations

[1] The uncle here referred to was Mr. Alexander Rogers, a resident of Baltimore.

were delivered, by two very young men of the name of Rogers and Saunders, which he complimented very highly, but particularly the first, which he said was delivered by Mr. Rogers. The thought immediately struck me that it was you, as you evinced some talent for oratory, and the subject opened a wide field for the display of it. It made me feel a momentary degree of pride, until reading farther I saw that William and Mary did not participate in the festival. This made me doubt whether you were the person, or some other of the same name. My principal object in now writing to you is to ascertain the fact. The writer says he hopes to be able to procure the first oration. If it be yours, I hope it may be published, that I may get a look at it. . . .

The following extract illustrates the character of this youthful oration, which may be found in full in the "Richmond (Va.) Enquirer" of June 4, 1822 : —

. . . "The first Virginian colonists bade a final adieu to the thronged land of their nativity. Having taken an affectionate farewell of their friends and dearest relations, they steered toward the ample shores of America. . . .

"As they sailed into the Chesapeake, they viewed this spacious bay with admiration and delight, and found themselves enclosed in a vast amphitheatre formed by the distant forests which skirted its blue waters. The jutting points of land opened, as they advanced, into broad extended shores, or retired as if by enchantment. While the eye surveyed the rich exuberance of vegetation, and the diversified tints of the foliage which painted the varied landscape on every side, the heart dilated with the exulting anticipation of unequalled felicity, and the enraptured imagination dwelt only on dreams of delight. Beauty and grandeur appeared everywhere around; and in the ardent glow of enthusiasm, the now joyous ad-

venturers represented the country as an earthly
paradise.

"In exploring this interesting scene, they entered
the spacious opening through which the Chesapeake
receives the tributary waters of the majestic Powhatan.   A permanent resting-place, favorable for the
establishment of a plantation, was now sought; and
the peninsula on which we are this day assembled
was the spot distinguished by their choice; Jamestown, consecrated by their toils and sufferings, became
the seat of the first colony within the present limits
of Virginia."

The young orators of Jamestown were always firm
friends.   The following letter is given to show their
boyish assumption of knowledge of life and men : —

TO ROBERT SAUNDERS, JR.

RICHMOND, October 13, 1822.

DEAR ROBERT, — I have not for a long time been
more out of humour than I am at this moment.   Fully
an hour ago I came upstairs determined to write
you a very amusing letter.   It occurred to me that an
occasional departure from my usual dull style of writing
might prevent your being weary of my correspondence.
Now, the cause of my ill-humour is this, — I have been
sitting ever since in a retired apartment, ready to catch
at whatever started in my mind that might afford you
entertainment, but after trying to stimulate my invention by every means in my power I have been unable
to elicit even a single pleasant conceit.   Two or three
snail-paced ideas have indeed crept across my mind,
but they are not of the kind I want.   I find my brains
are too heavy and viscid; the little wriggling maggot
that stirs up witty fancies is unable to move in them.
Alas!   I must content myself with my usual dull,
insipid style.

I agree with you in believing that there is a great

deal of villainy among men.   I fear few who consult
their experience can believe otherwise.   Young persons
who have had little intercourse with mankind are not
apt to be of your sentiment, however; they generally entertain a more favourable opinion of the world than
ordinary experience will support.   This arises from the
unsuspecting benevolence which is the natural character
of youth.   Viewed through this medium, man appears
encircled with the halo of every virtue.   Experience
draws a very different picture, in which the halo of
virtue is changed for the veil of hypocrisy.   This
painful contrast is perceived more or less by every one
upon first entering the busy world.   I am prepared for
it myself; but so long as my dear friend remains unchanged, I will be contented.

Dear Bob, I am quite impatient to see you again.
It seems almost an age since I left Williamsburg.
Indeed, as the time of our departure from Richmond
approaches, the days appear to move more and more
tardily.   In one week from this I expect we shall be
on the road; then my impatience will give me no rest
until the journey is ended.   The anticipation of again
enjoying your company is delightful.

Your sincere friend,
WILLIAM B. ROGERS.

It will be observed that in October, 1822, William
was in Richmond.   Hither the father had come, partly
to escape the dangerous climate of Williamsburg but,
on this visit, more particularly to superintend the publication of his text-book.   In the course of a letter
addressed to Thomas Jefferson, Dr. Rogers refers to
his son William, who seems to have been his assistant,
as follows : —

[About 1823.]

SIR, — I take the liberty of sending you a copy of a little work[1] which I prepared for the use of one of my classes in William and Mary.

The students who attend our courses are generally very deficient in preparatory schooling, and a great proportion of them appear to be altogether incapable of steady application, from the want of early discipline. My " Introduction," etc., was arranged in some measure with a view to the improvement of mental discipline; its plan being convenient for regular recitals, at the blackboard, or otherwise, and it is believed that familiar acquaintance with its contents may enable the student in natural philosophy (who is duly prepared in mathematics) to pursue more general reading with satisfaction and enjoyment, and to encounter future difficulties in the science with confidence and alacrity. . . . I have followed what is, perhaps, a very common, and is certainly a very natural inclination. A professor who loves the science which he teaches will be fond of treating it in a manner as a favorite child, by dressing it according to his own fancy, and by presenting it in that attitude which he supposes may most effectually secure to it, at first sight, an approving glance or a kind sentiment.

The demonstrations of the 14th, 35th, 68th, and 93d propositions are by my second son, who is now in his twentieth year, and has a very extraordinary passion for physico-mathematical sciences. About half a dozen other demonstrations are taken without alteration from the writings of Dr. Robinson and Dr. Thos. Young. All the rest of the work is my own method and language, my several guides being Newton, Robinson, Monge, Young, etc. . . .

[1] *An Introduction to the Mathematical Principles of Natural Philosophy,* by P. K. Rogers. Richmond, 1822.

In the letters of 1822 and 1823, there are frequent references to William's delicate health or actual illness; and the other brothers, as we shall see, were by no means robust.

JAMES TO WILLIAM.

BALTIMORE, December 19, 1822.

DEAR BROTHER, — The receipt of your letter was to me a source of real pleasure, for I have nothing more at heart than your health and welfare. I only hope that your sickness may not lay the foundation for serious and troublesome complaints so often the consequence of bilious disease. However, you are under the eye of a physician whose parental care will not allow anything serious, if possible, to occur. A short time after I returned to Baltimore from the country, I was apprehensive, from a pain in my side, that I had not completely recovered from the attack I had while there; but I believe now I am perfectly free from any local affection.

For the sake of improvement I attend some of the lectures in the University, and particularly the chemical lectures, by which I have had an opportunity of testing Dr. De Butts's acquirements. Dr. Murray, whose works I have read, I have found to be his right hand man. I have myself made so much progress in this beautiful science that I would not exchange my knowledge of the subject for that of the Doctor. I have for the sake of improvement written an introductory lecture on chemistry, which I should like you to see, if I had any convenient way of forwarding it; perhaps in your next letter you may suggest some plan of doing so. . . .

William, until the autumn of 1825, spent his winters in Williamsburg, and from the following letter it appears that in 1823 he was giving much time to the study of the classics : —

JAMES TO WILLIAM.

February 27, 1823.

DEAR BROTHER, . . . I was pleased that your apology for delay in writing was attention to the study of Greek, and not indisposition, which I feared existed, and indeed I am not disposed to view this as a trifling one, when I consider your habits of close application, in which you are so abstracted from everything but what you are at, as to be very liable to forget answering such letters as mine, in which there are no points of interesting character presented to your reflecting mind. Your views with respect to the beauties of Homer I make no doubt are correct, for although I have not studied the Greek, I love that idea of the language (I know not how I obtained it) which enables me to conceive it possible that no English translation can retain the majestic sublimity of the original.

I am reading also, for the sake of improvement in algebra, a Latin edition of Euler's elements of that subject, and for simplicity of style, clearness of conception, and accuracy of demonstration, he certainly cannot be surpassed by any. I never had correct views of this beautiful science, but since I have perused him I have been enabled to reason on abstract infinite quantity with as much precision as on determinate ones.

I am pleased Henry has made such rapid progress in his Latin, and that Robert is not altogether devoted to play.

I shall take an opportunity soon of sending you my introductory lecture by mail, that I may know whether you think me able to write introductory lectures. I read a short essay before the Medical Society of Maryland a few evenings ago, and from their conduct to me I judged they thought me in some degree qualified to write medical essays. The subject comprehended criticism on the popular use of mercury in

fever, in which I endeavoured to prove that this invaluable article was much abused by the alchymistic
physicians of the present day, who have as they think
found in it the long-sought-for Panacea, and for the
benefit of humanity make it their *unicum remedium*,
and dispense it with liberal and bountiful profu-
sion. . . .

In the next winter (1823–24) Dr. P. K. Rogers,
in writing to Thomas Jefferson, states that William
was engaged in mathematical studies : —

PATRICK K. ROGERS TO THOMAS JEFFERSON.

WILLIAMSBURG, March 14, 1824.
To THOMAS JEFFERSON, ESQ.

Sir, — The polite terms in which you are pleased
to express your estimate of that portion of my " Introduction " which has been printed could not fail to
give pleasure to the writer.   And the kind conclusion
of your letter claims more than formal thanks : it is,
in commercial phrase, a draft upon the affections,
which the heart is ready and willing to pay.   I intend
to indulge myself in the high gratification of making a visit to Monticello next July, and regret that I
could not without great inconvenience have done so
last summer.   With an ardent curiosity to see the
University, considerations (I cannot call them hopes)
are connected, which make me desirous to see you
as soon as the duties in which I am engaged will
permit.

There is something in the organization of William
and Mary which, independently of its location or
other permanent disadvantages, must forever prevent
it from being prosperous or successful; and while I
sincerely congratulate the friends of the University on
their success in the late session of the legislature, I
am inclined to think that when that institution goes
into operation we shall scarcely have occasion to open

the doors of the old college. Even at present there
is no reputation to be acquired here, and no encouragement to activity or zeal. Your comparative
view of the merits of the French and English writers
on mathematical and physical science is that which I
have long entertained. Two great works, however, in
the English language, those of Young and Robinson.
may be regarded as exceptions to the general standard of the English writers on the various branches
of mechanical philosophy. Yet, I confess, I am not
a convert to the theory of light and heat which is
so ably defended by the former, — the theory of undulations in a diffused universal medium. The latter, in his system of mechanical philosophy, which
is delivered in the happiest style of an experienced
teacher, avails himself of the best and latest investigations of his contemporaries of every country. . . .

The fluxional notation and idea must undoubtedly
give place to the differential, in England and in this
country, at no distant period. The clearness and
facility of the latter, compared with the obscurity and
the difficulty of the former, in the hands of beginners,
will soon fix the destiny of the two methods. The best
Scotch mathematicians have already decided in favour
of the differential method. . . . My second son has
almost completed a translation of the " Eléments du
Calcul Differentiel " of Bézout, for the use of his
younger brother, this being the only elementary work
to which he has access that treats the subject by the
theory of infinitesimals. He has himself been engaged
in reading the more abstruse and more perfect treatise
in Brewster's Encyclopædia. Although we have a
pretty large library in this place, we have very few
books of real use to the profession, unless those on
metaphysics, or what has been pompously denominated
the philosophy of the mind, are to be considered as
such. We have indeed the works of Bézout and La-
place, with several of the best treatises on chemistry,
and the systems of natural and mechanical philosophy

of Young and Robinson, which, after three years of
solicitation, were reluctantly imported and received
last summer. And of course we have access to most
of the old writers on physics and mechanics, from
Archimedes to Newton. . . .

I have hesitated to trouble you with the present
letter, aware that the correspondence which, at your
advanced period of life, you may still find agreeable
to sustain, must be with old and probably very distant friends. But reflecting that to read is less
fatiguing than to write, and that an acknowledgment
was really due for that assurance of welcome which
you have been so good as to give me, I came to the
determination to tender it in this form; and with my
thanks for the personal favour and sentiments of
purest respect,

I remain,

Your ob't servant,

PATRICK KERR ROGERS.

In October, 1825, William and Henry had both
removed to Baltimore to seek their fortunes, Henry
finding employment for a time with a retail merchant.
Ill health, however, pursued them, as the following
letters testify : —

PATRICK K. ROGERS TO HIS SON WILLIAM.

. . . Henry writes me that your indisposition continues unabated. I cannot, I am sorry to say, suggest
anything promising of utility beyond what your own
experience would direct you to. It is to be hoped
that a hard winter will do you service. . . .

WILLIAMSBURG, October 17, 1825.

DEAR WILLIAM, — I regret exceedingly that I have
not yet received any communication from the bursar.
I have feared that some of you may have been in

want of necessary articles to meet the inclemency of the season. There is now no expectation from Christian [1] until he comes to Williamsburg at the commencement of next month to make his usual settlement with the faculty. This delay of salary has given me unusual concern, as I had made your aunt Ramsay expect some money at the opening of the course, and as it is high time your uncle had payment for board. Both claims must be attended to in the beginning of next month. As I do not now expect to receive any money from Christian until he comes at the first of January, I have enclosed thirty dollars, with the view of providing any article which either of the three — James, Henry, or yourself — may particularly require. Shoes and good warm socks are indispensable, and unless Henry has got already supplied he must want a couple of flannel shirts.

I have been much disappointed in not receiving a letter from any of you by yesterday's mail. I am anxious to know how you and Henry come on in your new engagement [teaching], and how the business consists with the health of both. If you are able to continue those duties it will be a very important circumstance; you may, by a dignified and kind deportment to the boys, lay a sure foundation for an independent establishment for yourselves at some future day, should it suit in respect to your health.

I had hoped, on your receiving my last letter, or at least since Henry and you entered on your academic duties, to have had a letter of information. Do not fail to write immediately on receipt of this, or, if you should find it oppressive to do so, let James or Henry write. . . .

Your affectionate father,

P. K. ROGERS.

[1] The bursar of the college.

The rising University of Virginia now threatened the slender prosperity of William and Mary College. It was therefore proposed to remove the latter to Richmond. The following letter of Dr. Rogers refers to this proposal, and also illustrates the pecuniary difficulties of a professor's life in a poorly-endowed college : —

PATRICK K. ROGERS TO HIS SON WILLIAM.

WILLIAMSBURG, January 16, 1826.

DEAR WILLIAM, — I send enclosed an order of the bursar on the Bank of Virginia for one hundred dollars. This day he laid his books before the Society for settlement, and the dividend to each of the professors was unexpectedly small on account of the expenses in fitting up the college, and the additional salary to be paid out of his collections. I received only two hundred dollars, fifty having been deducted for rent to the 5th of July last. He has, however, pleasant news for us. Large amounts of interest long due will certainly be paid during the spring, and he assures us that he has not the least doubt but that, between this time and next July, every cent of arrears due the professors will be paid to them. There is remaining, after the present payment, about thirteen months' salary due to every one. This will be very fortunate for me if it is made good. But there will be strong pulling at the next convention in different directions: offices to be divided, professorships to be put down, removal and no removal of the college. Keep these things private. I shall have much curious communication for you and your brother when I go on to Baltimore, which I am afraid to put on paper. One thing is to me certain: the college will not, in any time to serve us, be removed from its present location.

Desire Henry to write to me frequently. He is the

youngest sojourner, and therefore I feel particularly desirous to know how he comes on.

Of the enclosed sum it will be proper to give your aunt Ramsay at least ten dollars, and make such payment to your uncle as you may all judge right, and apply the surplus to the use of those of you who most want necessaries. I shall be happy to find on my arrival at Baltimore that you all are to each other kind and liberal, and that your health and happiness improve. James should have a keen lookout for himself; an unfortunate squall in this place may render me unable to give him any important assistance.

I remain your affectionate father,

P. K. ROGERS.

The proposed removal of William and Mary College to the city of Richmond, referred to above, was advocated because of its unhealthy location, and also in the belief that only by its transfer to a larger and wealthier community could it compete successfully with the new " University" of Thomas Jefferson.[1]

In the autumn of 1826 the two brothers, William and Henry, opened a school at Windsor, Md., some fourteen miles from Baltimore. Robert, now thirteen years old, left his father and joined them in Windsor, attending their school and living in the family of Mr. and Mrs. Fitzhugh.

WILLIAM TO HIS FATHER.

WINDSOR, November 3, 1826.

DEAR FATHER, — I have seated myself in the midst of our school to write to you. I cannot, therefore, bestow much study on my letter.

Henry is much as usual, — still troubled with dys-

[1] See *U. S. Bureau of Education: Circular No.* 1, 1887; *The College of William and Mary*, etc., pp. 58–61.

peptic symptoms, and occasional pains in the breast.
Robert has had an attack of the croup, but through
the kind care of the family he is now well, though
not able to come to school. . . .

Our school has been nearly stationary since we
saw you. We cannot expect to make much more
than a support in our present situation. The profits
of the school would be sufficient to satisfy one of
us, as it would enable him to lay by something for
the future; but, as by the present arrangement they
must be divided between us, they will not enable us
to improve our circumstances. However delightful
the place and society, we therefore cannot regard
the situation as a permanent one, at least for both
of us.

Since you left town I have made inquiry respecting
the situation which Dr. Webster spoke to you about,
and which I declined applying for. I called upon
Dr. Stewart, who gave me particular information on
the subject. The gentleman who wanted a tutor is
Mr. W. Garnett, the husband of the lady who teaches
a very celebrated female school in Virginia. He has
three sons, whom he wishes to educate at home. They
are to be instructed in Greek, Latin, English and
Mathematics; and the tutor is to receive a salary of
four hundred dollars and his boarding. The salary
is handsome, and to one in my situation is very enticing. From the importance attached to the classical
instruction, I fear my qualifications would hardly be
sufficient. Mr. Garnett observes in a letter, from
which Dr. Stewart read a passage, that the person
whom he employs must have great patience, for he
must be content to teach without the use of the rod
or emulation. My present situation is truly delightful in every respect but one: it is not sufficiently
lucrative. But for this I would not change my abode,
with the same employment, for any other in the world.
I have felt anxious to have your opinion again on this
subject, ever since I heard that the place was still

open. Mr. Garnett is a visitor of the college; perhaps you may have seen him in Williamsburg. Teaching is much less profitable in Maryland than in Virginia. There, a classical teacher may in a few years lay up what will enable him to obtain a profession and begin the practice of it; here, unless he is so fortunate as to become fashionable in the city, he can only realize a support. You may, perhaps, hear of some situation in Virginia that would be desirable. If you should, please inform us.

I remain your affectionate son,
WILLIAM B. ROGERS.

N. B. — Do not from this letter infer that I am displeased with our present situation. I am highly pleased with it, but I feel that I ought to look to the future.

W. B. R.

In January, 1827, we find William delivering lectures before the Maryland Institute in Baltimore, and from his "Introductory" lecture quote a few sentences: —

"The general considerations which I have thus presented are such as the scene before me is calculated to suggest. I shall now conclude my preliminary observations with a few remarks relative to this institution, and then proceed to topics more immediately connected with the subject of the succeeding lectures. I need not in this place enlarge upon the usefulness of popular courses of scientific instruction; with respect to my own department, this, I hope, will be clearly evinced in another part of the present discourse. Of late years, the public mind, both in this country and abroad, has been much interested in the subject. In many places institutions calculated to render useful science attainable by the mass of society have been established; and such is the growing impression of their value that their number continues yearly to increase. Our own city has not been backward in this career of improvement. The Maryland Institute is, I believe, the second in point of seniority in the United States, and has now been upwards of a year in successful operation. During this period the public has had an opportunity of testing the advantages which it proffers. And may not its friends believe that the laudable sentiments which led to its erection have been more extensively and permanently impressed upon the public mind by the evidences which it has already afforded of its useful character? May they not hope that it has become, and will continue to be, an object of the kind regard and fostering care of our philanthropic citizens; that it will be cherished with the guardian attention which was in ancient times bestowed upon the vestal fire whose extinction was thought to be ominous of evil; and that, being thus enabled to diffuse the light of useful knowledge, not only among ourselves but to distant places, it will, by the invaluable results to which it may in time conduce, assist in irradiating with splendour the city which gave it birth? "

WILLIAM TO HIS FATHER.

BALTIMORE, January 25, 1827.
. . . My lectures continue to be well attended. On Monday night the room was crowded. I am at present engaged with the subject of astronomy, and have already delivered four lectures upon it, in which I have been much assisted by an admirable tellurian which has been loaned to me. It would be difficult to give you an idea of the beauty of this instrument. It was constructed by an ingenious young mechanic in this place a few years ago, and has since been in the possession of a teacher of a female school. It has suffered much injury from the ill-usage it has received, but is still of great value in illustrating many impor-

tant points in astronomy. It exhibits with great precision the relative motions of the earth, the moon, and Venus around the sun. The orbit of the earth is a horizontal circular ring, about six feet in its exterior diameter and six inches broad, upon which the signs of the ecliptic and the months of the year are inscribed. This ring stands upon four legs. The sun is a large gilt globe placed upon an axis, having the proper obliquity to the ecliptic. Venus is a silvered ball. The earth is a small terrestrial globe of about the same magnitude as that which we used to attach to a string and move around a candle. The parallelism of the earth's axis to itself is maintained in all positions, together with the diurnal and annual motions. A brass circle encompassing the globe in a direction perpendicular to the ecliptic presents its face always to the sun, and serves in a striking manner to distinguish the enlightened from the dark hemisphere. This instrument affords a clear explanation of the phenomena of the seasons, and the variations in the lengths of days, the equation of time, the apparent motion of Venus and the other planets, and a variety of other interesting particulars. As a means of illustration, I think it is infinitely more useful than an orrery or planetarium of the same magnitude. Embracing but a few planetary bodies, it is simple, and the movements it exhibits are conspicuous at a distance. I wish you could see it in operation. I am sure you would desire to have one among your apparatus.

Dr. Vethake is lecturing on the gases. I confess I do not admire the plan of his lectures. He first reads the lecture from a manuscript book, and concludes with the experiments. Do you conceive this a judicious course? It is objected to by many members of the class.

James is well and apparently in good spirits. He is a great hand at analysis. Mr. —— is becoming more of a saint every day. He is the most disgusting canter

I have ever seen. Although he is a member of the Institute he seldom attends, preferring to be present at prayer-meetings, class-meetings, etc.

I have become acquainted with Dr. Howard and Colonel Long, of the U. S. Engineers. They are very amiable men. I have been surprised to see the crudeness of their scientific knowledge on some subjects. Where principles are concerned, I have the vanity to think that I could sometimes set them right. . . .

WINDSOR, January 30, 1827.

DEAR FATHER, — Henry received a letter from you about three weeks ago. It was a very interesting one to us. We had been desirous of knowing the state of the college, and it gave us full information on this point. The playfulness of some parts of it delighted us, for every indication that you are happy gives us pleasure. We congratulate you upon having an agreeable companion in Dr. Wilmer.[1] The amiable disposition of that gentleman must be particularly pleasing from the contrast it forms with the very opposite character of his predecessor. It is like a mild, vernal sunshine succeeding to cold, changeful, blustering weather. It really gives us great satisfaction to know that you can have society congenial with your taste. . . . As —— has but one student, I think he can lecture from no other motive than the love of talking, which is with him a very powerful passion. So fond is he of the music of his own voice that I really believe, rather than omit lecturing, he would harangue the desks and benches. I believe his lectures have often transformed his hearers into objects hardly more intellectual. How I pity the luckless wight who must sit singly for three long hours listening to ——'s soporific discussions ! . . .

[1] President of William and Mary College.

HENRY TO HIS FATHER.

WINDSOR, January 8, 1827.

DEAR FATHER, — William had expressed a wish to write to you shortly after the receipt of your pleasing letter. I therefore deferred writing until I could have something worth communicating. . . .

As I have lately felt a slight recurrence of my dyspeptic feeling, Mr. Fitzhugh has, with his habitual kindness and attention, given me the use of a horse whenever it has been practicable. Indeed, I can never feel sufficiently grateful for the disposition to oblige us which they have all so continually evinced. A few weeks ago Mr. Fitzhugh procured from his brother in Baltimore the loan of a very fine-toned violin for my use. William has borrowed his cousin's flute, and with the aid of some of our old music we could enjoy ourselves extremely. As it is, we frequently play in unison. I begin to look forward with impatience for the return of summer, that it may afford us the never-failing pleasure of your cheering presence. . . .

The prospect now arose of a professorship for William in the Maryland Institute in Baltimore : —

WILLIAM TO HIS FATHER.

BALTIMORE, March 14, 1827.

. . . My principal object in this letter is to inform you that a respectable appointment will probably be offered to me, and to consult you with regard to the propriety of accepting it. You know Mr. Craig has been lecturing during the winter on Natural Philosophy in the Maryland Institute. Having resolved to remove to the Western country he intends to resign his professorship, and to endeavour to dispose of his apparatus to the Institute. I have lately had several interviews with him, and he has told me that if the Institute buys his apparatus he will endeavour to have me appointed his successor, if I desire it. With this view he has spoken to several of the managers, and there is much probability that the place will be offered to me. There will be some salary given, but for the first year or two it will be small. The institution is already more prosperous than was at first anticipated. There are at present 600 members, and they will no doubt greatly augment. Mr. Craig seems very anxious that I should obtain the place, and had proposed me before I knew anything of the matter. Henry thinks I should eagerly embrace this offer if it is made. I wish to know of you if you think I should accept the appointment. Am I competent, and in other respects would it be proper? I wish to do exactly as you will counsel me. . . .

The appointment, however, was postponed, as appears from the following letter from William to his father : —

BALTIMORE, March 31, 1827.

DEAR FATHER, . . . I have been disappointed in my expectation of obtaining a situation in the Institute. The managers after a great deal of delay have informed Mr. Craig that they cannot purchase his apparatus. They have been endeavouring to collect money for this purpose, but without success. I think if they possessed a proper spirit they would buy it at their own expense, rather than permit the institution to be without it. Had they purchased it, I would certainly have been appointed. As it is, I presume no appointment will be made.

Our school at present is small. Permanently we cannot look for more than a decent support from it. We are both very well contented. I confess I would have been better pleased with a station in the Institute, and I felt much satisfaction in the anticipation of an employment so congenial to my taste. It was with great pleasure I read your account of the improved condition of the college. Nothing would be more gratifying to me than to see William and Mary attended by numerous classes and enjoying the reputation it deserves. . . .

One reason for William's anxiety to secure the place in the Maryland Institute appears in a letter from Henry to his father, dated April 13, 1827. Henry's treatment of the professional outlook is also suggestive : —

HENRY TO HIS FATHER.

. . . William has apprised you of the failure of his hopes with respect to the Institute; nothing further has transpired, and I think nothing will. The managers have resolved to purchase a less expensive apparatus, not thinking it advisable to buy at present such unnecessary and costly instruments as a telescope and microscope. Whether they will apply to William or not we cannot tell, but some one should be appointed, and that soon, and I know of no other individual here who is at all competent to fill the station. They appear, however, so little interested in the prosperity and so incompetent to the management of the Institute over which they have been placed, that I fear it will soon fall through. It would have been a fortunate circumstance for us both had William been successful, as I might then have been enabled to lay by a couple of hundred dollars every year towards acquiring a profession; but now, being associated together, with the expenses of two and little better than the income of one, we cannot look forward to anything higher than a country school, the proceeds of which are both small and precarious. The school yields us at present about five hundred and fifty dollars, and we may calculate on an average of five hundred. This, it is true, is amply sufficient for every present expense, but the future is also to be thought of. Our duties are light and our leisure considerable; we think, therefore, that were we once entered upon the study of a profession we might prosecute it with considerable facility and but little expense. We expect shortly to have our lodgings and our school removed to old Windsor, where we can prosecute any study with far less interruption. We would be glad, therefore, to have some certain and definite object in view, but it is difficult to fix upon the choice of a profession, both law and medicine are so greatly overdone. In Baltimore there are no less than ninety graduates in medicine. This is enough to destroy all confidence of success. The law likewise has its difficulties, but there appears to be in this State a better opening at the bar. To a young man, there is little prospect of success in medicine unless he settles in an unhealthy neighborhood, and to us health will always be a matter of the first consideration. William says he will write to you soon, and deliver his thoughts pro and con at greater length. I believe he has abandoned all thoughts of the Institute. James has received a proposition from Mr. Tyson, but what it is I do not know. I suppose, however, he has written, and you know more of the matter than I do. When we saw him last, which is some time since, he appeared to think that his prospect in the country was a gloomy one. . . .

JAMES TO HIS FATHER.

April 20, 1827.

DEAR FATHER, — I am now at Windsor, which place I have visited for the purpose of consulting my brothers upon the same subject I desire to consult you upon. Isaac Tyson, the chemical manufacturer, is desirous that I take the same office in the factory which I had last summer. He is willing to dispense with a written contract, and would substitute in its place a promise to the same amount. With any honest man, the one would be as obligatory as the other. He has made arrangements so as to change

the situation of the experiment room to a more airy
and agreeable part of the premises, and also to improve the manufacture of chlorine, so as to render
it not so unpleasant to the operator. He is willing
to allow only 350 dollars salary the first year and 400
the second.

Upon reflecting upon my present prospect and situation, and consulting with my brothers, I have thought
I should accept the situation. For a long time I have
had no practice to attend to.

Your affectionate son,

JAMES B. ROGERS.

The summer vacation at the college followed and
appears to have been uneventful, except for the death
of Dr. Wilmer, President of William and Mary. At
the opening of the college session in the autumn, an Introductory Address was delivered by Dr. P. K. Rogers.
Beginning with an eulogium of Dr. Wilmer, Dr. Rogers
proceeded to a careful consideration of important educational questions. From this part of his address a
few characteristic paragraphs are quoted: —

" In the most extensive acceptation of the term, Education comprehends everything — whether systematic
or accidental — which contributes to develop, improve,
and determine the powers of the mind, the tendencies of the passions, and the affections of the heart.

" To promote the happiness of the individual, to raise
him to the higher standard of worth and excellence, to
render him not merely a harmless but a valuable member of the community of men, to give him the disposition and the power to be useful to his companions in
the frequently difficult and cheerless journey of life, and
to prepare him for the happiness of a future world, are
the great ends to be kept in view in the education of
every human being. And this is equally true whatever

place in society he may occupy, from the humble walk
of the cottager to the throne of national authority. . . .
"The advantages derived from the science of natural
philosophy are of two kinds, indirect and direct. The
former consists in a happy discipline of mind, a conscious satisfaction in the possession of a species of
knowledge which increases our power and independence, enlarged views, and a chastened and well-regu-
lated imagination. . . . While the study of natural
philosophy restrains the thoughts within the limits of
reality, it at the same time affords abundant scope for
the sublimest conceptions, and the most excursive flights
of imagination. Carrying us beyond the boundaries of
sense, it weakens each selfish feeling, by interesting
us in everything around us. It is the best preparation
for the study of mind ; for the rigour with which its
researches are conducted, and its cautious mode of reasoning by induction or inference from ascertained
phenomena, check that rage for verbal disputation
which has, from the time of Plato to our own, impeded
the progress of the human understanding. . . .
"Metaphysics, in an extended sense, may be considered as the science of ultimate induction. . . .
. . . "It is impossible to draw a definite line between physics and metaphysics as applied to external
things ; nor is it by any means necessary. But in all
our general theories, whether philosophical or physiological or theological, the mind rests at last on some
ultimate conception which is purely metaphysical."

Early in the autumn of this year William was a
second time appointed to lecture in the Maryland
Institute.

WILLIAM TO HIS FATHER.

BALTIMORE, October 31, 1827.

. . . I have just received a reply to the note
which I addressed to the Committee of Lectures of
the Institute. It will not be in their power to afford

more than two hundred dollars to each lecturer. This sum will be guaranteed, and they will be enabled in time to enlarge the salary. They expect two lectures a week for three months. I wish to know if you would advise me to accept the situation on these terms. . . .

BALTIMORE, November 11, 1827.

. . . I had determined to engage in the Institute before your letter reached me, and had informed the managers that I would accede to their proposals. . . . After I had written to you to request your opinion, I regretted having done so, and thought that you would be best pleased that I should judge and act for myself in the matter. Henry's health at present is as good as it was in the spring, and he is confident of his ability to conduct the school alone.

BALTIMORE, December 9, 1827.

. . . I delivered my introductory lecture on last Monday. It was received with the most flattering applause, and although my colleague, Dr. Vethake, is an experienced lecturer, having been a professor at Carlisle,[1] I believe I did not sink on being compared with him. On Thursday I gave the first lecture of my course, which I have understood yielded great satisfaction. I spoke extemporaneously, assisted by a few heads methodically arranged. . . .

BALTIMORE, December 27, 1827.

I am progressing with my lectures in the Institute, and I believe the class is well pleased with them. Our philosophical apparatus has not yet arrived, but we expect it daily. Henry has seen a list of the articles which have been ordered for the Institute, and has probably enumerated some of them to you. I long to obtain the handling of them. If I had the use of them at present, I am confident that I could give great *éclat* to our Institution. As it is, though I do not possess a single philosophical instrument, my lectures are very

[1] Dickinson College, Carlisle, Pa.

well attended. My class is at least as great as that of
my colleague, who has a tolerable chemical apparatus
at his command. I make great use of the blackboard,
and manage to communicate the more obvious principles of the science pretty clearly by means of drawings
and diagrams. My last lecture treated of uniformly
accelerated and retarded motion and projectiles. In
the preceding lecture I exhibited the experiment of the
guinea and feather by means of a small air-pump,
which was lent me by a member of the class, and this
is the only important one which I have been able to
produce since the commencement of the course. . . .

HENRY TO HIS FATHER.

BALTIMORE, January 1, 1828.

. . . Though labouring under the great disadvan-
tage of want of apparatus, William is still able to
command large and even increasing classes; that of
yesterday evening considerably exceeded two hundred,
a larger assembly than any they hitherto had had. It
appears that the lecture-room can contain only about
three hundred persons. I cannot refrain from expressing my surprise at William's great success, aided
as he is by little more than the blackboard and
chalk. . . .

WILLIAM TO HIS FATHER.

BALTIMORE, February 19, 1828.

. . . The course in the Institute will soon terminate.
Dr. Vethake will conclude his lectures on Saturday
week, — the 1st of March, — and I shall finish nearly
at the same time. The want of apparatus has compelled me entirely to omit several subjects in my department. This, though a matter of regret to me,
may prove advantageous to my course in the winter,
as it will enable me to give it an air of novelty. I
have really been surprised to see my lectures so well

attended, though entirely destitute of the usual attractions of a popular course. Last week I lectured upon the tides and the theories of the earth. I took occasion to expose the absurdities of Captain Symmes's hypothesis, which had gained many advocates in Baltimore, and my criticisms appeared to excite much interest in the class. There is some talk of connecting an English and Mathematical School with the Institute. It is highly probable that this will be effected in the ensuing spring. Should it be soon, the managers are desirous that I should undertake the management of the school. They will meet on Monday next, when I shall receive more definite information on this subject. I think when I have completed my course I will pay you a visit. I wish to see the old college, and particularly your apparatus-room, and I am desirous of examining the electrical instruments which you have constructed. . . .

HENRY TO HIS FATHER.

BALTIMORE, April 12, 1828.

. . . I have been less punctual in writing, as William has personally and by letter informed you concerning my health and whatever else it would interest you to know. I was pleased to hear that you advised my joining with him in the contemplated school to be established in the Institute. This change of circumstances will be highly acceptable, as I foresee, from its present declining state, that I would have to relinquish my present establishment in the country. My connection with William, though it must for the present be in a subordinate capacity, will eventually redound, I think, to my advantage. Even now his reputation is considerable, and the approaching winter will no doubt augment it. . . . William is at present engaged in maturing a scheme for the regulation of the school, to be offered to a committee of managers for their approval. . . .

WILLIAM TO THE GOVERNORS OF THE MARYLAND
INSTITUTE.

BALTIMORE, April 13, 1828.

TO THE COMMITTEE OF THE INSTITUTE:

Gentlemen, — In obedience to your request, I submit the following hints towards a plan and regulations for the High School about to be established in the Maryland Institute. . . .

1. The aim of the school being to impart such knowledge and to induce such habits of mind as may be most beneficial to youth engaging in mechanical and mercantile employments, the study of mathematics will be an object of primary attention, and will, it is expected, be pursued to a considerable extent. The earlier classes will be instructed in arithmetic, reading, writing, grammar and geography; the more advanced, in algebra, geometry, mensuration, surveying, navigation, perspective, etc., and perhaps in English composition. The latter grade of scholars, after having made a certain proficiency in their mathematical studies, will be taught the elementary principles of astronomy, mechanics, natural philosophy and chemistry, and will be permitted to attend the lectures in the Institute in aid of their scientific studies, as a reward for their diligence and improvement.

2. Classical studies are not within the scope of the school.

3. The number will be limited to fifty.

4. To obtain admission into the school, the pupil must be able to spell correctly, read with facility, write a fair hand, and perform arithmetical computations at least as far as the rule of three.

5. The price of instruction will be eight dollars per quarter, in which the expense of fuel, pens, slate-pencils and other stationery, and books, is not included. . . .

The subject of railways was now beginning to be actively discussed, and William early contributed to the popular interest in the subject by experimental lectures on the principles involved.

HENRY TO HIS FATHER.

BALTIMORE, May 3, 1828.

. . . William has lately delivered to very crowded assemblies a couple of lectures on the subject of Railroads, which have greatly roused the attention and gained the interest of the people here. By the assistance of some beautiful models, he rendered them both instructive and entertaining. Indeed, such was the eagerness displayed by the populace to become better acquainted with the principles of an undertaking in which they are all interested, that the lecture-room could not contain more than half of those who endeavoured to gain admission. This he finds has operated favourably in advancing his new undertaking, and when the August holidays shall have freed the children from their existing engagements we expect an accession that will fill the proposed school to our limit of fifty. William will write in a few days, informing you more particularly of the progress we are making. . . .

WILLIAM TO HIS FATHER.

BALTIMORE, May 19, 1828.

DEAR FATHER, — I received your letter of the 14th this afternoon. I believe the " low spirits " of which you complain is inherent in the family; for Henry and myself are sometimes affected with it, although we have never been able to assign a reasonable cause for our depression. It is not to be wondered at that in your situation the mind should occasionally fall into this state. It is the natural consequence of the monotony of a village life. But I hope a visit to Baltimore in July will exhilarate you. I should have written to you before this to inform you of the progress of our plans, but I was desirous of first ascertaining our prospects of success. I am pleased that it is now in my power to tell you that they are encouraging. We opened school on Monday last with ten pupils, and the number has since been augmented to seventeen. In addition to these, we have the promise of many others who, being engaged in other schools, cannot with propriety be withdrawn until the expiration of their current quarter. These included, our list numbers about twenty-four. This is not a bad beginning. . . . I have no doubt that in less than six months our school will be in a very flourishing condition. The school-room, which is one of the lower apartments in the Institute, fronts on Charles Street, and is airy and tolerably commodious. Our hours of duty are from eight to half after eleven in the morning, and from half after two to five in the afternoon, making six hours in the day. Robert, who left the country last week and boards with us at Mr. Trego's, has entered the school. He appears to be perfectly satisfied with the change, and is in good health and spirits. The week before last, Henry and I paid a visit to Philadelphia for the purpose of inspecting the High School of the Franklin Institute. We remained there two days, and would willingly have prolonged our stay if it had been in our power. Philadelphia has greatly increased in extent and beauty since my boyish days, yet I did not feel altogether as a stranger in it. I soon became familiar with its streets, and recognized many scenes of my juvenile frolics. I visited the parts of the city in which we used to reside, and felt a peculiar interest in viewing the house in Ninth Street and the old University. We could not obtain an interview with Uncle James[1] until the morning of our departure. He

---

[1] Mr. James Rogers, a merchant of Philadelphia, often referred to later.

treated us with cordiality, and expressed a wish that we would make a longer stay in the city. He is quite gray, but nevertheless appears to enjoy almost youthful hilarity. He inquired particularly respecting your health and situation. . . .

HENRY TO HIS FATHER.

BALTIMORE, June 7, 1828.

. . . James is quite well. He is actively employed in the discharge of his duties, which require, indeed, through the day, an unremitting application. I think he displays, from his success in many delicate and complicated processes, and from the certainty and accuracy of his final determinations, no ordinary acquaintance with the difficult operations of refined analysis. Indeed, I have no doubt but that he will one day be among the first practical chemists in the country.

I feel my impatience to see you rapidly increasing as the time draws near, and find myself daily and almost hourly estimating the shortening period which must elapse before that time arrives. Secluded as I am in a great measure from any society in which I could mingle with any degree of comfort, and debarred from any substitute I might find in books, from the oppressiveness of the season and the effects of the confinement attendant upon school, I am continually wishing for your enlivening company. I feel an eager longing for those cheerful moments which an intercourse with you has never failed to bring. I believe I shall never cease to look to you as a guardian spirit. The sense of security which I always have when possessing your advice has afforded me many of my happiest hours ; and, now that I am embarking in an arduous business, the value of your counsel will be highly prized. I hope you will bring with you your violin and music. . . .

BALTIMORE, June 26, 1828.

DEAR FATHER, — We have been expecting a letter from you for some weeks, and have become apprehensive that you are unwell. I hope you will write to us immediately. We look forward with pleasure to your arrival in Baltimore, and our impatience increases as the time at which we expect you approaches. We are all pretty well, though some of us are enfeebled by the warmth of the season. Robert is quite hearty. Henry and I have found our engagement very fatiguing. We have recently instituted a plan in the school which enables us to relieve each other on alternate days. The mode in which teaching is usually conducted renders it as servile and laborious an occupation as that of a ditcher. Teachers in our cities find it necessary to devote the whole of their time to the concerns of their occupation. Some of them keep their schools open for more than eight hours in the day. Surely their health must ultimately sink under such confinement. We are employed in the school only six hours, and find this period sufficiently long.

James has a companion in his chemical engagements, — a young gentleman recently from France, a pupil of the celebrated Thénard. He is the most scientific young man I have ever met. With an intimate acquaintance with chemistry, theoretical and practical, and a knowledge of all the important principles of physical science, he combines a large fund of general information. We find his conversation very interesting. He is able to describe from personal knowledge many of the distinguished scientific characters of France and England.

You have perhaps heard of the solemnities which are to take place on the 4th of July. On that day the construction of our railroad will be commenced. A procession, in which all professions, dignities, and trades will be embodied, will march through the city

to the spot (about two miles from town) at which the
great work will be begun.   The spectacle will no doubt
be imposing.   The mechanics, merchants, farmers, doctors and lawyers have been busy for the last two weeks
in making arrangements to unite in the procession. On
this occasion the Freemasons will display all the decorations and paraphernalia of their order; the carpenters
will exhibit the implements of their trade and a house
moved on wheels ; the sailors, a full-rigged ship, trans-
ported in the same manner; and it is said that the
manufacturers will work a spinning jenny and loom
as they move along, and with the aid of the tailors
will produce a summer coat before the procession has
arrived at the point of its destination, which they will
present to old Mr. Carroll to be worn during the ceremonies of the day.   Mr. Carroll, who, in consequence
of the estimation in which his public services during
the Revolution are held, is called upon to officiate on
all occasions of general interest, is to break the first
ground for the railroad with a silver trowel and pick.
I must now close with affectionate wishes for your
health and happiness.

As has been stated in the previous chapter, Dr. P.
K. Rogers came northward this year as usual and
was stricken by malarial fever at Ellicott's Mills, Md.,
where he died on August 1, 1828.   How great this
blow was to his sons will be understood by those who
have read the preceding letters. Two months after
his death, in the autumn of the same year, William was
chosen his father's successor in the chair of Natural
Philosophy and Chemistry in William and Mary College, and thenceforward became, in large measure, the
head of the family.

Hon. A. H. H. Stuart, a pupil of Dr. Patrick
Rogers and a life-long friend of his son William Barton Rogers, has kindly supplied some recollections of

Dr. Rogers, and of life at William and Mary in 1824–25, as follows : —

" About the middle of October, 1824, I left my home in Staunton, Va., to become a student at William and Mary College. I was then seventeen years and a few months old. The Faculty of the college consisted of Dr. John Augustine Smith, President; Dr. Patrick Rogers, Professor of Chemistry and Natural Philosophy; Ferdinand Campbell, Professor of Mathematics; and Judge James Semple, Professor of Law.

" Some delay was caused in the commencement of the exercises of the college by the great celebration of the surrender of Cornwallis, which was held at Yorktown (twelve miles distant from Williamsburg) on the 19th of October, and was attended by General Lafayette.

" The professors were all men of ability and admirably qualified for the duties of their respective positions; but the financial condition of the State and other causes tended to reduce the number of students in attendance to about thirty. This paucity of numbers led to a more free and familiar intercourse between the students and the professors, and with each other, than would have existed if the number had been larger. There was no regular curriculum in force, and each student was at liberty to select the studies he would pursue. . . .

" Dr. Smith, the President, resided in a spacious brick mansion, known as the ' President's House,' situated on the north side of the lawn of four acres which lies in front of the college. Professor Rogers occupied a similar house on the south side of the lawn, and known as the ' Brafferton House.' The other professors lived some distance from the college.

" In 1824 Professor Rogers was a widower. His family consisted of four sons, viz., James, William, Henry and Robert, all of whom, in after life, became distinguished scientists and professors. James, the

oldest, had completed his education and left Williamsburg before I entered college. . . . William had graduated with great distinction a year or two before I
entered college, and was looked up to with the respect
and almost reverence with which college boys regard
those who have won high college honours.

"Henry was, I presume, near my own age. We
were classmates and friends, and, although it so
happened that we did not meet in after life, I noted
with great pleasure every step that he made in his
onward progress to the success and distinction which
he so richly merited. Robert was, during my sojourn
in Williamsburg, an active, vigorous, and sprightly
schoolboy, apparently thirteen or fourteen years of
age. In form and features he was much more like his
father than either of his brothers. My most vivid
recollection of him is as a diligent flyer of kites on
the lawn! He, like his brothers, attained great distinction.

"Dr. Patrick Rogers, at the time I became acquainted with him, was about sixty, or possibly sixty-
five years of age, and a man of imposing presence. He
was about six feet in height and was massively framed.
I presume he must have weighed from 180 to 200
pounds. His hair was as white as snow, and his com-
plexion ruddy and healthful, and contrasted beautifully
with his snow-like hair. His face was distinctively
Irish in its general appearance. His manner was deliberate and dignified, but courteous and affable. In
temperament, I judge, from the readiness with which
his face would flush with each emotion, that he was
sensitive and excitable. He was devotedly attached to
and proud of his sons, and on more than one occasion
I was struck with the interest which he showed in the
amusements of Robert. . . .

"Dr. Rogers was a very learned man, and a most
able, faithful instructor, and seemed desirous of keeping pace with the events of the day. As an illustration, I will refer to a single interesting incident.

About the middle of the session, the newspapers of the State were teeming with accounts of the mysterious ringing of the bells in the elegant mansion of Colonel John Taylor, of Mount Airy, in King George County. The bells would commence ringing violently all over the house without any visible human agency, or cause for so doing; and there was much speculation as to the true cause. In a few days thereafter, when the doors of Dr. Rogers's lecture-room opened, the eyes of the students were greeted with the extraordinary spectacle of a whole system of bells, in different parts of the room, ringing in concert, without any apparent cause for their activity. After we had looked for some time at the wonderful spectacle, they were suddenly and simultaneously silenced, and the professor then proceeded with a delightfully instructive lecture to show how the result had been accomplished, by currents of positive and negative electricity, thereby explaining all the phenomena connected with the Taylor mansion on scientific principles. . . .

"Dr. Rogers lived a somewhat secluded life, mingling but little in general society. His time was devoted to study, the society of his sons, and the direction and supervision of their education. He enjoyed the reputation of being a profound scholar, and I can bear testimony that he was a careful and faithful teacher, singularly successful in his illustrative experiments before his class."

CHAPTER III.

1828-1835.

William succeeds his Father. — His Introductory Address. — Correspondence of the Brothers. — Life in Williamsburg. — Henry appointed Professor of Chemistry and Natural Philosophy in Dickinson College. — James Professor of Chemistry in a Baltimore
Medical College. — His Marriage. — Henry leaves Dickinson College. — With Robert, is engaged on Railroad Surveys in New
England. — The Cholera. — William visits North Carolina. — Narrowly escapes Drowning. — Henry visits England. — His Impressions of English Men of Science. — He returns to Philadelphia and
lectures on Geology at the Franklin Institute. — Geological and
Chemical Investigations of the Brothers. — Henry appointed Professor in the University of Pennsylvania. — Proposals for Geological
Surveys. — Appointment of William to a Professorship in the University of Virginia.

As we have already seen, it was the custom at
William and Mary College for a professor to mark
the formal opening of the year by an introductory
address. In the previous year (1827) this address
was delivered by Dr. Patrick Rogers, who began by
eulogizing his lately deceased friend, Dr. Wilmer,
President of the College, and passed on to remarks
on education, some of which were quoted in the last
chapter.

By a chain of natural causes William Barton
Rogers, now Professor of Natural Philosophy in the
Maryland Institute, and already well known as a

successful teacher and lecturer, himself a graduate of distinction of William and Mary College, was chosen to be his father's successor, and the duty of making the opening address in 1828 devolved upon him.

The election occurred on October 13, 1828, but before that time, in accordance with a custom prevailing at the college, the young man and his friends secured and forwarded to the governors numerous testimonials in his favor. In this connection the following letters are of interest: —

HENRY TO WILLIAM.

BALTIMORE, October 1, 1828.

DEAR WILLIAM, — I received on Saturday last your interesting letter, and immediately set about executing the commissions it contains. On Sunday I had some conversation with Mr. Hasard, in which he appeared to enter warmly into your interests, engaging himself to procure forthwith the credentials of the engineers, Colonel Long and Dr. Howard, — the latter of whom I find is at present in town, — and promising at the same time to convene the managers as soon as practicable, in order to procure from them as a body collectively the testimonials which you have desired. This was done last night, and, upon my mentioning to them in a note your wishes, they passed a resolution authorizing the secretary, Mr. Latrobe, to draw up a letter to be signed by the chairman, Mr. Lucas, and himself, on behalf of the board as a body. I succeeded on Monday in seeing Dr. McAulay, and was cordially received. I then saw Dr. Potter, who, with equal politeness, has afforded his attestation, protesting characteristically that, had he been aware of your views and wishes, he would have voluntarily afforded you his name. You have therefore letters from Drs.

Baker and Potter and two from the engineers, together
with general ones from our managers and the Faculty
of Washington College.[1]

Dear William, inform me soon of the aspect of
your affairs, for I feel a powerful interest in the result
of your exertions. I have heard many persons express their deep regret at the likelihood of your
removal to Virginia, and some of them, I suppose, are
looking around them in despair for some individual to
supply your place. One or two with whom I have
conversed have looked to me, thinking me the only
·alternative they have. Mr. Hasard, who is anxious
for the preservation of the school and is really desirous that the Institute should flourish, has suggested to
me the expediency of remaining here, saying there can
be little doubt of my succeeding you; that I could
employ an assistant in the school; and that, with the
aid of the expected apparatus, he did not question my
ability to afford them ample satisfaction. This is a
subject which I wish you to revolve well in your mind,
and on which, when you have leisure, to express your
full and decided opinion.

BALTIMORE, October 3.

In fulfillment of the promise stated in the envelope
of the package which I forwarded the day before yesterday, I now transmit a very gratifying letter drawn
up by Colonel Long, and signed by himself and Captain McNiel. I was not a little surprised to hear from
Mr. Hasard, who has been active in procuring this
letter, that it is the opinion of both those engineers,
with whom he himself agrees, that your ultimate advancement would be more promoted by your remaining here. They state that there is now opening in
this country an extensive field for highly respectable
and lucrative exertion in the growing spirit for works
of internal improvement demanding the superintend-

[1] The medical college in which James taught.

ence of scientific men. This I have thought it my duty to communicate, and shall for the same reason suppress my own opinion.

The college was formally opened on October 27, and on November 12 there appeared in the " Phœnix Ploughboy," published in Williamsburg, a report of the young professor's introductory address, prefaced by an editorial comment: —

" The following address of Professor Rogers, introductory to his course of natural philosophy, was delivered a few days ago in the College of William and Mary to a numerous and attentive assemblage of ladies and gentlemen. We could not avoid listening to our youthful professor with lively emotions, as, with the animated warmth of true filial sensibility, he adverted to the recent melancholy event which had left that chair vacant to which he was now appointed by the Visitors of the Institution." . . .

ADDRESS OF PROFESSOR ROGERS.

In entering upon the duties which have been devolved upon me by the governors of this institution, I am impressed with feelings which it is difficult to describe, — feelings that arise from the peculiar relationship in which I stand to the revered individual whom I have succeeded.

To have returned to the scenes of my early youth — scenes hallowed in my bosom by every fond and pleasurable sentiment; to be enabled to renew the delightful associations which even the absence of several years has but slightly impaired; to tread again within these consecrated precincts, where at every step the remembrances of former years are awakened into animated existence, and where the very air I breathe seems almost to speak of companions dear to my affections, of social study and collegiate ambition — is, I confess, attended with emotions of the purest and liveliest satisfaction. And I may be permitted to add that these sentiments are heightened by reflecting on the circumstances in which I am about to renew my connection with these scenes, and to become again an inmate in the halls of my venerable *Alma Mater.* But, alas! mournful considerations sadden these reflections, and, indulging in them, gratification is converted into grief.

To your sensibilities I will commit the task of appreciating the feelings I experience when, with the affections of a cherished son and pupil, I view the objects that surround me, associated as they all are with the recollections of a venerated parent and preceptor. Should I conduct you to the apartments in which for a series of years, with the calm dignity of true philosophy, he imparted to his pupils whatever is useful or sublime in physical science; should I display to your view the beautiful collection of philosophical instruments in which he took such pride, arranged with characteristic neatness and symmetry, and in some degree the products of his own ingenuity and zeal, — you would feel these traces of his recent presence with a melancholy force, and friendship would sympathize with filial tenderness in the engrossing sorrow of the scene.

Were I gifted with the chastened though pathetic eloquence which flowed spontaneously from his pen; could I imitate, even at an humble distance, the touching pathos with which at the opening of the last course he paid the tribute of grateful eulogy to a colleague dear to Williamsburg, to the college, and to himself, — I would gladly present you with a picture of his diversified excellencies worthy of such a subject. But I feel myself inadequate to the task. Nor is it necessary that I should attempt it. I feel assured that by those of you who knew him his memory will not be forgotten. But his intellectual qualifications and attainments, his humane sensibilities, his paternal regard for the youth under his preceptorship, his devotion to the interests of the college, his candor, his innocent simplicity of heart, his inflexibility of principle, and the lofty spirit of independence which shone in all his thoughts and actions, will long be cherished in your affections, and his name, in association with that of his late revered colleague, will continue to be repeated with eulogy by those who shall have the interests of this institution at heart, until these ancient halls shall have ceased to be visited by the votaries of knowledge, or until whatever is eminent in intelligence or exalted in moral character shall have ceased to be subjects of admiring and grateful recollection.

I trust, in thus giving expression to the feelings which arise from the circumstances in which I am placed, I shall not be regarded as an ostentatious panegyrist, or an obtrusive claimant of your sympathies. I have felt, in assuming the functions but recently exercised by my beloved father in the college, that some offering of the heart was due to his memory, and demanded as well by the warmth of filial affection as by a sense of the obligations of justice and filial duty.

But, quitting a theme upon which, however natural, it is profitless to dwell, I would for a moment address myself to those who are about to become inmates of this institution. Towards you, gentlemen, I am henceforth to be placed in a relation of the most interesting character, one in which my interests will be in a great measure mutual with your own, and in which the happiness and success of both will be much promoted by a continued reciprocation of kindness, friendship and esteem. You must be aware that on my part such a relation involves duties of an important and sometimes extremely delicate nature, — duties embracing not merely the judicious fulfillment of a course of scientific instruction, but the enforcement of those laws which have been established for the regulation of the college, and with the observance of which your collegiate acquisitions and subsequent advancement in life are not less intimately connected than the reputation and prosperity of the institution to which you are attached.

In assuming my functions in the college, it is natural that I should be desirous of conciliating your respect and kind regard. I would fondly hope that the mantle which has descended to me, though no longer graced by the paternal character with which age had invested my predecessor, may still, through a zealous devotion to your interests, be viewed with reverence and affectionate estimation. From my own experience as a student of this college, I am aware of the feelings with which, under certain circumstances, even the noblest and most ingenuous youths are accustomed to regard the collegiate authorities. I know they do not always advert to the community of interest by which the preceptor and pupil are naturally united to each other, but sometimes look with dissatisfaction, if not hostility, upon those who certainly should be among their best and most valued friends. Such feelings are much to be deprecated, and I sincerely desire never to become the object of them. It is, therefore, that I would here willingly begin that intercourse of kindness and mutual confidence which I shall ever labor to maintain, by giving you the assurance that I shall esteem it my duty, as it will be my delight, by every means within my power, to contribute to the success of your studious pursuits, and to your general happiness and welfare, and by claiming from you in return a share of that cordial goodwill which, with generous ardor, you dispense to your associates in letters, and your participants in study, emulation and honour.

After these remarks, which I trust will be received in the spirit in which they have been dictated, I would solicit your attention to the views which I shall present in illustration of the *history, nature* and *utility* of Physical Science generally, and particularly that

WILLIAM AND MARY COLLEGE, WILLIAMSBURG, VIRGINIA

"The Brafferton" on the right

department of it which is usually denominated Natural Philosophy.   In presenting these views I propose, —

First. To allude to the relative proficiency of the ancient and modern worlds in Science and the Arts.

Secondly. To exhibit some general ideas in relation to the material world; and,

Thirdly. After defining the science of Natural Philosophy, and tracing the limits which separate it from Chemistry, to adduce a variety of illustrations to evince its utility. . . .

Among the letters of congratulation upon his appointment, the first which we find came from his uncle, James Rogers, of Philadelphia.   After the death of the father, this uncle plays an important part in the family affairs.   He is described as having been a gentleman of courtly and most agreeable manners. IIis friendly attitude towards the orphan brothers is illustrated by the following postscript of a letter addressed to Henry some months later: "At all times command my services and my money too.   So long as used and necessary for your comfort or respectability, I tender you both."

His letter to William was as follows: —

JAMES ROGERS, ESQ., TO HIS NEPHEW WILLIAM.

PHILADELPHIA, October 29, 1828.

MY DEAR WILLIAM, — I congratulate you upon your success in obtaining the situation in William and Mary lately filled by your much-lamented father.

While we all mourn the great bereavement we suffer in the loss of so near and beloved a relative, I feel some consolation in the assurance that his excellent example, devotedness and great attention to the education and morals of his sons will be treasured up by them as a most invaluable inheritance. I am anxious to know how your brothers are occupied. . . .

BALTIMORE, November 3, 1828.

It is really to me a source of the proudest exultation that, by the mere influence of unpatronized, unobtrusive merit, James and yourself are likely to acquire well-founded respectability and a permanent success. Continue, William, to exercise the same prepossessing disposition which has gained for you here many real friends, and you will grow in the respect of your colleagues and the students, and inspire in the inhabitants a deep-rooted and enduring attachment. Their sympathizing veneration for the exalted character of our father sways my mind with a gratitude more powerful than I deemed myself capable of entertaining, and their regard for Robert oppresses me with a softened love.

During the past week I attended most of the introductory lectures in each of the rival schools, and discovered a vast superiority in those delivered by James and his coadjutors. James surprised and fascinated his auditory, without one exception. To me it was a most gratifying spectacle to witness the rapt and approving attention of many who were unprepared for such an intellectual treat. I could read in the according smiles and tokens of the professors their high estimation of his abilities, and the pleasure they received from his elegant production.

The reference to James in this letter shows that he had already begun his connection with a medical school, lately opened in Baltimore as a rival to an older and well-established school. James's hopes of success in this lectureship, though brilliant in the beginning, soon faded, and both he and Henry sought for places in the Maryland Institute. Their letters during this period to William, who now had an assured position, are numerous, and alternately buoyant with hope and heavy with discouragement. But however dark the outlook, they never sought counsel of William without obtaining a sympathetic response.

HENRY TO WILLIAM.

BALTIMORE, November 14, 1828.

I have attended the post-office for some days past in anxious expectation of receiving a letter, but until to-day have always returned disappointed and disheartened. . . . .

Dear William, I have been subject for two weeks past to the most deep despondence. A sense of friendless destitution is ever rising to shadow with its gloom my liveliest aspirings; it requires for its suppression the utmost exertion which my fortitude can sustain. Oh, how I sometimes deplore the necessity of my absence from you! each succeeding day seems only to heighten my regret. You will not think me unreasonable in my repining when you reflect on my utter loneliness, — on the harassing incertitude of mind arising from the inexplicable delay in the arrival of the apparatus, and on the precarious condition of my health.

Scarcely a half hour elapses but my mind steals insensibly away from its occupation, to dwell in musing on you and Robert, surrounded as you are by the tranquillizing yet animating influence of your own avocations, so happily blended with the refined society around you. I cannot think of Robert, with his gentle, tender disposition, but a rising gush of feeling overcomes me. Do be explicit about his health and welfare. Let him know that I cherish towards him, as towards yourself, an affection that agitates me when solitary with an irrepressible solicitude. . . . I feel

in your absence a void of all the objects of my regard;
and in the spontaneous swellings of a long-cherished
love I vainly seek for something to allay its fervour
in giving it direction.   I never thought till now that
I could derive gratification from caressing a dog. . . .

If you knew the uncontrollable eagerness with which
I expected a letter by each mail for the last six days,
and the sharp disappointments which attended my applications at the office, you would find time to give me
at least some intimation of yours and Robert's health.

Dear brothers, the most unbounded love to both.
Farewell.   HENRY.

WILLIAM TO HENRY.

WILLIAMSBURG, December 6, 1828.

DEAR BROTHER, — The disappointment with which
I perused the beginning of your last letter was mingled
with a sentiment of indignation at the culpable neglect
which has marked the conduct of the Managers of the
Institute.   Yet, while a sympathy in your hopes and
your laudable ambition to become eminent rendered
the information contained in your letter painfully dis-
appointing, the prospect of welcoming you to our Virginia home, and of enjoying society once more so
peculiarly congenial to my feelings, more than counter-
balanced these unpleasant sentiments, and induced me
almost to wish that there was no longer even a possibility of the arrival of the apparatus, or of the occurrence of any circumstance which might protract your
absence.

I trust, in the event of the non-arrival of the apparatus, you will not hesitate to leave Baltimore immediately.   Your health and enjoyment would be greatly
enhanced by a residence in hospitable old Williamsburg.   You might prosecute your studies at leisure
with the facilities which the college would furnish, and
improve your qualifications for situations similar to
that which you have been expecting in the Institute.

It is indeed almost the only wish of my heart which is not fulfilled that we might all live together. . . . I have just concluded my lectures on caloric, to my own satisfaction, and, I am well assured, in a manner agreeable to the class. No little difficulties arising from want of instruments, or from imperfection in those we possess, or any other trival circumstances connected with my duties, give me the slightest uneasiness or perplexity. I employ every accessible means of illustrating my subject in an intelligible manner, and when instruments fail me I have recourse to explanations. The want of apparatus is certainly a serious difficulty in the way of a lecturer. But I believe that one course delivered under these circumstances is of more value as an exercise to the professor than half a dozen assisted by the usual auxiliaries.

Both James and Henry finally obtained, and filled for a time, the places which they coveted in the Maryland Institute, the former the lectureship on Chemistry, the latter that on Natural Philosophy, though in Henry's case at a reduced stipend ($150 for three months' service). Accordingly, William's cordial offer of refuge to the latter was not accepted and the winter was spent in Baltimore. Thus it happened that here Henry formed the acquaintance of Miss Fanny Wright, an apostle of Fourierism, of whom he writes to William: —

" The populace of Baltimore throughout all last week have been wonderstruck by the matchless eloquence of a most daring reformer. Miss Frances Wright, a coadjutor of Owen the Harmonist, and joint conductor with him of the ' Harmony Gazette,' an infidel in all religion and an avowed opponent of existing institutions, has, in association with a gentleman of the name of Jennings, been preaching a crusade throughout the chief of the Atlantic cities. A prodigy in learning, in intellect and in courage, she awes into deference the most refractory bigots. . . .

"Unable, through the narrow-minded policy of the proprietors, to procure the use of any other room sufficiently capacious, she was compelled to lecture in the Belvidere Theatre. Fancy a woman nearly six feet high, majestic in her mien, and with a countenance betokening a long indulgence in the most refined and philosophic thought, with her short hair unbound and in ringlets on a head which would have graced Minerva, standing before a multitude in the delivery of strains written in a style of unsurpassed elegance, and delivered with a grace which Dr. Barber could not equal: — think, William, that I witnessed this and much more in reality, and then I think you will excuse my fervour. But I am unjust in withholding the mention of her rarest peculiarities. To be more explicit in my account, her native country is Scotland, and her birthrights were wealth and all the refined luxuries of aristocratic Europe, but for her noble intellect these seem to possess no fascinations; from her early youth she forsook them to devote her time to study in all branches, even the abstrusest. Well versed in the languages and learning of antiquity, she associates what is rarely their companion, — a comprehensive acquaintance with the absolute sciences of modern times. After spending her youth in the acquisition of all these, she conceived the noble design of enlightening by her labours the views of mankind. Her independent mind, spurning obedience to the self-invested authority with which ecclesiastics have ever endeavoured to trammel the actions and even the thoughts of men, and actuated in her attempts by views based on the soundest philosophy, she has devoted her life to the promulgation of sound principles and just knowledge. Renouncing the enticements of her former sphere of life, she has suffered an ample fortune to become impaired in the dis-

charge of her arduous undertaking. She is now intent
on procuring, in the chief cities of the country, the establishment of " halls of science " appropriated to the
instruction of all orders of society, in every demonstra-
tive department of human learning. According to the
plan proposed by her in her lectures, these should ac-
commodate, gratuitous of cost, from three to five thousand persons each. They should have attached to them
lecturers on all the certain sciences, libraries and apparatus, and extensive schools; but in them she would
have the existing methods of instruction totally sub-
verted, and their place supplanted by others far more
rational. That you may know more accurately her
views, I should inform you of the purport and topics
of her lectures. Her first was on free inquiry, tending
to lull the prejudices of those who recoil at the discussion of subjects at all implicating religion. The two
subsequent ones regarded knowledge, its importance,
its true nature, and its source primarily in the senses:
this had a powerful bearing on the substantiality of
religious belief. The fourth lecture was devoted to a
disproof of the justice of any science of theology, and
contained some highly philosophical discussion on the
distinction between belief and knowledge. In the last
she treated of morals. The whole might be regarded
as a happy extension and application of the sound philosophy of Brown to the existing condition of human
institutions; but there were throughout such clearness and reach of thought, sublimity of diction, and
often such powerful philippics against the clergy, that
every mind seemed spell-bound throughout the term
of her lectures. To *you* I need communicate but one
circumstance to impress a just conception of the rare
acuteness of her mind. In an interview with her which
I sought, after much conversation, — all displaying a
transcendent genius, — she spoke of the true nature of
mathematical truth, denied its foundation in abstrac-
tions, and dwelt on the importance of communicating
its first principle, through *perception.*"

BALTIMORE, January 6, 1829.

You would be surprised at beholding the entire re-
verse of popular sentiment as respects the Institute.
James, though he acquits himself in an admirable
manner, has but a handful of two or three dozen yawn-
ing and lounging listeners. My own classes are as
slender, and to all appearance as little edified. Now,
though I am conscious my manner has been unassured
and consequently tame, yet, in thought and subject
it should have been interesting. I certainly can avow
with no undue self-praise that, adopting as a guide
the notes which you had left me, I inculcated in the
three last lectures an enlarged and critically correct
philosophy. I have said I feel no disappointment at
our own inauspicious circumstances, but I do feel provoked at the inattention and mismanagement of the
managers. All must be ascribed to them, and so entirely have they weaned the popular regard that, under
present feeling, no efforts of the lecturer can avail to
regain it. They seem, however, conscious of their
dereliction, and determined to adopt in future more
strenuous means of promoting our interests. I am
therefore contented with the present, and only solicitous to accomplish myself in my profession.

The town has been all on the *qui vive* for some days
past in witnessing the exhibition of a newly invented
railroad friction wagon, the contrivance of a Mr.
Winans, of New Jersey. The invention is certainly
valuable; in the exhibited model, a half-pound drew,
on level rails, 1,000 pounds!

Dearest brother, could I convey in due expression
the dictates of my surcharged emotions, you might
rightly appreciate the devotedness of my affection. I
have lately, for the first time, adequately conceived the
amount of gratitude I owe you; you have been to me
a moral master, a steadfast friend and an enlightened
tutor. I owe to you much of my acquisitions, but I
owe you more, — the mental independence of erroneous

views : you have always inculcated in me the purest
virtues and the most enlightened philosophy. But
for your valuable precepts, I should never have enjoyed the proud gratification of my present engagements. Under your guidance I anticipate that Robert
will prove an accomplished scholar and a virtuous
man.

What think you of Miss Wright and her plans? I
find it necessary to be guarded in my expressions, but,
thanks to our lamented Father and yourself, I enjoy a
precious freedom from the despotic sway of false and
perverting doctrines. Williamsburg is, I suppose,
almost enveloped in the Bishop's cassock.

At this time the young Williamsburg professor was
apparently keeping bachelors' hall, with two of his
colleagues, in the Brafferton, the home of his earlier
years.

In spite of Henry's melancholy mood, William
expresses his satisfaction with the family prospects,
and adds to a letter addressed to Henry interesting
suggestions on the art of lecturing : —

WILLIAM TO HENRY.

WILLIAMSBURG, January 12, 1829.

DEAR HENRY, — I was pleased to find by your last
letter that yourself and James are progressing in your
professional duties in a manner so satisfactory to yourself and your auditors. From the moment in which
the prospect of your present engagement was presented, I experienced delightful anticipations of the
honour and advantage you were about to derive from
them, and felt an assured confidence of your eminent
success. Believe me, even were my own circumstances
less rich in sources of satisfaction than they are, the
consideration of the happy success which attends you
both would of itself be sufficient to impart content

and tranquillity to my mind. Every letter that I direct to James and yourself elates my thoughts. I feel that I ought to be proud of such brothers, and of being one of three who, though youthful, are already so honourably distinguished from the general mass of society.

The " unassured manner " to which you allude, as a cause of occasional embarrassment, is a difficulty with which all who are entering on a career such as yours are obliged to contend. Lecturing is in some respects to be considered as an art, and perhaps the same remark may be applicable to public speaking of every description, even the more eloquent displays of the pulpit, the senate and the bar. Much practice is requisite to acquire such a degree of readiness as will be satisfactory to the speaker, and enlivening to his auditory. In my opinion, a very important requisite in public speaking is zeal, or perhaps I might even say enthusiasm. With respect to my own exertions, I have always observed that my success in exposition is proportioned to the earnestness with which I engage in it. Too minute an attention to accuracy of phraseology will infallibly induce hesitation of manner. It is even better to allow an inaccuracy of expression to pass uncorrected than to become involved in confusion by an attempt at amendment. The importance of this remark I have learned from experience, and think it cannot be too deeply impressed. You will find that as you progress you will acquire increased ease and power of expression, and you will sometimes be surprised at the facility and effect with which you deliver yourself. Even in the midst of your disquisitions, you will on some occasions become your own auditor, and will enjoy a singular species of satisfaction from witnessing your own exertions, as if they were those of a distinct individual.

We are all perfectly well, and as happy as we can be without the participation of James and yourself.

Assure Mr. Keyser that I do not forget my duty to him, and that I intend writing to him by the next mail. He is a gentleman whose friendship I have always valued highly. Of his excellent father[1] I cannot think without feelings of almost filial affection. You may inform the old gentleman that I have applied the platina sponge and wire to several useful and interesting purposes in my lectures, and not without acknowledging my obligations to a scientific friend in Baltimore.

In the autumn of the same year (1829) Henry became a candidate for the chair of Chemistry and Natural Philosophy in Dickinson College, Carlisle, Pa., to which he was formally elected in January, 1830, while in his 22d year. "Whilst connected with the college he edited ' The Messenger of Useful Knowledge,' a monthly magazine of popular scientific character, and also containing essays on educational, literary and political subjects, and valuable information from foreign journals."[2] To this journal, edited by his brother, William contributed occasional essays, notably one on "Dew."

With the arrival of the autumn, and the opening of another academic year, William returned as usual to Williamsburg. To his uncle James, in Philadelphia, he writes of the contrast between life in a country college and that offered by a large city : —

WILLIAMSBURG, November 8, 1829.

DEAR UNCLE, — To you, who reside in a busy, populous city where every hour gives birth to occurrences of interest, the details of village transactions would

[1] This was probably the china merchant (p. 15).
[2] *Dickinson College*, by Charles F. Himes, Ph. D., Professor of Natural Science. Harrisburg, Pa., 1879.

appear trivial and contemptible. Nor is the news
which originates with us calculated to excite the curiosity of a stranger. Our town, like others of the
same grade, is a favorite abode of that daughter of
Satan, *Gossipry*, whose restless tongue from house to
house rings, untiring, "its eternal larum," and whose
wrinkled visage, "spectacle-bestrid," is seen invading
the privacies of intercourse, and introducing discord
and confusion into the domestic circle. Heaven be
praised! she has yet permitted me the undisturbed
enjoyment of my fireside, and I trust she will thus
continue to observe her distance. I pity the luckless
wight upon whom she has once fixed her "scrutiny
severe."

Our college has opened with encouraging prospects,
but at the present stage of the course no correct estimation of the ultimate amount of students can be
made. Our number will at least equal that of the
former session; most probably it will be greater. My
own classes are perhaps the largest in the institution;
and that in the department of Natural Philosophy has
not been equalled for the last ten years.

It has too often been the case in the United States
that medical schools have been created largely for the
sake of fame or financial gain to their owners. The
one in Baltimore, in which James was a professor,
appears to have been an example of this kind.

JAMES TO WILLIAM.

BALTIMORE, November 22, 1829.
. . . Washington College may, by a very fortuitous
concourse of events, acquire a reputation which, in a
pecuniary point of view, shall be valuable to its professors, as an unworthy and undeserving nephew acquires an unlooked-for fortune by the death of a
rich uncle who dies intestate; or it may for a time

attract the wonder and incite the curiosity of the
searchers after medical honours by the wildness and
attractive novelty of its emanations, dignified theories,
strange compounds of philosophy and poetry, fact
and fiction, — things captivating to the young medical
mind, and producing impressions as evanescent and
illusory as is the reputation they would seem to bestow on their author. You may understand my allu-
sions when I inform you that Dr. M. has discovered
that the *whole medical world*, from the days of old
Father Hippocrates down to the present time, has been
in the midst of error in accounting for the phenomena
of life, and in leaving out of consideration the wonderful agency of the compound of *oxygen*, electricity,
and caloric, in forming the nervous fluid, while the
blood is undergoing its various mutations in the animal economy. . . .

William now began to win success as a teacher : —

ROBERT (AGE 16) TO HENRY.

WILLIAMSBURG, December 6, 1829.
. . . William has his hands full, having to lecture
twice every day. His class are advancing very well
indeed, and they are all very much pleased. William
has divided his classes into four divisions, which are
called *clubs ;* he meets one of them every night of the
week except Saturday and Tuesday, and the students
attend with the greatest alacrity possible : there is not
the least disorder among them, either at college or
at the table; they are sociable, but polite, towards
William. I put my name down on the matriculation
book, and made the 55th student. I attend, as a re-
citing student, five classes, —William's four and Mr.
Empie's. William has made a number of fine models,
and is making many more, to explain conic sections,
spherics and all solids. Two or three students were
at first very much opposed to mathematics, but now

they have become very much delighted with the subject. The subject on which William is now engaged
in chemistry is light; he will soon finish it, and then
go to electricity. He has been so very busy that he
has not been able to finish your piece, but is now
writing it. He says you shall receive something for
the "Messenger" every month. The subject on which
he is now writing is Meteorology. If I meet with
anything in my reading, I shall transcribe it and
forward it to you. There will be more studying this
year than usual, on account of there being monthly
examinations, keeping the students always on the
spur.

The Faculty, finding that the students are so well-
behaved, permitted them to meet in the society at
night. We had last night a question which is as old
as the society itself almost; it was, "*Should the
Right of Suffrage be Extended?*" I opposed the
measure at present, but I said that the lower classes
of society be first informed, and then they would
know their rights better, and therefore maintain them;
but under the present ignorance they might make
bad use of them were they extended.

Meantime, William's interest in popular education
remained unabated, and his fertility in suggestion is
illustrated by a letter addressed to his brother Henry
at Carlisle, Pa.: —

WILLIAM TO HENRY.

WILLIAMSBURG, December 15, 1829.

I approve highly of the plan of popular lectures
which you have in contemplation, and feel assured of
its beneficial results to yourself and the society of
Carlisle.

Upon reflecting on the plan which you have proposed to yourself, a variety of topics have suggested

themselves as appropriate to popular elucidation. You
have yourself hinted at astronomy and meteorology
as presenting extensive fields for the selection of interesting materials. . . . An exposition on the theory
of projectiles, embracing an account of the experiments of Robinson and Hutton and Rumford, and
simple illustrations of the resisting agencies of the
atmosphere and other fluids, might prove highly interesting to a popular audience. My students are always
delighted with the subject, and it is so susceptible of
simple illustrations that all would find it perfectly
intelligible. On this head Dr. Robinson would be
your best guide. As the subject of internal improve-
ments has excited much attention in Pennsylvania,
might not an exhibition of the comparative advantages of railway and canal transportation be presented
to your citizens with interest and advantage? You
are aware that various particulars of a curious nature
to the uninformed might be introduced in connection
with this subject. Thus the equilibrium of forces on
an inclined plane; the application of the laws of cen-
trifugal force in the meanderings of the road; the
property of the curve of swiftest descent; the laws
of friction; the modification of animal or mechanical
energy by the velocity of the motion, together with a
general account of the properties of steam and the
structure of the steam engine, — would supply curious
and interesting matter for several discourses. At
present I can make no further or detailed suggestion
on these subjects; but in my next, and in succeeding
letters I propose to transmit such hints as I may from
time to time think likely to prove useful to you in the
prosecution of this plan, and in your general business
of instruction. Perhaps in doing this I shall contribute but little to your aid.

N. B. — Would you believe that I am reported
through town to be engaged to Miss ——, and not
without her countenance? But of this, Mum! Heaven
defend us from gossips!

Into the ear, and we may truly add into the heart,
of William his brothers still always poured the story
of their many troubles and their sorrows, as the letters
which follow abundantly testify : —

JAMES TO WILLIAM.

BALTIMORE, December 13, 1829.

DEAR BROTHER, . . . It seems as if I was peculiarly selected for the sport of adverse fortune. . . .
Our classes this season were small ; the proceeds arising from mine, together with some monies I had received as registrar of the college for matriculation fees,
were laid aside.   After having liquidated my debts,
I had about $100, which I left hung up in one of my
coats in the room I thought secure.   While I was out
some villain entered my room, stole the coat and some
articles of clothing of much less value.   No search has
been able to detect the thief, and in all probability he
will riot on the proceeds of my labour.   Dear brother,
I am thus left almost penniless, and, with the exception
of two or three tickets I expect to sell some time in
the winter, know not where to look for money. . . .

Ducatel, of the Institute, has lately become very
sociable, and invited me to assist him in one of his
lectures on galvanism.   This I did not refuse, in consideration of my respect for *him*, although I entertain none for the managers . . .

I have received from Philadelphia the deflagrator,
and made some of the most brilliant experiments with
it ever made in Baltimore.   My poverty has compelled
me to solicit indulgence of the artist for some time,
and to delay the other instrument, the calorimeter.   I
have invented a little classification of the subjects of
my lectures for the more easy comprehension of my
class, for which I have received some commendation.
I will make a fair copy and transmit it soon, if you
have curiosity to see it.   It may, perhaps, furnish you
with a hint.

HENRY TO WILLIAM.

CARLISLE, January 2, 1830.

. . . I cease to believe that I have an identity entire, and almost feel myself but the fourth member of an individual. There is a nature common to us all, and only one happiness amongst us all. So little do I feel myself of separate existence from my brothers, that often I assume successively the place of each, and in his emotions contemplate the other three. It is therefore with the sensation of a private sorrow that I sympathize with James in his distress, and it is my own regrets I seem to be enlisting when I call on yours. . . . Pecuniary means James would have if you should concur with me in deeming him privileged, from his wants, to employ a portion of the funds of our poor, lamented parent. Five hundred dollars would make his long-harassed heart sing in joy, and it would afford him means of accomplishing a sure success. After relieving him from all embarrassments, it would contribute enough for apparatus and other expenses essential to the undertaking. Did our own circumstances render us less able to lend future aid to Robert, I could feel more reluctance to such an appropriation; or, did I rely less on the noble and affectionate temper of that generous boy, I should not venture in such unreserve to propose my hints. I think I have fair reason to expect my place and salary to be permanent; yours are already so. With these we can well assist our brothers till their equal merits procure them equal recompense.

The object of my letter is that you may think of these things, and to make you the assurance of my coöperation in whatever your judgment will decide in aid of James's circumstances. To relieve the distress he must suffer I conceive a duty. I am not dictating, William. I know the ample soul which you possess, and if I have a liberal feeling of my own, I know how much it is due to you. My only object is to mention my thoughts, and leave all with you.

CARLISLE, December 23, 1829.

. . . We see the universe in parallax, nor shall we rectify our judgment of its aspect till we perceive that we are not the centre. You spoke truly of the great extent of the topic that I have chosen. Science is, indeed, a hill, for from it we behold the widest of all prospects. . . .

Perhaps you entertain occasionally a wish to learn something of the tenour of my pursuits and the circumstances of my situation. I have foreborne hitherto to speak of the condition of this college. Since the session began, all around me has been suspense; every effort to procure a president has failed. . . . Care for my ultimate success in life never influences much my happiness. I have few social delights, as I am destitute of your presence and feel an extreme reluctance for society. But I do not deem my solitude a privation, except when I think of you, and I receive more than a compensation for the absence of heartless acquaintanceships in the exquisite and soothing enjoyment that I can derive from science. Oh, how one may revel in pleasures of true knowledge! Secluded from men, we may mingle in wider and closer fellowship with Man; we may dwell with him through all past ages, and wherever he has made abode. And thus lonely, to all but ourselves, we may wander wherever thought has strayed, amid all that was or is or shall be in the history and destiny of Nature and the human race. Only in the deepest privacy can we visit the sealed solitudes of Nature. Amid thoughts like these do I find my pleasures in the present. Shall I speak of my ambitions in the future? to whisper them would be too loud. Of late I have minded not the petty vicissitudes around me, for change is busier within me; in new powers of vision I behold new scenes and new paths in the field of enterprise. William, I have strange thoughts sometimes, when I reflect how little good we do our fellow-beings, and how much we might; how many truths important to human welfare we cherish, yet tremble to avow. Are there not frequent periods of self-upbraiding when your sagacity discloses how profitless to real good are all the fine talents and extensive knowledge you possess? For myself, I feel an exalted incentive to pursue knowledge. A fever has been born in my heart that will never leave it.

Tell me how you enjoy the present session, and give me a full narration of all your performances done or fancied. . . .

HENRY TO WILLIAM.

CARLISLE, February 2, 1830.

. . . I did not discern till recently how prostrate must be the independence of all who take their hire of a nefarious priesthood. But now I find full amply that the tenure of my station must be a deep hypocrisy, and an oppression and ignominious servitude. Some evenings since, I attended a pleasant party at which the choicest society of the place was present. To gratify the company the host produced his violin, and all united in a dance. Now I, poor devil, knew no reason why I should not with the rest taste the gaiety of the evening, nor could I apprehend that any should scruple at my conduct. In deference, therefore, to the mistress of the house, I danced, and saw in the same cotillon two of the trustees of our college. But, behold, in due time I was notified through a private interview with one of our priestly rulers how greatly I had acted amiss, and was made abruptly to know how little my greatest services might avail me to retain my place should I disavow the requisitions of their church, or fail in my conduct and expressions to coöperate in rendering the college a school of religious discipline. Now this was gross tyranny and insult, and my soul burned to defy

it. Then it was that I felt the lofty spirit of my
father in me, and I answered that, if such must be the
fetters I must wear, then Dickinson and I must part;
but I afterwards softened my expressions and all was
appeased between us. Since, I have held myself mute
and continue cautious. I think I have fair expectations of reëlection in the spring, but certainly I should
forfeit all chance of such an issue were I not now to
bow low to dictation.

I cannot rightly tell you how much and how anxiously I have lately pondered my future conduct in
life. My mind seems destined to struggle along between the decisions of policy and the ardent determination of a bolder virtue. . . .

There is in recent years much criticism of the
Congress assembled at Washington. It would seem
that the doings of this body in 1830 did not inspire
universal respect, and those who insist that the former
times were better than these may be interested to
peruse the following estimate of Congress by a young
contemporary professor : —

WILLIAM TO HENRY.

WILLIAMSBURG, February 13, 1830.

. . . Who that is inspired with just ideas of the
true interests of society can witness the proceedings
of our Congress, the assembled learning and talent
of our country, without disgust and shame? How
trivial, and how foreign from the happiness of the
people for whom they act, are the subjects they discuss
and the measures they decide! and how false, and
often vicious, the principles by which they affect to
regulate and improve the condition of society! For-
getful of the moral nature of man, they seem to regard
him only in a legal point of view, as the proprietor
of land and other possessions. They legislate as if

national and individual happiness were synonymous
with extensive property, and dependent upon the
arithmetic of ledger calculations. Their hall of council is the very headquarters of selfishness. There the
agents of the several States assemble, not to digest
schemes of diffusive moral benefit, but by argument
or intrigue to drive interested bargains for their constituents, and all their proceedings are little better
than a miserable scramble after wealth and power.
Witness these engrossing questions, — the Tariff and
the Public Lands, — in which each section of our
country is agitated by hopes and fears concerning its
own prosperity, and which, however they may be decided, can influence their real happiness only in a very
slight degree. . . .

WILLIAMSBURG, February 26, 1830.

. . . This morning I exhibited nitrous oxide to several of my students, and in some instances with the
most powerful effects. I have myself inhaled it twice
in private, and found its operation upon my system to
be somewhat peculiar. It imparts to me a sense of
omnipresence. I lose all feeling of relation to the
earth or sublunary things, and seem winged away
through boundless space, the only sentient being in
existence. My emotions are pleasurable, but their
characteristics are vastness, grandeur, sublimity and
solitude. The influence of the aerial draught continues for a long time, and as it subsides I become
gradually sensible of my presence upon the ground,
and look around me with the haughty disdain and
towering importance of the Great Mogul.

Throughout the correspondence thus far, William
appears to have refrained from offering unsolicited
advice to his brothers, except on the all-important
subject of their health. But now he writes more
freely.

WILLIAMSBURG, March 27, 1830.

Be not discouraged by the present state of circumstances. The literary institutions of our country are numerous, and the demand for men qualified as you are is daily augmenting. A year, perhaps less time, may open you a way to distinction and emolument. Be on the alert, be vigilant in watching for the propitious opportunity, and with unrelaxing perseverance labour in improving the eminent qualifications you already possess. In the season of disengagement from the duties of instruction, do not abandon your studious pursuits. Do not permit your armour to rust, but keep it well burnished by continual use, and be ever ready for the field. Above all, my dear brother, be not too diffident of yourself when a favourable occasion is presented for a display of your claims to the attention of the community. This is not a country in which retiring merit is ever likely to be rewarded. There are no kind patrons of genius, ever ready to assist its efforts, ever active in drawing it forth from the haunts of obscurity and want. Here talents cannot succeed without enterprise, and every man is expected " to achieve his own greatness." The community will only give you credit for as much as you display, and they will not seek to educe your hidden resources. You must present yourself before them boldly, frequently and impressively; you must almost obtrude yourself upon their notice: by such means their good opinion must unfailingly be secured, and, once obtained, you may bid defiance to disappointment. . . .

In the summer of 1830 William with Robert visited Henry in Carlisle. The following letter of William to his uncle refers to his friendship with the Empie family : —

WILLIAM TO HIS UNCLE JAMES.

CARLISLE, August 14, 1830.

DEAR UNCLE, — Mr. Empie and his most excellent lady have ever been among my most cherished friends in Virginia. In difficulty or in sickness I have always experienced their heartfelt sympathy and their tenderly affectionate attentions. They are to me indeed as brother and sister, and the apprehension of their serious indisposition, of which I have received some accounts, excites my most painful solicitude. Should you ever become acquainted with these valued friends, you will sympathize in my affection for them.

In company with Henry and sometimes Robert, I make frequent excursions to the neighbouring mountains and valleys, and derive from them improvement both in health and information. We have already explored, both botanically and geologically, a considerable region of the surrounding country, and we still continue these enlivening expeditions. . . . Amid the various jealousies and hostilities which have for many years prevailed in town and college, and which still continue to disturb the peace of both, I have been pleased to find that Henry's prudence and manly openness have conciliated the esteem of all, and that he is generally respected for his abilities and science. . . .

Another academic year opened in October, 1830, and found William at his post in the ancient college. Troubles were brewing, however, for Henry at Carlisle. James had been violently ill during August, and in the autumn, after his recovery, had terminated a long-standing engagement by marriage to Miss Rachel Smith, of Harford County, Maryland. To eke out his income he soon after entered with a partner into the business of an apothecary in Baltimore; but this essay was doomed to failure.

Meantime the professorship of mathematics in William and Mary became vacant, and the classes were carried on temporarily by William, as the following shows, with acceptance : —'

WILLIAM AND MARY, November 11, 1830.
The students of my classes, unknown to me, met this morning and entered into resolution to solicit the Visitors to make no appointment now, but to continue me in the mathematical chair, at least to the end of the course. . . .

As was anticipated, the Visitors met but made no new appointment and the classes continued under William's direction. Henry, meantime, found the position at Carlisle less and less to his liking, and finally in the spring of 1831 resigned. James continued in Baltimore, in constant financial difficulties, but towards the summer saw a ray of hope, having secured a lectureship for the next year in the Maryland Institute.

In these troubles of the brothers William gave them unfailing sympathy. To Robert he gave a paternal protection, to James constant and substantial aid, and to Henry encouragement and counsel.

During the summer of 1841 William, Henry and Robert went North, in the hope of securing for Robert work under Captain McNeil who was engaged in locating some of the new lines of railway then projected in New England. Robert soon found employment under Captain McNeil and his associates included some who afterwards achieved eminence in engineering, notably Mr. E. S. Chesbrough.

As he was now out of employment, Henry appears
to have determined to join one of the numerous surveying parties then in the field, and on September 10
he proceeded from New York to Providence, R. I.,
by steamboat, and thence by stage-coach to Boston.
Robert accompanied him, and the experiences of the
young men on arriving in New England were interesting.

HENRY TO WILLIAM.

BOSTON, September 25, 1831.

. . . For the last week we have been entirely in
the country, prosecuting our surveys with great activity, and it was necessary to ride seventeen miles to get
here.   During our excursion so far, we have met with
nothing to annoy us; the weather has been uniformly
serene and soft, and the country we have traversed as
beautiful as taste could wish.   Our operations being
at present directed towards Taunton, we have pursued
a line nearly due south; this at first led us, on quitting Boston, close upon the heights of Dorchester, the
site, you are aware, of the American redoubts during
the Revolution; and in all that vicinity we enjoyed
a scenery varied and pleasing beyond description.
Passing on, we reached the foot of the Blue Hills,
directly beneath the magnificent quarries of the celebrated Quincy granite, and, deviating slightly to the
east, we avoided the rocky barrier in our path by
penetrating the range through a deep valley.   We
witnessed, of course, all the interesting works connected with the quarries, and beheld from their summits by far the noblest scenery in the neighbourhood;
in the distance, a grand and lovely view of the ocean
and its islands, and beneath us the fair-built city and
the rich meadows, fields and woods of its vicinity.

During our stay in the neighbourhood of Quincy, we
made that pretty village for the time our home, but
for the last three days we have tarried for lodgings

and meals in the interesting village of West Randolph. Our practice is to halt at the nearest town, or, if one be not accessible, at the nearest country inn, when we approach it within about three miles ; there we stop generally about two or three nights, until our operations carry us too far beyond it. Taking breakfast before commencing the day's business, thrusting a few biscuits into our pockets, we labour on without intermission until the approach of sunset; then, confiding our instruments to our labourers, we seek our place of rest for the night, enjoying our suppers with no little relish, and spending the evening with books, or amusing conversation with the people about us. . . .

Robert and I amuse ourselves sometimes in practising topography, an art of the first importance ; after sketching the local features of the ground around us, I often make some observations on its natural history, especially the nature of the trees and rocks. Griswold has mentioned my habit to the Captain, reporting, I presume, something in praise of my geological information: the Captain requested me to-day to record a series of geological observations throughout our route, stating that such things will be beneficial to my prospects. So much for a little science ! ! ! I should not omit to state that, though volunteers, we receive the full recompense usually given persons who do our duty, each of us getting now $1.25 a day. This of course will not continue after we quit the field, but for the present it more than defrays our expenditures.

ROBERT (AGE 17) TO HIS UNCLE JAMES.

SEEKONK, MASS., Friday, September 28, 1831.

. . . We have concluded most of the important surveys of the season. We have been from Boston to Taunton, and from Boston to Providence, and there yet remain some short distances to be surveyed before we shall have finished all our outside work. . . .

When in Virginia, I have often heard the activity

and the stirring enterprise of the North put in contrast with the languor and listlessness of the South, and I had been led to form a different opinion of the New Englanders from that which my past experience would justify, though they are indeed an active and stirring people; yet their enterprise does not seem to be at all enlarged, but confined to each one's own petty interests, entirely disregarding those of another. One thing is the fact, however, that I have never seen any part of the country so well calculated to leave a good impression upon the mind of the traveller as the environs of Boston. Everything has the appearance of utmost neatness and care; the houses are all built in good taste, with beautiful lawns of grass before the doors, all bearing the appearance of greatest comfort: here, with a million or so of income, I might live the life of a happy bachelor. . . .

The winter of 1831–32 was passed by William in Williamsburg, and by Henry and Robert in New York. Reference has already been made to the influence which Fanny Wright and her doctrines had produced upon Henry. During this winter he saw much of Robert Dale Owen and others belonging to the same movement, and became so much interested in their plans that, in spite of his uncle's disapproval and William's reluctant assent, he determined to cast in his lot for a time with the reformers and, in furtherance of this purpose, decided to travel with Owen to London.

HENRY TO HIS UNCLE JAMES.

NEW YORK, May 12, 1832.
. . . My own feelings assure me that I, not for one moment, have been careless as to how you and William would look upon my schemes. These schemes I have

long had in contemplation ; but in coming to my decisions about the career I was selecting, I fully appreciated the distress which I saw I would occasion you.
My decision was by no means rashly made ; I may say
that for the last two years I have almost incessantly
deliberated upon the matter. You have frequently
told me that you did not think any one authorized
to run counter to public opinion ; so far I saw that you
must censure the course I was tracing out for myself,
and so far I felt a disposition to alter my views. But
conviction, a sense of conscientious duty, has been too
strong. This William is aware of, for my trip last
winter to Virginia was for the express purpose of giving him my intention and hearing his sentiments. I
cannot think, therefore, that I have proceeded rashly.
I have well studied the state of opinion among that
part of society who favour my plans, and feel convinced
that they will not fail. I cannot see that I have much
to fear from popular odium, even among those who will
object to my use of the Sunday. My main object is
to be useful. Sunday is the useful day for the purpose,
therefore I select it. Again, were my schemes to fail
and all the world to scout, my true happiness would
still be greater than any I could have by taking a
course contrary to my convictions.[1] . . .

About Europe, — should William have his views
altered by what you wrote him, and now disapprove
of my going, I do not go. Should he still approve, I
must obey my conviction of its propriety, and adhere
to my first intention. I shall not take his generosity
unless I have his judgment.

Henry finally sailed from New York, on the ship
" Washington," on May 19. Robert, when the spring
opened, returned to his surveying near Boston. This
was the year of the great invasion of cholera and, as

[1] The use of Sunday here referred to was for lectures to working-
men which were later given in London.

the time for the annual migration from Williamsburg
approached, William wrote to his uncle : —

WILLIAM TO HIS UNCLE JAMES.

WILLIAM AND MARY, June 21, 1832.

DEAR UNCLE, . . . You will be surprised that I
am preparing for a journey South before I can join you.
Mrs. Empie and family have determined to pass the
summer among her relatives at the seaside, near Wilmington, N. C. The health of Mr. Empie is such that
he will be compelled to spend the season in travelling
and at the Virginia Springs. He cannot then accompany his lady and her children to their friends. A
pressing invitation from several persons in Wilmington
has been given me to attend Mrs. E. thither and remain there during the summer. The deep obligations
of kindness and maternal affection which I owe to this
inestimable lady would alone require as a duty that
I should do everything to contribute to her safety and
convenience. But, moreover, she is exceedingly infirm
and delicate ; her family is large, and consists mostly
of very young children ; and the journey is long and
somewhat fatiguing. How, then, could I in friendship withhold my assistance from her in these circumstances ?

. . . Some anxiety has been occasioned in my mind
in reference to Robert's safety by recent accounts of
the cholera. Should it extend to Boston, would he not
be in greater danger than in Philadelphia? Oh, what
anguish should I suffer if I had reason to believe that
it prevailed in his vicinity! My dear uncle, if you
think there is any likelihood of his being placed in
the way of this terrible scourge, please write to him
immediately and request him to return and await me
in Philadelphia. . . .

In September William informs his uncle that
he had lingered near Wilmington, N. C., partly on

account of the cholera, " the terrible pestilence by which even your healthful and cleanly city has been assailed." Here, also, he almost lost his life.

WILLIAM TO HIS UNCLE JAMES.

WRIGHTSVILLE, NORTH CAROLINA, September 13, 1832.

. . . I have already described the village in which I have spent most of my time. The Atlantic Ocean is not much more than a mile in a direct line from our house. The intervening space is occupied by rich meadows of sea grass, with creeks meandering through them, and communicating with the sea by inlets made by breaks in the low sandbanks which form the shore of the ocean. The roar of the breakers, which are very heavy on this coast, is now sounding with a noise like that of distant thunder in my ears.

About ten days since, I went with a party of gentlemen on a sailing excursion in a small boat, such as is commonly used in the waters of the Sound. We passed before a brisk wind through the nearest inlet, and sailed for some time on the bosom of the ocean ; we then proceeded to return to the Sound by another inlet lower down on the coast. Our pilot, however, steered us into the very midst of the breakers. In an instant, surrounded by the raging waters piled like mountains on every side, our boat was turned over, and ourselves precipitated into the boiling and foaming waters. We clung with difficulty to the boat, while the irresistible tide carried us out farther and farther into the ocean. For half an hour we remained in this situation, until I, who had been seized with cramp, had given myself up as lost, and all were ready to sink in despair. Providentially some fishermen had witnessed our disaster, and, coming to our assistance in a strong and well-manned boat, rescued us from a terrible fate. I lost my watch, shoes and waistcoat. . . .

Letters in due season arrived from Henry, the absent brother. These reported that he would soon return, and he in fact actually embarked from London in the autumn. But a series of westerly gales arising, the ship was unable to proceed beyond the English coast, and after struggling for some weeks with the elements, during which time the vessel was driven to and fro, sometimes advancing and sometimes retreating and again lying at anchor, all having been long sick and the captain of the vessel having had his arm broken, Henry and his friends decided that the best thing to do was to give up the attempt and return to London for the winter. His letters contain much of interest, especially many valuable glimpses of contemporary men of science in England; and as the young professor was one of the earliest of American scientific men to report his observations, somewhat copious extracts are given : —

HENRY TO HIS UNCLE JAMES AND HIS BROTHER WILLIAM.

LONDON, November 14, 1832.

. . . I am very comfortable at Mr. Owen's, 4 Crescent Place, Burton Crescent, London.

. . . A few evenings ago I met Tully, the great optician.[1] His microscopes are reported the finest ever invented, and certainly, from what I saw of one which he made for our host, I can well believe it. Not the wildest accounts which we have ever heard of the microscope equal what I witnessed. During the evening we made the very interesting discovery of a 'valve in the pulsating system of a minute object like a cabbage-louse. . . . Going home with Mr. Tully, he mentioned to me that the attempts of Mr. Faraday and the Royal Society's Committee to procure optical glasses have not succeeded. He says by using a *borate* of lead their product is too dense to sort with crown

[1] One of the inventors of the achromatic microscope objective.

and plate glass in achromatic lenses, besides having
other defects. Tully has contrived a little instrument
by which he rules with a diamond 12,000 parallel
equidistant lines in one inch on glass, giving the most
perfect micrometer ever made, and enabling one actually to measure thus the minutest infusoria. It was
truly curious to witness, on the back of the plant-louse
I before spoke of, a number of bell polypi swinging
to and fro on slender stems, erecting themselves,
expanding their fibrillæ, and catching the minutest
monads. . . . Turner [1] is in every sense a gentleman.
I am present at his lectures almost daily. He experiments very much and in beautiful style, most of his
instruments being on a large scale. To-day, treating
of hygrometers, after showing us all the varieties, he
presented one of his own, the most simple and perfect
of all. It is merely a cup of silver two inches by half
an inch, gilt and burnished outside. A few grains of
freezing mixture, half nitre and half sal-ammoniac,
are dissolved and stirred with a small thermometer on
which you mark the dew points. Some days since, he
brought before us a pyrometer of Daniell's which I
had not known. It is a bar of plumbago bored to
receive a rod of malleable iron, and a shorter rod of
clay to act as index. The plumbago prevents oxidation. . . . This evening I go by invitation to a soirée
of the professors and friends of the University.

Faraday is at present on electricity at the Royal
Institution. Yesterday he was melting the metals,
etc., by the most powerful battery I ever beheld, with
two enormous machines in full action. Three days
ago it was electrical light, and a more successful and
splendid series of experiments could not be performed
by any one. Faraday's style of lecturing and experimenting reminds one of Paganini's playing: so easy,
so adroit, *so much execution*. When I listen to his
fluent and eloquent delivery, my thoughts wander
home to you, William; and with tenderness and with

[1] Edward Turner, Professor of Chemistry in University College,
London.

a sweet pride I think of the greater powers possessed by my own dear brother. Yes, William, I have already heard several lecturers, reputed among the best in Europe, and I will vouch for it that with equal aids you shall outshine them all.

You are aware of the discoveries of Ritchie in electro-magnetism; he is Professor of Natural Philosophy in the London University. He is conducting two courses, — one profound, the other more exclusively experimental. I have an invitation to attend either. He is a Scotchman, deeply scientific, and a clear lecturer; but, strange to say, while Turner has in chemistry nearly three hundred students, Ritchie has barely twenty or twenty-five, — not more, I hope, than your own class. It should cheer you when you learn that the singular distaste of the age for natural philosophy is not restricted to Virginia. Biot, in Paris, had often not above half a dozen. . . .

I was introduced some days ago to Loudon, the botanist and gardener. He is a Scotchman, has lost his right arm, and is a truly amiable man. He seemed extremely rejoiced to meet an American. . . . I may mention that the news reached this city a few days ago of the death of Professor Leslie, of Edinburgh, who breakfasted with us at Mr. Owen's in the summer. The same day he was with us he went to Court and was knighted. The honours accorded by the philosophic world will long outshine the already withered laurels of the King. With many here, there is a feeling that philosophers ought not to wear the empty decorations of the Court. Dalton,[1] like a man of sense, lately refused a knighthood, though warmly proffered. . . .

HENRY TO HIS UNCLE JAMES.

LONDON, December 14, 1832.

. . . Dr. Turner, last night, introduced me to the Geological Society of which he is secretary. I shall have fine chances for making myself a geologist by

[1] John Dalton, the famous chemist and natural philosopher.

the free access I may have to the Society's superb
museum. I was introduced personally to several of
the members, De la Beche, Lyell, Babbage and
others. . . .

One of the papers read [at the Royal Society]
will prove a highly important one to men of science,
as it contains some fundamental discoveries in electro-magnetism. It is by Ritchie, of London University, whom I very well know, and with whom I had
last night some very instructive chat. As you are a
reader of the scientific journals, you may have seen
something of Mr. Faraday's very brilliant discoveries
concerning the production of electricity from magnetism, which created much noise here last winter. This
subject Ritchie is now exploring with great success,
and has already in this paper reduced all Faraday's
researches to one simple *universal law.* I attend his
lectures habitually, and esteem him one of the first
natural philosophers of the age. I go likewise to the
Royal Institution, where Brande and Faraday deliver
perhaps the most perfect course of chemistry anywhere
given. . . .

My chances here are now truly golden ones, for I
am on such easy terms with several men of science
that they place every opportunity open to me; and it
has become my consuming ambition to retrieve my
mistakes by devoting myself to those studies which
will please my friends and procure me an honourable
name. It annoys me, however, when I think how
soon I must leave these fine opportunities, almost
immediately, as it were, after I have broken the ice.
Such has been William's generous kindness that I
can hardly excuse myself in thus reaping advantages
which should in justice be his and not mine.

I feel a strong wish to ramble a little in England
before forsaking Europe forever. . . . My expenses
are very small, and this is some consolation when I
think how much I have taxed William. I have
glorious means before me for studying geology, espe-

cially if I were to steal a month or six weeks in pedestrian excursions. . . .

HENRY TO WILLIAM.

LONDON, January 5, 1833.

DEAR WILLIAM, — . . . It would be no easy matter to describe the Christmas doings in England, though it all seems to centre in but one indulgence. This eating nation seems to devote all its energies at this time to plum-pudding, and energy enough does it require. The lectures throughout London being suspended, I embraced the holidays to make a short excursion with an acquaintance into the country, to see a little of England's geology. He being, like many of the English, an excellent walker, and knowing how beneficial the exercise is always to myself, we went on foot, and shaped our rambles toward the lower end of Kent. Leaving our place of lodging in London in the evening, we walked sixteen miles, a light frost on the ground, a bright moon above, a smooth footpath leading us over hill and dale, the mists of night sleeping in the valleys, and once in every while a solitary horseman on patrol saluting us with the protecting words, "Good-night."

We passed several villages, with their gray church towers, every spot teeming with the records of old England's stormy history. But it was when we reached our inn that I recognized in full strength in what land I was staying. Entering the little parlour, I thought I saw some picture from Smollett or Fielding, — a bright coal-fire, and around a table near it the host and several sturdy farmers, each pipe in hand, a pot of beer at his elbow, and all busy at the truly English game of cribbage, — the short breeches and gaiters and deep waistcoats were so like my own early picture of English rural life.

The next day we went twenty-four miles by one o'clock to Maidstone, a fine old town on the Medway,

studying the country as we went, and culling specimens of all the rocks passed. My great object was
to procure fossils, and I wished, therefore, to reach
the district called the Weald, in the clays of which
they are so abundant, and where those immense remains of saurians, etc., are chiefly found. We were
likewise to go to the Island of Sheppy, in the Thames,
but a change of weather prevented our reaching
either and drove us hastily up to London. I learned
much from this ramble, and I also found myself
stronger from the exercise. Sheppy is a formation
where they find an immense deposit of extinct fruits
and seeds, all similar to those now growing in the
tropics. A parcel of these I have, and shall take
home with me a collection of them. . . .

You may remember, my dear William, that years
ago in Baltimore we read in the "Edinburgh Review"
an article on the Hazelwood School, near Birmingham.
I am very good friends with the proprietors of that
fine school. Two of the Messrs. Hill possess a branch
school seven miles from London, and now, during the
holidays, old Mr. Hill with the whole family are up
from Birmingham at Bruce Castle, where I go to-morrow to dine and stay a day or two. The older Hill,
the founder of these very superior schools, was formerly a great friend and espouser of Priestley. The
elder son has just been returned to Parliament for
Hull, and is a great favourite with Brougham. All
the brothers — there being four — are men of fine
education and first-rate talent.

. . . The papers are all making comments on the
resistance of South Carolina to our government, and
on the President's memorial, the general sentiment
being one of sympathy with the South, and of surprise
that we should find any bone to quarrel over. Alas!
the true condition of America's politics is but little
understood here. . . .

The dread of the cholera affected the prosperity

of William and Mary College, which had long had
the reputation of possessing an unhealthy situation.
The classes were smaller than usual, and to William the outlook for the old college, now threatened
by the growing prosperity of its formidable rival, the
University of Virginia, was discouraging. Something
of this feeling must have been reflected in his letters
to Robert, who writes : —

ROBERT TO WILLIAM.

New York, January 7, 1833.

DEAR WILLIAM, . . . It grieves me that you are
subject to strains of melancholy such as your last
letter seems to have left you in ; but really, my dear
brother, I think you have little, very little, cause thus
to be sad. Your career has been one of success, virtue and usefulness, but of the latter, perhaps, less
than your benevolent heart would lead you to desire, and certainly less than your abilities would enable you to perform: wherever you may be placed,
you cannot fail to find yourself comfortable and independent ; you will make friends wherever you
go, and with your powers and acquirements you are
sure of success in whatever undertaking you may em-
bark. . . .

It has always been, and always will be, I think, my
craving to follow, in some measure, in the track of
my brothers, — to become a teacher. I know of nothing that I should like better than to be an instructor in a school. . . . Engineering holds out but very
few inducements, for only those who have been educated at West Point stand in the way of promotion,
and can look forward to certainty of success ; they
alone are sure of constant occupation in the profession.[1] . . .

[1] Civil engineering, as a distinct branch, had hardly yet arisen. The
only " engineers " were military engineers from West Point.

NEW YORK, March 1, 1833.

. . . I believe, but I am not certain, that I mentioned in my last letter that I had given four lectures, the first and second on chemical affinity, the third on electricity, the fourth on testing and analysis; and, as a powerful agent in effecting decomposition, I introduced galvanism, making use of a *voltaic pile* of a *hundred plates ;* the experiment with this succeeded finely. I decomposed water, the bubbles of its two gases flying off in copious and constant streams, being received into small glass, graduated tubes, which indicated exactly the proportion of their volumes as two to one. I also decomposed sulphate of soda, using three cups, and putting the salt in the middle one and an infusion of cabbage in the two end ones; it was beautiful to remark that that at the positive end turned *red,* while that at the negative end turned *green.*

WILLIAM TO HIS UNCLE JAMES.

WILLIAM AND MARY, February 22, 1833.

. . . Of local news, my dear uncle, I have none to transcribe ; of the general public news of the day, you are doubtless much better aware than I. Is not the threatened tempest to be averted by measures of conciliation now proposed ? Will the present brightening prospects again be overshadowed by the fatal obstinacy of either or both the contending parties ? Are we to have peace or fratricidal war ? These questions daily agitate and concern my thoughts, but of the course of events I feel but ill qualified to judge. Can you not enlighten me on these points by views derived from your better knowledge and ample experience ? Another subject on which I feel interested to learn your opinion is the doctrines sustained in the proclamation. You know in general they are anti-Virginian, though there is a large party in the State inclined partially to embrace them. In this part of the State the politics are ultra-Southern. Here, therefore, the proclamation is almost universally condemned.

I understand that Mr. Rives, our minister, has given such dissatisfaction to the legislature that a proposition has just been offered in that body requesting him to resign his seat in Congress. Mr. Tyler, who expected to be excluded, has been elected by a majority of one. Mr. Leigh has not returned. . . .

WILLIAM AND MARY, April 15, 1833.

. . . From Mr. Joseph Cabell, a Visitor of the University [of Virginia], and a very particular friend of mine, I have lately received very strong hints of the probability of a vacancy in that institution in the current or following year. Possibly the preparations now in progress towards the institution of the Girard College have led to this prospect on his part. Should such a vacancy occur, I have reason to expect from him and others all the assistance requisite to assure my appointment. Of these subjects, it is needless to say, I speak to no one but my brothers and yourself. . . .

These were the days of " nullification," and the political references are to the proclamation of the President (Jackson) in response to the action of South Carolina.

Henry, after much hesitation, decided to remain in England until after the meeting of the British Association, which occurred in June at Cambridge. His stay appears to have been of the highest service to him, and through him eventually to all the brothers. So attractive did he find his scientific and especially his geological work, that this appears to have rapidly overshadowed in importance the purely philanthropic objects which had carried him over the sea. Still his interest in the latter did not cease, and he even gave public lectures in the halls of the reformers. But his pursuit of science became constantly more eager, and before long he was honored by an election as Fellow of the Geological Society of London. His experiences are fully detailed in letters to his brother William and his uncle James. We quote the following extracts : —

HENRY TO WILLIAM.

LONDON, February 14, 1833.

. . . Parliament is in full tide of debate, and a crisis of deep interest is close at hand for England and, above all, for poor, unhappy Ireland. The miseries in that devoted land pass conception. I have acquaintance with two or three of the more aristocratic families from Ireland, whose relatives are in the Commons, and their description of the country would truly appall you. O'Connell is taking a very elevated position, and has already waged a most tremendous attack upon the King's address. He will either effect the Repeal of the Union, or Ireland will be in open insurrection before another year. . . .

It is highly amusing to observe the determined style in which Cobbett forces the proud and scornful aristocracy of the House of Commons to give attention to his scoldings. He has been flogging some of the high spirits most rarely. O'Connell, as you will see by the papers, is laying about him with a very heavy hand.

LONDON, March 6, 1833.

I should mention that at the last meeting of the Society a very curious communication was read from Brewster[1] on the origin of the diamond. From examining the effects of polarized light on certain minute cavities in it, he comes to the conclusion that it has been originally soft like a gum, and he gives to it a similar source to the amber. I hardly know what to think

[1] Sir David Brewster, Scottish natural philosopher.

of the notion. About every two weeks the President
of the Society, Mr. Greenough, who is an extremely
wealthy and munificent man, entertains the members
and other friends at his house in Regent's Park. I
have access to all his parties, and such luxury in
science I have never before seen. His library and
cabinet are a scene of perfect enchantment. He is a
very cordial old man. I met there Babbage, Ure,
Lubbock, Davies, Gilbert, etc., but none so awakened
my admiration as Babbage.

At the last conversazione in the Royal Institution,
Faraday's lecture was on the nature and cure of dry-
rot. He detailed a series of very elaborate and successful experiments now making by himself and others
on the efficacy of solutions of corrosive sublimate in
completely preserving timber, canvas, etc., from decay by this malady, which he showed us to result commonly from parasitic vegetation. Wheatstone lectures
there to-morrow night on some of his own discoveries
in vision and sound.

And now for politics. I have heard Daniel O'Connell, not only in the House of Commons, but in an
immense assembly of the National Union, and certainly none but a son of poor, despised Ireland could
display such eloquence, at times so tremendous and
terrific, and at moments so melting and so tender.
He looks a very Hercules; and from his sturdy, coarse
frame, bull neck, and ploughman air, no one on first
sight would ever suspect him the man of genius which
he is. O'Connell is making a desperate and powerful
opposition to the Irish Coercion Bill, as it is called;
and, should you see in the papers the despotic nature
of the yoke to be imposed on that country, you will
not wonder at the frenzy it excites among the Irish.
Still, I fear the bill will pass, and what new act will
follow in this fearful drama the fates who brew the
mischief only know. O'Connell's influence in his
country is supreme, even to exciting the people into
tranquillity. If he escapes the vengeance of his foes,

and runs his career unharmed, I am pretty sure that liberty in Ireland will triumph. . . .

LONDON, March 30, 1833.

. . . I think I mentioned to you my expectation of becoming a Fellow of the Geological Society; on Wednesday last I was regularly nominated by Turner, De la Beche[1] Murchison, and several others, and my card suspended for a few weeks prior to my election, which now, however, is certain. It will be a source of some pleasure to me, more especially when I remember, as I always shall, the kind and friendly way in which Turner, De la Beche, etc., have taken me by the hand. Mr. Greenough, the President, also expressed very kindly his pleasure at finding that they were to have a young and active fellow-labourer on the other side of the Atlantic. This silly bit of F. G. S. and the other points mentioned, together with a strong desire to see a little of England out of London, decide me to remain longer than I contemplated. De la Beche is occupied with a geological survey of Devonshire, Cornwall and most of the South of England just now, for the great ordnance maps, under the direction of Government, and he desires that I shall visit him in Devonshire to study the subject practically from nature and from his lessons. This I esteem a great privilege, as it will fit me, as you perceive at once, to do the like at home, whenever the pursuit may prove desirable. And I shall take notes, collect specimens, and I doubt not, in the exquisite air of Devonshire, get fat and rosy cheeks.

De la Beche is bringing out an entirely new edition of his work in very perfect form. He very kindly offers to put the new edition proofs in my hands when I go, sending the remainder after me as they appear, that I may *republish* it with *notes* of my own,—a mark of regard that I value. He leaves the thing quite to my option, but will give me the chance, whether I accept or not. What think you? Could we not do something good in this way in your vacation, you

[1] Sir H. T. De la Beche, English geologist.

doing the authorship, I doing the geology with you?
. . . I was at the great Priestley dinner, saw all the
great men of the age in science, — Faraday, Dalton,
Cummings, Daubeny, etc., — and heard them speak.
Faraday is a *prodigious* favourite. So is Turner. . . .

LONDON, May 22, 1833.

. . . Since my visit to Oxford and return to London I find I should be resigning chances of improvement, of a kind and importance I was not aware of, by
returning home at once. Being now a Fellow of the
Geological Society, I should by right become a member of this Annual Association of the Philosophers of
the Kingdom, they admitting me to a full share in all
their proceedings and privileges, with an especially
welcome reception by them as a foreigner; so, many
of the members, Faraday, Sedgwick of Cambridge,
etc., tell me. . . .

My intercourse with the men of science is every day
becoming more easy and valuable to me. I go, free of
ceremony, to almost any of the societies, once every
week to the Royal, and, now that Faraday and I are
familiar, without even a member's ticket, to the Royal
Institution. Faraday is, I fancy, the leading man now
in England, and I shall not be surprised to witness his
fame much augmented; he seems to be certainly on
the train of some very important discoveries in regard
to electricity. He reads a paper at the Royal Society
to-morrow night on a new law he has discovered in
electric conduction.

I went to Oxford under excellent auspices, previously acquainted with one or two of the professors
and taking letters. They entertained me for two days
most hospitably. I was present at their society, where
I met the whole body, went to several lectures, saw all
the colleges, museums, Bodleian Library, etc. Dined
twice in College Hall, with the Professors and Fellows
in their gowns and caps, at Magdalen College, and
attended them in great state to Chapel, the most beau-

tiful piece of Gothic, by the way, I have ever seen, and with the finest choir of boys. Had I not been tied by my trip to Bath, I should have stayed with them a week, for invitations to meetings, dinners, etc., were crowding upon me the morning I left.

I am getting now some little insight into good society in London, and am invited to dinner oftener sometimes than I wish. I go to dine with a gentleman to-morrow where I shall meet many very eminent men. I only wish my dear brother William were here to partake, as he would more beneficially than I can, of the good spirit thus shown me. . . .

After Henry's return in the summer the brothers William, Henry and Robert appear to have been together until the autumn, probably in Philadelphia. On the opening of the college William returned to Williamsburg, while Henry and Robert remained in Philadelphia, the former offering lectures on geology to the public to be delivered at the Franklin Institute, the latter attending the medical school of the University of Pennsylvania. James meantime continued to live in Baltimore, and still retained his connection as Professor of Chemistry with the struggling medical school to which reference has been made. Robert's ingenuity and mechanical skill, for which he was noted, as well as other matters, are touched upon in the following letter : —

ROBERT TO WILLIAM.

PHILADELPHIA, November 15, 1833.
. . . James, being desirous of having a galvanometer, and not minutely aware of its construction, desired me to send him one. I took some pains, and have made him, I think, a very beautiful and complete instrument. It is on the plan we last proposed as best, that in which

straws are used : the lower one, to sustain the needle,
I made four inches long, so that it might be astatic.
At right angles to the magnet I placed a very fine
straw; this, as an index, vibrates over an arc of 60°.
The arc at the sides and end is walled by a rim of
paper, and on the top is an arc of glass, the whole to
protect the needle from agitation ; it acts finely.

Since finishing this, Henry and myself have been
busily engaged in preparing for his lectures, which are
to be delivered in the Franklin Institute. You cannot
imagine what a beautiful set of models to illustrate
crystallography we have made ; they are constructed
of glass, which is put together by means of gum and
small slips of colored paper. They not only present
the simple and primitive forms, but also illustrate the
resolution of one crystal from another. Henry is at
my elbow, and bids me ask you to give him as many
hints as to the method of treating the subject-matter
of lecturing, etc., as you can, and to write very soon,
as he delivers his first on this day two weeks. He at
present thinks of treating first of Physical Geology,
or the present existing causes modifying the earth's
structure. The Institute is attended by an over-
flowing class, and I doubt not that Henry will show
them that he understands the subject and do himself
much credit. . . .

William's attention was now turned more and more
to geology. The powerful stimulus which Henry had
received in London towards geological investigation
seems to have been an impulse which reacted also on
William, who set on foot inquiries into the marl, greensand, and other deposits of Virginia [1] that soon brought
him into public notice, and into correspondence with
some of the foremost men of the country.

In the following spring he was attacked by a severe

[1] See *Geology of the Virginias.* Appleton, N. Y., 1884.

illness, characterized by chills and fever. During
his absence in Philadelphia, to which place he went
to recruit his health, his friend and colleague, Professor Dew, addressed to him a letter giving news of
Williamsburg : —

FROM PROFESSOR T. R. DEW.

WILLIAM AND MARY COLLEGE, April 23, 1834.

You have no doubt heard from Mr. and Mrs. Empie
all the news which our miserably dull city can furnish.
We are travelling our eternal round of dulness and
insipidity as usual, — lecturing, to me more intolerable
than ever.

. . . Dr. Peachy proved to me, as logically as the
47th problem is demonstrated in Euclid, that we are to
have ten students from Frederick alone next year, and
numbers almost innumerable from other quarters. I
am afraid this good news will neither stop your chills
nor make you strut. I have reason to believe more
strongly than ever, however, that if next year is a
failure like the present, the Visitors will consent to a
removal of the college. Be therefore of good cheer,
and continue present sacrifice for future fame. . . .

An interval of more than six months occurs in the
series of letters. It is probable that the brothers (except James) were together during the summer. It
would appear that William was occupied in field-work
in Virginia and with investigations of mineral springs.
It was during this period that the first important
scientific publications of the brothers began. In June,
1834, William addressed two communications to the
"Farmer's Register," of Virginia, and at about the
same time made his first contribution to "Silliman's
Journal."

The contributions to the "Farmer's Register" (vol.

ii.) are entitled, "Some Observations on the Tertiary Marl of Lower Virginia," and "Further Observations on the Green Sand and Calcareous Marl of Lower Virginia." These are dated from William and Mary College, June 26 and June 27 respectively. Later in the same year (1834) "Silliman's Journal" contained two articles by William, and one under the joint authorship of William and Henry.[1]

In the following letter, Henry refers to a correspondence with the elder Silliman, professor at Yale and editor of the "Journal" in which the brothers were now publishing the results of their researches. The letter affords a good example of the incitements to work which the brothers constantly supplied one to another, and also the variety of their scientific interests : —

HENRY TO WILLIAM.

PHILADELPHIA, November 28, 1834.

Having received a very friendly letter from Silliman in which you are as much interested as myself, I enclose it, to save the trouble of copying, and to put you fully in possession of his expectations from us. . . .

If you furnish him anything on the Virginia Springs, it can only be a mere report, which would, perhaps, if carefully drawn up, be calculated to whet the appetite for your book, which I assume is a good deal talked of. . . .

I begin to think that we shall hold enviable ground by and by if we persevere. Can you help me to some references upon the subject of the twinkling of the stars, a matter I am writing on for the American Philosophical Society. . . .

Remember my advice about your book; never

[1] *Experimental Enquiry into Some of the Laws of the Elementary Voltaic Battery*, vol. xxvii. pp. 39–61.

more than two hours' writing per day, and no copying.

Will you have anything, however short, for the Philosophical Society in three weeks? . . .

I have had a letter from James on electro-magnetism which I shall soon send you. . . .

I wish much you were here. Can you not collect some geology about the coal mines of Richmond? . . .

Keep a sharp lookout for the eclipse, but you will scarcely get this in time. . . .

The following refers to a possibility which had arisen of William's appointment to some position in Philadelphia, and also to an attempt about to be made to induce the Legislature of Virginia to inaugurate a geological survey of the State, such as Massachusetts, Maryland and Tennessee had already instituted.

WILLIAM TO HENRY.

WILLIAM AND MARY, November 30, 1834.

. . . Firstly, of the contents of your letter so far as relates to myself. I owe many kind thanks to Dallas [1] for this evidence of his friendly regard, and I hope he will feel assured of the grateful pleasure with which his proposal affected me. Of the expediency of my accepting the offer I really know not what to think. I have endeavoured disinterestedly, and in calm prudence, to weigh all the reasons and motives pro and con, and I confess I am still in doubt. Had the opening occurred last season I would have embraced it, perhaps without hesitation. But now that the college is decidedly looking up, my health improved, and (I may say it without vanity) my reputation in Virginia rapidly rising, while at the same time a much wider field of exertion seems likely to open before me, I feel that the advantages of a situation in Philadelphia, great as they

[1] Dallas Bache, afterward Superintendent U. S. Coast Survey.

are from every point of view, are less decidedly pre-
ponderant than they would have been at any former
time. Yet when I recur to the still doubtful nature of
my hopes of public employment in geology in Virginia,
and also the precarious tenure by which my health
must always be held in this climate, I almost decide
for a removal. So far as reputation in the community
is concerned, I believe that I shall soon have no com-
petition among the scientific men of the State. Letters
are coming to me every mail asking advice on the
subject of marl or some other thing. All these things
are in favour of my present residence. If I could be
certain of obtaining the geological appointment this
winter, I think that would decide me to remain here,
unless, indeed, it could be combined with my duties
in Philadelphia. To obtain such a situation from the
legislature, or, indeed, to urge them to any measure of
the kind, will require great activity, not only of me but
of all my friends. . . . By the first or second week in
January, I should know what the legislature can be
prevailed upon to do. In the mean time might you not,
as you have already proposed, undertake the "Journal,"
etc. ? I wish you to give me your opinion on the point
by return of mail. I am sure that I could eventually
do well in Philadelphia, but here I have already
obtained firm footing, and this is what "gives me
pause."

I have been waiting for a private opportunity to
forward shells, etc., to Philadelphia, but I shall wait
no longer. In a few days I despatch them to Norfolk,
thence to be sent by packet. Of most of the specimens I shall retain a sample myself, marking what
I send and what I retain with the same number or
letter. I wish Conrad[1] and yourself to name the
shells as numbered, so that I may thus learn through

[1] T. A. Conrad, American paleontologist, Philadelphia. These
shells were described by W. B. Rogers and H. D. Rogers in a series
of contributions to the American Philosophical Society, 1835, 1837,
1839.

you their true denominations. Many of them I know already. If you have received the November number of the " Register " you will find in it my article on Artesian Wells. . . .

WILLIAM AND MARY, December 22, 1834.

. . . You speak of my intended publication on the Springs. I am very anxious to have it ready by an early day, but I feel still more solicitous to have my results complete and perfect. For nearly a month past I have been daily at work in further analysis. Having water from many of the springs, I went over some of my summer's work, and pursued the same process with several springs which I had not then examined for saline matter. I was alarmed to find in the latter that the barytic precipitants usually directed would throw down but a small portion of the carbonic acid in the water. I had ascertained in the summer that free carbonic acid was scarcely at all affected by nitrate of barytes, and I was soon induced to prepare some artificial carbonated water holding up a little carbonate of lime. I found the barytic salt precipitated only a minute portion of the carbonic acid. Hence you see that Murray's formula will not apply to waters of this kind. With my admirable marl apparatus,[1] however, I can determine the carbonic acid exactly from a given quantity of solid residuum obtained by evaporation; so that I can correct the deficient quantity of carbonic acid, which, however, I find to be excessively slight in the White Sulphur. Of course, you see it will be necessary to go over all the Springs with this view. Had I the analyses to perform again I could with my present knowledge obtain my results with far less labour than I went through in the summer.

On January 1st I hope to put pen to paper in beginning my work, but in the mean time I must be extremely busy. What I have said about the inade-

[1] See *Geology of the Virginias*, p. 10.

quacy of the barytic tests is, I suppose, known to
chemists, but it is nowhere insisted on. My marl
apparatus now comes into most admirable play. I
did use it occasionally in the summer, but all along
imagined that the other process was sufficient. . . .

On January 6, 1835, Henry was elected to the professorship of geology and mineralogy in the University of Pennsylvania, and on January 2, to membership
in the American Philosophical Society.

WILLIAM TO HENRY.

WILLIAM AND MARY, January 21, 1835.

. . . Nothing is doing yet on the subject of geology
in our legislature. Gregory is here, and tells me that
a proposition will probably be introduced as soon as
the agitating subject of electing a Senator shall have
been finished. I have great hopes of obtaining the
work. Your views of the best mode of prosecuting a
survey would be of great interest and use to me.
Please let me have a copy as soon as possible.

When William Martin comes on in the spring, you
can embrace the opportunity of sending me Lyell and
any other works that you may think useful. Please
also to obtain for me the following articles, and send
them by the same or an earlier opportunity : —

1 platinum capsule, such as I had a year ago.
1 lb. of absolute alcohol (French).
Half oz. oxalate ammonia.
Half lb. distilled muriatic acid (pure).
Half lb. distilled nitric acid.
1 four-ounce phial of phosphate of ammonia.
1 foot of small platinum wire for blowpipe.

These can all be obtained at Smith's. My alcohol,
with all the economy I have used, is almost exhausted.
The gill which I had at the opening of the course has
been used at least ten times in analysis, and, though

carefully distilled off in each operation, a portion of course is lost. . . .

In furtherance of the interests of the survey, William went to Richmond and, after appearing before the legislative committee having the matter in charge, was awarded the privilege of addressing the lower body, or House of Delegates, which he did on February 9, 1835.

WILLIAM TO HENRY.

RICHMOND, February 11, 1835.

I fear you have been anxious on account of my unusually long silence, but I am sure that the contents of this letter will more than compensate you for your anxiety. I have been here for more than a week, though when I left Williamsburg I designed to return in a day or two. The object of my visit you have already guessed. I am almost certain that I shall accomplish it. A geological committee has been appointed by the legislature to report upon a survey. Unprepared as I was, I appeared before the committee two days ago, and, in an harangue of an hour and a half, so interested them in the matter that the members of the legislature requested me to make an address to them publicly on that subject. With but a few hours' warning and without a note, and without even casting a thought upon how I was to address them, and with only one illustration (a magnified section), I marched into the hall of delegates yesterday evening at half past seven. At least three hundred persons had already appeared, and many more crowded in afterwards. At my right were Mr. Stannard, Mr. Wickham, and several of the judges of the Court of Appeals; around me on all sides were the numerous members of both Houses of Assembly. It might well have daunted a stouter heart than mine. But a scarcely momentary tremor gave way to the conscious feeling of the importance and dignity of the occasion, and I stood forth boldly and advocated, I think powerfully, the cause of geology, developing a few of its most important truths, and displaying the benefits which it proffered to Virginia. I was listened to with a riveted and deep attention, which satisfied me of the interest which I excited; and without once halting or stammering or becoming confused I went on for upwards of an hour, and when I closed loud words of approbation followed me. Stannard and others, here esteemed great critics, have been pleased to pass high encomiums on my address, and its effect upon the legislature is acknowledged to · have been great. What think you of my being asked for a copy of my address for printing? I don't remember a syllable of it now.

Friends say that the legislature will authorize a reconnaissance this year, and of course I shall have the management of it. You must help me all you can. . . .

The movement for the establishment of a geological survey of Virginia came before the legislature in the form of "Certain Memorials from Morgan, Frederick and Shenandoah Counties praying for a Geological Survey of the State, with a view to the Discovery and Development of its Geological and Mineral Resources." These petitions were referred to a select committee of the General Assembly, who submitted (in February, 1835) a lengthy report. This is published in full in the "Geology of the Virginias," pp. 754–762. The following letter shows that this report of the committee was prepared by Mr. Rogers: —

WILLIAMSBURG, February 27, 1835.

. . . Yesterday I received the printed Report of the Geological Committee, together with the bill, which has by this time probably passed its third reading and goes up to the Senate. The report was drawn up by me, and has been adopted and fathered by the Committee without a syllable of change. It was pronounced good. The bill will authorize the appointment of a geologist, and if needful a topographer, by the Board of Public Works, the joint emoluments not to exceed $3,000. It contemplates a reconnaissance in the first place, after which there can be no doubt of a complete and extensive survey. I am told that there is little doubt that the bill will pass; but even if it should not now, next year it certainly will. The daily papers of Richmond have lauded my efforts in a very complimentary style. So much you see for a little enterprise. How much I wished for two or three of your drawings at my public lectures! With the aid of one of the engineers, I copied on a large scale a portion of Conybeare's European section by way of illustration, and this was all I had. I hope Robert will come as soon as he is able, and if you can spare several of your drawings I would find great use for them.

Have you, or can you get for me, a set of platinum wire weights? I have called on your kindness in so many ways that I am really frightened at the amount of trouble you will incur, but don't let anything I ask take you from important engagements. Robert will now have no lectures to attend, and he will execute my commissions readily, I am sure. . . .

An Act establishing the survey was passed on March 6, 1835, and William was soon after appointed to conduct it. Henry began about the end of May, 1835, a similar reconnaissance of the State of New Jersey.

WILLIAM AND MARY, March 25, 1835.
Your last letter, stating your hopes of being appointed to make the reconnaissance of New Jersey, gives me great delight. I trust that we shall spend many delightful and profitable days together in the field. Your suite of rocks would be very acceptable. Can you procure a small specimen of strontianite to bring on, or have you any of the strontian or barytic minerals in your collection? I found a mineral in the calcareous slate this summer which I judge to be of this nature. I am about to examine it. Bring on specimens of the New Jersey fossils. How I long for Dr. Hayes's work and Sowerby!

I have found a *Crepidula* new to me. It is very smooth on the exterior, and the beak turns up beautifully so as to resemble the *Crepidula communis arielis* of Lea, only more beautifully rounded at the back. . . .

On February 4, 1835, Mr. Rogers was elected to membership in the Virginia Historical and Philosophical Society of Richmond. After his appointment as Chief of the Geological Survey, other societies in Norfolk and elsewhere in Virginia, as well as the more important American Philosophical Society of Philadelphia, offered him membership, either active or honorary.

But now a far more important step than any he had yet taken was near, — namely, his removal from the malarious climate of Williamsburg to the more salubrious and elevated region of Charlottesville. Early

in August Mr. Rogers received notice of his election
to the chair of Natural Philosophy in the University
of Virginia, and soon after signified his acceptance.
He was now in his thirty-first year, and had been
for seven years Professor of Natural Philosophy and
Chemistry in the College of William and Mary.

SEAL OF WILLIAM AND MARY COLLEGE.

CHAPTER IV.

PROFESSOR OF NATURAL PHILOSOPHY IN THE UNIVERSITY AND DIRECTOR OF THE GEOLOGICAL SURVEY OF VIRGINIA.

1835–1842.

The University of Virginia. — William appointed State Geologist. — First Report. — Lack of Assistants. — Henry Geologist of New Jersey and Pennsylvania. — Robert graduates in Medicine. — Disturbances in the University of Virginia. — James Professor of Chemistry in Cincinnati. — Formation of the Association of American Geologists and Naturalists. — Student Riots. — Opposition to Geological Surveys. — Chemical Analysis. — Ill-health. — The National Association for the Promotion of Science. — Beginnings of the Smithsonian. — Discovery of Infusorial Earth. — Chairman of the Faculty of the University killed by a Student. — Vain Efforts to save the Survey of Virginia. — Henry presides at the Second Meeting of Geologists and Naturalists in Philadelphia. — Removal of James to Philadelphia. — Lyell visits America. — A Journey to New England. — Geological Discussions. — William and Henry present their Memoir on the Physical Structure of the Appalachian Chain, at the Third Meeting of Geologists and Naturalists in Boston.

THE University of Virginia occupies a peculiar position among American institutions of learning. Founded by an ex-President of the United States as an embodiment of novel and liberal ideas of university education; supported chiefly by the State, free from sectarian control, and open to all classes of the white population; governed on the part of the State by a Board of Visitors, and on the part of the instructors by the Faculty itself which was without a president and answerable only to this Board; located in buildings expressly designed as an historical architectural setting for a thoroughly modern establishment, and fearlessly discarding obsolete or obsolescent educational ideals;—the University of Virginia has, from the outset, been entirely unique. Thomas Jefferson, its founder, after long public service and residence in Europe, conceived and carried out the establishment of the University, secured for it the support of the Commonwealth, and imposed upon it not only its architectural plan, but to a great extent its peculiar educational features. Jefferson himself was a graduate of William and Mary, but he did not hesitate, in the interests of freer and higher education, to view with complacency the overshadowing and even the absorption of the old College by the University.

The University was opened to students on March 7, 1825. It had therefore been in operation for ten years only when William Barton Rogers was called to it from the College of William and Mary. Ever since the Rogers family had been established in Williamsburg in 1819, they had suffered severely from the climate. In summer they had been compelled to migrate northwards, and in winter they had felt its ill effects. References to the unwholesomeness of Williamsburg as a place of residence abound in the correspondence covering the entire period from 1819 to 1835, and some citations have already been made. Doubtless the vitality of all the brothers suffered from this cause; and to show that they were not peculiar in this respect, the following from the President of William and Mary may be quoted:—

THE UNIVERSITY OF VIRGINIA, CHARLOTTESVILLE

Rotunda and Lawn

WILLIAM AND MARY COLLEGE, April 1, 1836.

MY DEAR SIR, — I have just distributed your sugar to the children as a means of comforting them, for Adam, Charles, Susan and Lucy have all had chills this morning. The rest of us, thank God! are well. There seems no prospect of our ever enjoying health in this wretched place, though we were to spend our lives here. My own health is not good; I have very little appetite, and have had more or less of febrile symptoms for the last six weeks. . . .

Charlottesville, on the other hand, proved to be an excellent and wholesome location, and Mr. Rogers's health improved. Of his first impressions little or nothing, unfortunately, has been preserved. But with the coming of the spring, after his first winter at the University, he wrote to one of the Empie children a rhapsody on the season : —

UNIVERSITY OF VIRGINIA, May 14, 1836.

DEAR KATE, . . . Spring is now exulting in the hills and valleys; graceful and lovely is the livery she wears. The soft green of the tender grass and grain that overspreads the fields and meadows; the deeper hue of the luxuriant clover; the rich coloring of the verdure that spreads its ample folds even to the summits of the mountains, — are a delicious luxury to the eyes. Our gardens and lawn are beautiful beyond description. Just now the early roses are turning their blushing cheeks to the kisses of the sun, and the flowering locusts stand around on our lawn like bridal nymphs arrayed in white plumes and flowing lace. Odours are wafted by every breeze, and the songs of the spring birds awaken many a tender and many a sad remembrance. Surely this world is beautiful, and God is good. . . .

There is abundant evidence that Mr. Rogers's departure from William and Mary was deeply lamented by his many friends in Williamsburg. In this connection brief extracts of letters, the first from his friend and former colleague, Professor T. R. Dew, and the second from Mrs. Empie, the always devoted friend of the brothers, may be quoted: —

FROM PROFESSOR T. R. DEW.

WILLIAM AND MARY COLLEGE, November 2, 1835.

It makes me sad indeed to take my seat to write to a friend with whom I have spent so many happy hours, and laboured so many years in our old college. I miss you exceedingly; your rooms are as yet closed, and when I stroll up and down the old piazza the college presents *to me* quite a desolate aspect. I am almost tempted sometimes to wish you here again, in spite of all the advantages which I know you will realize at the University.

Our old college has opened under better auspices than I anticipated; the number of matriculates this morning was thirty-nine, and I believe there are several more in town to subscribe. . . . I now really think that if we had you with us the college would have been thoroughly resuscitated, for the present at least. . . . My dear fellow, I wish most cordially I had you here to accompany me in my long and solitary rides; I think in one more year I should become quite a famous geologist without reading. . . . I suppose by this time you are fairly under way at the University. Have you trouble in governing your students? How often do you meet in faculty? Is your health good? . . .

FROM MRS. EMPIE.

WILLIAMSBURG, December 7, 1835.

. . . Christmas is almost here, and your coming a daily subject of conversation. The children talk of it with delight, and Lucy sings it over and over. . . . Old Mrs. Peachy gave a splendid party (she says to the college). Every student was invited, and, would you believe it, Mrs. Sally P. danced! Col. Mac. gave also quite a grand entertainment, at which (report says) both married and single became gentlemanly merry. Mr. Bright had a stylish dining company on Friday. . . .

The Act of the legislature establishing the Geological Survey of Virginia was passed, as already stated, on March 6, 1835, and Professor Rogers was soon after appointed geologist in charge. Thus began a public and official service which was continued by his reappointment annually for the six next succeeding years. Thus also began that investigation of the geology of Virginia which was his most extensive contribution to natural science.

His public plea for the establishment of a survey, and his appointment as its director, occurred while Mr. Rogers was still at the College of William and Mary, and probably this was one reason for his call to the University of Virginia, although he was already well known to men of science. Joseph Henry, then Professor of Natural Philosophy in Princeton College, and afterwards the eminent Secretary of the Smithsonian Institution as well as President of the National Academy of Sciences, wrote of Mr. Rogers : —

FROM PROFESSOR JOSEPH HENRY.

NASSAU HALL, PRINCETON COLLEGE, July 6, 1835.

Mr. William Rogers, of Virginia, is well known as an ardent and successful cultivator of science. I am personally acquainted with him, and have a very high opinion of his talents and acquirements. He is one of those who, not content with retailing the untested opinions and discoveries of European philosophers, endeavour to enlarge the boundaries of useful knowledge by experiments and observations of his own.

Should Mr. Rogers's life and health be spared, I am confident that he will do much towards elevating the scientific character of our country.

It is worthy of remark in this connection that the young man of whom it was thus predicted that he would " do much towards elevating the scientific character of our country " became in after years Professor Henry's successor in the presidency of the National Academy of Sciences. To him also, in this capacity, fell the honorable duty of pronouncing the eulogy of that Academy on Professor Henry.

To his academic duties and to the work of the survey Professor Rogers faithfully devoted the earlier years of his service at the University of Virginia. The winter of 1835–36 was comparatively uneventful. His first Report, giving the results of his reconnaissance of Virginia and accompanied by a colored profile section of the State, cost him much labor, not only in the field in the summer of 1835, but also at his desk during the following winter. In all his work at this time he was cheered by the ardent affection, sympathy and aid of his brother Henry. The latter was living in Philadelphia, and during the winter was engaged chiefly upon his own first Report of the geo-

logical survey of New Jersey. Robert was in Philadelphia studying at the medical school of the University of Pennsylvania. James, who had now a family
of small children, held a Professorship of Chemistry
in a medical school in Cincinnati. Henry became
interested in a movement for the establishment of a
geological survey of Pennsylvania, of which he was
destined to be the head. The attempt proved successful, and in 1836 he was the director of the geological surveys of both Pennsylvania and New Jersey.
He also found time in the same year to assist William
to some extent upon the survey of Virginia.

Robert, meantime, was drawing near to the end of
his course as a medical student. His experiences well
illustrate some of the methods of medical education of
the time : —

ROBERT TO WILLIAM.

PHILADELPHIA, October 9, 1835.

. . . Our summer course has not yet closed ; it will
finish at the end of this month, when the winter session will immediately begin, and then I shall be tied
indeed, listening for eight or nine hours daily to lectures, and catching what time I can for reading up on
them. . . .

PHILADELPHIA, December 16, 1835.

Heartily do I wish that the days were longer. My
studies are crowding faster than ever upon me, and
my thesis is yet unfinished, I might almost say un-
begun, for many of the most important experiments
are to be performed. This moment have I been released from my last lecture (and it is now past nine
o'clock), chasing from room to room since nine this
morning. And yet I shall have to drop my pen in a
few minutes to prepare for to-morrow's lectures. . . .

Samuel Haldeman[1] is in town, and is quite full of

[1] Geologist and distinguished philologist.

the geology of his neighbourhood. He is desirous, I believe, of making with Henry's assistance a geological map of that section of the State.

In analyzing some of the marls which Henry left for Casamajor and myself, we find that, upon the addition of ammonia to the digested marl, and subsequently by heating, as directed by the books, to thorough dryness, a substance is sublimed which is by no means solely chloride of potassium, but in large amount muriate of ammonia. You had better repeat this, and see what suggestions you can make to relieve us from this difficulty. We find that, by continuing the heat to redness, we volatilize the ammonia; may not some of the chloride of potassium also be driven off?

I wish you to think of the subject of my thesis. Can you not devise some method by which I can separate the colouring matter from the saline matter? for I consider it a discovery that is extremely difficult, and has never yet been done, though generally considered as effected by simple means, such as pressing the clot between bibulous papers. In this even Berzelius is in error, and therefore I am particularly desirous of a method unobjectionable, as many of the experiments heretofore performed have been made upon the presumption that it was pure colouring matter employed.

Dr. Hare is now upon pneumatic chemistry, and my opportunity for experimenting has just arrived; but my lectures engross all my time, and it would sometimes seem even more, for the duties of several hours are sometimes pressed into one. This, therefore, you will not consider a short letter for one so much a slave as I am. . . .

It was reported this evening that New York is still on fire, and that six hundred houses have been already consumed on the East River side.

March 20, 1836.

. . . You will be much pleased to learn that I am successfully through my examinations, and that I have not merely passed, but have acquitted myself in the eyes of the Faculty with much credit. My thesis I handed in but a few days before I appeared for my examination; it was read by all, and all complimented me highly. Dr. Chapman was the first to meet me when I entered the "green room." "Mr. Rogers," said he, "we have all read your thesis attentively and with great pleasure; it does honour to yourself and to the University. You need not be at all alarmed, you are perfectly safe." He then asked me one question, which I answered, slapped me on the back and said, "You'll pass." Dr. Hodge then began a conversation about my thesis, and ended with saying to Dr. Gilman, "I resign Mr. R. to you, sir, and if you deliver him as well as he can deliver I shall be perfectly satisfied." Dr. Gilman said I had got myself into a difficulty, for "any one who writes such a thesis is pitting himself against the Faculty, and they are sure to try to stump him." But instead of this he asked me two of the simplest questions he could think of, and turned to Dr. Hare and said, "Dr., it is your turn." The Dr., without lifting his eyes from a newspaper he was reading, called out, "I pass this gentleman." Materia medica came next. Dr. Wood not being present, Dr. Chapman asked me, "What is opium?" and one or two similar questions. Dr. Horner treated me equally kindly. They then all rose to congratulate me.

This morning was the time I had fixed upon to start to join you, but yesterday I received information from Dr. Horner (the Dean) that the Faculty had passed a resolution to have my thesis printed, and another awarding me a medal to be presented at "Commencement" (on next Saturday the 26th), and were therefore desirous that I should be there to receive it. A committee of the Faculty have been appointed to have it made. They are not sure that it will be ready in time, but, should it not, the form will still be gone through. I have therefore to postpone the time of my departure till Monday, the 28th. . . .

The young state geologists were hardly at the head of their respective surveys before a very serious difficulty arose in the total lack of properly fitted assistants. There was no scarcity of young men willing to become salaried assistants, but the experience of the brothers in Virginia and New Jersey the previous year had shown that young men competent to make investigations in field geology were extremely rare. As this was a difficulty which promised to continue, William, who was necessarily confined to his university duties, appears to have felt it so keenly that he even thought seriously of resigning his professorship in order to give all his time to the work of the survey. Accordingly, it was decided by the brothers that Robert should for the moment abandon the idea of practising medicine and become William's assistant in Virginia.

HENRY TO WILLIAM.

PHILADELPHIA, April 10, 1836.

. . . Our great and pressing dilemma is for competent geological assistants. The country does not afford them: they are to be made *by us,* and patience is therefore indispensable, for bear in mind that under no circumstances ought the State to look to us for detailed work; *that* is to come from the assistants. Be not teased by what you hear, but quell the impatience we have awakened, by pleading the importance of maturing plans and getting duly organized with fitly instructed assistants ere we go minutely to work.

These popular schemes are too apt to be abortions, and better do little than go wrong at the start.

In regard to your survey, I propose to join with Robert and Maxwell in about twelve days at furthest, consult with you and lead them to the scene of operations, and get back towards the 20th of May, or sooner if I can, with Maxwell, who is to be my reliance in Pennsylvania with J. Fraser. Then, for a second permanent assistant for you, I am at a loss. Mr. Espy, who has a strong leaning to geology, would spend his vacation from the 20th June to September with you and try what he can make of it, so that, if he should find himself likely to make a geologist, he would give up his school and become your second permanent assistant. He could not do so, however, for less than $1,500 clear of travelling expenses, but thinks we might in a year induce the State to add a small appropriation for Meteorology, a thing really of vast practical moment to an agricultural people, especially as he would do it by teaching a better knowledge of the climate and the means of foreseeing storms, etc. I design to give all my New Jersey appropriation for assistance in that State, taking to my share the labour only. Perhaps after a while I may shuffle it off to some competent successor, and then if Robert wants to resume medicine I could again take his place. Keep of good cheer, and in due time we shall see all things go on well. As to opposition and detraction, of course I look for this, but I feel certain we shall ultimately prove ourselves foremost in the ranks. I am sending to Europe for several important works, and by next winter we shall be fully equipped for doing our tasks scientifically. Heed not the impatience you witness; it is the inevitable consequence of our state of society and institutions. It cannot harm us if we do not feel it. The New York survey is ruined by attending to the popular impatience. General Dix, who drafted their plan, confessed to me in a letter how much the good of the measure has been marred by it, and this is the secret of their great appropriation, $26,000 per annum. . . .

Robert alone looked with some disfavor on this plan, and especially as he had just been appointed physician to the almshouse. But he cheerfully set aside his own preferences for the common good and prepared himself to enter the service of the Virginia survey under his brother William, who cordially approved of the plan.

WILLIAM TO HENRY.

UNIVERSITY OF VIRGINIA, April 25, 1836.

. . . I am now at electricity, and have a good deal to do in the lecture-room. Next week I shall lecture at night as well as in the day, in order to finish this subject within the week. I have yet to treat of Galvanism, Magnetism, Electro-Magnetism, Optics and Astronomy, and I shall be prodigiously hurried. I am in great distress about my book upon the Springs.

I look with great satisfaction to Robert's aid. I am sure that physical science will open better prospects for him than medicine. But I can well appreciate the reluctance with which he will suspend for a time his medical pursuits. Should he come on as I expect in May, I want him to scour the Northern Neck for marls and fossils, which he can do before the climate becomes unsafe. . . .

With the opening of the season for field-work in 1836, William's assistants continued the work begun during the past year, the legislature having voted an appropriation. Owing to his duties at the University Professor Rogers could not join them at the outset, but that he carefully superintended and directed their work the following extract from a letter to one of them testifies : —

UNIVERSITY OF VIRGINIA, April 18, 1836.

. . . You must keep a keen lookout in the vicinity of Norfolk, and in extreme eastern counties in general, for deposits newer than the Miocene. You and Robert both fell upon strata seemingly of this character at the mouth of the Rappahannock. You remember the peculiar oyster, of very long figure and thick hinge, associated with clay of a darker hue, and in the same neighbourhood with the gypsum. Look out for a recurrence of these things. . . .

Let your notes always be very ample, for it will be far easier to compress from abundant materials than to remedy imperfections in detail. Remember you are to draw up the results of your aquatic tour, and with such modifications as I may see to be useful, this will be incorporated in my Report. Take the temperatures of such springs and wells as you meet with, noting their probable depth. . . .

When released from duty at the close of the session, Mr. Rogers joined his assistants in the field. Robert also was by this time engaged in field-work in Virginia, so that, with Henry at work in New Jersey and Pennsylvania, all three of the brothers were thus simultaneously engaged during the summer. The following from William to Henry gives some idea of the character of his work: —

CHRISTIANSBURG, October 29, 1836.

MY DEAR HENRY, — I reached this point yesterday and have been kept within doors by bad weather. This morning we had a fall of hail and now it is raining. To-morrow (Monday) morning I shall set off for some of the coal seams in the vicinity of Blacksburg, and shall probably ride into the mountains near the Botetourt line. I am on the ridge that separates the

Mississippi and Atlantic navigable waters. An extensive district between this and Newbern, which is about twelve miles a little south of west, exhibits horizontal strata of limestone, and this circumstance has probably contributed to make the impression that this is connected with regions to the west, in structure and character.

The sandstones which occur here, as a part of the series of calcareous rocks, are remarkable for a beautiful pisciform structure, like that of the specimen from Scott County which Wyndham Robertson gave us last winter in Richmond.

I have seen and examined the strange and interesting regions of the lead-salt and plaister, and have taken some useful notes. I shall cross the Blue Ridge at Buford's Gap on my way home, about the middle of next week, and I expect to reach the University by Saturday.

I have heard nothing from Philadelphia since my departure from the University, and I have become exceedingly anxious and impatient to know how you and Robert are coming on. I do not know how Robert is now employing himself in Philadelphia, but I suppose at analysis.

I am glad to be so near the close of my excursion, for, although I have seen a great deal to interest me, my time has been so restricted, and my means of locomotion often so very indifferent, that I have sometimes grown quite impatient, though never weary. Besides, I have felt a painful solicitude, which I have rarely experienced before, on account of being cut off from all intercourse with my brothers. I feel, too, that without their companionship I am but half myself, either for labour or enjoyment. When, my dear brother, can we be so circumstanced as to work and enjoy ourselves in concert? This is what I now desire more than anything else.

Of James I have not heard a syllable for a long time. I presume he has written to one or both of you since reaching Cincinnati. When you write, let me know all about him. I am anxious, too, to hear from our dear Uncle. I hope his health improves. Please to remember me affectionately to him.

When, my dear Henry, will you join me at the University? I shall be looking for you in November. I have a great deal to do, — my notes to put in form, my Report to write, and my lectures to the engineering class, in addition to the others. But I keep a stout heart and work on, for I think I can do it all.

What would I not give to have you here! and I feel this longing now, not so much from the want of your valuable help as from the affectionate concern for your welfare and happiness which seems to gather fresh strength as we are more separated. I sometimes, too, feel a sort of awful foreboding that time and distant occupations may wean us from each other. The tears start and my heart sickens at such a thought. God grant that this may never, never be. Life to me would be worthless without the love and society of my brothers.

Excuse, my dear brother, these perhaps foolish thoughts, and do not suppose that I indulge them. Are we not too much to each other for such things ever to be possible? A thousand blessings upon you both, my dear Henry and Robert. Write to me often. I shall write as soon as I reach home, where I expect to find letters from you.

Your affectionate brother,
WILLIAM.

The cordial relations existing between Henry and the English geologists are illustrated by a letter from John Phillips, Esq., then Assistant General Secretary of the British Association for the Advancement of Science, who, writing under date of September 2, 1836, in his official capacity to request Henry "to prepare a continuation of your [his] report on the

Geology of North America, to be presented at the next meeting of the Association at Liverpool, in September, 1837," adds to his official request the following personal letter:—

JOHN PHILLIPS, ESQ., TO PROFESSOR HENRY ROGERS.

YORK, September 28, 1836.

MY DEAR FRIEND, — After I wrote this official circular last year, I received your most welcome letter containing the notice that you would give us at the next meeting the continuation of your report, and I laid my "form" aside as needless.   But since, a few days ago, I saw Professor Bache, I have resolved to give you a few lines in addition to this letter of request, though to say truth I have been and I am so drowned in occupation that all my correspondence is in danger of utter ruin through the mere distraction of my mind.   First of all, be assured that the continuation of your report is most earnestly desired by the geologists of England, who received the former part with great favour and thankfulness at Edinburgh.   Mr. Lyell and Mr. Murchison, as well as your humble friend, explained the bearing of many of the questions discussed, and the whole meeting concurred in the sentiments of approbation with which your labours were mentioned.   Some person or persons in America sent over to England a rather strange critique upon what he or they fancied to be your report (the very imperfect abstract which was put by some person unknown into "Jameson's Journal," I believe), and this paper I threw in the fire.   Others received this critique as well as myself, and treated it in the same manner.

. . . It would be a fatal error if you should suppose your reputation unsafe in the hands of the Engglish geologists, who are, it is true, very ill-informed of the state and progress of science in America, but who are, believe me, too well instructed in the merits of your zealous labours, not to do you the fullest justice. Have no doubt on this point, I entreat you, but send us the continuation of your work for the next meeting in September in Liverpool. . . . By the bye, I have never yet obtained possession of the Trilobites you were so good as to say you had sent me, nor do I know at all how they came, nor to whom addressed. Perhaps you had intended them for the Geological Society, as the specimen you last sent, which I confess I do not understand, nor have I anything very like it. My last volume on Yorkshire geology contains 420 species of organic remains from mountain Limestone alone, and of them 320 are new!

The return of the autumn found Professor Rogers again at his post at the University. But evidence abounds in the letters of this period, and those immediately following, that his position was in many respects difficult. His double service (to the State and to the University) and his frequent enforced absence appear to have excited the envy of some of his colleagues, while his outspoken disapproval of the behavior of the student-body served to make him for a time an object of dislike to the unruly. The situation, therefore, became irksome, especially after certain disturbances which now interfered with the quiet of the academic life.

On November 12, 1836, a serious infringement of the rules of the University took place, and led to the summary dismissal of seventy students. " The grounds of the sentence of dismission set forth in the sentence were, that the students included in it had introduced firearms within the precincts, without lawful authority, and avowed their determination to keep them in their possession, notwithstanding the enactments of the institution and the express prohibition of the Faculty; and that these offences were greatly aggravated by the circumstance that they were the result of an illegal combination between those students."[1]

It was one of the rules governing the University that "No student shall, within the precincts of the University, introduce, keep or use weapons or arms of any kind, or gunpowder."[2]

"A voluntary association of students, styling themselves the 'University Volunteers,' had organized and brought arms within the precincts, apparently without being 'aware that to do so it was necessary to obtain the leave of the Faculty.' Application being made to the Faculty, leave was granted on certain stipulated conditions essentially similar to conditions attached to similar leave in former years. One of the (seven) stipulated conditions reserved to the Faculty the right to dissolve the corps for violation of the prescribed conditions or 'whenever the interests of the University shall in their opinion require it.' . . .

"These conditions, on being communicated to the company, were not acceded to. . . . On the contrary they resolved 'to resist the authority of the Faculty.' . . . And the second night after the refusal of the company to accede to the conditions prescribed, disturbances commenced by the frequent firing of a musket or muskets on the lawn and elsewhere in the University, which was continued on the following night. . . .

"And on the night of the meeting of the company, at which their resolutions of combination and defiance were adopted, the breaking up of the meeting was immediately followed by an outrageous riot, during

[1] *An Exposition of the Proceedings of the Faculty of the University of Virginia in Relation to the Recent Disturbances at that Institution,* December 16, 1836.

[2] Chapter iii. 3, *Enactments relating to the Constitution and Government of the University of Virginia,* 1831.

which there was a continual roar of musketry on the
lawn and in other parts of the University for an hour
or more, apparently intended to celebrate the triumph
supposed to have been already achieved by the combination, or to intimidate the Faculty into submission.
And subsequently their determination to carry their
resistance into effect was marked by every circumstance which could indicate deliberation and contempt
of the authority of the Faculty.[1]

"On the sentence being made known, about four
o'clock on Saturday, a scene of unparalleled disorder
and violence was immediately commenced, which with
little intermission was continued until late on Sunday
night. The acts committed during the nights of its
continuance, particularly the second, were altogether
different in their character from those which have
usually distinguished college riots, — they were the
outrages of an infuriated mob. Our houses were
attacked, the doors forced, and the blinds and windows broken. And there is reason to believe that,
not content with this, they contemplated proceeding
to the desperate extremity of entering our houses for
the purpose of attempting personal violence."[2]

The dismissal of seventy students, which followed,
naturally created a profound sensation and aroused
much criticism, but after order had been restored the
Faculty resolved to allow "to reënter those of the
dismissed students who should make application for
readmission, on their disclaiming participation in the
principal acts of riot and violence which had been
committed, or, if they could not do so, on their making proper atonement therefor."

The whole matter led to the lengthy statement, or
"Exposition," from which the foregoing extracts have
been made, prepared by Professor J. A. G. Davis,

[1] *Exposition*, etc., pp. 11, 12.   [2] *Exposition*, etc.

then Chairman of the Faculty and Professor of Law. The "Exposition" is dated December 16, 1836. Among Mr. Rogers's papers is a draft of a letter addressed to J. H. Pleasants, Esq., editor of the "Whig," Richmond.

TO J. H. PLEASANTS.

UNIVERSITY OF VIRGINIA, December 20, 1836.

I send you by mail a copy of the "Exposition" of the Faculty of the recent disturbances here, and of the course which they pursued in relation to those students who were involved in them. This paper, very clearly drawn up by the chairman, sets in a just and proper light all the incidents which occurred, the measures adopted by the students and by the Faculty, and the laws upon which the measures of the latter were founded, and by which, as I think, they were not only fully justified, but rendered absolutely imperative. Perhaps no necessity for such a detailed exposition existed, but as from more than one quarter sentiments of approbation of the conduct of the students have been heard, and as it appeared obvious to us that these expressions of approval were founded on imperfect or mistaken knowledge of the facts and law of the case, it was thought that a more detailed view of the matter than had yet appeared was, to say the least, expedient.

I am fully aware of how much your time must be occupied with public matters. Yet I take the liberty of requesting you to read the "Exposition" herewith sent, and, without desiring you to give it a place in the "Whig," which I know would be inconvenient if not impracticable, I would ask you, in case you find the opinion you formerly expressed to be no longer tenable, to make a remark to that effect, whenever convenient, in the "Whig."

There are many students with whom your former notice possessed much weight, and some of them have

probably been delayed in reëntering the University
by the confirmation thus given to their views by so
high an authority. Without in the smallest degree
intending to sway your opinions, I would remark that,
in case you agree with us in the justice and propriety
of the course we pursued, — and of this accordance I
feel almost certain, — an intimation to this effect would
probably decide the course of several who from mistaken pride are now holding off, though extremely
desirous of resuming their studies in the University.
About forty of the dismissed students have returned
to their studies under the resolution of the Faculty
by which they are conditionally admitted.   Others
will no doubt follow their example, and it is therefore
desirable for their sakes, as well as that of the institution, that an erroneous view of the laws and of the
recent action of the Faculty should not be counte-
nanced by those in whose opinions they confide, so as
to become an obstacle to their return.

Only four years later, Professor Davis himself
was shot down before his own door and killed by a
student celebrating the anniversary of this riot of
1836.

The survey of Virginia was continued in 1837, and,
Henry having resigned his connection with it, James
(who was still Professor of Chemistry in a Cincinnati
medical college) was appointed to become one of William's chief assistants.

TO HIS BROTHER HENRY.

UNIVERSITY OF VIRGINIA, April 30, 1837.

. . . I have written at great length to the Board of
Public Works asking their approbation of the appointment of Aiken and Hayden, formally announcing
your resignation, and recommending James for the
place. I have also given a detailed view of the pro-

posed organization and plan of operations for the
season, with which, I have no doubt, they will be
greatly pleased; and in addition to all this, I have
given a schedule of the expenses which will be incurred, as far as I can make them out, and accompanied with such of the particulars connected with the
prospects of the work as I thought would make them
fully acquainted with our views, and add to the interest they already feel in the prosecution.

I look forward with cheering confidence to the
progress of the work, whatever may be the difficulties which from time to time we may have to encounter.
But I need not say, my dear Henry, how much of this
confidence would be withdrawn, did I not feel that in
your wider experience and clearer science, I shall
still possess a resource in cases of embarrassment.
When you first announced your intention to resign,
the pain I felt was much greater than you probably
imagined; but in the kind and generous tender of assistance with which you accompanied your resignation,
I felt my confidence renewed. How, my dear brother,
can I sufficiently express my sense of the affectionate
concern you manifest in whatever is interesting to
my health, happiness or reputation? When I think
of the enduring strength of the fraternal ties which
unite us in mind and sympathy, how ardently do I
long for the arrival of the time, which I cannot but
think will come, when we shall all be together, as in
childhood, in the same house, and prosecute our researches in a happy concert of activity!

Since you left I have regularly taken a ride of
five or six miles before breakfast, and have been so
much refreshed by the exercise that I intend keeping
it up. . . .

UNIVERSITY OF VIRGINIA, May 9, 1837.

. . . I paid two visits, of two days each, to the Blue
Ridge since you left, and have explored very closely
in the caves near Rockfish and Turk's Gap. I have
seen the fucoidal sandstone in large beds upon the

west side of the Ridge, gently sloping to the west and
lying upon the rocks of the Ridge. I brought home
from Turk's Gap more than a dozen fragments of
the sandstone with impressions. The stones are all
straight and parallel. I was amazed upon this visit
at seeing how much I had previously been deceived
by the cross joints of this rock, giving it an almost
vertical and slightly eastern dip; but I caught the
beds in large mass very gently sloping to the west.
On Saturday (to-morrow) I go again to Turk's. . . .

What a disastrous train of difficulties have come
upon the country! I greatly fear that our institutions
of learning will feel a share of the pressure next
season. The Governor has convoked the legislature
on the 12th of June, but what they can do I cannot
imagine. . . .

The last few lines refer to the financial panic of 1837.

FROM HIS BROTHER HENRY.

PHILADELPHIA, May 20, 1837.

. . . I found matters in the money world in a sad
condition on my return here. How I wish you had
some time ago transferred all the spare funds you can
command to this place, as for some time to come it will
not be at all easy for me to bring on Virginia paper
without a loss ! . . .

PHILADELPHIA, June 14, 1837.

. . . Uncle is mending in strength, I think, daily.
But pecuniary matters weigh on him to the detriment
of his health. The fact is, he indiscreetly embarrassed
himself by going too far into the stocks, and has been
obliged to sacrifice a little, and fears he shall have to sacrifice more. Had he only some ready means now in his
hands all would be right for the future, I believe. I
found him this morning nervous on the subject of his
commercial credit, which has always stood without a
tarnish. . . . He enjoined me not to desire you to lend
him anything, for he says he has no right that any

should be without the use of their money but himself, who has played the fool. Still, I know that if you could bring on one (or, better, two) thousand, he would secure you in sound stocks, for which you could afford to wait a year or two, while you will lift a weighty load from his spirits. Indeed, I fear he has nearly abandoned the idea of going to Europe, in consequence of his apprehension of not having available funds without a present heavy sacrifice. He knows your generosity, and he bade me therefore be silent on the subject of his money troubles. Don't let him know I have mentioned them. . . .

Never did I want your succour and counsel more than at the present time. I stand in a truly trying situation. You shall hear.

The Government Engineer of the Delaware Breakwater some time ago objected to the Gneiss rock of Chester quarries, owned by the L——s, connections of Dr. P——, and preferred the unstratified trappean rocks of quarries near Wilmington. The Secretary of War requested the Committee on Science and Arts of the Franklin Institute to give their opinion on the comparative fitness of the two rocks. P——, the chairman of the committee, placed me on the sub-committee of ten, eight of whom were escorted, at the expense of government, to all the quarries and to the breakwater. This sub-committee was nearly filled by P——'s personal friends. A partial, one-sided report was framed; at this juncture I came in from the country. Much regret was expressed that I had not given them my aid as geologist. I was even told I had neglected a public duty.

The chairman of the sub-committee, James W——, required me to aid him by my geological knowledge, calling on me in public meeting of the big committee to describe the rocks by their right names. I said I would not even name them until I could go down to the quarries, for I knew the bearings of names. Thus drawn in, I required him to pilot me over the ground,

and I went to the quarries. My convictions went contrary to the majority of the sub-committee in their
report, for I preferred the trappean rocks. I also convinced Mr. W——, against his will, and brought over
to my views a majority of the sub-committee. I was
then called upon by him and the rest to draw up a
report for him, which I did, embodying the views
expressed in the sub-committee. Meanwhile W——,
having thus shuffled off the responsibility of the report
on me, hangs fire, no doubt from the influence of
P——, and slinks behind my back. After numerous
long sessions (some of them five hours!) in sub-committee, we took into general committee three several
reports, one being mine, the official one being only a
set of meagre resolutions, signed by five out of ten,
and not by W——, who was for pure neutrality. For
three sessions of the general committee I had to defend my report and views against all P——'s influence, which is mighty, but I foiled him by a vote of
eighteen to fourteen. Though fairly out-voted, he has
to-day called the general committee together for to-
morrow night, in hopes of having the vote reconsid-
ered, and I am compelled, after losing a whole week
already, to remain in town and renew the fight. The
stake is a very heavy one, — some hundred thousand
dollars; my responsibility is, therefore, very painful.
Thus far I have stood my ground against every sort
of unfairness, attack and ridicule, having succeeded
in carrying with me nearly all the true friends of the
Institute. He has packed the committee, bringing
against me such men as Dr. M——, whose chemistry
I very soon dissolved. I am proud to say that, by
abstaining on my part from all personality and keeping cool, I have won the confidence of the leading
men of the institution, while he (Dr. P——) has made
sad work with his reputation. I know I shall have
his enmity and that of his adherents, but I know also
my strength, and therefore I do not fear. . . .

Robert was not in the field in 1837, but was engaged as an analyst in Philadelphia, and afterwards in the University of Virginia.

ROBERT TO HENRY.

PHILADELPHIA, July 24, 1837.

Yesterday afternoon Dr. Caldwell, of the West, called upon me, asked my age, my occupation, and if I had ever lectured, and then made me the offer of the Chair of Chemistry in the Medical School of Louisville. From his representation and that of persons I have since seen, there seems little doubt that the Louisville school will far take the lead of that at Lexington. One great advantage which the former will have is that it will be located in a large town (of 30,000 inhabitants) with ample facilities for anatomical instruction and an extensive hospital. The people of Louisville have presented the Faculty with $100,000 and land to erect a building upon. Dr. Caldwell seems perfectly sanguine of its success. The class at Lexington last winter was two hundred and fifty.

I did not, however, make him a certain answer, though I had little expectation of accepting, and knowing pretty well what would be the wishes of yourself, William and Uncle. I told him I would consult you forthwith, and when I heard from you, would give him a definite answer. Please, therefore, give me your views. The offer is a compliment to me, if nothing else. . . .

Bishop can make for me a battery (in a few weeks) of 8,000 pairs, with all the arrangements very complete and on an improved plan, for eighty dollars. Though this seems a good deal, yet it is very cheap, and I want such a battery very much. What say you? Shall I have it made? Will you and William not divide with me the expense? At any rate, had I not better order it? I think I shall be repaid by the discoveries I hope to make.

Do not forget to answer me upon these two points at once, — the school and the battery. . . .

PHILADELPHIA, August 28, 1837.

. . . I look forward with great pleasure to my work, and hope to get through with a great deal of valuable analysis in the ensuing season.

There are a great many matters of research, especially in galvanism and electro-magnetism, I am anxious to pursue. The journals are teeming with articles on these subjects of the deepest interest. I can scarcely pick up one of them without running half frantic. . . .

UNIVERSITY OF VIRGINIA, September 20, 1837.

. . . I learned shortly before I left that the engineers, to whom was entrusted the breakwater question, had decided and reported in favour of the L——'s rocks. Dr. Emerson told me, however, that this decision is not at all a reversion of your report, but that the question put to them was quite a different one from that which the Institute had. It was not which was the most suitable rock for the breakwater purpose, but "Was the L——'s rock, at its price, a suitable material?" No comparison of the values of the two rocks for the purpose was asked. You will not, therefore, feel mortified at the result, as you would otherwise have been. It is a great shame that W—— and others who have acted so meanly in this matter should reap the benefit of their conduct, while others who would have gladly avoided the discussion should be made the sufferers; but I trust it will all speak for itself, and things turn out as they should.

William has a class of seventy, — very promising indeed for the time, and quite as large as at this time last year. . . .

148 *GEOLOGICAL SURVEY OF VIRGINIA.* [1837.

UNIVERSITY OF VIRGINIA, September 27, 1837.

. . . The joint examination along the Potomac is
the thing that I most of all desire. It is the only
plan by which we can finally dispose of the difficult
question of the age of our valley coal in comparison
with yours.

The southwestern counties present a strange state
of things. I am at a loss to imagine what Troost [1]
is making of the same formations in Tennessee. There
is really an alternation of Limestones, Slates and
Sandstones dipping east nearly from the Great Flat
Top to the Blue Ridge! I expect to derive valuable
lights from even a brief inspection of your formations.
We have truly a sublime work in our hands, and I
cannot but think that we shall bring it to a successful
termination, if only time enough be allowed to make
our labour as minute and extensive as is necessary.
I have the "Geological Transactions," and the "Scientific Memoirs" which were ordered for the University Library at my instance. The "Transactions"
contain all the admirable papers of Sedgwick, Murchison and Fitton of late published. I am feasting upon
these matters.

UNIVERSITY OF VIRGINIA, December 4, 1837.

. . . Tell Robert that the method of analyzing iron
ores, which I described to him, appears thus far to
succeed. By avoiding much excess of the acetate of
potash, and by boiling the mixture for some time, the
liquid passes through the filter as clear as distilled
water, and will scarcely indicate the presence of iron
by the addition of ferro-prussiate. From this liquid
the Manganese and Alumina may be readily separated.

I from time to time enjoy a great treat in reading
some of the late valuable papers in the "Geological
Transactions."

[1] State Geologist for Tennessee.

In one of Sedgwick's I have lately read on the Magnesian Limestone, I find some interesting views in regard to concretionary structure. How admirable those papers are in all respects!

What lights do the geologists of New York seem to have attained! If you can spare time, my dear Henry, write me particulars. . . .

. . . Oh, how I long to be in Philadelphia! Solitude is, after all, no friend to Science. My chief stimulus of a truly exciting kind is received from your letters, and sometimes, as for instance to-day, they impart new life to me, and really make me happy in scientific ardour and hope. You must therefore, my dear Henry, write to me as frequently as possible.

HENRY TO WILLIAM.

PHILADELPHIA, December 11, 1837.

. . . Dr. Daubeny [1] is in Philadelphia, and means to be here two or three weeks. I have met him, and exchanged pretty long conversations with him. This morning he called to give me a copy for you of his " Report on the Present State of our Knowledge of Mineral and Thermal Waters," read last year at the British Association, and now in print in the last volume, which we have not yet received. He told me as soon as I had read it to send it on to you; this was in consequence of my telling him of your forthcoming work on the Mineral Waters of Virginia. He wishes to see you, and I offered him a letter to you. At first his plan was to take the University in his way going South; but as the thermal springs of Virginia, which he means to see if possible, are not easy to reach in winter, he has taken my suggestion to go by Norfolk and Charleston and New Orleans, thence to the thermal waters of Washita if possible, and to come back here by Cincinnati, Guyandotte, the springs in Virginia and your University. He is likely,

[1] Charles G. B. Daubeny, M. D., F. R. S., English geologist and chemist.

therefore, to visit you about the early part of April, as he intends to sail for England on the first of May. . . .

He has already told me that he agrees with me in the propriety of rejecting the European names of strata, and says that we shall have Greenough with us also. In Whewell's work on the Inductive Sciences, many sound and broad views are set forth in agreement with our own, so that we are in the right road.

WILLIAM TO HENRY.

UNIVERSITY OF VIRGINIA, December 18, 1837.

. . . You ask for my method of examining the Virginia anthracites. I follow the same steps as with the bituminous coal. Our anthracites all contain some volatile matter, partly aqueous and partly bituminous. This is estimated in the gross by the loss of weight by heating in the perforated crucible. . . .

Bravo! your letter of the 11th has just come. You are well, at least so I infer from your silence on the subject.

I shall start some more analyses of coals and several lignites I have.

I congratulate Robert and you on the possession of a snug laboratory. I feel, had I been provided for some time past as I now am, I should have done a great deal more, and more accurately. Where can I procure Whewell's work to which you refer? . . .

HENRY TO WILLIAM.

PHILADELPHIA, December 18, 1837.

. . . I see Dr. Daubeny frequently. Saturday evening I passed at Clem: Biddle's with a small party of gentlemen in his company; to-night I am invited by Isaac Lea to meet him at his house. I am getting my specimens in a condition of arrangement to show Daubeny, wishing to let him see what we have been doing. By the spring we shall all be able to let him see more; your sections and mine will then, I hope, be all drawn. He is very amiable, and I am sure you will like him for absence of all pretence. . . .

WILLIAM TO ROBERT.

UNIVERSITY OF VIRGINIA, January 3, 1838.

One of my buggy horses (not Billy) was taken sick yesterday morning, though apparently quite well before, and about tea-time died in a sudden spasm. . . . I do not know when I felt more sad than upon Levi's coming into the laboratory, and in a mournful and scarcely articulate voice telling me, "Jimmy is dead." He was an excellent draught-horse, and not bad under the saddle. Young, well-proportioned and of excellent temper. Poor fellow! how many a hard pull has he made for us up the steep mountains in Hampshire and Hardy during the summer and fall! I could really weep over his loss. . . .

You cannot imagine how much pleasure I have received from Henry's and your late letters, in which you speak of scientific matters, and mention the conversations with Daubeny, and the favourable impression made upon him. I have never before felt so strongly desirous of being with you in Philadelphia as of late.

By the bye, I shall require to renew the pot of my blast furnace ere long. The anthracite is actually melting it down. Such a heat! Why, when the door is opened, it dazzles like the interior of a glass or iron furnace. . . .

HENRY TO WILLIAM.

PHILADELPHIA, February 10, 1838.

. . . Robert informed me a few days since of brighter prospects for Bache. That the preliminary school of Girard College will be commenced, there is not much doubt, though the council is disposed to hang back as far as it dare. Bache is not without his troubles, but he will ultimately succeed, and with glorious results, for his mind contemplates a noble and very wise system for the instruction of the orphans.

The Virginia survey had now been going on comparatively smoothly for nearly three years. In 1838,
however, opposition began to develop in the legislature, and Professor Rogers henceforward experienced
the difficulties which beset many scientific enterprises
dependent on state appropriations.

TO HIS BROTHER HENRY.

UNIVERSITY OF VIRGINIA, March 8, 1838.

When I wrote you two days ago, I was in high
spirits in relation to my various tasks, for I had just
heard from Mr. Brown that the printing of my report
in 8vo form had been determined on, and was about
to be commenced by Sheppard. But I fear there is
trouble in store for me. By yesterday's papers I see
that some resolutions offered by Mr. Harmon, to aid
the circulation and to enlarge the edition of the reports, met with great opposition, and that a long debate occurred, in which the merits of these documents
were freely discussed. This proceeding strikes me
as being very indelicate, at the same time that it is
obviously absurd. How can those gentlemen pretend
to judge of my reports? I take for granted that
some sneers have been cast upon my labours; and the
thought of a legislative body employing itself in
venting spleen or exercising wit upon a paper of
which but a very few of them have any adequate
comprehension, really fills me with indignation. It
shows, too, that I have been mistaken in confiding in
the good sense and good feeling of our legislature,
and will destroy much of the satisfaction I have heretofore enjoyed in the prosecution of my tasks. I hope
that, when I hear definitely of what has been done, I
shall find that I now exaggerate its importance. Immediately before adjournment, it appears that Mr.
——, who opposes improvements of all kinds, made a
motion to suspend further printing on the subject for
the present, which was carried.

The internal improvement question has lagged on very tardily, and I really fear that nothing important will be done, after all the talking that has occurred. Had I been in Richmond, no difficulty would have arisen in regard to my report, because in the first place I should have prevented any doubtful or over-zealous movement, and in the second I could have made full explanations satisfactory to all.   As it is, I am at the mercy of the ignorant or the illiberal. . . .

Do not suppose I am in despondent mood.   On the other hand I am labouring on hopefully and cheer-fully.   These difficulties are only what were to be expected, though from the perfect smoothness of the voyage hitherto I have been ill-prepared to encounter a rough sea. . . .

In 1838 many intelligent people in the Middle States embarked in a speculative enterprise for the cultivation of the *Morus multicaulis*, or mulberry, with a view to the rearing of silkworms which feed upon its leaves.   A feverish speculation in these trees developed and ran like wildfire throughout all classes of the community.[1]   The Rogers brothers did not es-cape the infection, and suffered a heavy loss of time, energy and money.   Of the last William was the principal loser.   That they were not alone among educated people in this strange infatuation, the fol-lowing, concerning certain professors of the Univer-sity of Virginia, shows : —

TO HIS BROTHER HENRY.

UNIVERSITY OF VIRGINIA, March 14, 1838.

. . . Robert arrived just in time to aid us by his counsel in planting our buds.   We had not buried them enough, and though they were beginning to shoot, they were doing so less vigorously than he says

[1] See article, " Silk," in *Johnson's Encyclopædia.*

they should. Bonnycastle is wanting buds. Harrison
will soon be desirous of making a little venture, and I
suppose Griffith and Cabell will follow suit. . . .

The immediate predecessor of the present American Association for the Advancement of Science, was
the Association of American Naturalists and Geologists. The following letter from Professor Edward
Hitchcock, of Amherst College, State Geologist of
Massachusetts, to Professor Henry Rogers, relates to
the genesis of the parent society : —   .

AMHERST, MASS., April 4, 1838.

. . . I shall be very happy to receive a copy of
your forthcoming Report upon the Geology of Pennsylvania, and will forward you mine upon certain
points of the economic Geology of Massachusetts.
You will see I have been compelled, as indeed I have
been in all my publications on the subject, to bring out
many things in an immature state. The thing of
principal interest in my report will be a new method
of analyzing soils, by my friend, Dr. S. L. Dana, who
is unquestionably the best chemist in New England,
and who is well acquainted with geology. . . .

. . . But, to cut the matter short, I want that you,
with such other geologists as you choose to associate
with you in Philadelphia and New York, should forthwith appoint a time and place and issue a circular
summoning a meeting of our geologists. And it seems
to me important that this should be done this spring,
before the state geologists take the field for another
campaign. Let each man be invited to bring with
him any specimens he may wish to be examined, and
let it be understood that several days will be spent
together, and if you think proper, that an association
will be formed. Perhaps one or two public lectures
might be given during the meeting, or some of the
discussions be made public. I feel so strong a hope that

you will listen to these suggestions that I will venture to name the individuals in New England whom I think it would be desirable to invite; some of them I have seen within a few days past, and they express a deep interest in such a plan: Professor Silliman, Professor Shepard, Dr. Percival, New Haven; Dr. C. T. Jackson, George B. Emerson, President of the Natural History Society, Professor Charles B. Adams, Boston; Dr. Samuel L. Dana, Lowell, Mass.; Professor Cleveland, Brunswick, Maine; Professor Hubbard, Darmouth College, Hanover, N. H. I suppose that New York or Philadelphia would be the proper place of meeting. It is quite customary for many from New England to go to the former city about the middle of May to attend the religious anniversaries, and might it not be well to have the geological meeting about the same time? I submit the whole, however, to your better judgment.

The following refers to a subsequent visit of Professor Hitchcock to Philadelphia, and his continued interest in the new project: —

HENRY TO WILLIAM.

PHILADELPHIA, September 26, 1838.

. . . The chief part of to-day I have spent in company with Professor Hitchcock, who, making a brief visit to the city, called on me. He is an engaging, unpretending, and guileless man, and is an ardent enthusiast in his pursuit of science. . . . He sees and admits already the want of philosophy in all those who, like himself, have used old names for our strata; and he said unasked that he had perceived that I had found a key to the geology of the greater part of the United States. He is very impatient to witness a summoning of the geologists into an association, and says those of New England will obey the call most cordially. He thinks we should commence it here or in New York. What say you to our trying it for next spring and in Philadelphia? Take this into grave consideration, and give me your suggestions as to whether it were better to delay the movement until a General Association for all the Sciences can be brought about, or to make it now for geology merely.

Every consideration touching anticipations of the future convinces me of the importance of our executing this winter, you your important task on the Springs, myself my Report to the British Association, and both of us jointly a general essay on the Geology of the Appalachian region. Whether I go abroad or not, I think I can do much towards these. . . .

WILLIAM TO HENRY.

UNIVERSITY OF VIRGINIA, April 14, 1838.

. . . I have two noble barometers from Green, and two boiling-point thermometers. All these instruments were put to the test the day before yesterday. We took them in the new buggy up to Turk's Gap, leaving one of each at Harris's, low down in the Gap. Aiken and I proceeded with the others to Turk's Mountain, which is a very prominent point to the left, and a little west of the top of the road. This peak is composed of No. 1 Sandstone, full of the lithodomous impressions. Its height above Harris's is upwards of 1,800 feet. The thermometers gave results beautifully consistent with the others. We then went over into the valley and made observations on the South River, Hayden all the while making simultaneous half-hourly observations of both instruments at Harris's. The next morning we went to the Black Rocks, a still higher point of the ridge, composed of Sandstone No. 1 ; this gave us about 1,900 feet. I am delighted with the thermometers, which have been admirably constructed by Green. They are graduated to tenths of degrees, and will admit of being read to fortieths, which corresponds to about twelve feet. I made a preliminary trial, as follows: Finding the boiling-point on the floor of my laboratory, I then transferred the instrument to my bedroom and marked the difference, which was easily noted. I then measured the vertical distance of the two, which was twenty-nine feet, while by the usual rule, deduced from the boiling-point, it was twenty-seven! I have great hopes that these instruments will help us in approximating to the topography. They are quite portable, and could be carried in a girdle. . . .

Aiken has not seen the formations as they occur in our two northern districts, and goes to James to study them with him and Hayden. His numerous profiles (more than twenty), taken last year, I have been going over with him, and I think that I have clear ideas of the whole Southwest. But great and rapid changes of the members of the series occur, which no one but ourselves could have detected. . . .

TO HIS BROTHER ROBERT.

UNIVERSITY OF VIRGINIA, April 19, 1838.

MY DEAR ROBERT, — Peace has come at last, but not without leaving many uncomfortable recollections of late scenes, which are not soon to be forgotten. In my last I believe I intimated something of a riot either anticipated or actually in progress. This was produced in consequence of the refusal of the Faculty to allow a ball on Jefferson's birthday. You must know that a ball permitted on the 22d was so disgraceful in many particulars as to excite general disgust. One of our students was within an ace of perishing by *mania a potu* in consequence of excess. Both his physicians despaired of him for some hours. I therefore, with others, decidedly opposed a second ball, and through some treachery, where, I know not, my vote was disclosed to the students, together with some expressions calculated to wound their pride, which I never even dreamt of using. On the birthday night, tar-barrels were burned on the lawn, the belfry broken open and the bell rung nearly all night. Numerous students in disguise, with firearms, paraded the lawn, assailed the doors and windows of some of the professors known to be unfriendly to the ball, and more particularly my own. At the same time the most insulting ribaldry was used, and their violence was such that neither I nor those in the house considered their persons safe. Accordingly we prepared ourselves with firearms. On the next day the Faculty convened, and, in the midst of our session, the chairman was personally threatened by one of the offenders. By my instance, the action of the Faculty on the accused was suspended until the next day, and then another and worse scene of violence was presented that night. The following morning we acted, and the next night the dastards made a deliberate and almost silent attack upon my house, scarcely molesting any one else. They broke in my front door, stoned my house on all sides, and for half an hour one of them amused himself by breaking the glass of my back windows. The night was dark, and he skulked behind the wall, and it was impossible to watch, or he would have been inevitably shot. Aiken and Hayden were with me at the time. All is quiet now. The body of the students, of course, reprobate the transaction, but here is the evil, — their reprobation is not active, and it is only by being so that the institution can be saved. Our police is worthless; two or three rowdies can with impunity stone our dwellings, destroy our property, peril our lives, and take from us that quiet without which the situation is unworthy a man of science. Three days have elapsed since the sentence, and still one and perhaps more of the offenders are in the precincts. The very man who doubtless broke my windows I met this morning on the lawn. Can an institution be permanent thus governed? or can a professor consent to the degradation of such a life? I am determined not to do it, and, my dear brothers, I write to you to ask your counsel. The pecuniary sacrifice of leaving the University would be great, but I shall have a support left, and I can doubtless ere long have more. I shall have time at my command, and my reputation as a man of science, which I of course have much at heart, will be more promoted by having more time for research. I have read Henry's Report with great pleasure. How far it surpasses in true science and broad philosophical views all the others I have received! I have received the Maine, Ohio and Maryland reports of this year. My own I place above either of them, but it does not come up to Henry's. . . .

I have this moment received Henry's letter announcing the happy news of his success, and by the same mail a letter from Auditor Brown saying that our state printer declares that the 10,000 copies of my report cannot be printed. What think you of that? Business is sadly conducted with us.

Tell Henry to write to me at once, and let me have the views of all. Were I able to pass the winter in Richmond I could effect everything I want.

UNIVERSITY OF VIRGINIA, June 26, [1838 ?].

MY DEAR ROBERT, . . . The day of my intended departure was that on which my lectures were to close. But with a heavy heart, and thinking only of you, I went over to my lecture-room half an hour before the opening of the lecture, and to my astonishment I found the room already almost full. Students, persons from the country and from Charlottesville, thronged in until at length they were obliged to stand, every bench, chair, etc., being crowded. It was evident that high expectations had been excited, and all this from my having at the previous lecture announced that at the next I would close my course. Valedictories are not customary here, and I had not intended to give one. Thus put upon my mettle, however, and feeling that there was

something at stake, I struck off, after briefly conclud-
ing astronomy, into general topics of Philosophy,
Education, etc., and if I am to judge from the profound attention of my audience, and the remarks since
made, I was successful. I know I have done better,
and had I received your cheering letter before the lecture I should have been quite another man. Yet I
believe that I have gone through my course with a
good deal of *éclat.* Next year I may look for a very
large class. . . .

Maxwell has completed twelve of the county maps,
and will make a short visit to Philadelphia, after finishing what he is now engaged upon. . . .

. . . Mr. Maury's Navigation is briefly and moderately reviewed in the last "Southern Literary Messenger." You will probably be able to recognize the
writer of this trifling paragraph. I wish to show the
kind people of Fredericksburg that we apppreciate
their hospitality and friendship.

FROM HIS BROTHER HENRY.

UNIONTOWN, FAYETTE CO., PA., August 29, 1838.

. . . It cheers me to learn the excellent progress
you have made in developing your intricate Appalachian Geology. What a noble mass of materials
we shall have in two or three years! I am sincerely
glad that James works so well. Of Robert's fine
talents for practical geology I have spoken.

Earnestly do I hope that nothing has interfered
with your design of visiting Tennessee, for the more
I witness of my own region, the more confident do I
grow in the retentiveness of type of our several formations. Indeed, I shall be surprised if our thirteen
formations do not help us through the whole Appalachian basin. I wait impatiently to know your views
as to things in Tennessee. . . .

I believe nearly all your sulphur springs are in
Formation XI. Now only remark the uniformity of
things. The *only* spring in Pennsylvania resem-

bling those of Virginia is one on the Portage R. R., in Formation XI., and, though less powerfully medicinal, it has every external seen in your sulphuretted waters. . . .

TO HIS BROTHER HENRY.

UNIVERSITY OF VIRGINIA, March 2, 1839.

. . . My experiments on the Magnesian Limestones are perfectly conclusive. I have more than twenty which have hardened almost into stone. Of these, some contain much and some little silica, none any considerable proportion of Alumina or Iron. But while they have set so completely, others, containing much silica with the lime but no Magnesia, show no disposition to cohere under water. Thus it seems proved that in our Limestones the Magnesia is the water-setting agent.

I am desirous of knowing when the " Phil. Trans." will come out. If it were not probably too late, I would write for insertion in it an account of my mode of analyzing Magnesian Limestones, and a description of the experiments on the Hydraulic Limestones. I have now no doubt that good water-lime may be procured in a thousand localities in Virginia and Pennsylvania, not only in No. II., but in No. VI. and No. VIII. What think you of the Natural Bridge and Chimney rocks being chiefly of this variety?

Remember me kindly to Dr. Hare and family. How do I envy him the relief he is soon to have from the labours of the lecture-room! My year's task is not much more than half done, while his is nearly finished. To be able in about a month to mount my nag and spend the spring in the mountains, or in explorations anywhere, would be indeed a pleasure; and if you were along it would be beyond everything else delightful. . . .

UNIVERSITY OF VIRGINIA, March 2, 1839.

. . . I have to tell you of another disgraceful outrage committed by students. Two of them, not long
ago dismissed, made an attack upon Dr. Harrison
yesterday morning as he was returning from lecture,
one striking him with his fists while the other applied the horsewhip. This ruffian deed took place
in the presence of nearly one hundred students, of
whom only two or three attempted to interpose, and
they not efficiently. The rest, though as they say
strongly disapproving the outrage, looked on with
folded arms ! ! . . . When they had finished the exploit, they mounted horse and rode towards Lynch-
burg, but it is hoped the officers, who are in pursuit
of them, will yet overtake and apprehend them. . . .

UNIVERSITY OF VIRGINIA, March 26, 1839.

. . . I really forget whether I mentioned in my
last that the two fugitives, of whom I have written,
were overtaken, and that in their desperate struggle
to avoid being seized, while defending themselves with
deadly weapons, one of them was shot badly in the
shoulder. He is, however, recovering from the wound,
and it is fortunate for our peace and safety that he
is, for the day after the occurrence attempts were
making, by the exhibition of his bloody coat to groups
of students on the lawn, to excite sympathy, and to
inflame them against the officers and the Faculty. I
think now that quiet will be restored. . . .

In 1839 Professor Rogers encountered in the legislature further opposition to the survey, but Virginia
was not alone in its attitude towards geological research.

RICHMOND, April 1, 1839.

I was on the eve of despatching a letter three days ago from the University when I learned that it was necessary for me to set off at once for this place, as the survey was in peril. I came with all speed, reaching here on Friday night. I found that, after a warm debate in which unwarrantable liberty had been taken, by dint of the powerful advocacy of Southall, Kinney, Hodges, and other talented members, the suspension was voted out by a majority of seventy-six to forty-eight. It has yet, as a part of the Revenue Bill, to pass through the Senate, where I learn it is in still greater danger. . . .

I have no time now to tell you of the absurd speeches that have been made in and out of the House, the old falsehoods regarding the Walton Mine, the objection to my spending so small a time in the field, etc., etc. An ignoramus who could not put two words correctly together made an attack in which he attempted to paint me as I addressed the House last year, having a handful of stones before me, such as he could pick up anywhere in the roads in his county; some were red and some were white, and some speckled; and I talked such an outlandish lingo that he did not understand a word I said, and he doubted whether I did myself. But, after this farce, Southall rose, and I am told made one of the most forcible and overwhelming replies to all opponents that was ever heard in the House. . . .

PHILADELPHIA, April 9, 1839.

. . . The Ohio survey has been suspended; that of Maine also; and Ducatel is now quaking in his shoes. Thus goes on the reaction I predicted three years ago. . . . Conrad, Vanuxem, and Hall of the New

York survey, called on me the other day to get me to move once more in getting up a Geological Association. It was proposed to meet early in April next year, and meanwhile to write to our friends engaged in state surveys; none others to be admitted. I consented. I could not refuse, as I was in this quarter the original mover; we can, however, think of it. If we only had time this summer to complete our General Memoir, we might join them with advantage; but I fear we shall have no time. What think you? . . .

In April, 1839, Mr. Rogers was thrown from a carriage and seriously injured: —

JAMES BROWN, JR.,[1] TO W. B. R.

SECOND AUDITOR'S OFFICE, April 15, 1839.

. . . I condole with and congratulate you at the same time on account of your "unlucky accident" and recovery from it. I sincerely trust you will not again be in such danger of a broken neck, considering how difficult it would be to mend it, and how much more difficult still to find another such head upon any other neck. What with your escape and your victory in the legislature, your elasticity of mind and body will be so great as to be productive, I hope, of some thirty or forty pounds more of flesh on your bones than you now have, by the time you complete your summer excursions. The fact is, you overwork yourself in both respects, and unless you can manage to diminish your labours you will wear yourself out before you get through with this job. Let me hear how you get on occasionally. . . . Why do you pay postage on letters of business with the public?

[1] Auditor of the Board of Public Works of Virginia.

MR. ROGERS TO HIS BROTHER HENRY.

UNIVERSITY OF VIRGINIA, April 22, 1839.

. . . I have looked into Murchison and am in raptures with the work. In many of his drawings of Silurian fossils, I think I can at once recognize the portraits of some of ours. . . .

Had geologists commenced their observations in the United States, would they have made the distinction of Silurian and Secondary? Is there any evidence of any great epoch of convulsion after the deposition of our Appalachian series, more than after the deposition of IV.? Do not the red rocks continue among the coal measures after the transitory actions which produced XII.? and do we not in X. and XI. mark the gradual approach to the conditions necessary for the production of the great coal seams of the West? For my part, it seems as natural to make three groups — I. to VII., VIII. to IX., X. to XII. — as two. . . . I believe I remarked to you when here the singular coincidence in strike of the older Slates in Wales, Cumberland, etc., and our Blue Ridge and Appalachian series. Murchison's work shows this in the Silurian rocks very remarkably. He also points out numerous cases of inversion, such as occur along our Blue Ridge, in I. and II., his Limestone dipping beneath his Sandstone, as ours. With what delight could I labour with you in comparing the results, so beautifully put forth in this work, with our own! . . .

The end of the academic year found Professor Rogers thoroughly exhausted: —

TO HIS BROTHER HENRY.

UNIVERSITY OF VIRGINIA, June 20, 1839.

. . . It seems to be the impression here that no increase of the vacation will be granted by the Board

of Visitors, as several of them are thoroughly opposed
to it, and none would agree to it but on condition of
reducing the salaries and fees proportionately. We
are all utterly worn out, pale and emaciated. But
our masters think we have light tasks, and seeing us
at this beautiful season when all is bright and attractive around, and when our duties have terminated,
they are unable to appreciate the amount of our
toil. . . .

The vacation of 1839 was spent largely in the field
in prosecuting the survey of Virginia, and the autumn
passed without special incident. Already, in the minds
of the brothers (Henry and William) those ideas of
the great Appalachian System which they afterwards
developed with so much success, were taking practical
shape.

WILLIAM TO- HENRY.

. . . S—— is a capital fellow in the laboratory,
and will make a first-rate analyst. B—— is, I am
sorry to say, very far his inferior in mind and in
application. So much for the difference between
being schooled in the Appalachian and the Alleghany
Geology. . . .

How fully and deeply does my heart respond to
the wish that we could be together in our travels
and in all our labours! What is interesting to me in
Science loses half its power to charm because my dear
brothers are not by to share in my enjoyment. But I
have acquired the habit of late, whenever I feel de-
spondency creeping over my thoughts (and this not
unfrequently occurs), to look forward to the cheerful
prospect of our happy reunion ere long; and when I
dwell upon this cherished theme I find my spirits
never fail to be braced and enlivened.

Robert's method of peroxidating manganese is beautifully simple. This would at once place the manu-

facture of chloride of lime on a sure foundation, and render it immensely profitable. . . .

Reference has often been made in the foregoing pages to an uncle, Mr. James Rogers, a merchant in Philadelphia. Reverses in business, the sequel of the dark days of 1837, now led to the removal of this uncle to Charlottesville, where he found a warm welcome and a home with his nephew William.

JAMES ROGERS, ESQ., TO ROBERT.

UNIVERSITY OF VIRGINIA, March 8, 1840.

DEAR ROBERT, — I arrived at this delightful spot on Tuesday morning before breakfast. William received me with great kindness and affection: he had a room comfortably fitted up for my accommodation, which I now occupy, surrounded with books, pamphlets and newspapers. I ride frequently, and walk several miles daily, often accompanied by your brother when he has a leisure hour.

I have, since my arrival here, enjoyed the change of scene and charming weather of the past week in a degree far beyond my expectations, and the influence on my spirits is very great. I have really had comparative composure and happiness since I left the scene of my pecuniary misfortunes. . . .

Throughout this year (1840) Professor Rogers was in feeble health. He writes : —

UNIVERSITY OF VIRGINIA, March 18, 1840.

MY DEAR HENRY, . . . My only trouble now is on the score of health. My throat is pretty well, but I am gnawed continually by dyspepsia. How many days has this vile tormentor caused me to lose ! But I trust I shall be able to shake it off by care in diet and by active exercise. . . .

April (?), 1840.

. . . My health is now rapidly improving, and I hope that in a week or two I shall be in my usual condition. This fine weather has invited me out among the flowers, and I have been planting the seed with which I was so kindly furnished by the ladies. When I go down again, I shall be tempted to beg for more matters to ornament my garden.

I hope my good friend is quite well, and that Mrs. B. and the ladies are enjoying the sweet air and bright verdure of the season. Oh, that I could rest for a week or two with kind friends in Richmond! I should be worth a dozen of what I am now. . . .

FROM H. C. WILLIAMS, ESQ.

WASHINGTON, D. C., May 26, 1840.

DEAR SIR, — We have recently organized a Society[1] here, the object of which is to form cabinets of

[1] "In 1840 two important national societies were founded, — the National Institution for the Promotion of Science, and the American Society of Geologists and Naturalists, — the one an association with a great membership, scientific and otherwise, including a large number of government officials; the other composed exclusively of professional naturalists.

"The purpose of each was the advancement of the scientific interests of the nation, which seemed more likely to receive substantial aid, now that the money bequeathed by Smithson was lying in the Treasury vaults waiting to be used.

"The National Institution, under the leadership of Joel R. Poinsett, of South Carolina, then Secretary of War, assisted by General J. J. Abert, F. A. Markoe, and others, had a short but brilliant career, which endured until the close of the Tyler administration and had an important influence on public opinion, bringing about in the minds of the people and of Congress a disposition to make proper use of the Smithson bequest, and which also did much to prepare the way for the National Museum. The extensive collections of the National Institution, and those of the Wilkes Expedition and other government surveys, were in time merged with those of the Smithsonian Institu-

Natural Science. We shall take in every branch, and the specimens received from the Exploring Expedition, those collected by Dr. Owen in Wisconsin and Iowa, together with those now in the possession of the Department, will make a very handsome beginning. You will be written to officially on the subject, as we shall address a circular to the scientific gentlemen of this and foreign countries, to the Executive of the several States, and to the governments in friendly correspondence with ours, requesting their aid. The Society was formed under the auspices of the Secretary of War; it will be a governmental matter, but private individuals, for a while, will have charge of it on their own account. By next winter we anticipate such a fine collection that Congress will be induced to make a handsome appropriation to carry on the enterprise. Gentlemen of all political parties are active members of the Society, among whom may be mentioned Mr. Adams, Colonel Benton and Dr. Linn. One of the professors from Princeton College took an active part in forming the Society, — his name I can neither spell nor pronounce, — Colonel Totten, Colonel Abert, Mr. Markoe, Professor Hall, and some second-rate scientific men, with a lower order made up of myself. General Patton and some

tion, and, having been greatly increased at the close of the Centennial Exposition, began in 1879 to receive substantial support from Congress.

" The Society of Geologists was not so prominent at the time, but it has had a longer history, for in 1850 it became the American Association for the Advancement of Science. Although it dated its origin from 1840, it was essentially a revival and continuation of the old American Geological Society, organized September 6, 1819, in the Philosophical Room of Yale College, and in its day a most important body. Its members, following European usage, appended to their names the symbols, 'M. A. G. S.,' and among them were many distinguished men, for at that time almost every one who studied any branch of science cultivated geology also." — G. Brown Goode, *Origin of the Natural Science and Educational Institutions of the United States*, pp. 66, 67. 1890.

others are the working members. Mr. Markoe has
a splendid collection. Dr. Hall's ranks next, then
Messrs. Abert's and Totton's ; these gentlemen will
make large deposits in the cabinet of the Society so
that it will be complete in the first instance in Mineralogy, and very full in Geology. We indulge very
sanguine hopes of being able to perpetuate the Society; the government will have so large an interest in
it that it must remain, and if we can keep up the
spirit in twenty persons, there will be no danger of a
premature death, as in the case of the Columbian Institute. When you again pass this way, it is to be
hoped that we shall have enough to engage your attention for a day at least, and, as I live within forty
yards of the building we shall temporarily use, you
will be pleased to make my house your stopping-place.
It will afford me infinite pleasure to show you our
collection, and introduce you to such of our members
as you may not be acquainted with.

On August 22, 1840, Professor Rogers was informed of his election to membership in the National
Institution for the Promotion of Science, and the following is his letter of acknowledgment : —

TO H. C. WILLIAMS, ESQ.

UNIVERSITY OF VIRGINIA, September 8, 1840.

DEAR SIR, — The hurry of our first collegiate week
must be my apology for having delayed replying to
your gratifying letter, and tendering my acknowledgment for the honour of being enrolled among the members of your new Institution for the Promotion of
Science. Though from the number and urgency of my
other scientific engagements it may not be in my
power to contribute such aid to the Society as to render me really deserving of membership, I heartily
promise you whatever help it may be in my power to
give, and I hope that the early completion of some

of my present tasks will enable me ere very long to become a more efficient auxiliary.

Not knowing exactly the scope of the Institution, more particulary as relates to your meetings and public exercises, if any, I take the liberty of suggesting, as likely to prove useful in giving greater publicity to your proceedings, the delivery of occasional or regular lectures on subjects of natural science during the winter. A few able discourses of this kind, by the interest they would excite in the enlightened minds then assembled in Washington, might conduce more to your prosperity than, even with your observations of the effects produced by analogous means in regard to other matters, you would be inclined to suppose. From my own experience I can confidently say that in this country a most ready sympathy is always accorded to the aspirations of those devoting themselves to practical science, whenever its claims are justly and adequately set forth. Probably you have already projected such a plan of public discourses. If so, as the only means at present in my power of forwarding your views, and in token of my sincere desire to promote the highly laudable objects to which you propose devoting yourselves, I will promise to take a part in these discourses, at some convenient time during the winter, to the extent of one or two lectures.

I am much pleased with the Address you have been kind enough to forward to me, and send you a copy of my last Report, for the Society. As soon as I can procure copies of my other Reports, I will send you an entire set.

With best wishes for your health, and for the success of the Society, I remain, dear sir,

Your obedient servant,

WILLIAM B. ROGERS.

FROM H. C. WILLIAMS, ESQ.

WASHINGTON, D. C., October 10, 1840.

DEAR SIR, — A variety of engagements has prevented my acknowledging the receipt of your letter and
last annual Report. I took the liberty of showing your
letter to Mr. Secretary Poinsett, who expressed himself highly pleased with your suggestions. We have
contemplated the delivery of lectures, but that will
depend upon our receiving the Smithsonian bequest.
An effort will be made this winter to blend the two
Institutions, and as the dividend of the bequest now
exceeds thirty thousand dollars, there is an income
sufficient to compensate several professors, and the
sum already accrued can be applied to the purchase
of a library and philosophical apparatus. Mr. Adams's
project [1] stands in our way, but that obstacle is not
regarded as insurmountable. Mr. Poinsett asked me if
I thought that you could be induced to accept of one
of the professorships. My reply was, that I believed
you were much attached to the University, but if the
National Institution was established on the broad basis
that had been contemplated, the liberal salaries to the
professors, together with the disposal of their time
during the recess of Congress, being inducements, as I
thought, you might regard an offer of the kind in a
favourable point of view. Should this scheme succeed,
the professors will have to be taken from the colleges
and universities of this country; the most distinguished gentlemen will be selected, and we shall have
to propose larger salaries than a state institution can
afford. I think the Secretary has his eye on you for
Geology or Natural Philosophy. I think it right to
put you in possession of this conversation. Mr. Poinsett will deliver an oration before the Society some time
during the winter. Now we are busily employed in
preparing to make a good show by the meeting of
Congress; from that body we have received the favour

[1] See *Pop. Science Monthly*, January, 1896, p. 294.

of $500, and at the ensuing session some further appropriation will be asked. In a few days Dr. Owen's collection will arrive; but the specimens sent home by the Exploring Expedition will remain untouched until the squadron returns.

FROM J. R. POINSETT, SECRETARY OF WAR.

WASHINGTON, December 28, 1840.

SIR, — At the last monthly meeting of the "National Institution for the Promotion of Science," it was unanimously resolved that an effort should be made to have a course of lectures delivered during the present season on the several subjects which occupy the attention of the Institution, as the best means of promoting its designs, — securing the favourable notice of Congress, and procuring the coöperation of men of science throughout the Union. The duty was assigned to me, as senior director, of soliciting for this purpose the services of the members of the Institution, and of professors and gentlemen in the neighbouring cities and States.

The high opinion entertained by the members of the Institution, and my own estimate of your attainments and qualifications, induce me to address myself to you with the hope that it may be consistent with your inclination, and with other engagements, to deliver one of the series of lectures at as early a period as may suit your convenience.

Should it be in your power to confer upon the Institution the favour of complying with this application, it will be left entirely to your judgment to select such a subject as you may think best adapted to promote the objects of the Institution.

With respectful consideration, I have the honour to be, sir,

Your most obedient servant,

J. R. POINSETT.

PROFESSOR W. B. ROGERS,
    University of Virginia.

In 1840 Mr. Rogers made the important discovery that large deposits of "infusorial earth," now so-called, occur in Virginia. His first reference to this subject appears in a letter to his brother Robert.

UNIVERSITY OF VIRGINIA, July 1, 1840.

DEAR ROBERT, . . . What do you think? The light white earth from the Rappahannock Cliffs, which you thought some years ago might be carb. of magnesia, but which we proved to be very pure silex, turns out to be a mass of *Infusoria.* This is a *discovery.* I find also that the light and very white silicious earth contained in our iron ore in the hollow nodules, etc., is largely composed of *Infusoria* of a different description.[1]

During the summer of 1840 William and Henry met in Philadelphia, and proceeded northwards as far as Canada and New England. They started on August 21 "with the double view of geological inquiry and wholesome travel." Mr. James Rogers (the uncle) remained in William's house at the University. The part which he played in the bachelor housekeeping became more and more important, and the arrangement was clearly of mutual benefit.

MR. ROGERS TO HIS BROTHER HENRY.

UNIVERSITY OF VIRGINIA, September 14, 1840.

. . . Be assured, my dear Henry, I shall avoid taxing myself with all unnecessary labour. I am as yet lecturing but three times a week, and will at no time meet my classes more than six times. The remembrance of my prostration last session would be of itself sufficient motive to avoid excessive labour, for I have not yet recovered from the shock I then sustained.

[1] See *Geology of the Virginias,* p. 438.

With less power to make strong temporary exertion, my health is certainly better than it was last autumn. Uncle has greatly improved my household arrangements, and with far more comfort and retirement, we are living much more economically than heretofore. I have found him so judicious in managing, that I commit all these matters to his direction. He will, of course, continue with me this winter, and will be the only guest I shall have. I am making a study of my large room upstairs, where I am now seated, and using the room below exclusively as a dining and receiving room. With a stove instead of the Franklin, and the front windows boarded up, I shall make myself quite snug.

You ought all to seek agreeable society as often as possible. I hope James will not continue so recluse as he has been, nor ought you, my dear Henry, to omit frequent if not daily social relaxation. Most heartily do I wish society were on a footing to render the cost of its enjoyment less. But at all costs it should to some extent be enjoyed. . . . Tell James, as soon as he has time, to make out the details of his analaysis of the meteorite and send it in a letter. I will draw up a little account in our joint names which he may read before the Society, or dispose of otherwise as he may think proper. Would it not be well for me to give a brief account of the infusorial beds of Virginia, which you might present to the Society along with some of the specimens which you have?

UNIVERSITY OF VIRGINIA, November 9, 1840.

. . . Uncle has become quite the oracle of the neighbourhood on the subject of the elections. He has shown far more knowledge and sagacity as regards the results than any other person here. He is quite well and cheerful. . . .

PHILADELPHIA, November 9, 1840.

. . . I fear the death of your able colleague (Bonny-castle)[1] may a little embarrass your own course. But bear in mind how small is your stock of strength, how heavy the tasks you have already set yourself to do. I like Goethe's motto, " Be like a star that never resteth, but hasteneth not." The best portion of life is surely yet before us; not, however, if by over-toil we lose the capacity to enjoy it. Do take these hints well to heart. You know how much I would wish to say on this topic if I had the space. . . .

A perusal of letters already given in this chapter will suffice to show that a dangerous spirit of insubor-dination existed in the student body of the University. The climax was reached on November 12, 1840, the fourth anniversary of the so-called " Military Rebel-lion," when the Chairman of the Faculty and Pre-siding Officer of the University, Professor John A. G. Davis was, unhappily, murdered by one of the stu-dents. Professor Rogers's comments upon this affair, made two days later in a private letter, indicate the prevailing sentiment of the Faculty.

TO HIS BROTHERS IN PHILADELPHIA.

UNIVERSITY OF VIRGINIA, November 16, 1840.

MY DEAR BROTHERS, — This morning I assisted in laying another of my colleagues in the grave. My kind friend, and long my bosom companion, Davis, died on Saturday evening of a wound received on the preceding Thursday night! He was shot in cold blood in front of his own door while watching the movements of a student who, disguised and masked, was making

[1] Charles Bonnycastle, Professor of Mathematics in the University of Virginia.

riotous noises and firing a pistol on the lawn. The assassin retired a few paces from Mr. Davis before firing, and then deliberately discharged his pistol, the ball from which penetrated the abdomen obliquely, and, passing through to the hip bone, terminated its course about half an inch beneath the skin. At first, and indeed until after his death, the wound was not considered of a mortal character, but supposed to be rather superficial. He died a Christian hero, blessing his family and his weeping colleagues and friends assembled around his bedside.

Those engaged in the atrocious murder have been arrested, and he who fired the fatal ball, as well as his chief and perhaps only accomplice, are in confinement. The students to a man joined in the pursuit of the villains, and it was by their efforts they were secured. They have also been active in collecting the evidence, which, as it now exists, convicts the principal of murder in the first degree, probably. Not the smallest provocation is urged in extenuation of the deed. No violence was attempted by Davis, but he was mildly exercising the proper supervision which appertained to his duty as Chairman. The murderer, quite a youth, so reckless of consequences, remained in the University the next day until arrested by his fellow-students. He has since been tried by a Court of Magistrates, who found the chain of evidence irresistible, and committed him to prison. The bullet was extracted after the death of Professor Davis, and its peculiar form and marks were distinctly recognized by one of the students, who, on the morning of the fatal day, had lent the pistol to the assassin, little suspecting the horrid tragedy of which it was to be the instrument. It appears that the perpetrator of the crime, from all accounts a heartless though determined villain, had no particular grudge against Davis, but was determined, as he had before been heard to say, that he would shoot any professor who attempted to discover him while engaged in a riot. . . . The con-

duct and feelings of the students on this occasion have
shown that they are entirely worthy of the high opinion the Faculty had formed of them.

Of the afflicted family of poor Davis I cannot speak
without weeping. Mrs. Davis was for some time
bereft of reason. . . .

Bache has written to me in behalf of Courtenay for
the Mathematical Chair. I shall reply to-morrow. I
should like Courtenay as a colleague very much. How
disastrous has been the history of this session, — the
death of two of our professors, and that in the latter
instance under circumstances so peculiarly afflicting.
But I trust the event will prove a salutary warning,
and in the end be a public benefit.

I am quite well. To-morrow we shall resume our
lectures. . . .

The University gradually became calm once more,
and Professor Rogers returned to his scientific studies.

TO HIS BROTHER HENRY.

UNIVERSITY OF VIRGINIA, December 3, 1840.

. . . I wish much to have a talk with you about
scientific matters. Could I have obtained a sight of
Ehrenberg, I would have drawn up a paper for the
" Transactions " in relation to our infusorial formation. You know I found that potash is absent from the
ashes of coal and lignite and mineral charcoal. I am
inclined to believe that this is due to the solvent
action of water, and am now trying to determine
whether common charcoal, largely washed with hot
water, does not lose all or part of its potash. The
last number of the " Philosophical Magazine " is quite
interesting. I am impatient to see the Memoirs of
Murchison and Sedgwick on the Devonian rocks. I
suppose you have them in the last number of the
" Geological Transactions." . . .

UNIVERSITY OF VIRGINIA, January 5, 1841.

. . . As for my tasks, they are indeed making but slow progress.   I have, however, begun my Report in earnest, though I have not the time, were I inclined, to devote many hours to it daily.   My time is so broken up by other concerns that continuous writing for more than an hour, or at most two hours, is impracticable.   I am determined to make my Report a short one, and to endeavour, if possible, to hand it in by the last of this month.   It is supposed by some persons here that the Legislature may adjourn early next month, but of this, having heard nothing official, I feel quite doubtful.   As yet nothing has appeared in the papers, or otherwise reached me, to indicate the temper of the Legislature.   I am not without strong hopes, by my personal interview with some of the members in Richmond, of obtaining the full appropriation for another year, and I am proceeding with the early part of my Report upon the assumption of being thus permitted to continue.   Thus far we have expended about 36,000 dollars, and have been a little less than five years at work upon our new organization ; whereas, when the appropriation was solicited, I calculated upon expending about 50,000 dollars, and requiring six years for the completion of our operations.   This you see, makes quite a strong case when I refer, as I am now doing, to my Report of 1836. . . .

In showing the *infusoria,* you ought to use both Raspail's and the other microscope.   The former shows you the whole mass of fine particles as portions of an exquisite gauze-work of rotifer-like fossils.   Use the next to the highest power.   The other best displays the rings.   These rotifer objects form by far the greater portion of the substance, and are, I think, quite peculiar.   They do not occur in Ehrenberg's Tertiary, and mark, I think, the older character of this, approaching the chalk. . . . I find the specific gravity of the infusorial earth from the Rappahannock to be only 0.334 !! . . .

HENRY TO WILLIAM.

PHILADELPHIA, January 8, 1841.

. . . Our communication was well received. Next time I shall introduce your discovery of the infusoria. There will be a copy of Ehrenberg here in two months. Goddard has now a superb microscope. I shall examine your specimen, and if I can, but not just yet, will send you drawings. The first treat you allow yourself should be one of these splendid instruments. If I could get a sale for my magnetic instrument, it would go far to get us a microscope. . . .

WILLIAM TO HENRY.

UNIVERSITY OF VIRGINIA, January 18, 1841.

. . . My delay in Richmond was made necessary by the interests of the Survey, which could only be fairly represented by myself. . . . The Legislature is mainly composed of liberal gentlemen, though of little knowledge in matters of science, and I have little doubt of their making a sufficient appropriation for publishing next winter. One of the members, who on Friday last made an incidental attack upon the Survey, came to me yesterday, and after seeing the map and sections, and conversing with me for an hour, stated his determination to give his active support to the bill, and has made the same statement to Southall, Dorman and others. Thus, you see, I have been quite as successful in my visit as I could have hoped, — indeed more so than I hoped. But I had much anxiety and toil, and I am very glad to be again quietly at home. . . . Though much occupied during the day, I enjoyed most of my evenings at Richmond, and most heartily did I wish that all of you could partake of the music, etc., which I enjoyed at Stannard's, Cabell's, Lyon's, etc. How I sighed for leisure ! So many kind, engaging friends, to be merely looked at for a day or two and then left !

Such attractive young lassies, whom I wished to know better, but was compelled precipitately to leave! Really, my dear Henry, you ought to see the female society of Richmond just now. I know you would be charmed by it, as I am. . . .

TO HIS BROTHER ROBERT.

DEAR ROBERT, . . . My sojourn in Richmond was full of pleasure. My many dear friends there, Mrs. Empie and Mrs. Guathmay especially, did everything to make me comfortable and happy. The favourable prospects of the survey, at first not anticipated, and the success I met in my public lectures there and in Petersburg, all prepared me to enjoy with a keen relish the kind hospitalities of my numerous acquaintances, whose invitations awaited me every day. But how sad the contrast experienced here! The stupid dulness and unvaried monotony of the University never before weighed so heavily upon my spirits as they have for the last ten days. I feel that I am but half-alive here, and am more than ever resolved, when able, to quit the scene for one more congenial to my tastes and more likely to promote my happiness. . . .

WILLIAM TO HIS BROTHERS.

UNIVERSITY OF VIRGINIA, March 5, 1841.

MY DEAR BROTHERS, — I forget to whom I wrote last, but it makes no difference. My letters are for all.

We are as dull as a mill-pond in a deep hollow where no breeze can touch it. My heart longs for the cheering impulses of society with my brothers and with the busy world. . . .

UNIVERSITY OF VIRGINIA, March 8, 1841.

. . . Matters here are as usual, — too dull, almost, to engender a pun, though Mr. —— makes the effort now and then. Like a busy hen, he cackles whenever he feels the inward motion towards wit, but he does not always produce the egg.

Kiss both the boys for their uncle, and tell Rachel I long again to see her and them.

The fate of the Geological Survey of Virginia was now determined by the Legislature, and commented upon by the Director in a letter to Judge May of the House of Delegates : —

TO JUDGE J. F. MAY.

UNIVERSITY OF VIRGINIA, March 13, 1841.

DEAR SIR, — By this morning's papers I find that the appropriation to the Geological Survey is to be discontinued on the 1st of January next. It is probable that you in proposing this, and the other friends of the work in acceding to it, were not aware that the geological year, as we call it, commences on the 1st of April, and that in making this appropriation the Legislature is in reality only appropriating for nine months, and not, as I presume they supposed they were doing, for another *year.* In stating to you and Dr. Leyburn by letter that one more year would enable me to bring the work to a close, or so near it that I could myself carry it to completion, I had in view keeping all my assistants busily occupied in analysis and arranging the cabinet during the whole of next winter. The bill recently passed will entirely preclude this, as, soon after their return from the field, they will leave me, and the mass of chemical and other details which would devolve upon me would compel me to abandon the writing of my final Report, upon which at that time I designed to be exclusively engaged. Indeed, without the assistance of the corps in the laboratory and at the drawing-table, and in arranging the cabinet, during the whole of next winter until the expiration of the geological year, I should feel incompetent to perform the task of drawing up my Report without great additional delay.

As I imagine it was the intention of the Legislature to continue the appropriation for another year, I hope that the bill recently passed may be either so modified or explained as that it may not cease in January next, and my assistants may be continued throughout the winter, so as to complete another geological year.

FROM JUDGE MAY.

RICHMOND, March 16, 1841.

DEAR SIR, — Yours of the 13th was received this evening only. The appropriation bill is beyond the reach of the House of Delegates, and probably now of the Senate. If I had not offered the order in the form in which it is, one for an *immediate* repeal of your law would have been offered and carried. Even after it was engrossed, when the House for the first time perceived its true character, there was a motion and a large vote to reconsider it, in order to strike out the words " from the 1st of January next," so as to make the repeal forthwith. If the work be nearly completed by the 1st of December next, the next Legislature might perhaps make some further appropriation for its completion, but nothing can be done in favour of it at this session.

In great haste, I am, dear sir,

Very much yours,

J. F. MAY.

With this state of affairs and the slender hope of a continuance of the survey as a result of an appeal to the next Legislature, Professor Rogers had to be content.

TO HIS BROTHER HENRY.

UNIVERSITY OF VIRGINIA, March 22, 1841.

MY DEAR HENRY, . . . In regard to my survey, I think I told you in yesterday's letter that I have but small hope of procuring any further appropriation. I think, therefore, I shall call in my assistants early in the fall, say the middle of September, and give them work to do in the laboratory and among the minerals. But on these points I wish to consult you.

UNIVERSITY OF VIRGINIA, April 2, 1841.

. . . By the 10th of this month my corps is to muster at the University, and by the 15th I hope all will be in the field. Slade, Briggs and Ridgway will remain, but I am very doubtful in regard to Samuel Lewis. . . .

I find that my Infusorial stratum is growing more and more important. It forms a heavy bed in the Stratford Cliffs on the Potomac, where, however, it is far less pure than on the Rappahannock or near Richmond. The finer and purer mass is a first-rate polishing material, equal to rottenstone. You will see some account of it in my Report for this winter, of which I send you several copies by Mr. Briggs. . . . Should you attend the meeting (of the Geologists and Naturalists), if you think it worth while you might mention my discovery of the infusory stratum in the Tertiary, and the other curious fact of the absence of potash from the ashes not only of coals but lignite and mineral charcoal.

The Second Annual Meeting of the Association of American Geologists and Naturalists was held April 5–10, 1841, at the Academy of Natural Sciences, in Philadelphia. In the absence of the chairman, Professor Silliman of Yale, Professor Henry Rogers presided at the opening session. The official report of the proceedings may be found in the "Transactions" of the Association, pp. 11–41.

FROM HIS BROTHER JAMES.

PHILADELPHIA, April 10, 1841.

. . . I can only say one word respecting the meeting of geologists. It was pretty fully attended, and its deliberations were conducted with much spirit and were highly interesting. . . .

You can well understand how pleased I am to have it in my power to inform you that I have not been altogether neglected, but that a few days ago the Faculty of the University of Pennsylvania, in the most prompt and complimentary manner, appointed me Professor of Chemistry in the Summer Institute, and Robert as my assistant. This place, you recollect, was occupied by Mitchell. . . . We regard the position as a highly favourable one, as it places us in the best possible road to something better here, and associates us with such men as Jackson, Chapman, Horner, Hodge, Ball and Hare, and makes me Hare's representative during the summer, in fact identifying us with the interests and character of the University. In a pecuniary point of view, it can prove but little serviceable the present year, as I believe the class does not number more than thirty or forty. But all connected with it are devoted to its success as the child of the University, and assure me that next summer the class can be made to reach one hundred. . . .

WILLIAM TO ROBERT.

UNIVERSITY OF VIRGINIA, April 14, 1841.

MY DEAR ROBERT, — Your letter was read by myself and uncle at tea this evening with a relish I cannot describe. How truly does my heart rejoice at the opening now afforded to James and you! . . . There are several important subjects in a chemical course which I think are generally passed over for want of simple and accurate methods of exposition. Among these may be mentioned the computation of the specific gravities of the compound gases; the calculation of the quantity of vapour in air or a gas under given circumstances of temperature, pressure, etc.; the laws of atmospheric pressure; and in fact most of the *exact* subjects relating to general physics. I think no chemical course in a medical school ought to dispense with an exposition of the fundamental principles of mechanics and hydrostatics, although they are scarcely ever referred to. Undoubtedly they are of more importance to the physician than magnetics, electro-magnetism, much of electricity, and the theory of chemical forces, as well as a great deal of what is treated under the head of caloric or thermotics. This year, perhaps, it would be too late to make any innovation in this respect; but I would certainly recommend hereafter, as adding interest and value to the course, the introduction of a few lectures on these important principles in mechanical science. When I go on in the summer, if you ask me, I will give your class two or three lectures of this kind, embracing such topics as are professionally most useful.

TO HIS BROTHER JAMES.

UNIVERSITY OF VIRGINIA, March 18, 1841.

. . . I have been greatly occupied for the last two days in looking over the papers handed in at our English examination, and, together with Dr. Harrison and Professor Howard, was engaged in the completion of this troublesome task until eleven o'clock last night . . . Our English examination embraced seventy students, of whom twenty-nine failed to pass for want of a moderate acquaintance with spelling and grammar. Of those unsuccessful, five or six are candidates in the medical school.

PHILADELPHIA, Sunday, April 18, 1841.

. . . James delivered his introductory on Friday last. It was really very fine, mostly extemporaneous; the best part, indeed, was entirely so. He will very soon win for himself the reputation of being the best lecturer in the city. . . .

The following concerning Professor Rogers's discovery of "infusorial earth," already referred to (pp. 174, 184), is from the well-known microscopist, Professor J. W. Bailey, of the United States Military Academy at West Point: —

WEST POINT, April 25, 1841.

DEAR SIR, — Please accept my thanks for your Report for 1840, and my hearty congratulations on your important discovery of the *Infusorial Stratum.* This discovery may justly be considered as the most interesting which has been made in the country for a long time, and I can fully sympathize with you in the joy you must have experienced in making it. I feel some private pleasure in the discovery, as it confirms a prediction I ventured to make (in an article on fossil *infusoria,* published in Hitchcock's final Report for Massachusetts), "that, as we have vast quantities of living marine species of silicious *infusoria* upon our seacoast, it is probable that they may be found abundant in our tertiary deposits when properly examined." It had long been my desire to have an opportunity to visit a tertiary region of the United States to look for these things, but you can well understand that a professor of chemistry, mineralogy and geology, who has to hear two sections a day ten months in the year, has little time for original research. So the prize of discovery has fallen to other and far more worthy hands, and I rejoice with you at the good fortune you have had. . . .

A paper by Professor Bailey, giving many references to the Virginia *infusoria* discovered by Mr.
Rogers, afterwards appeared in the " Transactions of
the Association of American Geologists and Naturalists," 1840–42.

FROM ROBERT TO HENRY AT HARRISBURG.

PHILADELPHIA, April 28, 1841.
We have no news since I last wrote. James is
even improving in his lectures, if there were room for
improvement. The students appreciate his enthusiasm and clearness. I am sure it is the shortest hour
of learning they have in the twenty-four. I could
not but remark the other day the strong expression
of satisfaction upon all their countenances as he finished his explanation of electric attraction. I am
looking with anxiety to the action of the Senate [re-
garding the Geological Survey of Pennsylvania]. . . .

WILLIAM TO HIS BROTHERS.

UNIVERSITY OF VIRGINIA, May 1, 1841.
My DEAR BROTHERS, — I am delighted to hear
that James is so rapidly winning his way to fame as
a lecturer, and I doubt not, my dear Robert, that you
will find the task easy and pleasant. You ought to
have an ample blackboard, or other equivalent space,
for chemical formulæ and drawings. I presume you
will make use of brief heads of your lectures as re-
minders. Do not attempt to crowd too much in
a single lecture, and avoid the common error of experimenting for the eye and not for the understanding. Every experiment ought to be accompanied by
a full and clear explanation, and this cannot be rendered too explicit and elementary. Cultivate a deliberate and distinct enunciation without sacrificing earnestness and animation of manner. Above all, do not
attempt to be over choice in your phraseology, but

use the language suggested at the moment. I believe that many an one has failed in making an interesting speaker from being thus fastidious at the beginning. There is nothing in which habits are sooner formed and more difficult to remove than public speaking. In my view, the very first thing to be sought is a feeling of ease and confidence, and this, when the subject is thoroughly understood, you cannot fail to secure at the outset by giving play to some enthusiasm, and, as Rutledge advised, "speaking right on," even though at times your phrase may be obscure, inelegant or even incorrect. But I need not give you counsel, as I know you will soon learn to satisfy yourself, and that will be your best criterion of success. As you are now commencing a career in which you may expect to be professionally engaged (I hope hereafter in a more productive sphere) for many years and perhaps for life, it will be well, as soon as you have leisure, to devote some time systematically to a course of general as well as chemical reading. I think we have all of us erred in reading too little, though for the most part this has been in consequence of our engrossing and laborious pursuits. The highest eminence as a lecturer cannot be attained without a general culture of mind.

I am anxious to learn the results of Forbes's observations on internal heat as detailed to the last British Association, and I believe reported in a condensed form in the "London Athenæum." I wish one of you would examine that, or any other full account you can find of the proceedings, and give me an abstract of the numerical results, if they are announced. . . .

The fate of the Geological Survey of Pennsylvania was still uncertain : —

HARRISBURG, April 25, 1841.

MY DEAR WILLIAM, — To give you some idea of the tribunal to which I have to bow, one Senator, who a few days ago told me the survey ought by all means to be finished, uttered himself thus : " Mr. Speaker, I shall vote against this appropriation, on the ground of its unfairness to other sciences of like nature with this geology. The bill, sir, makes no provision for phrenology, physiognomy, animal magnetism, and the highly important science of *water-smelling;* it is partial, and I will vote against it." This was his whole speech. I anticipate a long debate to-morrow, but the chances are in my favour. If it is annexed to the big bill in the Senate to-morrow, there is but little doubt of its becoming a law.

I forgot to mention Mr. Boyé as one of my assistants, who would most gladly enter your corps. . . .

Think not, my dear William, that being indolent with my pen, I am not constantly by your side in my thoughts. As I travel, though behind you, the same path of care, I grow daily more convinced of the extent and worth of your sacrifices and undeviating love for your brothers.

HARRISBURG, May 4, 1841.

After many fluctuations of anxious hope, I am at last relieved by the final passage of the bill embracing the provision for completing the survey. The whole revenue bill had been vetoed by the Governor, but has passed each House by the constitutional majority of two thirds, as the papers will show you. I am now ready to go home and engage my thought once more upon my professional business. . . . It rejoices me to think that we may yet complete our surveys. I shall now have leisure and spirit to give you my aid during the next eighteen months in bringing out your final Report, if you desire assistance. . . .

The session at the University of Virginia ended un-eventfully, and the summer appears to have been spent to a large extent in geological excursions to Canada, New York and New England, as the following letter indicates : —

WILLIAM TO HIS UNCLE JAMES.

HUDSON, N. Y., August 20, 1841.

I have travelled so far, seen so many sights in New York, Canada, etc., that I cannot think, even did time permit, to enter upon a sketch of our movements. Henry, who made a rapid trip to Philadelphia, joined me at Albany yesterday, and brought me the letters you so kindly forwarded as well as your own. . . .

Lyell, the geologist, arrived in this country a few days ago, and we met with him this morning in Albany. He is at present in the keeping of some of the New York geologists, but will be in Philadelphia with Henry, and in Virginia with me, in the autumn.

Robert, who made a short trip with us to the West as far as Niagara, is in Philadelphia, and quite well. James had not returned from Virginia when Henry left Philadelphia, but had been lately heard from by his family, and was well. The letters from my assist-ants were all satisfactory, and relieved me of much anxiety which I had begun to feel. . . . I have not been much upon the highways, and have not met a soul whom I knew from the South in all my ramblings.

You see John Tyler has been true to his old prin-ciples, but the veto [1] is producing a wonderful hubbub in New York. In the main, I think it will render the President more popular than before. . . .

TO HIS BROTHER ROBERT.

UNIVERSITY OF VIRGINIA, September 11, 1841.

. . . Since my summer's rambles with Henry I have been unable to shut out the contrast between

[1] Of a bill to incorporate a national bank.

the region in which I live and the highly cultivated nature and society of glorious New England. I have, therefore, felt less than usual the pleasure of returning to my home. I have been mortified and provoked, too, at finding so much illiberality among a portion of the community here on the subject of religion, as displayed in the bigoted publications which appeared during the summer respecting the appointments of Sylvester and Kraitzer. Would you believe it, that a series of essays has been published condemning the Visitors for the appointment of a Jew and a Catholic, and sweeping charges at the same time made against the character, literary as well as moral, of the University! These have been chiefly published by two of the religious papers, but have not passed without eliciting the sympathy of some of the other prints, though in the main condemned by them. . . .

By recent accounts from Sylvester,[1] we learn that he will not leave England until the middle of October, and will, therefore, not assume his duties here until early in November. This I most deeply regret, for I fear it may prevent my absenting myself during October. Such long and serious interruptions have occurred of late years in the studies of the students that they are beginning to complain. But do not suppose I have given up the intention of being absent in October. . . . I have had a long conversation with Jefferson Randolph to-day, who says that he does not think the University will be injured by the fanatical publications referred to. He and the professors are in good spirits as to our prospects, though they do not expect a class of more than two hundred this year. I trust that in another year better times will favour all our plans, and I do most ardently desire, my dear brothers, that we should all cultivate a spirit of cheerful confidence in the future. . . .

[1] J. J. Sylvester, English mathematician, afterwards Professor in Johns Hopkins University, and finally in Oxford.

FROM MR. (AFTERWARDS SIR) CHARLES LYELL TO PRO-
FESSOR HENRY D. ROGERS.

SCHOHARIE, N. Y., September 19, 1841.

MY DEAR SIR, — As I promised to let you know
something of my movements before I reached Philadelphia, I now write to say that I hope to be there
to spend five or six days with Mr. Conrad about the
24th inst., and if about the last day or two of this
month I could join you, and find you at leisure to start
me, at least, on a tour of ten days, so as to see some
good section of Pennsylvania, I should be very glad.
I ought to see the higher grounds as much as possible,
because I might attack the less elevated ones in December after the snow is on your mountains. I must
be at Boston on the 13th of October, and hope to be
fairly in the field again the beginning of December,
after giving some lectures, which perhaps you may
have heard I promised to deliver at the Lowell Institute. I am much pleased with what I have seen
of your geology in the Blossburg coal down to the
sandstone below the Trenton limestone. Certainly,
the history of things which preceded the Coal and
Old Red is far more fully written here than in Europe, and it will take years before justice can be done
to it.

Have the goodness to let me find a letter from
you at the post-office, Philadelphia, to say when and
where we could meet after the 29th of September.

Believe me, my dear sir,

Ever most truly yours,

CHAS. LYELL.

WILLIAM TO HENRY.

UNIVERSITY OF VIRGINIA, October 3, 1841.

. . . I entirely concur with you in the plan of your
proposed journey and your scientific intercourse with
Mr. Lyell. My own reflections for a week past on

this subject have impressed me with the importance of securing his good will, and if possible his friendship, by showing to him the high philosophical import of our labours, and informing him frankly of all our scientific plans. I also feel as much or more than ever, the necessity of devoting some time this fall to the preparation of a memoir setting forth our leading views and discoveries, and am determined, if possible, to join you in Philadelphia for that purpose. . . . I confess I have been pained at the smallness of my class, but this has now ceased to give me concern. No students have arrived for ten days past save two or three in the professional schools, so that I remain *in statu quo*, being still below forty. . . .

My great cause of concern in regard to this year's classes is produced by my wish to have command of funds for our common purposes. From present prospects I am likely to fall short by $1,000 of my usual income from the University. . . .

FROM HIS BROTHER HENRY.

PHILADELPHIA, October 13, 1841.

MY DEAR WILLIAM, . . . I returned to town yesterday after a tour of eleven days with Mr. and Mrs. Lyell and McIlvaine. We went by the way of Reading to Pottsville, Mauch Chunk and Beaver Meadows, returning by Easton and the Delaware, through Trenton. If Lyell has been half as well pleased and satisfied with me as McIlvaine and I have been with him and his accomplished wife, I shall congratulate myself. I deem him a man quite too high-minded to encroach on the literary rights of others, and have many kindly feelings toward him for the friendly interest he has shown in our future scientific progress. Lyell came over at the invitation of Mr. Lowell, and intended to return in December, but now means to remain a year. This of itself shows how much our geology, and of course the exploring

of it, can interest the Europeans. His plan is to go
South through the Tertiary after his course of lectures, and in April to return North and proceed at
once to Canada and Nova Scotia, where he will be
at work until July. One grand object with him will
be a comparison of our Atlantic Tertiary with the
European, to test the applicability of his nomenclature
to this country. Having seen so much of the Tertiary
of Europe, spending one entire summer in the Crag
of England and all last summer in the South of
France, he is perhaps, of all the English geologists,
the best fitted to establish the true relationship of our
tertiary beds to those of the old hemisphere. To this
delightful task Conrad has shown himself unfitted by
his preference of the closet to the field. It will gratify
you to hear that Lyell already pronounces the beds
we have always named *Miocene* to be truly such.
After his return to Europe he will probably read a
paper on this whole subject, and I gather has an intention of reading a memoir also on the Geology of
Canada and Nova Scotia. Speaking of the latter, he
expressly told me he would avoid describing the organic remains which might be common to the New
York lower rocks until Conrad's labours were published, unless, indeed, these were so delayed as to im-
pede the progress unnecessarily of all research. . . .
Lyell thinks there is a close and even remarkable relationship between the silurian and our Appalachian
fossils; also between the coal formations of the two
countries. Now, as to the gradations from the silurian
fossils into the coal fossils, — perhaps the most interesting problem of all, — we may take this, if we are
diligent, into our own hands by collecting largely
from the marine limestones of our Western coal-fields,
and from the silurian beds in For. XI. and that portion of the series. In order to do this, Lyell recom-
mends us to procure the new work just published by
Phillips on the Devonian fossils, in which he has been
aided by the English government. Having Murchison

on the Silurian and Phillips on the Mountain Limestone, we have only to procure this last and collect largely and we shall have the whole subject before us. . . .

PHILADELPHIA, October 16, 1841.

MY DEAR WILLIAM, — I entertain a strong hope of seeing you in a little more than a week. With what we have to guide us in the way of specimens, we may succeed in determining the true paleontological relations of For. XI. This once done, we shall, I think, be prepared to attempt a subdividing of our eleven marine formations. What think you of the following classification?[1] —

Call all our rocks below the bottom of XII. the Appalachian System. Make a triple subdivision of these thus : from the bottom of For. I. to the top of V. one group or series ; from the top of V. to the top of VIII. an other ; and from the top of VIII. to the top of XI. the third; designating the first by some Greek compound, — the Appalachian morning, the second the midday, the third the evening. According to this scheme, the morning of the Appalachian epoch would coincide almost precisely with Conrad's lower Silurian series ; the Appalachian midday with his Middle and Upper Silurian series (for he terminates the upper with the top of the olive slate, For. VIII.); and the Appalachian evening would embrace the Devonian period, and perhaps a great part, or all of the mountain limestone, or marine carboniferous. Now my chief hesitation is in regard to cutting off For. XI. from the coal measures so abruptly ; and yet, as the latter are chiefly terrestrial and all our eleven lower rocks are marine, it seems proper enough for purposes of classification. By this plan we can find a designation for each of our formations exempt from the difficulties of either numerical or geographical reasoning. What think you, then, of attempting, with the

[1] For a note on the geological nomenclature and classification adopted by the brothers, see Appendix to vol. ii.

assistance of Dr. Harrison, to compound three words equivalent to "morning of day" before the coal, or simply "ancient morning," etc.?

I have now by me all the late parts of "Geological Transactions of London," in which are some good figures of Devonian fossils. I think in the space of one year, with proper method, we can conquer this whole subject. In the meanwhile, if we deem it inexpedient to commit ourselves to a nomenclature before studying our fossils better, we have plenty to do with our pens at the grand dynamic questions of our geology. I did not state in my last how greatly I astonished Lyell at the breadth of some of our results and doctrines connected with *structure.* Though incredulous for the first day or two, even as to the thickness of our rock, I quite made a convert of him before we parted.

Collect your recollections and notes in regard to slaty cleavage; for as a part of structure we ought to treat of it, and I think we can do it in a manner to make even Sedgwick consent to become a learner. For example, I see in this State no exception to this law, that the cleavage planes have a dip and strike closely coincident with what I want termed the *anticlinal and synclinal* planes, the deviation being some coefficient of the resistant to the cleaving presented by the stratification of the rocks. . . .

Your affectionate brother,

HENRY D. ROGERS.

PHILADELPHIA, October 22, 1841.

. . . With less than a month at our disposal we can hardly perfect a memoir so as to be ready for the press, and I think that whatever we do now we ought to do well, cost what time it may. It is my firm resolve to occupy two years on my final Report if necessary, rather than further impair my health, or let my six years of toil in the field tell for nothing. I shall, therefore, ask nothing this winter of the Legislature in aid of publication, but report myself as having begun my final report. This I can present nearly ready in January, 1843, and while it is going through the press employ a few more months upon it. The public will be better satisfied in the end, and it is for the *end* we ought to exert ourselves. I hope you will prevail on your Governor to make fit allusion to your survey; but have a care that he does not commit you by promises in your name, as I was treated by Governor Pennington, of New Jersey.

I am, at a moderate rate of diligence, setting my house to rights; that is, opening the specimens you and I gathered and placing them temporarily in drawers, thus saving you two or three entire days when you come. Opening the things you got at Schoharie, I readily understand your exultation at getting such a prize. In truth, our summer's work tells well, even in the way of specimens, when one reflects upon the quarters from whence they are derived.

We shall be able to set in a clear light some essential points in the Lake Erie geology, but to adjust the whole of the Western stratification is not for us to attempt yet. Hall will probably try it. From what Lyell told me I looked to see a paper from Hall in the October number of Silliman. We shall probably see his conclusions in the January number. He says that Niagara limestone expands westward until it becomes in Iowa twelve hundred feet thick. If he has gone much by the organic remains, there will be much for others to revise in his work before many years; but let us await patiently his paper. The establishment of the true order of succession of organic remains of the Appalachian rocks will be a work of years and by many hands, and none will come to sound results but those that go upon an independent stratigraphical basis. You will be cheered and delighted, when you read the proceedings of the British Association at Plymouth, to notice the views of Phillips and especially of Sedgwick on this subject. We are on safe ground, and shall have the support of the best of the European geologists in defence of our methods of research. Lyell is

rather too much for identification by organic remains,
but he also would admit us to be right if we were to
set forth our whole opinions in a clearly reasoned
paper. But it is in the department of dynamic geology
that, being foremost, we ought to be especially prompt
in publishing. Reading Darwin on volcanic phenomena in the Andes in " Geological Transactions," I have
been particularly struck with confirmatory evidence
of the soundness of our idea of a pulsation having
caused anticlinal axes. I am sure the doctrine will
meet with acceptance. . . .

PHILADELPHIA, October 29, 1841.

MY DEAR WILLIAM, . . . The grand point to
establish at the very outset is our nomenclature, and
to render this acceptable, I know we ought to be very
sure of our ground in the grouping of the formations.
A slight readjustment of the groups need not mar the
permanency of the classification.

I am now strongly inclined to a five-fold division,
there being as gradual a passage into the coal period
as into that of any of the other groups. Two periods
are wanted, I think, for the rocks below the bottom
of VIII., — one for those in VIII. and IX., one for X.,
Cambrian limestone, and XI., and one for the coal
rocks. But instead of the five names proposed by
Parke, I have another set to suggest offered by Mc-
Ilvaine. They are, Eōan, Ante-meridian, Meridian,
Post-meridian, and Hesperian, some of them having an
analogy in origin to your own. McIlvaine, for whose
judgment in such matters I entertain a high respect,
advocates his own more Latin set of terms, on the
ground of their being not altogether strange to our
language, and of their being readily understood and
remembered. I like them myself, but wish to hold
the whole matter over until you are here to consult.
If we had but taken the precaution to collect during
the past season a full suite of fossils from the rocks
above VIII., we should have felt ourselves at this time

prepared to propose definitely the boundaries for our upper groups, and I am, even as it is, in hopes that your own collection from the Greenbrier limestone, with the few I have, may avail us much. The organic remains of the upper part of VIII. and of IX. are of still more consequence to us as forming the ground-work with Conrad for his American Devonian. Please bring with you all fossils bearing on our researches; we can do much when together in determining their relations. Do not forget the subject of cleavage, and, if you do not find it too troublesome, put your sections and colored maps in your trunk. . . .

Anticipating the arrival of Professor Sylvester, Mr. Rogers went to Philadelphia for a visit.[1]

FROM JAMES ROGERS, ESQ., TO HIS NEPHEW WILLIAM.

UNIVERSITY OF VIRGINIA, November 17, 1841.

. . . I found it would be very difficult to dispose of your gray geological horse, except at a price much below his value. . . . I am much gratified to learn you are all well, and I can hardly express the satisfaction I feel at James's success as a lecturer, and have no fears but erelong something more lucrative will present itself as the reward of talent and industry. . . . For several days we have been anxiously looking for the arrival of Professor Sylvester. We learn he lost all his baggage in Boston; this may have detained him. Perhaps you may have met him in Philadelphia on his way hither. My love to all.

I am, dear William, your affectionate uncle,

JAMES ROGERS.

The joint paper referred to in the foregoing letters was read on December 3, 1841, before the Phi-

---

[1] The Chair of Mathematics had been filled by Mr. Rogers since the death of Mr. Bonnycastle.

losophical Society of Philadelphia, and is entitled, "Observations on the Geology of Western Peninsula of Upper Canada and the Western Part of Ohio. By William B. Rogers, Professor of Natural Philosophy in the University of Virginia, and Henry D. Rogers, Professor of Geology in the University of Pennsylvania."

WILLIAM TO HIS BROTHERS IN PHILADELPHIA.

UNIVERSITY OF VIRGINIA, December 6, 1841.

Late yesterday evening I got home, after a rather uncomfortable ride. . . . All my colleagues, except Emmet, are well, and the faculty, students and others attached to the University are all greatly pleased with Mr. Sylvester. He was terribly embarrassed at his first lecture, indeed quite overwhelmed, but has been doing better since. He has a good deal of hesitation, is not fluent, but is very enthusiastic and commands the attention and interest of his class. . . . On Saturday I saw in Richmond Mr. Southall, Mr. Lynn and other members, who all appeared to think that the Legislature will accede to my proposition. I shall to-morrow set to work to draw up two or three pages by way of report, and will send it down by the close of the week. I think that by a strong representation thus made, and by letters to several influential members in both Houses, I shall be able to secure my object. . . .

As I am about to have my sections all made out by Ridgway, I write to you to tell me what scale we fixed upon when we talked on this subject. I have forgotten. . . .

Your devoted brother,

WILLIAM B. ROGERS.

PHILADELPHIA, December 11, 1841.

. . . I greatly interested him (Lyell) by telling him of your discovery of the oölitic date of the Richmond and Fredericksburg strata. The fishes which he and Silliman lately got in Connecticut show, he thinks, an early New Red period. This agrees with my doctrine in "New Jersey Report," that our red shales began directly after upheaval of the coal. Can you not send a sketch of your fish scales from the Middle Secondary? The *Teneopteris* in Brogniart agrees well with your sketch. . . .

PHILADELPHIA, December 13, 1841.

. . . I am just now working at an abstract of our paper for the Bulletin, and retouching two or three pages of the memoir itself. On second thoughts I felt I had gone too far in giving it as our opinion that the limestone over the pitted rock is the equivalent of the Onondaga. I am much more inclined to regard it as a new interpolation, and to view the Onondaga as thinning out in Canada before we reach Goderich. This is borne out by the fossils, which are not those of the Onondaga any more than those of For. VI. Nor do they appear to be those of the Seneca limestone, though more allied. All this is far more in accordance with our general doctrines, and is the safest ground to take. I have found new evidence of the identity of the Sandusky and Goderich rocks in laying open a part of a trilobite in the latter, identical with a tail you perhaps recollect we have in the former. I took several specimens to Conrad, and think they are nearly all new to him, and this is another inducement to modify somewhat our manner of setting forth our notions of the relations of the Western rock to the Limestone at Buffalo. . . .

Do you not think it our wisest course to give ourselves first to those chapters of the memoir which treat

of structure ? In this way, working on with our sections
and maps at the same time, while our assistants are by
us ; we can do the other portions at a later time, even
in the spring, if necessary, with the advantage of
seeing such publications as may issue this winter.
The classification, especially all from For. VII. to For.
IX., is a critical part of our work, and we ought to
have Phillips's new book on Devonian fossils by us
first. It ought soon to arrive, two copies. Lyell, who
has it, says he thinks, by the analogies of the fossils,
the whole of our For. VIII. ought to go into the Silurian. He does not know what we are at. . . .

TO HIS BROTHER ROBERT.

UNIVERSITY OF VIRGINIA, December 21, 1841.

. . . I have received a letter from Redfield in reply
to some inquiries I wrote on the subject of fossil
fishes. The fish of the New Red coal is very nearly
allied to, though not the same as, one of those in the
Middle Secondary. It is described in the July number of "Silliman" under the name of *Catopterus
macrurus.* I incidentally mention in my present report my belief that, while the Fredericksburg sandstone refers itself to the Oölite period, the Richmond
coal appertains to that of the Lias. From the occurrence of the *Posidonomya* in our Middle Secondary,
I should infer its being, at least in part, quite late
in the New Red, or about the period of the Keuper.
This shell, I think, ranges from the Keuper to the
Bunter sandstone. I believe that our shell, and that
figured by Lyell and Brogniart, are identical.

Lyell in his letter expressed a wish to go with me
into the Richmond coal district for a day or two. . . .

FROM CHARLES LYELL, ESQ.

CHARLESTON, S. CAROLINA, December 28, 1841.

MY DEAR SIR, — Your letter was forwarded from
Richmond to me here. I took for granted, from the

non-arrival of the mail from Charlottesville two successive days, — in consequence, as they told me at the
post-office, of the snow, — that it would be impossible
that we should arrange a meeting.

Guided by your Report, I collected sharks' teeth
and casts of *Crassatella* in the Eocene greensand of
Shockoe Creek; saw well the infusorial bed, and the
impressions of leaves and casts of several shells in the
overlying sands, — Miocene? I should have been glad
to learn from you how to feel sure that the lowest
sandstone and coarse gravel at the bottom of the
ravine were really Secondary, that the infusorial bed
was Eocene and not Miocene, though I have no reason for preferring the latter. . . .

I shall be glad of your letters about the Wilmington district, and shall order them to be forwarded
here immediately.

I have nearly determined not to return South till
after the Meeting of Geologists at Boston at the end
of April. If you could then go South with me and
show me the Richmond coal, and show me the way
over your mountains of Western Virginia, I would
then take that route to Ohio. I shall be glad to find
a letter from you at Philadelphia, where I shall be
the first week in February, mentioning whether this is
possible. I am going by Augusta down the river to
Savannah. So far as I have gone, the fossils strongly
confirm the correctness of your identification of the
Williamsburg marls with the Miocene groups of
Touraine and the Suffolk Crag, according to the
results of my tour in France last year. See "Geological Society Proceedings." The analogy of forms is
very satisfactory, even independently of the per-
centage of recent species.

Believe me, my dear sir,

Most truly yours,

CHARLES LYELL.

HENRY TO WILLIAM.

PHILADELPHIA, January 14, 1842.

My DEAR WILLIAM, — By this time you will probably have got our abstract in the "Proceedings of the
Philosophical Society," and also Silliman's, containing
Mr. Hall's paper. I think he is wrong in calling the
limestone at head of Lake Erie the Niagara limestone,
the pitted rock appearing to be the lowest stratum
there exposed. Still his paper covers a great amount
of ground. I am making the Blue Limestone of Cincinnati an equivalent of the Salmon River and Pulaski
group, and he staggers me, and still more in half
admitting, as he does, the rock at the water level of
Cincinnati to be the Trenton Limestone. I shall not
be satisfied until I go there myself; a few fossils are
hardly enough. He clearly recognizes the Oölitic
Limestone in Indiana and Missouri to be the equivalent of Carboniferous Limestone, but he ought to have
mentioned, as we do, that Troost had already established it to be such. The perusal of his paper has
confirmed me in my purpose of visiting Tennessee
and Alabama this spring, if possible. Let us once
fairly trace your S. W. types into those States and
unite them with the rocks on the Ohio, and we shall
have material for a general treatise and map on the
Appalachian System. If we were to resolve to clear
up this Southern work during the coming spring and
summer, we might get certain portions of our work,
say that treating of the structure of the mountain
chains, ready to read to the Association in April, and
leave the rest for a season of more leisure, to be all
incorporated into a special volume. What think you?
Pressed as we shall be, I hardly see how we can get a
general memoir ready by June for the British Association. If we could spend two months together, we might
accomplish much. . . .

Conrad has actually read descriptions of all his
new species to the Academy, and the plates are soon

to be put to press. I rejoice at it; now we shall have something to go upon. I am on the committee on his paper. He proposes now this classification: From bottom of the series to *Tully Limestone* inclusive, Silurian, *our* Silurian. The Lower Silurian ends *with* the Clinton group. Middle Secondary commences with Niagara shales and terminates with Oriskany sandstone, which, he says, is well developed in Pennsylvania, Kentucky and North Alabama. Tully Limestone, and the Upper Secondary, Ithaca and Chemung groups and Blossburg Old Red he calls Devonian. Onondaga Limestone he finds at Falls of Ohio.

I think that Hall is not far wrong in his views of the western strata, if we accept what he says of the Trenton Limestone, etc.

Ought we not to get something ready for the spring meeting, and would a chapter on our anticlinal axes, etc., be appropriate? We could take time to study the organic remains next summer and mature our classification, the foundations of which ought to be well laid. . . .

WILLIAM TO HENRY.

UNIVERSITY OF VIRGINIA, February 5, 1842.

. . . We have just had a large meeting of the students to form a Temperance Society, and quite a respectable number have taken the teetotal pledge for the college course. This I deem the happiest movement for the University that has ever been made, and I make no doubt that a large proportion of the students, if not all, will eventually join. If so, we shall have no further riots or other serious violations of law, and our places will be infinitely more desirable than they ever have been. Besides, the effect upon the community of such a society being known to exist here will dissipate the unjust prejudice which exists against us, and I look for a very large increase of numbers. You will smile at my earnestness, but in truth I know that 99-100ths of all our troubles spring from drink, and that too, generally wine. . . .

I am glad that you are paying more attention to your lectures in the University. Nothing but practice is wanting with any of us to excel in this offhand kind of composition. In fact, I think that it is the genius of the family, and depends upon a peculiarity of temperament in which we all share. For my own part, I find that when I am strong, as I have been this winter, I absolutely revel in some of my better themes. . . .

I suppose Mr. Lyell's course is now under way. How happy would I be could I be present at his lectures! Please tell him for me that I greatly regret not to hear him, and remember me very kindly to him and Mrs. Lyell.

If possible, in the spring I would spend a week or two with him geologizing in Virginia. Whether this will be in my power I shall better be able to say by and by.

Give my and Robert's and Uncle's love to dear James and Rachel and the children, and do both he and you write soon to

Your devoted brother,

WILLIAM B. ROGERS.

FROM HIS BROTHER HENRY.

PHILADELPHIA, February 13, 1842.

. . . I conveyed your message to Lyell. He seems much to wish for an excursion with you. He talks of crossing Virginia to Guyandotte, going to Cincinnati, then North to Lake Erie, to get into Western New York and Canada, after the Boston meeting, and he would, I think, be glad of your escort through Virginia. I am not satisfied with the published abstract of his letter to the Geological Society, describing the results of our visit to the anthracite region in October. He told me he had sent it as our joint work; now he has taken, or is made to get, the lion's share. . . .

UNIVERSITY OF VIRGINIA, February 21, 1842.

MY DEAR BROTHERS, . . . Tell James that Robert and I were delighted to-day with Graham's mode of showing the decomposition of fluosilicic acid by passing through water. Each bubble, as it rose through the liquid, became encased in a film of silica. Probably he has made the experiment, which I never did before. If not, he should present it to his class when next on that subject. . . .

Your devoted brother,

WILLIAM B. ROGERS.

FROM HIS BROTHER HENRY.

PHILADELPHIA, February 22, 1842.

. . . The great point to settle is the best line of division between the *meridian* and *post-meridian* series. Conrad now makes it the top of the Tully Limestone, but this is too local for us. I think with us the question is nearly reduced to this: shall we take the bottom of VIII., or shall we divide VIII.? Phillips's book on Devonian fossils has not yet arrived. . . .

As has been already stated (p. 183), the Geological Survey of Virginia was to have come to an end on January 1, 1842, but after many delays a bill was passed extending the time for its completion to April, and making for it a further appropriation of $4,000.

The third annual meeting of the Association of American Geologists and Naturalists convened in Boston, April 25-30, 1842, and the brothers William and Henry Rogers were present. It was at this meeting, on the 29th of April, that one of the most important papers ever published by them was read. It was entitled, "On the Structure of the Appalachian Chain, as exemplifying the Laws which have regulated the Elevation of Great Mountain Chains generally," and appeared in the "Transactions" already refered to.

After the death of Professor Rogers in 1882, among the notices which appeared in the public prints was the following, by one who was present, referring to this meeting : —

EXTRACT FROM A LETTER OF JOHN L. HAYES, ESQ.[1]

CAMBRIDGE, MASS., June 4, 1882.

In April, 1842, I enjoyed the privilege of attending, as one of the youngest members, the meeting of the Association of American Geologists and Naturalists, held in the city of Boston, at the rooms of the Boston Society of Natural History. This association was remarkable from the circumstance that nearly all its members were practical geologists, actually engaged in conducting the geological surveys then in process in the different States. The discussions were of the gravest character and of profound interest, as all were seekers for instruction from each other, for guidance in conducting the surveys and completing the reports. The meeting in Boston, as compared with three others which I attended elsewhere, was a particularly brilliant one. Its President was Dr. Morton, of Philadelphia, so distinguished for his researches in anthropology. Its appointed orator was the venerable Professor Silliman, the father of American geology. Not less distinguished among the associate members present were the admirable State Geologist of Massachusetts, Professor Hitchcock ; the almost inspired observer of natural phenomena, our own Dr. Charles T. Jackson ; Emmons, of New Jersey, the expositor of the Taconic System ; the brilliant French astronomer Nicollét; the mineralogist Beck ; the paleontologist Hall ; the microscopist Bailey; the zoölogist Gould ; the philologist, as well as naturalist,

[1] An amateur geologist of Cambridge, Mass.

Haldeman; the eminent merchant, and promoter of New England industries, Nathan Appleton, to whose munificence is due the publication of the proceedings of the association; and the brothers William B. and Henry D. Rogers, the former (the elder) then the State Geologist of Virginia, and the latter of Pennsylvania, and each a representative, as professor, of the principal university in the respective States. To complete this brilliant circle, Sir (then Mr.) Charles Lyell, the recognized head of English geology, was present, an interested listener and active participant in the debates.

Notwithstanding the able address of Professor Silliman, the elaborate paper of Professor Hitchcock, and the frequent and interesting remarks of Mr. Lyell, the marked feature of this meeting, which continued for a week, was the reading of a joint paper by the brothers Rogers upon the physical structure of the Appalachian chain, as exemplifying the laws which have regulated the elevation of great mountain chains generally. The expression " reading a paper " conveys a most inadequate idea of what was a remarkable oratorical effort. The brothers, William and Henry, who must always be associated together, as there was an absolute unity of effort in the great work of their lives, their geological observations and deductions, had been for several years studying, respectively, different sections of the same great geological field, the Appalachian chain, the one in Virginia, and the other in Pennsylvania. With the natural desire of the representatives of the South to make a favourable impression on the occasion of their first appearance in New England, they selected the meeting in Boston for giving the grand results of their labours in the peculiar field of American geology which it had fallen to them first to explore. A grander geological theme could hardly be imagined. It related to the physical structure of a mountain chain 1,300 miles in total length, extending from Vermont to Alabama, and 100

miles in its greatest breadth, consisting of beds of Silurian, Devonian and Carboniferous formations (adopting terms applied to similar formations in England),
arranged in elevated parallel and narrow ridges, sometimes 100 miles in length, but with strata so folded,
warped, contorted, fractured and eroded that science
had sought in vain to find a key to their original
structure. Yet the genius of the brothers Rogers had,
like the Egyptologist with the papyrus roll, unfolded
the inverted and contorted strata, spread and smoothed
them out, as it were, in an open book, and showed
them to the eye of science as originally horizontal
deposits, continuous with the rocks of the great western coal-fields. But I can hardly even glance at the
scientific conclusions of this paper, as my simple
object is to describe the manner of its delivery, and
the impression it made upon its hearer.

The brothers, by their happy and amiable faculty
of thinking and working in concert, more than dupli-
cated their individual power. In making their joint
exposition — for the " paper," as delivered, was purely
an oral statement — William Rogers took upon himself the more modest but really more difficult part,
of describing the phenomena, leaving to his brother
the part of explaining the theory of the phenomena.
Nothing could be more pleasing than the working together of these two minds toward the same end.
Both were in the heyday of manhood, with the enthusiasm of youth and the fervour of their section still
unabated. Their ambition, it is true, was hardly
concealed, but it was an ambition which produces
noble efforts. Those who know the elegance of diction and manner which characterized the later address
of the elder Rogers can partially conceive of the
effect he produced by the fluent and graceful oral
statement of the complicated phenomena of this
hitherto mysterious mountain chain, — a statement in
which there was not one moment of hesitancy, nor
a word which was not the most fitting. But they

cannot conceive of the delight which was given to the admiring hearers by the restoration of these disturbed formations to their primitive symmetry, and by the revelation of the laws of structure which determined the conformation of the vast and singular mountain range.

This paper, or what purports to be the same, is published in the "Transactions" of the Association. I have frequently read it since. To me it is now comparatively tame in expression. It lacks the inspiration of the scene and the men, the illustrative diagrams, the emphasis of voice and finger pointing out the distinguishing phenomena, and the fervour of spontaneous utterance. The impression I have of this exposition, as delivered, is that, next to the Phi Beta Kappa oration of Wendell Phillips at Harvard, it was the most lucid and elegant effort of oral statement to which I ever listened. It may be true that eloquence is but a secondary quality in the philosopher but, in respect to the matter of this memoir and the general researches and deductions of the brothers Rogers here named, in their peculiar field of exploration, it may be safely asserted that they have made the most original and brilliant generalizations recorded in the annals of American geology, and have thrown light upon the structure of mountain chains generally, which entitles them to a place by the side of the great expositor of this subject, Élie de Beaumont, of France.

CHAPTER V.

PROFESSOR OF NATURAL PHILOSOPHY AND FOR ONE
YEAR CHAIRMAN OF THE FACULTY IN THE UNI-
VERSITY OF VIRGINIA.

1842–1846.

Robert appointed Professor of Chemistry and Materia Medica in
the University of Virginia. — His Marriage. — Henry presides at
Fourth Annual Meeting of Geologists and Naturalists in Albany. —
He lectures on Geology in Boston. — Fifth Meeting of Geologists
and Naturalists in Washington. — William and Henry elected For-
eign Members of the Geological Society of London. — Henry gives
a Course of Lowell Lectures in Boston. — William Chairman of the
Faculty of the University of Virginia. — Attack upon the Univer-
sity in the Legislature. — His Defence of the University. — An
Educational Document. — Student Riots. — Ill-health. — A Visit to
Lake Superior. — Henry removes to Boston. — Second Visit of
Lyell to America. — James and Robert edit " Turner's Chemistry."
— Plans of William and Henry for a Polytechnic School in Boston.
— A Summer Journey in New England.

ON the return of the brothers from the Boston
meeting of the Society of American Geologists and
Naturalists, they resumed their academic duties and
their regular correspondence. By the munificence of
Nathan Appleton, Esq., and other gentlemen of Boston, the proceedings of this meeting of the Society,
together with those of the two preceding meetings
held in Philadelphia, were published in a single
volume. In this was included the joint paper of
the Rogers brothers " On the Physical Structure of
the Appalachian Chain," as well as their individual
contributions.

PHILADELPHIA, May 9, 1842.

. . . Lyell and Nicollet have been sounding William's praise among our few confidential friends in a manner that has delighted me. Let us all stick to science in good earnest and we shall not repent the toil it costs.

Mr. Lyell afterwards induced the brothers to send an abstract of their paper on the Appalachian Chain to the British Association.

MARIETTA, May 19, 1842.

DEAR ROGERS, — Being here in the coal with Dr. Hildreth, I was curious to see the report of L——'s paper given in the number of the "Athenæum" which I received by post at Wheeling yesterday. As it contains much attributed to L—— on the structure of the Appalachian which you told me at Pottsville, and which I withheld in my *Stigmaria* letter to the Geological Society as being still your private property, I feel sure that you will not read the abstract without the same very uncomfortable feelings which I did. I could have wished that in your last short Report you had given two or three pages on your grand general results, which are now so widely *ventilated* (as Brougham would say), and are becoming such common property, to which others . . . may add original observations, mixing them up together so as no longer to know how much is their own, that if you do not take some steps in a periodical, or through some other channel, you will be involved in endless réclamations, as the French call them. No one can stand quiet and see others make off with the fruits of his labours, but the effect of having frequently to call out "Stop thief!" would be anything but desirable. It will be

long before I shall be in London, where I could explain.
The British Association meets some day in June at
Manchester. I hardly know whether a letter from
you to them would be in time. If so, I believe it
would not shut you out from a detailed paper at the
Geological Society, with sections, etc.

My wife sends her kind regards, and believe me,
dear Rogers,

Ever truly yours,

CHARLES LYELL.

HENRY TO WILLIAM.

PHILADELPHIA, May 30, 1842.

. . . The remarks of Lyell set me to pondering
as to my best course. I drew up a clear, condensed,
careful abstract, which when copied filled two fools-
cap sheets as close as James could write it. This I
despatched this afternoon with a separate letter to
Professor Phillips at Manchester, requesting him to
read it and show it to Sedgwick before presenting
it. . . .

On June 12, 1842, the brothers William and Henry
were notified of their election as honorary members
of the Boston Society of Natural History. Robert
had been appointed to fill temporarily the chair of
Chemistry in the University of Virginia in the place
of Dr. Emmett, who was absent on account of ill-
health.

WILLIAM McILVAINE TO HENRY ROGERS.

BURLINGTON, N. J., August 23, 1842.

. . . I give you an extract from a letter just received from Mr. Lyell at Halifax, dated the 16th
instant, as follows : —

" When you see H. D. Rogers tell him that early
attention was paid to his and his brother's paper at
Manchester, which gave rise to a full and animated

debate, . . . in which Sedgwick, Murchison, De la Beche, and Phillips took a part."

Robert was now appointed to the professorship in the University of Virginia made vacant by the death of Dr. Emmett.

WILLIAM TO ROBERT.

UNIVERSITY OF VIRGINIA, September 20, 1842.

MY DEAR ROBERT, — You have heard from Henry by yesterday's mail of your appointment. I have never seen so general a rejoicing as has been shown on hearing of your appointment. All the professors, Cabell, Howard, Harrison, Kraitzer and George Tucker, showed the greatest pleasure. You owe much to Cabell and Howard. The former, besides coming over expressly to help your cause, previously wrote to General Cocke about you.

As the Materia Medica is only once a week, you will have no difficulty in preparing in that department. Bring on two copies of Liebig's "Animal Chemistry."

You have the right to Mr. Bonnycastle's house. The Visitors have formally accorded it to you. I need not say how happy we all are, and how much happiness we look forward to.

McKennie is writing to you about text-books. Turner, he says, cannot be procured. You had best make inquiry on this point. Good-by, Professor ! !

WILLIAM TO HENRY.

UNIVERSITY OF VIRGINIA, October 2, 1842.

MY DEAR HENRY, — I reached this place late on Saturday night, having endured the discomfort of a crowded stage all the way from the White Sulphur. The tri-weekly arrangement having just been established, I found upon arriving at Callahan's that by giving up my seat I would be almost certain of deten-

tion for several days, as there were then persons enough
waiting to fill a stage. I thereupon, after a painful
struggle, relinquished my plan of pausing there to
complete the examination of Dunlap's Creek. I cannot tell you how much regret this disappointment
occasioned me. Indeed, so anxious was I to examine
V. in that quarter that I would have been willing
to take the *chance* of getting on. This leaves an important blank in my summer's observations. . . .

On my way from Callahan's to the Hot Springs, on
the road, I found in a neat cutting of the slate a new
locality of the *Orthoceras* limestone. It occurs below
the black wafery slate at which we commenced our
observations near the Hot Springs, and is near the
cement layers; several other fossils, all small ones,
are associated with it. I feel pretty certain that there
must be a narrow band, perhaps ten or twenty feet
thick, in that region, which should be regarded as the
representation of the Hamilton. I also found near the
top of the North Mountain, in walking up the western
slope, five or six bands of highly fossiliferous sandstone
and slate, containing a great variety of shells. They
were considerably below the base of IX., and are no
doubt Chemung. I brought one home with me. . . . I
have written this in great haste to be ready for the
Staunton mail, and shall have to send it to Cocke's
by the driver. I am quite well.

JAMES TO WILLIAM.

PHILADELPHIA, December 24, 1842.

MY DEAR BROTHER, . . . In a day or two I will
write to you both respecting the plan of a contemplated work of chemistry, with an outline of the arrangement which might be adopted. This I want to
submit to you both for such suggestions as you may
think proper to make respecting it, but more of this
in my next. . . .

HENRY TO WILLIAM.

I have opened James's letter, with his permission, to send you a hasty copy of a letter just received from Professor Phillips, of England, on the subject of our paper to the British Association. . . . Here is his letter : —

FROM THE CENTRE OF THE WOOLHOPE DISTRICT,
November 15, 1842.

MY DEAR SIR, — I am tardy in sending to you some account of the presentation of your paper on Elevation of Mountain Chains, at Manchester to the British Association, but in fact, my life is now that of a mere paleontologist, who has no proper notions of anything more recent than the chalk. My engagement with the Ordnance Geological Survey requires the devotion of a larger portion of my days and nights in active field hammering and closet reasoning, and there is yet a month of the former duty before I re-visit my dearly loved home at York. But to return to your paper. I received it just before the Manchester meeting, at which my official occupations were excessive, and then commended it to the President of the Section, Mr. Murchison, Professor Sedgwick not having arrived. Against my expectation the paper was appointed for reading on the first day, when I was so entirely engrossed with my duties as not to be able to appear. Sedgwick, however, had arrived, and there was a lively and continued discussion. The opinions of the geologists present were apparently at variance with you, but I am very much of the opinion that, had your views been put *en grande carte*, with large diagrams to show the mechanical reasoning, the result might have been different. There were several points in your argument which I approved and wished to advocate, but unfortunately my absence could not be prevented. I don't think the account of the discussion in the "Athenæum" very exact (so I heard from others), and in the Association reports, you know, we never introduce any statements but those of the authors of the papers. There will be a pretty full account of it in our next volume. . . .

On March 13, 1843, Robert was married to Miss Fanny Montgomery, a daughter of Mr. Joseph S. Lewis, of Philadelphia.

As the time appointed for the fourth annual meeting of the Association of American Geologists and Naturalists (at Albany) drew near, Henry, who had been elected at the Boston meeting in 1842 Chairman for that of 1843, wrote concerning it to William : —

HENRY TO WILLIAM.

PHILADELPHIA, March 30, 1843.

MY DEAR WILLIAM, . . . Dr. David Dale Owen [1] writes me that he will attend the Association at Albany, with papers on Western geology and a system of colouring geological maps, etc. I shall rejoice to see him, and hail his coming as a good sign. Is it not time for us to consider what we shall present? I presume it will be a fit occasion to come forward with our nomenclature and count on a discussion of its principles and details. We may derive profit from a timely discussion of it. What think you? If you agree, then we must soon each of us refresh his memory upon and turn over the various arguments of a general kind we have from time to time thought of in its defence. Of course we shall have to carry the war into Africa, and show the flimsy foundation upon which existing systems rest. What other matters shall we propose? . . .

PHILADELPHIA, April 8, 1843.

. . . Should you join me, I think we can essentially strengthen our present good position by presenting the outlines and principles of our nomenclature, which I

[1] Chief of the Geological Survey of Wisconsin.

am not, however, impatient to see produced. I have been looking rather extensively into the subject of earthquakes, with a view to its bearings upon all parts of our theory of flexures, and the grand fundamental doctrine of an interior fluidity; and I think we may in a joint paper, as a sequel to our former one, greatly strengthen our positions, and incite anew the attention of geologists to our views upon the broadest grounds. Such a paper I am collecting materials for industriously, in the hope that it may meet your consent that we send it this summer to the British Association, the leading members of which will have an opportunity at the same time to read our printed memoir. What say you to this notion? I fear it might be premature to send over our nomenclature until we have at least seen its fate here. . . .

WILLIAM TO HENRY.

UNIVERSITY OF VIRGINIA, April 18, 1843.

My dear Henry, — I have for the last three days been in doubt as to my attendance at Albany, and at last, though with no little reluctance, I have made up my mind to deny myself this gratification, that we may be the better able to secure our other objects the coming summer. We shall both wish to travel a part of the time for geological purposes, and I find that our means will be much restricted if I incur any more than necessary expenses now. By that time I shall receive a part of what is due from Davis's estate, some of which, however, I wish to hold in reserve for future occasions.

I could not attend the meeting without an absence of about two weeks, and, though Robert could very well supply my place with the junior class, my seniors would be idle, and in their present stage of study this would be a serious matter.

As James's classes are likely for the present to be quite small, I feel the more urged to economy in all

things. We shall soon, I am sure, feel the influence
of better times, and then I shall have coffers better
supplied. You can imagine with what reluctance I
have relinquished my intention of being at the meeting. Ever since the Boston Association, I have been
looking forward with much pleasure to it. But I
think I have decided prudently. . . .

UNIVERSITY OF VIRGINIA, April 23, 1843.

MY DEAR HENRY, . . . I write to request you to
make a verbal communication to the Society in my
behalf to the following effect: —

" Since my first discovery of the infusorial structure on the Rappahannock and at Richmond, as referred to in my Report for the year 1840, I have succeeded in finding a similar deposit at numerous other
localities, extending from the Potomac River to near
the southern boundary of the State. Among these
points may be enumerated the Stratford Cliffs, on the
Potomac, the vicinity of Westmoreland Court House,
and a great number of localities between the Potomac
and Rappahannock rivers, — the southern bank of the
latter, the vicinity of Newcastle on the Pamunkey
River, the James River below City Point, Petersburg
on the Appomattox River, and a tract above Dupré's
bridge on the Meherrin River. Further search will,
I am convinced, greatly multiply these localities, and
the observations already made are quite sufficient to
prove the wide horizontal extension of this interesting
division of our Tertiary series. Although in some of
the localities, as at Richmond, the structure reposes
upon beds containing Eocene impressions, and altogether beneath the Miocene strata, at other places, as
for example the Stratford Cliffs and Petersburg, it is
underlaid by unequivocal Miocene, and hence at these
places, if not generally, is to be referred to a position
in the geological series within and near the bottom of
the Miocene division of the Tertiary. I am, however,
inclined to the opinion that these strata are not all

upon exactly the same horizon, and that some of them lie in a higher part of the formation. Mr. Tuomey, of Petersburg, who has recently observed the deposit at that place, estimates the thickness at thirty feet. (See his paper in 'Silliman's Journal,' April number).

" In connection with these statements, it may be interesting to add that accompanying the infusorial material, I have found vegetable remains at some localities in great abundance. They are all imperfectly carbonized, still preserving their form and their fibrous texture, and they seem to be all referrible to creeping and apparently cryptogamous plants. From the specimens I am now collecting, I hope to be able to decide with some certainty as to their true character." . . .

HENRY TO WILLIAM.

ALBANY, April 30, 1843.

. . . Thus far I have done little in our own behalf, my time having been greatly engrossed by my duties as chairman and on committees. The attendance is nearly or quite as slender as it was at Boston, there being a poor turn-out from this region; but there prevails an excellent spirit, and there has thus far been decidly more solid work performed than last year. As to filling the chair, I find it laborious, but not at all embarrassing. The attendance at our discussions is very slender, this being a city of almost no taste for such matters. . . . Morton has failed to come with his address, and Silliman Sr., Gould, Ducatel, Locke, Taylor and yourself being absent, we were very much disheartened at first, as we have derived but a small contingent from this quarter. Lately we have been much more cheerful, and, as we talk seriously of going next year to Washington, we feel that we may yet reach a respectable point as regards numbers. . . . I think we shall meet in double the number at Washington, and we have cut out a first-

class deal of work. You and Robert are on committee to report on the chemical relation of the Coals
of this country, and James and Jackson, of Boston, as
a committee on Greensand. The large committee of
nine on Drift having done nothing, we have assigned
the task anew, — New England and New York to
Emmons, the West and Far West to Nicollet, and
the Southern boundary to you. I am on a committee
on coal plants.

The Governor has not yet signed the bill including
an appropriation for my survey; some doubt exists
as to his intention. I am to give *bond* for completing
the work, which I am willing to do if I can procure
it. But if, as some who heard the debate supposed,
I am also required to finish my report by next winter, I shall not accept the appropriation. . . . Coming
from New York in the same car with John Pickering,
of Boston, I had much delightful conversation with
him. He gave me to believe that I should certainly
succeed in Boston as a lecturer. . . . I would propose,
if it were possible for me to visit you (and I fear I
cannot for some weeks at least), that we should get
ready a brief paper conjointly, embody my investigations on earthquakes, and send it to the British Association for their approaching meeting. We could thus
strengthen our theory, and take occasion to reply to
the arguments of Sedgwick and others to the extension of the structural laws to Europe, and also on the
dynamics of the question.

WILLIAM TO HENRY.

UNIVERSITY OF VIRGINIA, May 27, 1843.

MY DEAR HENRY, — I am quite anxious for an
opportunity of replying to Sedgwick and the other
objectors to the theoretical views of our paper. Judging from the report of what he said, as republished
in " Silliman," I do not discover anything formidable
in his opposition. Indeed, both his and De la Beche's

objections are already in a great degree met in our extended paper.

De la Beche's comments appear to me to be feeble and without point. Thus when he says that, " while contortions of the strata sometimes assume the character of mountain chains, at others they occupy large tracts of low ground," he seems to have overlooked the effects of ulterior general subsidence as well as denudation. In adverting to our criticism of the theory of Élie de Beaumont, he has not rightly conceived the extent of deviation of the various parts of the chain he describes from a common direction, a deviation greater than that referred to by the French philosopher in some cases, as marking differences of epoch. In asserting that " the only force necessary for the production of flexures and contortions, such as he describes, is the lateral or tangential pressure," he has evidently failed to appreciate the evidence derived from the *laws of flexures* we have established. His reference to the structure of Russia, though well enough as a proof that our subterranean forces have not acted there, does not at all affect the question of their operation in Europe and this country. We have not pretended that our pulsations were propagated all around the hemisphere.

It would seem that Sedgwick does not regard the steepening of the flexures on the N. W. side as " favourable to our view of the origin of the contortions," and, from the language in which he is reported, he appears to think that the greater steepness, being " *farthest* from the centre of disturbing forces," is just what should not be the result according to our theory. What notions he entertains of subterranean waves I cannot imagine, but to me nothing in mechanics is more clear than the connection of such a force with a great progressive wave.

In reasoning from the form of the flexures and other phenomena presented by strata of such high antiquity, I do not see that much importance should

be attached to the *present level* of the region in which
they exist. The operation of an elevating as well as
tangential force — in other words, of a *wave* — does
not seem necessary to imply a *permanent uplift* of
the whole surface. Besides, in the Liège to which he
refers, we know not to what extent denudation or
subsidence may have depressed the ancient level of
the land. Sedgwick's idea of the mechanism of earthquake movement, which Dr. P—— in the Philosophical Society reproduced, is no better than any other
guess. The comparison of phenomena, and the actual
tracing of the movement with which you have lately
been occupied, is the true mode of discovering what
an earthquake is. . .

The Report of the Proceedings of the British Association for July 24, 1843, contains an abstract of the
joint paper on the Physical Structure of the Appalachian Chain.

The summer of 1843 passed without special incident, and another academic year began. October,
with its crisp coolness, came once more and brought
fresh inspiration for the new year.

WILLIAM TO JAMES.

UNIVERSITY OF VIRGINIA, October 14, 1843.

MY DEAR JAMES, — This clear, invigorating weather
reminds me of our October rambles together when you
were with me in the Survey, and I am still more for-
cibly reminded of them in pursuing my present task
of writing out the notes I took some weeks ago in
Rockbridge, Allegheny, and Greenbrier counties,
among the scenes of some of your most pleasing geological labours. My late tour has thrown new light
upon some important points in the development of certain formations there, and has enabled me to make a
useful collection of fossils. What think you of find-

ing the fossil ore on top of the North Mountain, beyond McCorkle's, and above the arch at Clifton Forge? I earnestly wished that you could have been with me in this journey, as much for my advantage as for that of your health.

From what I have observed of late, and what Henry has more than once mentioned in affectionate anxiety, I am fearful that you are destined, unless you practice the greatest caution, to suffer as seriously as even I have done from hoarseness and feebleness of the throat. This apprehension gives me many an uneasy hour, and makes me ardently desire that I were with you to persuade you to adopt every means of protection or care. I trust, my dear James, that you provide yourself in due time with flannels and thick winter-proof boots, and that you never venture out unprotected by these and by a good cloak or great-coat. My experience here has shown me that with these and warm gloves I may defy the cold and wet, and that frequent exposure thus arrayed is, even in bad weather, salutary rather than hurtful. . . .

Our classes have increased steadily though not very rapidly since I last wrote. We are much ahead of last season, and may, I think, reasonably count upon one hundred and sixty in all. Robert, who has been particularly lucky this year, has now sixty-six, and may calculate upon seventy-five. I have forty-two, and look for fifty. In these moderate expectations, however, we may be disappointed, but, should the ratio of increase with the time be the same as last year, these must be the results. From our numbers must always be deducted some two or three non-paying students. Between us, at all events, we may count upon one hundred and fifteen fees, which is a handsome improvement upon last session. From the character of our present students, I augur not only a quiet and successful course, but a great improvement in numbers and respectability for future years. Every one is struck with the very superior tone and breeding of the great mass of the new-comers of this season. Among those are a son of Watkins Leigh, of our good friend John Wickham, and of Bishop Johns. . . .

The occasional letters which passed between Professor Rogers and Professor J. W. Bailey, of West Point, reveal a pleasant scientific intercourse and the warm friendship which ever existed between them. Two such letters belong to this period.

TO PROFESSOR J. W. BAILEY.

UNIVERSITY OF VIRGINIA, October 22, 1843.

DEAR SIR, — I have been anxious for the last three weeks to inform you of an important extension of our infusorial formation, and to inclose you a small specimen for your microscope. You will, I am sure, be pleased to learn that I have ascertained the existence of this deposit in Maryland, where I have long felt pretty confident it would be discovered, and that it is thick and probably widely diffused. Its geological position, as at many of the Virginian localities, is near but above the junction of the Eocene and Miocene. The specimen sent you is from the neighbourhood of Piscataway. . . .

Though disappointed in my hope of meeting you in Albany last spring, and still later in my design of paying you a short visit at West Point, I trust I shall enjoy many pleasant interviews next spring in Washington, and by way of further recommending myself I shall take on specimens of all things worthy of your microscope that I can collect. We who are in collegiate harness may well envy the lot of those happy fellows who, free from all such restraints, can go whithersoever the love of research impels, and can devote all their hours of vigorous thought to extending the boundaries of knowledge. . . .

FROM PROFESSOR BAILEY.

WEST POINT, October 31, 1843.

One of your ever-welcome letters reached me yesterday, and its contents, visible as well as invisible, have afforded me much pleasure. I am glad to find that in spite of the harness you can still take flight into the fields of discovery. This new extension of our little pets into Maryland is truly interesting. I think we may now challenge the world to produce infusorial deposits equal in extent to those of which you made the truly "splendid" discovery. In America, in spite of old Buffon, Nature has done all her work on a scale commensurate with our immense territory. . . . As most of the forms in question are more abundant in the Petersburg specimen than in any others, I will now proceed to describe and figure some from that locality, that you may understand what I mean when I refer to them in mentioning the species in the Maryland specimens. First then, the gem of the whole, the most splendid animalcule ever discovered, is one which belongs to a genus which Ehrenberg called *Tripodiscus*, in consequence of his noticing three feet-like projections on the disc; but as our species has from three to seven of these feet, I propose to change the name to *Podiscus*, and our elegant species I shall take the liberty of calling *Podiscus Rogersi*. Ehrenberg's species was discovered by him in a living state in sea-water; he does not appear to have noticed it in the fossil state. Our species, which presents several points of difference from Ehrenberg's figure, is the largest animalcule in the Petersburg deposits; to the naked eye, it is as large as this circle, — O. Its surface is so elaborately marked that no engine-turning can surpass it in elegance, and it bids defiance to all my graphic powers to make a good figure of it.

I wish I could have you here for a while to have a long talk with you, and receive from your active mind that stimulus which sympathy in our pursuits and feelings never fails to impart. I am about the sole representative here of the natural sciences, and have to live in an atmosphere where all that is not mathematical is considered as unscientific. Of course, then, I meet with little sympathy or encouragement in my pursuits. Nevertheless, these studies carry their own reward, and render many an hour pleasant that would otherwise be tedious. I am amused, and at the same time pleased, to see how some of our American geologists are working up to views which you and your brother Henry advanced years ago, and which have but just been caught up with by some of our savants.

I close for want of room, but with feelings of most cordial regard.   Yours truly,

J. W. BAILEY.

Professor Henry Rogers, at the suggestion of Mr. George B. Emerson of Boston, and other friends, was at this time preparing to give in that city a course of popular lectures on geology.

WILLIAM TO HENRY.

UNIVERSITY OF VIRGINIA, November 5, 1843.

I have nothing whatever of local or scientific interest to tell you, but write simply from the impulse of the most affectionate sympathy in your present plans and prospects. You are now approaching the commencement of your course, for which no doubt you are by this time very amply prepared. And it is important that from the very beginning you should entertain the fullest confidence in your entire success, and suffer no misgivings to damp for a moment that animating sense of power which it is your right to feel. My own experience in popular lecturing has taught me how much the highest degree of success is dependent upon the extent to which this sense of confidence is felt at the opening and in the progress of the lecture; and hence it is my habit now, when on

such occasions I find anxiety or timidity creeping upon
me, to rouse my energy and, so to speak, new-nerve
my thoughts by a strong voluntary effort like that
which you witness in sprightly, imaginative children
in their heroic reveries. This curious effort of the
will, though hard to describe, you no doubt compre-
hend and have yourself resorted to. . . .

On Saturday last I delivered the annual address to
the Agricultural Society of Albemarle. It was all
improvised, and was intended to point out the true
dignity and the intellectual requirements of agricultural pursuits, and hence the demand for a high
grade of education in the training of those who are
to become farmers. . . .

FROM THE BOSTON DAILY ADVERTISER, 1843.

LECTURES ON GEOLOGY.

Professor Henry D. Rogers will deliver the first
regular lecture of his course on American Geology at
the Masonic Temple, on Tuesday, December 5, 1843,
at 7 o'clock. The lecture will treat of, — Means of
Geological Investigation ; Different Classes of Rocks ;
Series of Stratified Formations ; Scale of Geological
Time ; Central Heat ; Fluidity of the Interior of the
Globe ; Thinness of the Earth's Crust, etc.

WILLIAM TO HENRY.

UNIVERSITY OF VIRGINIA, December 18, 1843.

MY DEAR HENRY, — In regard to our Oölite coal
and superior rocks, my views, though not carefully or
finally made up, are briefly the following : I conceive
these materials to have been accumulated in a chain
of shallow lagoons and lakes extending some distance east of the present limits of the formation,
while the great primary surface to the west was, as
now, dry land. Supposing a subsidence of this tract
to have commenced in the region of the Chesterfield

Basin, we should in the earlier stages of the change
have the physical causes favourable to the production
of the coal, which, as you know, lies at or near the
base of the formation. This earliest-formed lagoon,
filled up with a rank growth of reeds, *Tœneopteris,*
etc., gradually sinking as the vegetable matter accumulated, would at length contain an immense thickness
of these exuviæ only requiring to be sealed in by
the overlying beds to form the coal. A more sudden
shifting of the level must now have occurred, attended
with violent wearing and transporting action of water,
by which the coarse grits above the coal were rapidly
accumulated. To this succeeded a gentler action,
giving rise to the fine micaceous sandstones which
lie above.   During all this time I conceive that the
region now occupied by the Fredericksburg sandstone,
extending to the South Anna River, had not yet been
brought within the limits of the sedimentary action.
But now, a second more sudden subsidence occurring,
and operating chiefly in the northern portion of the
tract, the belt from the South Anna to the Potomac
was overspread with coarse primary and Appalachian
pebbles, which at the same time mantled over the
Chesterfield and Henrico coal-fields ; and to this succeeded the more gentle actions, which, as the tract
gradually subsided, accumulated the materials of the
felspathic sandstone, with its lignities, silicified wood,
and other relics of vegetation.   As we cannot be certain of the absence of this formation beneath the
Tertiary even at a considerable distance to the south-
east, and as we know of its presence on the Appomattox, James, Rappahannock, and Potomac rivers
between the Gneiss and the Eocene, we cannot pronounce with confidence as to the extent of area over
which the sediment was originally spread towards the
east. Having found no decidedly marine forms in
any of these rocks, I cannot suppose it to have been
a coast deposit, although I am inclined to think that
the lagoons or the long inlet were but little removed

from the sea, even in the region of Chesterfield, and approached it still more closely towards Fredericksburg. I have no doubt that the formation prior to denudation was far more extensive than now, having seen traces of it far south of Appomattox.

In May, 1844, the annual meeting of the Association of American Geologists and Naturalists was held in Washington. James was a member of the Standing Committee and William and Henry attended and read papers, but no account of these appears in the correspondence of this period.

In a letter dated May 14, 1844, Mr. J. A. Lowell, Trustee of the Lowell Institute, proposed to Professor Henry Rogers to give a course of lectures on Geology before the Lowell Institute in Boston. The letter was addressed to the "Care of Professor W. B. Rogers, University of Virginia," and upon it William penned these lines : —

DEAR HENRY, — I have opened this most delightful letter, having a presentiment of what it contained, and I now close it to send it by this evening's mail. My heart rejoices with you over its contents.

Your devoted and happy brother,
WILLIAM B. ROGERS.

WILLIAM TO JAMES.

UNIVERSITY OF VIRGINIA, May 19, 1844.

We missed you, my dear James, at the Association. Next season you must arrange your affairs so as to be present. The place of meeting, New Haven, is, I think, well selected, and we may anticipate a larger session than we have yet had and a general interest of the community in our proceedings.

Why, my dear James, do you not write to us? We are desirous of knowing all particulars connected with the Institute and other medical schools, — what Dr. Hare is now about; how Frazer succeeds in his new place ; whether he intends retaining the place in the Franklin Institute, and other items of local and personal interest.

You have not told us anything about the little darling, — what is to be her name; whom is she most like; and many other inquiries which we would make in the first breath after seeing you, and which you can easily answer by pen. I trust dear Rachel has quite recovered. Tell her I think daily with brotherly affection of her and the children. I wish William and Henry could be here to enjoy our delicious strawberries and cream. The early fruits are unusually good and abundant, and we have strawberries, which cost only 6¼ cents. a quart, twice or three times a day. Before the year is out I shall reorder my household, fitting up my room to the exclusion of the cumbrous cases of minerals. Then I shall be able to have the boys with me in the spring when you can let them come to enjoy the fresh air, freedom and rustic pleasures of this region of verdure, fruits and flowers.

What are you now lecturing on, and what new arrangements have you made in your laboratory? Robert is just closing inorganic chemistry. I am beginning the imponderables, having allowed myself too little time to treat them as fully as I have been used to do. Tell me of any scientific news that has come to your knowledge. . . .

Your devoted brother,
WILLIAM B. ROGERS.

I hope you still continue to gather materials for your book. Depend upon it, you might do great things by such a work.

On June 1, 1844, Mr. Rogers and his brother Henry were informed, by the Foreign Secretary (De la Beche) of the Geological Society of London, that they had been unanimously elected Foreign Members of that Society; and in August, 1844, Mr. Rogers was notified of his election to membership in the Royal Society of Northern Antiquaries, having its headquarters at Copenhagen.

On the opening of the University in the autumn Professor Rogers was chosen by his colleagues Chairman of the Faculty, an event of great importance as it proved in the demonstration and the development of those administrative powers which afterwards characterized his life and labors in Boston. Reference is made to this appointment in the following letter: —

TO GEORGE TICKNOR, ESQ.

UNIVERSITY OF VIRGINIA, October 10, 1844.

. . . From the number of matriculates already enrolled, we have reason to anticipate a much fuller session than we have had for several years, and are encouraged to expect for the future a nearer attainment of that wider and higher usefulness which the great founder of the University had in mind in its establishment.

Nothing would please me more than a short visit to Boston during my brother Henry's course. But although I have sometimes indulged myself in dreaming of it, my additional duties for the present session, as Chairman, debar me of all hope of such a gratification. Perhaps early in May, during or after the meeting of the geologists at New Haven, I may steal a day or two to look in upon my friends in Boston and Cambridge, and at all events I console myself with the confident expectation of seeing them soon after the close of my duties here. You thus see how much my plans of literary and social enjoyment have been influenced by the impressions received during my late

brief but happy sojourn among you, and what anticipations of pleasure, before undreamed of, have been
awakened by the kind hospitalities of which I was a
sharer while in Boston, and more especially beneath
your roof. Be assured, my dear sir, that the pleasant
incidents of this visit recur often to my thoughts. . . .
In my heart I daily thank you and Mrs. Ticknor for
the cordial kindness that gave me the sense of home
in the midst of almost strangers, and proffered to me
the friendship which it will be my happiness to deserve and cultivate. And with a yet deeper gratitude,
let me add affectionately, I thank you for the interest
you have evinced in my dear brother's welfare and
scientific success, an interest that has won his warmest affection and contributes daily to his happiest
thoughts. . . .

From this letter and the next, it appears that during the summer of 1844 the brothers William and
Henry paid a visit to New England : —

TO PROFESSOR JOSEPH LOVERING.

UNIVERSITY OF VIRGINIA, November 1, 1844.

DEAR SIR, — I have of late often thought of the
promise I made you during my happy visit to Cambridge, but the academic harness presses too heavily,
thus early in the session, to allow me time for more
than a brief note in token of remembrance, and as
the vehicle of a small request. Erelong I shall have
greater freedom, and will most gladly do what I can
to continue by letter the intercourse begun so pleasantly during our interviews in Cambridge. Disliking
elaborate correspondence, I enjoy with the heartiest
relish a free, unreserved epistolary talk with the
friends I esteem. And such, I am sure, is your taste
also. Shall we not, then, indulge ourselves from time
to time in little friendly colloquies through the post-
office? It will be pleasant to interchange thoughts

about science, or society, or any other topics that may
arise, running "from grave to gay, from lively to
severe," and, although my poor counters will form but
a sorry equivalent for the good coin you may send,
they will always have the heart stamp of sincerity to
commend them to your regard. Among the items of
your first letter be sure to include a mention of your
lady, whose cordial kindness in word and manner
made me forget that she was not a friend of many
years. Please present me to her with earnest good
wishes and regards.

Dr. Schele tells me that Mr. Putnam's Phi Beta
address[1] has been published. I rejoice at it. Many
a worthless oration is preserved in the amber of typo-
graphy, but this, far excelling the dead flies thus en-
tombed, is amber itself in transparency. I beg of you,
therefore, to send me a copy at your earliest convenience; and I will be obliged to you also for one of
your catalogues for this year, in return for which I
will send you ours when published.

Our new colleague, Dr. Schele,[2] has made the most
favorable impression upon his classes, as well as our
little social circle, and is now quite domesticated
among us.

Begging to be very kindly remembered to Professor
Peirce, and hoping soon to hear from you,

I remain, dear sir, with sincere regard,
Your friend,
WILLIAM B. ROGERS.

FROM PROFESSOR LOVERING.

BOSTON, February 9, 1845.

MY DEAR ROGERS, . . . You have probably
heard before this of your brother's success [with his
Lowell Lectures on Geology] in Boston. He has

[1] Rev. Dr. George Putnam, of Roxbury.
[2] Schele de Vere, Professor of Modern Languages at the University
of Virginia.

only left us a few days since, much to our regret, and
I hope not without some long and lingering looks on
his part, back upon the city where he has made so
many sincere friends, and where he is so much loved.
I heard half of his lectures, and should have been
glad not to have missed any. He found a docile and
attentive audience, and a large one, too; and it is not
strange that his winning style of lecturing, his calm
eloquence, his chaste and beautiful language, and his
comprehensive views of his vast subject, should have
riveted the attention that was freely offered to him,
and stormed hearts that were by no means closely
sealed against him. The dignity of his thoughts and
the tasteful drapery in which they were enrobed were,
I assure you, fully appreciated, and produced their
full effect. Among the numerous acquaintances of
your brother I was but an humble individual, and,
although he gave me my share of his time, I only
regret that I did not see more of him. . . .

Your sincere friend,
JOSEPH LOVERING.

HENRY TO WILLIAM.

BOSTON, January 2, 1845.

DEAR WILLIAM, . . . A gentleman of this town,
Horace Gray, a highly respected and rich merchant,
interested largely in the iron manufacture, has requested me to undertake, some time in the summer, a
survey of a district near the Hudson, and ascertain
the practicability of starting furnaces there. It rests
with me to assent.

Kraitzer[1] gave a gratuitous lecture last night to
about one hundred and fifty persons of education.
They seemed greatly surprised, amused and struck by
his doctrines, which he expounded in a very able manner. He is certainly an extraordinary man; I am

---

[1] For a short time Professor of Modern Languages at the University of Virginia.

more than ever a convert to his grand generalizations concerning the organic genesis of language. Since he left the University his views have obviously settled into a more thoroughly compact and systematical theory, which to me is a truly sublime one.

Kindest love to Robert, Fanny and Uncle.

Your truly devoted brother,

HENRY D. ROGERS.

P. S.—I am concerned to notice by your letters that you are not at ease in relation to the University. Surely nothing can be done detrimental to its progress.

BOSTON, January 24, 1845.

MY DEAR WILLIAM, . . . A week since, I lectured before a Lyceum in Portsmouth to one thousand people, and on Monday and Wednesday of this week to a private class of about two hundred only. . . .

My friend, George S. Hillard,[1] whose Phi Beta Kappa address I believe you have read, insisted last week upon my making my home in his house, and here I am in his choice library, resting myself after my fatigue. . . . Among those whom I have met is Miss Sedgwick the authoress, who has just returned to her winter home in New York city, after a visit to her niece here for three weeks. I saw her frequently at Mrs. Minot's, and was greatly charmed by her benevolence of character and her highly cultivated and liberal mind.

. . . Have you seen a new work just republished by Wiley and Putnam, "Vestiges of the Natural History of Creation"? It contains many of the loftiest speculative views in Astronomy and Geology and Natural History, and singularly accords with views sketched by me at times in my lectures.

Write next to Philadelphia, where I shall be about this day next week. You know not how I pine to be

---

[1] George Stillman Hillard, author of *Six Months in Italy*, etc.

with you and Robert and Fanny for a season.   Kind
love to you all.
        Most affectionately,
                                HENRY D. ROGERS.

On December 22, 1844, the Committee on Schools
and Colleges of the House of Delegates of Virginia
was instructed to investigate "the past history and
present condition and influences of the University of
Virginia, with a view of forming their opinion upon
the question of repealing the Act of Assembly grant-
ing an annuity of $15,000 to that Institution." This
was the attack upon the University referred to by
Henry on the previous page.   William makes as light
as possible of his anxiety on this account, at the end
of a long letter on scientific matters.

                UNIVERSITY OF VIRGINIA, January 5, 1845.
DEAR HENRY, . . . We are quiet and comfortable,
but my neighbours think and talk of nothing but the
possible results of legislation upon our endowment. I
presume there is danger of a reduction, if not entire
withdrawal, of the annuity, but in my mind the probability is the other way.   Still Robert and I give ourselves as little anxiety as possible.

To this Henry, writing to Robert, replies : —

                PHILADELPHIA, February 11, 1845.
Things here look dismal enough to me after Boston.
There my mind and my heart had scope to unfold in ;
here, like a frightened coral, I draw myself within my
stony shell.   I am determined, however, not to give
way to the depressing influences which here beset me,
but to enter as soon as possible on a course of lectures. . . . I trust William has got home again without harm to his health.   I fear he has been working
too hard.   What you mentioned in your letter was

truly gratifying. I trust he will continue to maintain his high ground respecting the University. Its system needs only to be understood and carried out. Do you notice how they are stirring in Harvard an incipient reform? They have much to do there. What is to be the true extent of the lectureship department in the Smithsonian Institution? . . .

It devolved upon Mr. Rogers as Chairman of the Faculty to prepare a memorial to the Legislature of Virginia in defence of the University and its annual appropriation. There is evidence that he gave much time and thought to this work, and the lengthy Report of the Committee of the House of Delegates on Schools and Colleges " Against the expediency of withdrawing the fifteen thousand dollars annuity from the University " (Document No. 41, Session of 1844-45) was prepared by Mr. Rogers. This Report is of the highest interest, and of great importance in the history of American education. It is easy to detect in it abundant proofs of that educational breadth and insight which afterwards became so conspicuous in the foundation of the Massachusetts Institute of Technology in Boston. It is especially interesting to the student of the development of state universities, which have not infrequently had to meet and overcome attacks of philistinism similar to that which now menaced the prosperity of the University of Virginia. For these reasons, and because of its intrinsic interest, we give lengthy extracts from this document in the Appendix.[1] It should be observed that the annuity which it was now proposed to withdraw had constituted a prominent feature of the University's income ever since its foundation by Thomas Jefferson in 1818.

The next letter hints at some of the grounds of the

[1] Page 399.

attack upon the University, and suggests a union with
the Virginia Military Institute : —

FROM WILLIAM R. JOHNSON.

STAUNTON, February 14, 1845.

I have just returned from a visit to the Military
Institute at Lexington, and write to suggest to you a
scheme which occurred to me during that visit, and
which might be useful to the University.

It is to engraft upon the University, the Military
Institute, so as to avail the University of the appropriation, the cadets, the popularity, the popular feature of the free cadets, and the excellent system of
order and economy of the Institute. This seems to
me desirable when I consider some of the sources
of the prejudices against the University, her real or
apparent want of discipline and economy, or when I
look only at the frequent abuse which has been of
late unjustly heaped upon her, and the strong feeling
of hostility manifested in the present Legislature. . . .

This seems to me a favourable time to effect this
measure, if it be a desirable one. Some change in the
organization of the University, if not its total destruc-
tion, seems to be meditated by its enemies, on the
ground or the pretext of its expense and disorder ;
the military system seems to be the favourite of the
day.

I hope you will attribute my interest in the subject
to its true and main source, my ever warm attachment
to my Alma Mater, and accept for yourself my affectionate regard.

Yours respectfully,

WILLIAM R. JOHNSON.

To this Professor Rogers replied : —

UNIVERSITY OF VIRGINIA, March 15, 1845.

MY DEAR SIR, . . . As regards the feasibility and
success of the organic changes suggested in your let-

ter, it would be impossible for me at this time to
present my views and that of my colleagues in detail.
We all feel the importance of some system of police
capable of securing permanent good order and diligence among the students, and, consulting our own
feelings merely, would sincerely rejoice in a liberation
from the anxieties and annoyances of college discipline. Yet, when we compare the conduct and progress of our classes, and our relations to them, with
the like particulars in other leading institutions of
this country, we are far from being discouraged by
the result, and are still strongly hopeful of steady
and increased success, notwithstanding the ungenerous
enmity of those who, from prejudice or ignorance, are
labouring for our overthrow. . . .

Mr. Rogers had once more appealed to the Legislature for the means with which to publish his final
Report, but in vain, as the following shows: —

TO HIS BROTHER JAMES.

UNIVERSITY OF VIRGINIA, February 28, 1845.

. . . Next winter, I have little doubt, by timely
application and personal attention to the matter, I
can procure the appropriation for my Report which
has recently been denied. Mr. Brown writes that,
had I been able to devote one week to personal effort
with the members, he is sure I would have succeeded
this winter. But I am quite well pleased that I did
not, though I give no thanks to the Legislature on
that account.

We are just now enjoying comparative quiet within
the precincts; and as many of our most turbulent
spirits have been sent away, or have withdrawn, I
look for more comfortable times for the rest of the
session. My position as Chairman has devolved upon
me many unpleasant duties, and has kept me, until
now, in a state of almost unceasing anxiety. . . .

When will your lectures in the Institute terminate? The medical courses are, I suppose, now closing, and the great doctors' mill is making its last revolution preparatory to the process which is to send abroad the manufactured product stamped wholesale by the University branding-iron.

A renewal of the disturbances by the students of the University now caused the Chairman of the Faculty great anxiety, and marked the beginning of a new series of "riots" which finally became so serious as to cause the suspension for a week of all University exercises.

TO HIS BROTHER HENRY.

UNIVERSITY OF VIRGINIA, March 5, 1845.

. . . How heartily you must have enjoyed the confidence and society of Hillard, and how much pleasure you must reap from corresponding with him! Lucian Minor is the only person in all my acquaintance with whom I can have the luxury of free literary communion. He spent part of a day and a night with me and Robert lately, and did us both good by carrying us for a while away from our common subject of thought into the enticing realm of purifying and cheering letters.

Minor proposes making an abstract of my Report on the University, with his own comments, for the next "Messenger."[1] He says it is triumphantly convincing.

Spring is now fairly setting in. The lawn is growing green, the maples and poplars are in bloom, the lilac leaves are rapidly unfolding, and the violets shedding their tea-like fragrance in our gardens. Variable and blustering though generally mild weather has thus far marked the month, and we are anticipating a very early spring. Among the changes of the

[1] *Southern Literary Messenger.*

season, nothing pleases me so much as the lengthening of our daylight hours, and the exemption this usually brings from the annoyances and troubles among our students. . . .

TO LUCIAN MINOR.

UNIVERSITY OF VIRGINIA, March 6, 1845.

. . . With my ten-toe equipage, as Bonnel Thornton calls it, I journeyed to town this morning expressly to see you, and was sadly disappointed on learning that you had taken French leave of us and gone home. We were in hopes of enjoying another evening with you at my house and Robert's, when we might have looked into the grand tableau of Michelet's History, of which I spoke, and which I have since found, and might have indulged in many cheering and heart-refreshing literary rambles. . . . My pursuits of late years have been so entirely scientific that I have had little time or opportunity for gratifying the ever-present longing of my heart for the sweet recreations of general literature. There was a time when I could enjoy the luxury of pleasant journeyings amid those charming realms of flowers and fragrance and refreshing shade that spread in magic beauty around the slopes of old Parnassus; and, while listening with wrapt ear to the music of " Helicon's harmonious Springs," I have even fancied that I had a spirit within me that might some day respond to the divine minstrelsy of its swelling waters. But the muses, then but unwilling guides, have now, I fear, entirely forsaken me. You smile, no doubt, to hear that I should ever have indulged the conceit of mingling my triangle music with the harmonies of the poetic choir, but, to be candid, though I did not hope to win even a dry leaf of that laurel which first shaded the brow of the "blind old man" of whom the world disputes, and which has since enwreathed the temples of all the masters of the lyre, I did imagine that I might one day claim a homely garland of cedar for my song, and this I felt would be amaranth for me. But it was well that I was early turned from poetasting, and that severer guides pointed me to pursuits better suited to my capacity. Yet in the walks which I take through nature in quest of truth and demonstration, I recognize a poetry in earth and sea and sky, ruled in their cycles of harmonious actions, deeper and more sublime than ever muse untaught in science could inspire. . . .

Mr. Rogers's reference to "severer guides" will remind the reader of Matthew Arnold's lines: —

> " For rigorous teachers seized my youth,
>   And purged its faith and trimmed its fire, —
>   Showed me the high white star of truth,
>   There bade me gaze, and there aspire."

As long as he lived Mr. Rogers kept fresh and keen his love for poetry, to the reading of which he was fond of listening for hours at a time.

On the day when he wrote the last letter, he wrote to Professor Bailey, of West Point: —

. . . "It is a sad truth that the studies of men of science, fraught as they are with ennobling and fraternizing influences, are often perverted from those higher uses, and pursued mainly as the instruments of paltry gain and grasping ambition. When this is the case we witness the mortifying spectacle of a mind at once the abode of various knowledge, and of envy, malice and all uncharitableness; and we cannot but lament the insensibility of the unworthy priests of Nature who, while ministering at her shrines, are unpenetrated by her gentle lessons of kindness and world-embracing liberality."

The following concerning the "spoils system" is of contemporary interest: —

LOUISA C. H., VA., March 31, 1845.

Help me to help Mr. Polk from doing a great wrong, — nay (as Talleyrand says) much worse, — a great blunder. They say he will remove Blackford.[1] If he do so, where can proscription stop? It will be the most palpable and outrageous application of the spoils principle yet known in our government. The decapitation of Jonathan Roberts was a trifle to it, for he was old, and Mr. Tyler may have found him incompetent. But B.'s imperturbable temper, winning manners, shrewd knowledge of men, and tact in getting at their thoughts and at their blind sides, fit him preëminently for diplomacy, while he has a straightforward honesty that puts to shame and to rout the old-fashioned belief that the affairs of nations are to be successfully managed only by jobbery.

Whatever is done must be done quickly. I have merely drawn the hint of an address to the President, which I hope you will throw into such form as it ought to have, get it signed by all of the Faculty who supported Mr. Polk (including yourself), and send to him. If he go on with this spoils system, his political school will break down at the end of four years, or eight at all events. Then we shall have Bank, etc., all upon us, and they will not be half so bad as that system.

In April the "rioting" of students at the University of Virginia was resumed and carried to such a pitch that the civil authority had to be invoked for its suppression.

WILLIAM TO HENRY.

UNIVERSITY OF VIRGINIA, April 4, 1845.

. . . Since our last letter to you we have had some renewal of our college disorders, consisting chiefly in

[1] Chargé d'Affaires of the United States at Bogotá.

displays of indignation from students who had incurred punishment, and resulting two nights ago in a
most signal exposure by Robert of one of the band
of horn-blowers.

A number of the students turned out with horns
and drum, as they had often done this session, to sere-
nade the Professors and particularly the Chairman,
and in passing up Robert's alley some one of them
tapped upon the window shutters of his parlor, where
Fanny and a friend were seated. Robert was out at
the time, but on his return he found Fanny very much
agitated; and soon after, hearing the party again
approaching, he went out and took his station behind
one of the columns in the little alcove in front of his
house. As the musicians passed on, making their
infernal din, one of the marauders approached the
door, and was about placing his foot on the mat, when
Robert seized him by the cloak, and, allowing him a
little rope until he reached the grass, actually picked
him up in the presence of the whole crowd and carried him into the parlor, where the full blaze of the
lamp disclosed to us and the ladies who he was. None
of the bystanders attempted to interpose after being
warned by Robert that he was armed, and that if they
approached him it should be at their peril.

The young man thus apprehended, though occasionally noisy, has been rather a good student, though
very much of a coward. Adam Empie acted a very
manly part in arresting the excitement which this
bold exploit of Robert created among the students,
and in giving them a true account of all the circumstances. . . .

We have so large an admixture this year of cow-
ardly rowdies amongst us that some signal demonstration of the proper mode of dealing with them cannot
help being salutary, and it will be useful for them to
learn that we are prepared to punish their insults on
the spot. I think that we are not likely to have any
more of these very annoying occurrences. Certainly

the history of the session thus far has been most dis-creditable to the character of the students. Yet we have a large number of very well-disposed, correct young men, but no one among them of that moral weight and energy of character which might effectu-ally resist and break down the organized band of the idle and mischievous.

Almost every Faculty meeting witnesses a suspen-sion or dismission, and this had of course created much heart-burning, and awakened some vindictive feeling. Unfortunately, we have no way of compel-ling dismissed students to go home, and hence those from the far South linger for months about the tav-erns of Charlottesville, rioting in dissipation and tempting away their former associates at the Univer-sity. But enough of this. . . .

UNIVERSITY OF VIRGINIA, April 29, 1845.

It gives me real pain to be compelled to forego the pleasure I have been long anticipating in meeting my scientific friends and brethren at New Haven. Though I well know that the official duties which would de-volve upon me, were I there, will be far more satisfac-torily discharged by the member who may be chosen to fill my place, I would most gladly have embraced the opportunity of this meeting to evince my hearty zeal in the purposes of the Association, and my anxiety to extend still more widely the sphere of its scientific activity.

Public rumour and the newspaper have already spread far and wide the reports of our riots, and my professional brethren, who have doubtless all had some unpleasant experiences of this kind, can readily understand the urgent causes which compel my ab-sence from the meeting. The peculiar responsibility of my position as Chairman of the Faculty increases the necessity of my presence here; for although per-fect tranquillity has been restored, I am yet in the midst of a laborious correspondence connected with the action of the college authorities, and the inquiries and applications of the friends and parents of our pupils. . . .

We are now enjoying peace, the lectures are proceeding as usual, and some of those who in alarm retreated from the scene when the riots were at their height are beginning to return. . . .

Robert and Fanny have given you some of the details, and I am too much exhausted by anxiety and toil, and too sick of the disgusting scenes through which we have passed, to enter upon a history of the disorders. The annals of college disturbances could hardly furnish another narrative as disgraceful to the character of the youth of the country as the history of this would be. On such occasions generally the disorderly and rebellious have some real or supposed cause to allege as the provocation of their open defiance of the law. But in this instance, although many were questioned on the subject, no one attempted, until within the last day or two of the disorders, to assign any reason whatever for their systematic progress in disorder and outrage. The newspaper reports, ascribing the outrages to censures pronounced by myself and others in the lecture-room, are utterly untrue. The remarks made there by us were subsequent to nearly all the attacks, and after they had been continued with increasing violence for weeks. So, also, the statement that my severe enforcement of the regulations had produced general resistance. If I have committed any fault in my administration, it has been that of over-gentleness and not rigour.

We are now preparing a circular which will be sent to all the parents and guardians and printed in some of the papers. I drew up such an one as I thought most suitable, containing a brief narrative of facts, and an earnest setting forth of the importance of the step by the Faculty in calling in the civil power. My colleagues seemed to think that it was too earnest in manner, and are now, I believe, trying to freeze it down to suit their own timid notions of propriety.

We have now, at least, the comfortable assurance of quiet for the remainder of the session. But I confess, my dear Henry, that I feel so little sure of exemption from like humbling and disgraceful disorders in future that I intend earnestly to look about me for some other and more tranquil home. . . .

Of our prospects I am not very hopeful. Perhaps the Legislature may be induced to make some provision for our future police by establishing a Judge on the precincts, and exempting us from all duties but those of instruction. This is rather a dream than a hope.

The "circular" referred to above as having been prepared by Mr. Rogers is given in full in the Appendix.[1]

On May 27, 1845, Mr. Rogers was elected a Fellow of the American Academy of Arts and Sciences in Boston.

WILLIAM TO HENRY.

UNIVERSITY OF VIRGINIA, June 6, 1845.

. . . New schemes of organization are likely to occupy the Visitors, and among them one greatly talked of abroad, and I understand very popular with several of the Board, is the making the Chairmanship permanent, or perhaps appointing a President as at other colleges. Every one you know has his nostrum for college evils, and this seems to be in great favour just now. Some of the professors seem inclined to favour the plan, but I believe a majority object to it. The want of uniformity of administration is the objection to the present system upon which the friends of this scheme place their great reliance. This is, doubtless, a serious evil, but they have not adverted to the evils of the plan they advocate. Could we, by having a permanent Chairman, be spared individually the harassing cares and disquietude of our present system, I should almost be disposed to welcome the

[1] Page 413.

new plan with all its risks. But with no such relief from odious and onerous duties of discipline, the professors could reap no advantage from the change commensurate with the evils it might inflict.

What we want most of all is some effectual legal means of enforcing discipline by compelling evidence, and this can only be secured by legislation directed to that end. It seems, however, to be generally thought that the difficulties in the way of such an organization are too serious to justify the hope that with any recommendation of the Board the Legislature would be induced to frame a series of laws for the purpose.

You thus see we are on the eve of interesting discussions, if not momentous events. . . .

It may easily be imagined that Mr. Rogers needed rest and relaxation after his year of arduous and difficult service as Chairman of the Faculty, especially as this service was added to the regular duties of his professorship. He therefore turned his face northward and, after a brief stay in Philadelphia, made with his brother Henry a journey through the White Mountains of New England. It was on this journey that the brothers found themselves fellow-travellers with the family of Mr. James Savage, of Boston, whose eldest daughter afterwards became Mr. Rogers's wife.

Later in the season the brothers William and Henry visited the shores of Lake Superior, which Henry was under engagement to explore for Boston friends with a view to the location of copper.

The following incident is taken from Mr. Rogers's note-book of this tour: —

. . . "Here I found a congregation of eager travellers, preparing, some of them, to enter upon their lake rambles, others to return to winter on the inhospitable shores of the great inland sea.

"One of these persons especially excited my curiosity and conduced to my inward mirth. He had scarcely seen me landed when with oiliest speech imaginable he propounded question after question with a deliberation and searching personality quite overwhelming. He was accompanied by an oldish, plain, blunt man, who, without knowing the difference between a copper vein and a weathercock, had no doubt been selected by one of the countless mining companies of New York to explore and report to them, on the ground of his perfect honesty and singleness of purpose. The good, simple-hearted old gentleman told me an amusing story of one of his co-representatives of the mining corporation. This worthy, sent to the mining country to explore and secure proper locations, stopped on the way at Detroit, and was there found by my informant, quietly writing a detailed report of the location, with the contents and character of all of the veins, the whole material of his long document being derived from verbal reports communicated to him in Detroit. When the old gentlemen expressed surprise at his pretending to give a detailed account of the country without even looking at it, he promptly answered that he was quite certain of being able to furnish a much fuller and more accurate account of the company's location by availing himself of the information accessible in Detroit than by visiting and exploring the location in person. The report, drawn up by one who is, I suppose, an expert lawyer, — I forget his name, — will no doubt appear in print, and make quite a sensation on Wall Street."

When the time came for Mr. Rogers to return to the University, he left Henry at Lake Superior and travelled to Virginia by the lakes and Albany.

In his farewell letter to Henry the following occurs: —

SAULT DE STE. MARIE, September, 1845.

MY DEAR HENRY, . . . I shall be almost continually thinking of you, my dear brother, and shall never lie down at night without sending from a full heart my anxiously affectionate wishes towards you. While painting the wild scene around you, on the heaving waters, along the pebbly or the rocky coast, in the mazes of the entangled swamp, or upon the fir-spread couch of the tent, brightened and warmed by the blazing log-fire, I shall long earnestly that I were still the companion of your wanderings and toils, and the helper of your researches. . . .

On the lake steamer he addressed to Mr. George S. Hillard, of Boston, a friendly letter, to which the following was the reply: —

FROM GEORGE S. HILLARD, ESQ.

BOSTON, October 18, 1845.

I am much indebted to you for your kind and warm-hearted letter and the friendly interest it expresses. In making the acquaintance of you and your brothers, I feel that I have added much to my stores of social wealth. A man does not easily make new friends after thirty, at least a man so reserved as I am; but you and your brothers seem like old friends, and my nature flows into yours as readily as one stream into another. It is a great pleasure to me to have the opportunity of contributing to Henry's comfort, and to give him the refreshments and satisfactions of home. He is like a brother to me, and I look forward to a happy winter in his society. . . . You belong here, in dear Massachusetts, dear in spite of its stormy coast and barren soil, and were I a dictator, I would transplant you at once. And another thing would I do for you, — persuade you to surrender to the silken yoke of matrimony. You have too warm a heart and too domestic tastes not to twine some gentle being's name with yours. So pray, set your face northward and wifeward.

Our social life is relapsing into its usual winter channel. The season promises to be very gay, the natural consequence of a very prosperous year. Every interest in New England is in a palmy state of success; whether we are not, morally speaking, waxing fat and kicking, may be doubted. The native American party in this State is pursuing a most unprincipled and mischievous course, and I fear the most disastrous consequences from them. There is no greater evil in our country than the formation of parties upon collateral and immaterial issues, for the end is always to throw power into the hands of that party which pursues its ends with an arrow-like directness, which always presents an unbroken front, and which has a polypus-like power of reunion whenever it is severed. There are and can be only two parties in a country like ours: the conservatives and the destructives; I do not like this latter word, but you know my meaning, the antagonism of conservatism. Mr. Caleb Cushing delivered a lecture here, a night or two ago, which (as I learn, for I did not hear it) was very pernicious in its tendency. It was a glorification of our country and an abuse of all others, and an exhortation to do everything to advance the physical greatness of the country, to get all the land we can, and make ourselves as formidable as possible, but not one word of warning, or rebuke, no vibration of a moral chord. I have no patience with a public man who thus panders to the worst passions of the multitude, instead of elevating and improving them. . . .

The Savages are all well and hold you in fresh remembrance. . . .

The Lyells[1] are at the Tremont House, but I have not seen them. . . . Our new house will be finished before your next summer's flitting, and I shall depend

[1] Mr. Lyell had come to Boston to give another course of lectures at the Lowell Institute.

upon a long visit from you. We shall always have a "chamber in the wall" for any of your name.

As may be gathered from Mr. Hillard's letter, it had already been arranged that Henry should leave Philadelphia and make his home in Boston in the house of Mr. Hillard. This, on his return from Michigan, he did. Amidst his regular duties, William found time to write the preface to an American edition of "Turner's Chemistry," which had been prepared by his brothers James and Robert and which was now issuing from the press.

WILLIAM TO HENRY.

UNIVERSITY OF VIRGINIA, December 3, 1845.

. . . Robert is pushing on actively with some chemical matters in which we are jointly engaged, my share being chiefly that of office counsel, and he doing most of the laboratory work.

James writes that he has just completed the index, and that we may expect to have the book in the market in a few days. When you meet with a copy, I wish you to look over the article on Heat, which I think you will pronounce to be a great improvement upon Turner. . . .

My dear Henry, I revert hourly in affectionate sympathy to all your plans and interests, and more than ever long to be joined in labour and in social relaxation with you. You are right in your view of the advantages of the quiet we enjoy here for literary pursuits, and could we now and then exchange the monotony of our life for the happy excitement of a truly refined and stimulating intercourse, we could have no reason to complain. But I am cultivating cheerful contentment with things as they are, looking for happier conditions of life in the future— that future which I yet, even as when a boy, gild with a brightness which sober folks might deem poetical....

William had desired Henry to report to him concerning the feeling in Boston and at Harvard in regard to the advantages and disadvantages of having for a university a President, instead of a Chairman of the Faculty. The following opinion of President Quincy is now an educational curiosity: —

HENRY TO WILLIAM.

BOSTON, February 25, 1846.

... Yesterday in a long conversation with Mr. Quincy, the old gentleman told me that he deemed the functions of the President of the utmost relief to the Faculty. He had no duties as instructor, but his great business was to overlook the conduct of the young men, and by timely interference prevent bad habits, detect delinquencies, and administer reproof and punishment in all instances in which he could, apart from the Faculty. He will, he says, give any information the Visitors or Faculty may desire, and he sends, at my suggestion, a copy of his pamphlet to Mr. Cabell, Mr. Stevenson and Mr. Randolph. I shall mail them to-day....

The following letter probably marks the first step towards the intimate relations which now exist between the Lowell Institute and the Massachusetts Institute of Technology: —

HENRY TO WILLIAM.

BOSTON, March 8, 1846.

A few days ago I mentioned how my affairs were looking,[1] and promised to write again whenever I should gather any further knowledge of the intentions of the Corporation [of Harvard University]. ... It

[1] Henry Rogers was at this time a candidate for the Rumford Professorship at Harvard.

has been Peirce's darling wish for a long time past
to reorganize the Scientific Corps of the Faculty;
but this they cannot do, with —— in the way, and
he fears that if the Rumford Chair is filled without
other changes being made, a golden occasion will be
lost for the more thorough reform which he desires.
. . . If they can effect what they desire, they will
make a sort of extra-faculty school of science for the
use of young men who desire a scientific education
without the diploma of the college and without the
classics, etc., and who would not even be undergradu-
ates of the college. And they would place the Rumford Professor at the head, in the central position in
this corps, and select him for his practical familiarity
with the useful arts, — a man such as Treadwell might
have been if he had given himself to the chair only.
Whether this is a feasible plan, I am not quite prepared to say, so difficult would it be to find a mechanician, an accomplished engineer in the wider sense,
who would also be an able teacher; but if successful,
it would be a good thing for this community and for
the college.

But I have to speak of another interesting matter.
Mr. Lowell, with whom I have been talking, after mentioning the feature in the Lowell will which enjoins
the creation of classes in the Institute to receive exact
instruction in useful knowledge, requested me to give
him, in writing, the views I had just been unfolding of
the value of a School of Arts as a branch to the Lowell
Institute. My communication to the corporation has,
I am sure, made an impression on him, and it is possible he has seen, by what is there stated, the importance of teaching science in its applied forms in this
community. He is a very cautious man, desires never
to make a mis-move, fears to expand his Institute too
fast, and has had doubts of the practicability of at-
taching this sort of practical College to the Institute,
lest it might be too large an affair to build; but he
sees its value, and now is a fine occasion to inspire

him with the zeal which he is quite capable of feeling
in its behalf. His plan would be to teach the operative classes of society, — builders, engineers, practical
chemists, manufacturers, etc.; to admit in the first
year only in limited numbers, and to teach them regularly; to have, perhaps, two permanent and salaried
professors at the head of it, and to make up the rest of
the instruction by assistants and by teachers, who would
give courses of instruction occasionally on special
branches. How much I want you near me at this time
to aid me in digesting and submitting my views on this
important scheme to Mr. Lowell! If you and myself
could be at the head of this Polytechnic School of the
Useful Arts, it would be pleasanter for us than any
college professorship, for there would be less discipline, indeed, no more than with medical students.
At no distant day, if not indeed soon, Mr. Lowell will,
I hope, organize such a branch in his Institute; and if
he does not, you and I can surely get one founded here
by going about it in the right way. Let us give this
matter our earnest and sober thoughts, remembering
that if I get the professorship in Harvard, it will
rather promote the plan than mar it. Can you send
me a copy of our memorial on behalf of the Franklin
Institute for a School of Arts?[1]   I have none by me,
and shall write to-morrow to Philadelphia for a copy;
perhaps you have one, but what is better yet, give me
your ideas in a letter, however hastily expressed, as
soon as conveniently practicable, and tell me where I
can see what was said at the starting of the London
Mechanics' Institute, etc. Take Robert into counsel,
and draw up a scheme of study : enumerate the things
to be taught, the nature of the apparatus for instruction
aiming at economy, and show me your ideas of the
value of science in this its great modern application
to the practical arts of life, to human comfort and
health, and to social wealth and power.

[1] A Memorial to the Legislature of Pennsylvania, presented about
1837. (See p. 263.)

UNIVERSITY OF VIRGINIA, March 13, 1846.

Your interesting letter of the 8th inst. came to hand this morning. Your prospects of some acceptable place in Harvard are, I think, almost as good as could be wished, and should the proposed change be effected, I should count certainly on your success. Were this or any other promotion of your views to lead hereafter to a closer union of our labours by placing me also in the congenial air of Boston, I would indeed rejoice. Under circumstances so auspicious for effort in teaching and research we could, I am sure, both of us be more productive and far happier in our labours than can be now. Ever since I have known something of the knowledge-seeking spirit, and the intellectual capabilities of the community in and around Boston, I have felt persuaded that of all places in the world it was the one most certain to derive the highest benefits from a Polytechnic Institution. The occupations and interests of the great mass of the people are immediately connected with the applications of physical science, and their quick intelligence has already impressed them with just ideas of the value of scientific teaching in their daily pursuits. Besides this, the high prevailing taste, diffused from the upper to the inferior classes of society, inspires an earnest appetite for richer intellectual food than they can now readily obtain.

Mr. Rogers then goes on to formulate at length, in answer to Henry's request, a plan for a Polytechnic School in Boston (see Appendix [1]), and continues: —

I must hastily close. To-morrow, or at farthest on Sunday, I will jot down some details as to the practical bearing of the different branches of physics and

[1] Page 420.

chemistry, that Mr. Lowell may see how grand a field of beneficence lies before him.

Your devoted brother,

WILLIAM B. ROGERS.

UNIVERSITY OF VIRGINIA, March 13, 1846.

As to-morrow will allow me no leisure, I embrace the hour before bed to make some additions to the matter of my letter committed to the mail this afternoon, intending to complete on Sunday what I have to say.

The true and only practicable object of a Polytechnic School is, as I conceive, the teaching, not of the manipulations and minute details of the arts, which can be done only in the workshop, but the inculcation of all the scientific principles which form the basis and explanation of them, and along with this a full and methodical review of all their leading processes and operations in connection with physical laws. When thus instructed in applied science, the mechanician, chemist or manufacturer, clearly comprehending the agencies of the materials and instruments with which he works, is saved from the disasters of blind experiment, guided securely because understandingly in a profitable routine, or directed to the contrivance of new and more efficient combinations. Were it necessary at this day to adduce proofs of these practical fruits of instruction in physical science, we might boldly refer to the unexampled progress of every branch of the arts for the last fifty years as but the result of the general diffusion of a better knowledge of physical laws, which has flowed from the researches of men specially devoted to natural science. Bearing in mind, too, how few of the almost countless products of ingenuity, even in these times, are of real and permanent value, and how immense the number of utterly barren inventions, the laboured contrivances of acute but undirected or misguided minds, we cannot but believe that, with a proper training in science, the host of unprofitable inventors living within the last half century would have contributed innumerable really valuable aids to human industry, and have advanced the arts to a stage of far higher improvement than they have yet attained. What stronger argument on this head could be asked than a glance at the encumbered cases of the Patent Office in Washington.

Among practical pursuits there are perhaps none whose dependence upon the determinations of physical science is more generally recognized than those of the machinist, the engineer and the architect. Yet even in these professions, while all admit that many of the details are but immediate applications of the leading laws of mechanical philosophy, how few have formed a just conception of the variety and extent of the sciences they involve. In the first place, the materials used must be studied in their more important mechanical and chemical relations. The strength of beams of timber and metal of various shapes and dimensions, and placed in various attitudes in buildings or machinery, must be computed by formulæ derived from scientific researches. The direction and energy of the forces distributed to different parts of the structure according to the arrangement of the several parts, and the position of the load or other pressure, require also to be known, and can only be learned by an appeal to the principles of mechanical science. So also, the durability of the materials employed in masonry can only be safely inferred from a knowledge of their composition, and the chemical actions to which they will be subjected when exposed to the air or water, or both, or when submitted, as in the walls of a furnace, to intense heat.

The machinist should, moreover, clearly understand all the principles of equilibrium and of the composition of forces; in other words, the general doctrines of statics and dynamics, those of friction, whether sliding or rolling, the mode of operation of the various motive powers of which his mechanism is to be the conductor, and the methods of computing the relation between the force applied and the useful effect obtained, or, in other words, the economical value of the combination.

The road engineer, with as ample knowledge in all these particulars, should further have a good acquaintance with the mineral and geological character of the region in which he operates, should know when to interpret the appearances on the surface, either as an encouragement or warning, in directing his tunnels or other excavations, should be prepared to judge of the value of the rocky materials he encounters in building an embankment, and should be qualified to form an estimate of the relative advantages of different districts as influenced by the extent of the mineral products.

Instruction in all these and other kindred particulars, essential as it is to the fullest success in the several pursuits referred to, involves, it will be seen, no insignificant acquaintance with some of the leading branches of mechanical and even geological and chemical science.

If we turn now to the manufacturing arts, we shall find an equal, and in many cases even a more urgent demand for scientific guidance. . . .

The remainder of this letter has not been found; it formed a portion of the "Plan" given in Appendix C.[1] (page 420).

UNIVERSITY OF VIRGINIA, March 21, 1846.

DEAR HENRY. — Owing probably to the freshet in the Susquehanna, your letter of the 16th did not reach us until this morning; from the same cause I presume you will not have received my last, also mailed on the 16th, until now. In that and the preceding I have endeavoured to put forth the practical considerations which occurred to me as strongly recommending a Polytechnic School, and I trust you will find my sug-

---

[1] The missing portion was afterwards discovered, and is included in Appendix C.

gestions of use in drawing up the proposed memorial to Mr. Lowell. There is certainly no place on this side the Atlantic where such an institution would be more useful and popular. If well managed it would give Mr. Lowell just cause for being proud of the wise liberality of the appropriation.

After writing my last I remembered that in both my letters I had omitted to mention that I have no copy of the paper we drew up for the Franklin Institute, and that I do not think I ever saw it after leaving you on that occasion in Harrisburg. I trust you will be able to recover it in Philadelphia, as it contained a clear and forcible exposition of the subject, that might be of much use in framing your memorial.

. . . I long for an atmosphere of more stimulating power. College recluses are liable to become in some degree mentally asphyxiated, and to avoid this state ought, if possible, to plunge often into the more oxygenated air of active, bustling life. . . .

Robert and I will put our heads together at once to plan your laboratory arrangements. I have already written out a pretty full scheme for lectures on Water. This, with some additional suggestions, I shall transmit in a few days.

To-day is, you know, my day of double duty. I have lectured this morning on astronomy, and at three o'clock I lecture on geology. I must, therefore, reserve the completion of this until after my lecture. . . .

We are all quite well and enjoying the delightful weather of the last few days. Be of good heart, my dear Henry, we are together strong, and delays, or even disappointment of hopes, should not mar our satisfaction. By and by we shall command all we wish.

Kindest regards to Mr. and Mrs. Hillard. I wish them all the enjoyments of the opening spring.

UNIVERSITY OF VIRGINIA, April 5, 1846.

DEAR HENRY, — I am yearly becoming more impatient of the lifeless routine around me, and will indeed be most happy to join you in any such scheme as that of a Polytechnic Institution, either under the wing of the Lowell endowment, or other suitable and adequate auspices.

You will soon begin, even in Boston, to enjoy the soft air and freshening verdure and bloom of spring. I confess, my dear Henry, I *long* to be able to walk with you and other friends on the Mall, to take an exhilarating drive to Brookline, or Cambridge, or the other neighbouring points of attraction, but above all to feel the impulses of a higher social life, which have so stirred my thoughts in my visits to New England. This is Sunday, and my thoughts have been with you and those around you almost since I awoke. I have thought in kind affection of all my friends, and in fancy been with you in Pinckney Street, and paid a delightful visit to Temple Court where I began to feel so much at home. . . .

UNIVERSITY OF VIRGINIA, May 30, 1846.

DEAR HENRY, . . . Have you seen Murchison's "Russia"? All the reviews are trumpeting its praise. Some time ago I mentioned his having adopted the translation-wave theory of drift, which in the "London Athenæum" is highly commended for its force and originality. The "London Quarterly" calls his work the *opus magnum* of Geology. . . .

. . . Could I but command some two or three months of unobstructed leisure at a good working season and have my present holiday time for the field, I could, I think, do a good deal at the pen. But as I am placed, my hours are but remnants of the day, in which I still feel the fatigue or anxiety of college duties, and there is no social stimulus to refresh and enliven the mind wearied with routine. . . .

UNIVERSITY OF VIRGINIA, June 19, 1846.

. . . After spending a short time in and about Boston, I propose revisiting Lake Champlain to settle my doubts on some points of the geology referred to by Emmons. My sections of Vermont being thus completed, and the obscurities referred to explained, we will, I think, have an interesting paper on that region ready for the New York meeting.

I have lately been reading "Frémont's Journal," with his map before me, and felt an itching impatience to be able, united with you, to reap a portion of the great geological field west of the Rocky Mountains. From the very centre of Mexico, all the way to the Columbia, is a *terra incognita*, rich, it would seem, in geological phenomena. Must we not, some day, try our hammers on the Sierra Nevada, and trace the Oölite formation and others already reported of? Is it not interesting to find coal fossils west of the Rocky Mountains bespeaking the Oölitic period, and thus probably the counterpart of our little patch near Richmond? . . . It will be no news to tell you that the Senate are now discussing a treaty with England, and that in a day or two we may look for its ratification. This will give new vigour to enterprises of all kinds, and will prove, I trust, the seal of perpetual peace between the two nations. Of what solemn and stupendous importance to the world is this event! A war now between us and England would put back for generations the swelling tide of benevolence and world-sympathy, which bears on its breast the hopes and aspirations of the wise and good. We may now look for the prevalence of humane and pacific counsels among all the great nations, — for what England and we exemplify and adopt for international control must finally become the law.

You see, my dear Henry, I have nothing to write of but my own thoughts, but these will I know come to you warm with a brother's earnest affection.

CHAPTER VI.

1846-1853.

Arrival of Agassiz in America. — Foundation of Scientific Schools in
Harvard and Yale. — Seventh Annual Meeting of Geologists and
Naturalists in Boston with Mr. Rogers Chairman. — James appointed
Professor of Chemistry in the University of Pennsylvania. —
William proposes to resign his Professorship and join Henry in
Boston. — Degree of LL. D. from Hampden-Sidney College. —
Organization of the American Association for the Advancement of
Science. — Henry again visits Europe. — His Letters. — He returns
and lectures in the Lowell Institute. — Death of James Rogers the
Uncle. — William invited to lecture at the Smithsonian. — His
Marriage. — Journey to Europe. — Birmingham Meeting of the
British Association. — Return to the University of Virginia. — Dr.
Wayland of Brown visits the University. — Kossuth's visit to Amer-
ica. — Illness and Death of James. — Robert appointed his Suc-
cessor.

THE summer of 1846 found Mr. Rogers again in
Boston.

TO HIS BROTHER HENRY AT LAKE SUPERIOR.

BOSTON, July 17, 1846.

. . . I was at Cambridge day before yesterday with
Sumner, and after listening to the closing class oration by young Phillips on mathematics, and taking the
usual lunch in his rooms, we adjourned to Longfellow's,
where we had a very pleasant sociable family dinner.
Mrs. and Mr. Longfellow made very kind inquiries
after you. Mrs. L. came up to me as I entered, and
in a very cordial manner took my hand and bade me

welcome, all the time thinking it was *you*. Lovering
was as kind as usual, and has just written to ask me
to come down and see him and Mrs. Lovering at
Nahant, where they are staying for her health. I had
some talk, also, with Peirce and Gray, who asked in
friendly terms about you.

Mr. Rogers returned to Virginia in the autumn,
and Henry writes to him from Boston.

BOSTON, October 7, 1846.

DEAR WILLIAM, . . . Agassiz has arrived and
will lecture [in the Lowell Institute] after I do. He
is a most amiable, engaging and philosophic spirit. . . .
We shall see much of each other, and I shall draw new
power and impulse from him. Verneuil [1] sailed yesterday in the steamer.

Agassiz can help us much in our researches among
our older fossils. . . .

BOSTON, October 24, 1846.

. . . Tell me where it was we found the fish relics
in the Matinal Limestone, and say if you have the
specimens, and if they are undoubtedly fish-like. It
will be a very important point if we can be the first
to contradict the declaration of all geologists that no
vertebrates occur in the older Silurian period. Agassiz
says we ought to find them even there, and the laws of
progression be still maintained. . . .

WILLIAM TO HENRY.

UNIVERSITY OF VIRGINIA, November 11, 1846.

. . . It rejoices me to learn that you are satisfying
yourself in your lectures; [2] that you would please your
class I never had the slightest doubt. And what a
class you have! Eighteen hundred or two thousand
auditors, such as one commands in Boston, is, perhaps,
the very best audience assembled anywhere in the
world to listen to instruction in science. . . .

[1] Edward de Verneuil, a distinguished French geologist.
[2] On Geology, before the Lowell Institute.

UNIVERSITY OF VIRGINIA, November 15, 1846.

. . . S——, from whom I have learned a great deal of Boston and Cambridge gossip, tells me that Everett is endeavouring to do away with the elective studies and make all the students pursue the same course as matter of compulsion. This, I suppose, is in imitation of the English universities, and is, I think, a *great stride backwards.* Better far to make all the studies *free,* and place Harvard at once on the broad liberal basis of one of the German schools. I ought not, perhaps, to speak so positively, as after all perhaps Mr. E.'s views are not what are ascribed to him, and may be judicious under the existing arrangements at Harvard. . . .

Robert and I have been making powder-cotton [gun-cotton], of which so much is said in the papers. Robert has now a small quantity which flashes off so instantly as not to fire the gunpowder upon which it is placed. It leaves no stain, and gives scarcely a perceptible smoke. I suppose by this time the Bostonians have seen this interesting product, as its preparation is not difficult, and Jackson would have the means at hand readily to make it. . . .

UNIVERSITY OF VIRGINIA, November 29, 1846.

Have you seen the October number of the "Athenæum"? It contains a rather brief account of the doings of the last British Association, and among other things some remarks of Lyell concerning the Richmond coal. You remember that in Horner's address Lyell is made to intimate his doubt of the accuracy of my reference of these rocks to the Oölite period. Now in one of these latter statements he distinctly declares that Agassiz has pronounced the fish to be *Oölite,* and Bunbury has recognized the group of plants to be the same as those of Whitby.

Mr. Rogers was under engagement at this time to deliver before the Mercantile Library Association in Boston a lecture on " The Atmosphere, or the Balance of Nature in the Vegetable and Animal Kingdoms."

TO HIS BROTHER HENRY.

UNIVERSITY OF VIRGINIA, December 6, 1846.

The time is drawing near, my dear Henry, when I shall have the joy of meeting you and other friends.

We are enjoying great quiet as yet. The professors have been giving the students a succession of very pleasant parties, and the utmost good feeling thus far prevails with nearly all the young men. The only symptom of mischief that has occurred was the explosion of a log loaded like a cannon on the lawn last night a little after supper-time. We have no apprehension of any recurrence of serious annoyances this year. . . .

Is Dr. Jackson's vapour, which divides the public ear with gun-cotton, anything more than rectified ether?

The " vapour " referred to was in fact " rectified ether," and its use marked the discovery of anæsthesia by this agent.

The following letters from Lieutenant Maury are of historical interest : —

OBSERVATORY, WASHINGTON, November 23, 1846.

DEAR PROFESSOR ROGERS, — I send a copy of our observations for 1845, of which I beg your acceptance. I have also sent a copy for the University, with a letter to the President, requesting the advice and aid of the Faculty in relation to our future operations. It is probable you will see that letter; therefore I beg to put you in possession of my views and wishes more fully than I felt at liberty to express them there.

In the first place, you know that the Observatory is yet an illegitimate concern, smuggled into existence under the name of a "Dépôt of Charts and Instruments," a circumstance significant enough of the hostility, or rather prejudice, still existing in the minds of the lawgivers to an Observatory.

Now to be useful the Observatory must feel that it is on its own bottom, firm and stable. This want of stability impairs its usefulness and prevents it from carrying out its plans with efficiency. . . . Should the work of the Observatory so far meet your approbation and give you confidence as to its management, any act on your part would help us along which would tend to strengthen our hands here for usefulness.

There was a bill unanimously supported by the Committee on Naval Affairs last session for separating the Observatory from the Bureau of Ordnance, and giving it a Bureau of its own. That bill comes up for final action at the approaching session; its passage would be productive of much good.

FROM THE SAME.

OBSERVATORY, December 7, 1846.

. . . There is a bill before Congress to establish a Bureau of Hydrography, or Longitude, which embraces the Observatory. The passage of that bill would place the Observatory where it ought to be, upon its own bottom, and give it the *lawful* consequence in the public eye which it should have to facilitate its undertakings. As for reasons : —

First of all, there must be an American Nautical Almanac; it is the tangible fruit of our Observatory. The arguments in favour of it are, that every maritime nation of the least importance in Europe has its own Nautical Ephemeris, and that it would cost little or nothing, for the sales to merchantmen would pay for the expense of computation and publication. The arguments in favour of a Hydrographical Office are of a like character. Experience has taught all nations the importance of an office with authority to collect hydrographical information. For the want of such information, we have witnessed the failures of several enterprises in the Gulf of Mexico against the Mexicans, for with proper information, Conner's attacks upon Alvarado would not have been the mortifying failures they are.

As to a chart of winds and currents, you recollect, which the American Geologists so heartily seconded me in, after much labour, and writing page upon page on the subject, I have prevailed on the Navy Department to order *one* ship to collect such information. With a Bureau of Hydrography the Chief would have authority to give the proper orders in the premises and enforce them.

Notwithstanding this, I have, after much entreaty and boring, been allowed the privilege of overhauling the old log-books for information, which is like hunting a grain of wheat in a bushel of chaff, and of constructing a chart therefrom. With such meagre materials, I am constructing a chart of the Atlantic, one sheet of which — the Gulf of Mexico — is now in the hands of the engraver. There is no telling the value even of this much. What appeared to be disorder and confusion among the currents there are thus made to appear all harmony and arrangement. The currents in the Gulf turn out to be rivers almost as sharp, constant and as well defined as the Mississippi itself. In fact, by the information which this chart already affords, the average passage from Havana to Pensacola, or Mobile, will be shortened at least one half, for we have revealed to us a current of three or four miles an hour, of which vessels thus bound may avail themselves for nearly the whole distance. This current was not known before. Like the shoals and channels of an unsurveyed but oft frequented harbour, the true draft of water that can enter is not known until the surveyor takes the soundings from his note-book and plots them down upon the chart. Then for the first time he comprehends the shape of the shoals and sees the winding of the channel. So with these currents, when we come to put down the tracks of two or three hundred vessels, each showing currents, the crossing of these tracks enables us to assign both limits and strength with much precision.

You can enlarge upon the ideas thus hastily sketched. They are the things upon which the arguments for a separate and efficient organization turn. A memorial to Congress upon the subject, I suppose, would promote the object in view. Anything you may be pleased to say as to the volume of Observations, and the importance of having them regularly published, will help me on with an appropriation for the next volume.

Mr. Rogers, in reply to Lieutenant Maury, sent a recommendation to Congress in behalf of a Bureau of Hydrography.

In December, 1846, Mr. Rogers was offered the professorship of " Mineralogy, Geology and Agricultural Chemistry " in the University of Alabama. The salary mentioned was $1,700 and house rent. It is hardly necessary to say that he did not accept the offer.

It was in 1847 that the foundation of the Lawrence Scientific School at Cambridge was laid by Abbott Lawrence, Esq., afterward United States Minister to the Court of St. James, who gave for the purpose at the outset the sum of $50,000.[1] Professor Henry Rogers, in a letter dated June 25, 1847, refers to the gift, and states that Mr. Lawrence was treating with Agassiz for the professorship of Geology, and with Courtenay (at that time Professor of Mathematics in the University of Virginia) for that of Engineering. He adds: " Courtenay would be well qualified, but he would hardly take a place worth at present perhaps less than $1,000, and hereafter only $1,500." We cite these facts as a contribution to the

[1] *Memoir of Abbott Lawrence*, by H. A. Hill, pp. 108-116.

SUNNY HILL, LUNENBURG, MASSACHUSETTS

educational history of the time, for it is worth noting that a scientific school was begun in 1847 at one of our most famous universities, with an endowment of (originally) only $50,000; that the chair of Engineering yielded but $1,000, or less; while the man naturally sought for to fill it, and regarded as "well qualified," was a university professor of Mathematics, who had had no other engineering experience than that of a West Point graduate.

The Scientific or "Philosophical" Department of Yale was first organized and opened to students in 1847.

Mr. Rogers, on the arrival of his summer holidays, journeyed to Massachusetts and visited the family of Mr. James Savage at their summer home in Lunenburg. As many of the happiest hours of his life were passed here, we give a brief description of the place.

Lunenburg is one of the typical "hill-towns" of Massachusetts. It is but sparsely settled by a farming community, though distant only a few miles east from the bustling manufacturing city of Fitchburg. "Sunny Hill," the home of Mr. Savage, commanded fine views of Mount Wachusett towards the west, and of many lesser hills on the horizon. In one of the valleys not far off winds the Nashua River, and in another, just below the Hill, lies "Whalom Pond," a beautiful lake bordered by sloping fields and woods. Here in complete retirement, yet only some two hours by rail from Boston, Mr. Rogers found for many years the perfect quiet, and companionship with nature, which are the best refreshments of the scholar. In this hospitable home the brothers James, Henry and Robert were also welcome guests.

In September, 1847, the seventh annual meeting of

the Association of American Geologists and Naturalists which had been organized, as above stated, in
1840, was held in Boston. At this meeting it was
voted that the Association " should resolve itself into
the American Association for the Advancement of Science, and that the first meeting, under the new organization, should be held in the city of Philadelphia on the
third Wednesday (20th day) of September, 1848." [1]

Mr. Rogers presided over the last meeting of the
parent organization and, as chairman, took a prominent part in the establishment of the new Association.[1]
At the beginning of October he was again at his post
in the University of Virginia.

WILLIAM TO HENRY.

UNIVERSITY OF VIRGINIA, October 3, 1847.

. . . The more I think of our plan of a Polytechnic
School, the more confident I feel of its rapid and great
success. The Lawrence School never can succeed on
its present plan in accomplishment of what was intended. It can only, as now organized, draw a small
number of the body of students aside from the usual
college routine. It should be *in reality* a school of
applied science, embracing at least four professorships,
and it ought to be in a great measure independent of
the other departments of Harvard. Besides, Cambridge is not the place for such a school. It should
be in *Boston.* Thus organized and placed, it would
really cover the ground of our School of Arts, and
would undoubtedly become very popular and be highly
successful.

In the autumn of 1847 James B. Rogers was elected
to the Professorship of Chemistry in the University of
Pennsylvania, to succeed Dr. Robert Hare, resigned.

[1] *Proceedings of the American Association for the Advancement of*
Science (1849), vol. i. p. 5.

All the brothers turned to William whenever they needed counsel, and especially for assistance and criticism in their literary or oratorical efforts. James now invoked William's aid in criticising his introductory address to be delivered on assuming the new office, and William, as usual, lent his aid : —

WILLIAM TO HIS BROTHER JAMES.

UNIVERSITY OF VIRGINIA, October 11, 1847.

. . . The task is finished, and I send you the remainder of the lecture, six pages, which, added to the twenty-eight despatched yesterday evening, will, I think, be quite as much as you can read. . . . The subject of *life* is a ticklish one, you know, with theologians ; but the view I take leaves full scope for the spiritual, while it is, I think, the truly logical one. . . . This literary task just completed has cost me a good deal of toil, more, perhaps, than if from the very beginning I had struck out in a path of my own. But I enjoy, I cannot tell you how much, pleasure in feeling that it will relieve you of so much trouble and anxiety, and help you to launch your bark successfully on the wider sea you are about to navigate. . . . In haste and tired,

Your ever affectionate brother,

WILLIAM B. ROGERS.

TO HIS BROTHER HENRY.

UNIVERSITY OF VIRGINIA, October 13, 1847.

. . . Do you hear anything further of this Chair of engineering? . . . If the course were devoted to applied mechanics, of which engineering would form a part, it would be more promising. In truth this department ought to embrace experimental physics in all its practical bearings, including the principles of Mechanics, Hydrodynamics, Pneumatics, Thermotics, etc., as the basis ; and then the discussion of materials, and the principles of construction, and the motive powers, with the machinery through which they are applied. How I long, my dear Henry, to be with you. We have not for many a year spent a *working* season together. I am sure we could accomplish a great deal by such a combination. To this my heart now looks with a pleasure I cannot express. . . .

William, Robert and James were now comfortably established in professorships, and Henry was doing well as a lecturer and geological expert in Boston. Nevertheless, mainly on account of a feeling of isolation, William began to think seriously of resigning his position in Virginia and going to join his brother Henry in Boston.

WILLIAM TO HENRY.

UNIVERSITY OF VIRGINIA, October 20, 1847.

. . . James delivered his lecture no doubt yesterday. He wrote in good spirits; the laboratory was looking vastly improved by its new arrangement, and students were pouring in rapidly upon him. Notwithstanding the increased length of the session, the University was looking for a large class. Household arrangements were progressing in the new residence, and, in a word, all things looked bright, as they certainly ought to do. What a cause for continual rejoicing is this glorious success which James has had! That his course will be eminently satisfactory I am perfectly sure. The Introductory I regard as his only trouble, and hereafter I would advise him to make it an extempore one. I have great hopes that the happy circumstances in which he is now placed, and especially the large leisure and means they will give for renewing his health by wholesome travel and occupation, will be of great service to him in a variety of ways. . . .

Your letter, written immediately on your return, gave us great pleasure. I have since thought of you daily as one of the circle of dear friends at Sunny Hill, and have gone with you to the many beautiful points around, now so dearly familiar to my thoughts.

From some observations I made last year, I am doubtful of Dalton's Law, *that the amount of gas absorbed by water is in the exact proportion of the pressure.* We are constructing a new, and I think beautiful, arrangement for testing it, and whatever the results may be they will be worth publishing.

Things are very quiet here. The class numbers 196, and my colleagues are all in the greatest glee.

Would it not be well, as occasion offers, to sound some of the leading practical men in Boston on the subject of our scheme? . . . I confidently think that after taking time to digest courses of lectures on practical subjects, we might even a year hence command immense classes from the ranks of the mechanics, manufacturers and part of the merchants of the city. . . .

My heart is full of confidence, and I look forward with unmixed happiness to the time now approaching when I shall be able to join you in preparing for our common effort and our common engagement in the ample and grand theatre which Boston offers. . . .

UNIVERSITY OF VIRGINIA, November 3, 1847.

. . . But by and by, my dear Henry, we shall I trust be able, shoulder to shoulder, to win a position in which we may enjoy ourselves in science and socially, free from all anxiety and in a spirit of entire independence. We must be satisfied, for a time at least, with moderate success, and in wise culture and relaxation must seek that happiness which without them, wealth and a brilliant career cannot give. . . .

UNIVERSITY OF VIRGINIA, December 27, 1847.

. . . Robert and I pass much of our leisure time in the laboratory, where we are busy completing our observations on the solubility of minerals. An incidental result of much interest has disclosed itself since our determination of the great *volatility of potash and its carbonate*. We now see the reason for the absence of alkali from the ash of coals and lignite. *It is dissipated by the intense heat* necessary for their incineration; and for the same reason, it is obvious that the usual mode of finding the alkali in plants, by first reducing to ash, must involve serious loss. Powdered anthracite, etc., yield alkali readily by our extemporaneous process with CO_2 water! In this way, too, we can procure it from powdered woods of all kinds. . . .

So volatile is potash that the tache from a drop on platinum is dissipated in two seconds by the heat of the mouth-blowpipe. Lime is scarcely altered, magnesia is enfeebled, soda disappears in thirty seconds, and lithia in half that time. You thus see how different will be the behaviour of the tache from a feldspar, a hornblende, a serpentine, etc. Our experiments are so delicate now, that the *solution of the glass of the bottles* forms a source of embarrassment, and we are going to use more powder, shorter time and frequent agitation. You spoke in your last of sending an abstract to " Silliman : " I hope you have had time. At any rate, you must prepare an account of your geological matters for the next number. . . .

I form many a delightful picture of our future union in scientific labour. One of the first cares will be to fit up a neat working laboratory with all the more delicate equipments. There we can pursue analysis, and perhaps, if we chose, we might have a few pupils and then we might push on most happily our various matters of research. There are innumerable directions in which discoveries are readily within reach. In these late experiments scarcely a day passes without disclosing some new collateral inquiry, which, if followed, would itself prove the parent stem of others. The wide field of general chemistry is all to be re-explored, and is, I think, a far more inviting

and elevated ground than the organic chemistry which
is now so passionately occupying the majority of in-
quirers. The latter is becoming a complex mixture
of facts and mere interpretations, while the greater
number of chemists seem, in utter neglect of a sound
philosophical logic, to be setting forth mere formulæ
as the true pictures of natural relations. Berzelius is,
after all, among the wisest of them; and Liebig, with
all his genius, is, I fear, giving support to much error
as well as much novel truth. . . .

HENRY TO WILLIAM.

BOSTON, February 19, 1848.
. . . The business of framing a new constitution
for the Association of American Geologists need not
engross much of my time. . . .
I send you the advertisement of the Lawrence
Scientific School. I shall watch their progress with
interest.

The announcement of the Lawrence Scientific
School referred to is dated "Cambridge, February
17, 1848," and is issued by Eben N. Horsford, as
Dean of the Faculty. The following paragraphs may
be quoted: —

"Candidates for admission must have attained the
age of eighteen years; must have received a good
common English education, and must be qualified to
pursue to advantage the courses of study to which
they propose to give their attention. . . .
"The number and choice of studies to be pursued
are optional on the part of the students, who will,
however, be counselled on these points by the Faculty.
Attendance on the lectures and recitations is voluntary. For this, as well as other reasons, the government of the University wish wholly to discourage the
resort of young men to the Scientific School who do

not, in the opinion of their parents and guardians, possess that stability of character and firmness of purpose which will ensure a faithful performance of duty without academic discipline."

WILLIAM TO HENRY.

UNIVERSITY OF VIRGINIA, February 27, 1848.

. . . From the advertisement of the Lawrence School, I judge the authorities are very anxious to invite students to the department. . . . If they would put it on a right footing, making the courses numerous, full and practical, and under charge of professors having no other duties in the college, it would by and by command large numbers. . . .

In a couple of weeks I shall send in my resignation to the Rector. It will create quite a stir and occasion no little regret. Harrison and his wife are quite downcast about it. . . .

UNIVERSITY OF VIRGINIA, March 9, 1848.

. . . This week I shall draw up my letter of resignation, so as to send it to Mr. Cabell, the Rector, some two weeks before the required time. This I do in courtesy to the Board, that they may have the longer interval for choosing a successor. . . .

Mr. Rogers duly sent in a formal letter of resignation, and received from the Hon J. C. Cabell, Rector of the Board of Visitors of the University of Virginia, a courteous reply.

UNIVERSITY OF VIRGINIA, March 14, 1848.

JOSEPH C. CABELL, ESQ., *Rector of the Board of Visitors of the University of Virginia:*

Dear Sir, — I write to notify you officially of my intention to resign my place in the University at the close of the present session. From the nature of my future plans, I have been for some time anticipating

an early removal to Boston, but until recently I had
not entirely relinquished the prospect of a somewhat
longer continuation at the University, and I have,
therefore, abstained from making an earlier communication on the subject.

I need not say how much it will pain me to quit
the literary home where, with some cares, I have
had so large a share of enjoyment and such valued
scientific opportunities. Nor need I speak of my
regrets at leaving the circle of friends throughout
Virginia whose intelligent regard I have felt to be
one of the most grateful of the rewards by which my
humble but earnest labours have been repaid. For
the last twenty years it has been my privilege to aid
in the scientific training of the young men of the
State, and it would, indeed, be strange could I contemplate, without strong emotion, a change which,
however desirable in itself, breaks up the kind associations which have yearly added to my interest in
the intellectual progress to which they are contributing so large a share.

During the twelve years of my connection with
the University, I have learned to value more and
more the scheme of the organization, the method
and thoroughness that preside generally in its halls
of instruction, and the enlightened devotion to its
interests of the distinguished citizens who form its
Visitorial Board.

As I have hitherto deemed it an honour to be numbered among its professors, so shall I continue to be
proud of what it has done and is doing for the cause
of sound instruction in letters and science; nor shall
any interests hereafter make me indifferent to its
prosperity, or estrange me from that kind regard for
its faculty and governors, which I shall carry with me
into my new home.

　　　With great consideration and respect,
　　　　　　Your obedient servant,
　　　　　　　　WILLIAM B. ROGERS.

FROM HON. J. C. CABELL.

WARMINSTER, April 2, 1848.

MY DEAR SIR, — Your favour of the 15th inst., announcing your intention to resign your place in the University at the close of the present session, reached me on the 24th. I confess that this annunciation took me altogether by surprise and gave me great concern. I had regarded you as permanently settled at our Institution, and was not apprised that you had an idea of removal. I am very sure that the regret which you express at the contemplation of the approaching separation is not greater than that felt by myself and the rest of the Visitors and the people of the State, in consequence of the loss which the University will sustain by your retirement. In view of the manner in which the duties of the Chair have been fulfilled, it will be no easy task to find a worthy and satisfactory successor. I cordially wish you success in your labours upon the new theatre of exertion upon which you will soon appear, and likewise happiness and prosperity in all your undertakings.

I am, dear sir, very respectfully,

Your obedient servant,

JOSEPH C. CABELL.

PROF. WILLIAM B. ROGERS.

WILLIAM TO HENRY.

UNIVERSITY OF VIRGINIA, March 21, 1848.

. . . I have sent my letter of resignation to Mr. Cabell. By this time I suppose he is aware of my purpose. I have also made known the change to all my friends. Harrison and family have been informed of it for a month past. I did not suppose it would produce such a shock as it appears to have occasioned to all to whom I mentioned it. They seem really distressed and confounded. They have valued me even more than I imagined.

BOSTON, March 26, 1848.

. . . I am also to examine the two tunnels of the aqueduct[1] for the Water Commissioners, a work of two or three days, for a fee of $100 ; at least, so says Robert's old friend Chesbrough, their engineer. Thus, you perceive, I have at all times a little professional work in prospect. When you come here to live we must have an office and laboratory, and what with such work and with lecturing we can make a very fair income and be our own masters. . . .

WILLIAM TO HENRY.

UNIVERSITY OF VIRGINIA, March 29, 1848.

. . . Every day brings me some new evidence of the regret occasioned by my resignation. The students generally evince much concern about it, especially my own class, and the very considerable number who expected to be with me the next year. I understand they say my place cannot be filled. Of course I am pleased with these marks of appreciation, but not the less happy in the prospect of my change. I do not doubt we shall do well in Boston. But to be happy we must not be over-wrought or over-excited. Moderate efforts with steady but moderate aims, and a proper appreciation of home enjoyments apart from ambition, will best conduce to our happiness. . . . What stirring news from France! Heaven prosper the movement to the best results. . . .

UNIVERSITY OF VIRGINIA, March 31, 1848.

I hope to be able this afternoon to send you a short account of our experiments on the diamond, which were completed with an entirely satisfactory result

---

[1] The Cochituate Aqueduct.

this morning.[1] But time has not allowed, and as
to-morrow will be my day of double work, I shall
probably be unable to draw up the statement in question until Sunday. I will at that time give you a
brief sketch of our process for the analysis of graphite,
with a diagram and some of the results. The pro-
cedure for the liquid oxidation of the diamond is the
same, but the resulting CO_2, instead of being arrested
by PO_3 in a Liebig tube, is passed into lime water.
We are quite pleased to find the result unequivocal
and striking, and think it will be regarded by chemists as interesting and curious. It is certainly entirely
new. . . .

UNIVERSITY OF VIRGINIA, April 9, 1848.

. . . I shall lecture for Robert to the chemical class
this week (Robert being ill). The subject is easy, —
the metals, — and I shall have but two lectures to
give. I find lecturing on chemistry a very easy business, especially as I have Robert's admirably digested
notes to aid me. The present little practice will be
of service to me. My own course just now is particularly simple, so that you must not fear lest I should
be overworked. . . .

On Saturday, James closed his duties by the Address. In Horner's absence on a proposed visit with
Wood to Europe, James is to act as Dean. This will
involve but little trouble through the summer, but will
give him a good deal to do at the opening of the next
session. It is gratifying to see how highly he is appreciated in the institution. . . .

Professor Henry Rogers had, during the winter,
made an attempt to secure from the Legislature of
Pennsylvania an appropriation which should enable
him to publish his final Report. In this attempt he
was bitterly disappointed.

[1] " Oxidation of the Diamond in the Liquid Way," *Silliman*, vol.
vi. p. 110.

UNIVERSITY OF VIRGINIA, April 15, 1848.

. . . Ere this, my dear Henry, you have no doubt heard from Harrisburg of the fate of the Report. Robert and I have been grieving this morning at the thought that this disappointment will prove much more painful to you than we had at first supposed. The despondent tone in which you close the letter received this morning has given us pain. But is it not almost certain that in another year a wiser legislation will prevail? And even should it not, in a scientific point of view you can reap higher advantages by devoting your time, by moderate and steady efforts, to the production of a systematic work on American Geology. With easy labours of authorship and occasional lectures in the Lowell Institute or elsewhere, and your geological examinations, you will be abundantly employed for the present, and who can doubt, my dear Henry, that before long some more permanent scientific plan will offer itself, in which you or both of us can happily engage. It is true your faithful labours and your unbending uprightness have in many instances been cruelly repaid, but then how much have you won of the love and respect of friends who appreciate you fully, and how strong have you grown in the opinions of men of science and the widening circle of your acquaintance. See, my dear Henry, how much cause there is for cheerful views of the present and for bright confidence in the future. Since this time last spring how great has been our common gain in the almost unhoped-for advancement of James to his present enviable place. To "labour and to wait," the former wisely and moderately, so as to make our tasks a pleasure, the latter patiently and in cheerful hope; these should form our plan. How much of true enjoyment lies before us, especially when we can all more frequently unite in science and recreation. The call for accomplished teachers of science is daily and rapidly augmenting. In the large cities, and Boston especially, we can surely have abundant employment in this way. Did I not think so I should be really pained to give up my present position.

MR. ROGERS TO MISS LUCY SAVAGE.[1]

UNIVERSITY OF VIRGINIA, May 8, 1848.

. . . Nothing could exceed the beauty of the gardens, fields and woods around us here. The mock-orange (*Philadelphus coronatus*) is loaded with fragrant blossoms, the honeysuckles of various kinds are filling the air with sweet odours, the locust-trees are hung with clustering flowers of the richest fragrance, and a multitude of other plants are blooming, or preparing to hang out their honours in the sun. Among these the roses are especially full of promise. All day the sound of bees and birds swells delightfully on the ear. How often, dear Lucy, have I wished that you could be here to breathe the warm, fragrant air, and feast your eyes and heart upon the beauty and music of the smiling, happy scene. But you will soon all take flight to sweet Sunny Hill, where like pleasures await you, and where Whalom and Wachusett will smile a sweet welcome on your arrival, and where the harsh eastern winds will not dare to follow you. Thither, by and by, I too will hasten. Will you not listen for the sound of the coach wheels in the evening, as they toil up the gravelly slope of Clarke's Hill?

TO HIS BROTHER HENRY.

UNIVERSITY OF VIRGINIA, May 10, 1848.

Your view of our future in Boston must, I am sure, be correct. We can find much to do undoubtedly in the line you mention, and I confidently believe we can soon get up a Franklin Institute, or School of Arts, which will be a source of great pleasure as well as

[1] Youngest daughter of Mr. James Savage.

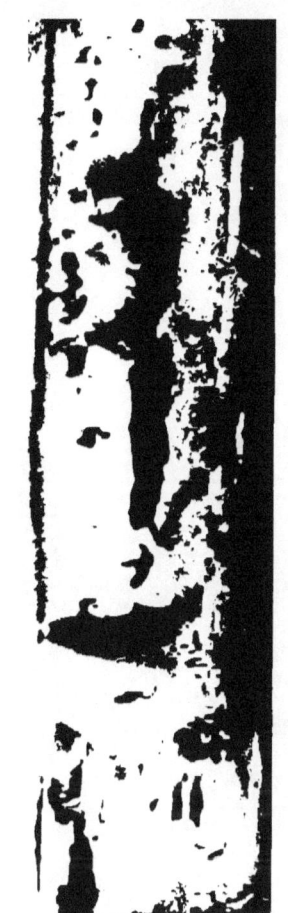

A VIEW FROM SUNNY HILL, LUNENBURG, MASSACHUSETTS

profit.   Could we not count certainly on large classes
from among the mechanics and merchants to patron-
ize lectures such as we could give on applied science,
and science in itself in its more elevated bearings?   I
am sure of it. . . .

TO HIS BROTHER JAMES.

UNIVERSITY OF VIRGINIA, May 12, 1848.

. . . We were delighted with your account of the
boys and Mary.   William [1] will become quite a politi-
cian, and no doubt a good Whig, during the Convention.   The skill he is acquiring in stenography may
be of much use to him and to you also.   I have often
wished that some one could have taken down my lectures on certain parts of my course; for I find that
in the free play of thought during the lecture I strike
out occasional new views or illustrations which I am
unable afterwards to recover, and which might be of
use at a subsequent time.

HENRY TO WILLIAM.

BOSTON, May 16, 1848.

. . . Letters have just come from Hillard from
Paris, where he arrived on the 23d day of the Elections. . . . Of the ability of the French for repub-
licanism I have not for a long while felt any serious
doubt.   Their political economy is not greatly to be
praised, but is our own?   In truth, the great science
of the adjustment of human labour is but in its infancy, and no country has hitherto legislated at all
upon commerce or labour with any light from the profound laws which experience is slowly evolving.   Certainly neither England nor New England need boast
of any wisdom in this branch of legislation, com-
prising indeed for the future, directly or indirectly,

---

[1] William Barton Rogers, 2d, eldest son of James B. Rogers, later
an assistant to his uncle Henry in the Geological Survey of Pennsylvania.

nearly all legislation. . . . I am at work on the new Rules for the Association,[1] a labour of some responsibility and trouble, as I am writing a few explanatory pages to go into the Circular. I think you will entirely approve of my Constitution, it is democratic, federal, flexible and expansive, progressive, with all the true conservatism these features imply. . . .

WILLIAM TO HENRY.

UNIVERSITY OF VIRGINIA, May 27, 1848.

. . . I see that in my new field I shall have more to do to make my reputation than I had anticipated. My position in the South for the past fifteen years has in some degree spoiled me. For a good part of that time my scientific rank has been fixed, and, as you know, I have been looked up to in Virginia and around as the authority in matters of science. My pride is not obstinate, or I should be concerned at the thought of having to take a lower place and again to work my way up the hill. But I do not doubt that I shall seek happiness in other objects than mere scientific rank or office, and ask only for independence and opportunities of being useful in teaching and research. . . .

HENRY TO WILLIAM.

BOSTON, May 30, 1848.

. . . Remember that at the American Association you will represent both yourself and me. I send you in two or three days the Circular for your suggestions and valued criticism before permitting the printer to strike off an edition. . . .

In spite of his determination to leave the University, Professor Rogers ultimately yielded to the solicitation of his friends in Virginia and the advice of those in Boston, and withdrew his resignation.

[1] American Association for the Advancement of Science.

WILLIAM TO HENRY IN EUROPE.

SUNNY HILL, August 14, 1848.

. . . What you say of Edinburgh and its environs in your letter to Mrs. B. touched my heart with a deep sympathy which you can easily understand. Even in this country in my journeyings I have once or twice caught those tones and looks of which you speak, which carried my heart back to the home of our childhood, and filled my soul with holy images of the loved ones that hung over us with such devoted affection. I verily believe, my dear Henry, that in spirit we truly sympathize with the Scotch character. Our philosophy will always take its mould from the closely analytic and inductive forms of the great teachers of Scotland. I can feel and think with a Brewster much more entirely than with a Whewell, or even with a Herschel. I trust, my dear Henry, you will see more of Scotland than in this first brief visit. There I am sure you could soon make good, enduring friends among the men of science. You will, of course, try to see Brewster and Forbes and Jamieson, etc. . . .

On August 4, 1848, Mr. Rogers was informed that the degree of LL. D. had been conferred upon him by Hampden-Sidney College in Virginia.

HENRY TO WILLIAM.

MERTHYR TYDVIL, SOUTH WALES, August 17, 1848.

. . . In Scotland I saw many of the northern geologists and some interesting portions of northern geology. Jamieson, Hugh Miller, David Milne, Maclaren, etc., among the men, and Arran, Glencoe, Glen Roy, the Highlands and Edinburgh among the scenes. I was both surprised and gratified to find our names familiar to the Scotch geologists, and really touched when I heard honest praise from Jamieson and others

of your own and Robert's chemical researches. I
passed nearly a week in Edinburgh and its vicinity,
and visited Melrose, Stirling and other scenes of
great beauty. At Glasgow I was hospitably received
by Nichol, and went thence to Arran, and afterwards
to the Highlands. Among my pleasures in the beautiful and grand mountains of Scotland, not the least
was my visit to the Parallel Roads of Glen Roy, and
my success in solving the problem of their origin. I
shall give my views to the Geological Society, and
in my next, if time permits, shall sketch to you my
theory. From Scotland, where I felt like a native,
who, after a life's absence, had wandered home to his
birthplace, I went to London to join Lyman,[1] and
came to Swansea.

The meeting of the Association has been one of fair
average merit, not a brilliant one by any means. The
geological section was somewhat spoiled by Sir Henry
De la Beche's presiding; he is excessively prosy and
wasted time fearfully.

Phillips has been a zealous and most useful friend,
and I shall have a glorious time this autumn in the
field with him in Derbyshire, with Ramsay in North
Wales, and Oldham in Ireland. De la Beche will
give me every facility. Brewster is very cordial and
kind, and so is Horner, Lyell's father-in-law. Lyell
was not at the meeting, being prevented by the illness of his own father. Murchison is in Italy, and
Sedgwick could not come. Sedgwick spoke lately to
Hillard of us both in terms of the warmest praise,
and I shall make him a special visit at Cambridge.
Daubeny was at Swansea, and invites me to Oxford;
he remembers you with much kindness. Sir Philip
Egerton invites me to Cheshire, and in fact, I have
more invitations than I can possibly accept. There
are about twelve of us here, at Dowlass Works, in the
luxurious mansion of Sir John Guest, and for two or
three days we shall have rare sport. Lady Charlotte
Guest is a woman of rare endowments and high intel-

[1] Mr. Joseph Lyman, of Northampton, Massachusetts.

lectual powers. We are already organized into sections, and to-morrow I entertain the company on the subject of earthquakes, with blackboard and chalk for my means of illustration. Wheatstone will give us some of his ingenious things, and Brewster is inexhaustible. Layard is here with his portfolio full of wonderful transcripts from the walls of Nineveh! friezes and inscriptions almost rivalling those of the age of Pericles, made by the Syrians eighteen hundred years before Christ.

I am losing the opportunity of a tour through the works, and you must therefore excuse my incoherent haste. . . .

When at Swansea I communed much with Owen, the naturalist. He is one of England's strongest men, gifted with an amazing perception of the profounder analysis of things. He was very cordial towards me, and I hope to profit by the intercourse on my return to London. I wish him to examine my specimens of *Mosasaurus* bones. . . .

WILLIAM TO HENRY.

UNIVERSITY OF VIRGINIA, October 13, 1848.

. . . Your last letter has given me and Robert more happiness than I can express. We have repeatedly followed your steps on our good maps, and I have tried to make myself, by reading and charts, more familiar with the Jura and Alps. What a glorious support for our generalization you have acquired in these journeys. I think you must be correct in referring to the Vosges as the great line of disturbance which has determined the form of the flexures. The rocks of that belt are, I believe, the old metamorphic, like our Blue Ridge and the region on its southeastern side. The existence of a great line of fault along Lake Neuchâtel would be interesting as forming a natural terminus to the series of related flexures. Just as is the case of the great lines of fault in southwest Virginia, etc., where the series of folds and flexures cease with the fault. But in the case you have been examining, the region beyond the fault (the Alps) has been subsequently very greatly invaded and disturbed, while with us the great Western coal-field has remained without disturbance. . . .

We see that the "Chemical Gazette" and Jamieson have republished our paper upon solubility of rocks, etc., but we have not seen anything of the communication on the absorption of CO_2 by sulphuric, which you read for us to the meeting. I am quite desirous that this should come out, as Noad and others have been denying our results, as formerly stated, and the brief paper sent you was, as I mentioned at the time, to satisfy those who were doubting on the subject. . . .

HENRY TO WILLIAM.

PARIS, October 25, 1848.

. . . I have had several interesting interviews with George Sumner, a brother of my friend Charles Sumner. He has been ten years in Europe, is very bright and full of historical and political knowledge, and is able to give me strange revelations concerning men and parties here. Just now all Paris is talking of the great chances there are that Louis Napoleon will be elected the first President; the day of election is set for the 10th of November. He is very weak intellectually, yet formidable from the blind veneration which the peasantry, especially of the south of France, entertain for the name Napoleon. Many people say that after him will surely come a king, Henry V. At present all is pacific in France, and externally Paris bears no marks of its recent turmoils. The National Assembly has finished with the Constitution, and the state of siege is withdrawn, and all without a sensation. My own belief is that France has seen the worst, and that with much political agitation for the next few years, she will gradually fit herself for republican forms, and resume her commercial activity.

HENRY TO ROBERT.

LONDON, November 5, 1848.

. . . As I stated in my letter to William I went to
the Institute and there saw Arago, Pouillet, Dumas and
other eminent men.   Subsequently, through the kindness of Pentland and De Verneuil, I saw and conversed
with Élie de Beaumont, Count D'Archiac, Valen-
ciennes and others.   Élie de Beaumont seemed right
glad to see me, and gratified me much by the manner
in which he spoke of the labours of William and myself in geology, and of the fraternal association of our
names.   He had read all we have written, and even
said, at the meetings of our Association.   My reception by D'Archiac was of the same flattering sort.
Being occupied on a work of the history of the recent
progress of Geology, the first volume of which is in
print, he. has been a careful student of American
Geology, and I found him well informed in relation
to our colours, which he seems highly to appreciate,
as I had already learned from his friend De Verneuil.

. . . Not only was it gratifying to find our names
well known in Paris by the geologists, it was more so
to perceive that the views we have contended for at
home, often in the face of a bitter opposition, meet
general approval.   Thus, our doctrine of flexures
being produced by an undulation of the crust will,
I feel convinced, meet a prompt reception by the
French geologists, even while many of the English
may hesitate.

LONDON, December 1, 1848.

I have returned from a visit of four days to Sedgwick, who entertained me in a most hospitable and
complimentary manner, at Trinity College, Cambridge.
He was delighted with our maps and sections.   I
dined at his table with Adams, Hopkins, Challis,[1]
etc., and had much pleasant chat with them there
and on other occasions about our geological generaliza-

[1] An English astronomer.

tions and other topics. I also saw Whewell, who is
certainly a Hercules in his way, and yesterday, at the
anniversary dinner of the Royal Society, sat between
him and Murchison. He asked me concerning some
points in my earthquake theory, and I entered into
the whole subject. He took a very large view of the
question, and pleased me by telling me not to be impeded by Hopkins's mathematics, for observation and
a common-sense view of the mechanism in such a case
was infinitely safer than the calculus. He said, moreover, what I had suspected, that Hopkins has passed
over greater unexplained elements to seize upon a
lesser one, and has been precipitate in deciding that
there can be no countervailing conditions connected
with nutation and precession. In fact, he thinks the
determination of thickness of the earth's crust, by
such a line of argument, quite wild. This gives me
new courage, for the geologists have had a supersti-
tious awe of Hopkins's mathematics, as Whewell says,
a lot of " Oxford superstition."

Professor Rogers, replying to a letter from a parent,
asking advice concerning the education of his son,
writes : —

TO JOSEPH ALLEN, ESQ.

UNIVERSITY OF VIRGINIA, October 7, 1848.

. . . We have as yet in this country no school of
mining and metallurgy, nor can your son procure at
any of our universities direct practical instruction on
this subject. At Harvard, the Lawrence School embraces a course of practical chemical analysis, and is
designed also to include a course on geology, but on
this latter subject, I believe provision has not yet been
made for instruction in mining and practical metallurgy. At Yale, the laboratory furnishes some facilities, but less ample than those of Harvard. At either
of these institutions he could, I think, obtain such a
knowledge of practical chemistry as would aid him in

his future vocation, and with this he should unite the study of mineralogy and geology, which, although not taught at those places to great extent, or with a systematic practical bearing, would throw a useful light on his pursuits. Were I to decide between the two institutions, I should be disposed to recommend the Lawrence School at Cambridge. . . .

In the beginning of 1849, Henry had returned from Europe, and was preparing to give a course of Lowell lectures on the Application of Science to the Useful Arts. William writes of himself and his classes to Henry in Boston.

UNIVERSITY OF VIRGINIA, January 26, 1849.

DEAR HENRY, . . . As I get on now with my classes, I think I shall be able to carry them through all that is needful in my department before the close of May, or at any rate, by the first week in June. The students seem all rejoiced at my coming back, and are willing to do all in their power to help on the course. The University has continued perfectly quiet from the opening of the session to this hour. At night not a voice is heard to break the general tranquillity. The kindest feelings prevail towards the college authorities. This is a truly gratifying state of things. . . . I weigh 135 pounds, which is quite a gain.

Early in March, 1849, occurred the death of Mr. James Rogers the uncle, some of whose letters have been given above and who had for some years made his home with William. In writing to one of the brothers, William says: " To me his loss is a sad blow, for he has for eight years past been my constant companion . . . and I feel truly desolate."

In May Mr. Rogers received a letter from Pro-

fessor Joseph Henry, detailing a plan for courses of
lectures in the Smithsonian Institution : —

SMITHSONIAN INSTITUTION, May 31, 1849.

PROFESSOR W. B. ROGERS :

My dear Sir, — Dr. Bache informs me that you
have made an interesting series of observations on
thunderstorms, from which it appears that storms
of this kind occur nearly at the same time, in patches,
along lines extending many miles in an east and
west direction. Please inform me whether your observations have been published, and if so, where I
can have access to an account of them.

We have commenced our courses of lectures in the
Smithsonian Institution, but shall not do much in
this line until after the meeting of Congress. The
plan we have adopted is that of inviting only those
who have distinguished themselves by original research, or those who can speak with authority from
their own experience on the subject on which they
lecture. Among those by whose assistance we wish
to make an impression on Congress, in the way of
improving the science of the country, are your brother Henry and yourself. I regret that our funds
are so much absorbed by the erection of the building,
that we are able to pay scarcely more than is sufficient to defray the expense, say twenty-five dollars a
lecture.

I remain, very respectfully, your obedient servant,

JOSEPH HENRY,

Secretary, Smithsonian Institution.

On account of ill-health Professor Rogers applied
for and received leave to close his courses at the
University somewhat earlier than usual. On June 20,
1849, he was married to Miss Emma Savage, eldest
daughter of Hon. James Savage, LL. D., author of the
"Genealogical Dictionary of New England;" and on

the same day sailed from Boston for England via Halifax, on the Cunard steamer *Europa.*

TO HIS BROTHERS IN AMERICA.

LIVERPOOL, Sunday, July 1, 1849.

. . . Our passage has been without any stormy weather, but excepting two days we have been continually in a thick, cold fog.

You will see in the paper that accompanies this a detailed account of the heart-rending casualty of which we were witnesses on Wednesday last, in the midst of the Atlantic. At a time when the fog was so thick that it was impossible to discover any object at a distance equal to the length of our own vessel, a ship of 400 tons, laden with iron and lead, and having on board 160 passengers, together with a crew of 14, advanced directly towards us. We were moving at the rate of 12 knots, and the approaching ship with all the speed her full-spread canvas could impart. Collision was inevitable, and it took place almost immediately after her sails were discovered from our deck. Our bow entered her a little behind the main hatchway, and, like an enormous wedge, actually penetrated nearly to the opposite side. An awful scene of silent horror ensued. Before the boats could be lowered to rescue the men and women and children crowding the deck, the vessel went down, and in the resistless vortex of waters carried down the greater part of those on board. Out of the whole, only about forty were saved, and of them but one woman, although there were forty women on board! . . . It was fortunate that our ship was so stanch at the bows, for the whole of the outer bow, or cut-water, was torn away, and even the main timbers beneath deeply lacerated. But not the slightest injury was done to her framing or butts. For a time, until this was confidently known, there was the most painful anxiety among those of us on board who understood the great peril in which we had been placed. Excepting this sad event, our voyage has been a very happy one. . . . Two or three of the passengers had been fellow-travellers of Henry, and knew me at once by our likeness.

The first sight of the Irish coast, near Cape Clear, and the view of that picturesque shore, as we sailed along and near it for many hours yesterday morning, filled my heart with a pleasure indescribably sweet and sad. I felt that its heathery hills and verdant slopes claimed something of a filial love, and spoke to me in our dear father's voice. God bless and prosper that beautiful but helpless land! We had a most charming run up the Channel yesterday evening and last night; and through the soft haze I this morning saw the bold outline of the Welsh mountains with an interest and delight which you can better imagine than I describe. My own dear brothers, need I tell you that I have more than ever tenderly and affectionately thought of you all. . . .

We reached London after a most charming journey. Mrs. Chapman [1] was expecting us, and had provided a comfortable room in a quiet part of the house. The position, 142 Strand, is good for sight-seeing, and the house is comfortable. . . .

TO HIS BROTHER HENRY.

LONDON, July 13, 1849.

. . . De la Beche has been extremely kind. Buckland gave up all the spare hours of last Sunday to us, and we breakfasted with him, attended service, and heard the wondrous harmony of the Abbey Choir and organ; then were conducted by him over all the Abbey, seeing many parts that are not commonly shown; then lunched with him. He spoke warmly of you. I have seen Playfair and Phillips, Mantell, Morris, Grant, Sowerby and Forbes, but as yet have missed Murchison and Mitchell. On our return from Scot-

---

[1] Wife of John Chapman, editor of the *Westminster Review.*

land I hope to see others, and, at any rate, I shall
meet them at the Association. . . .

Doubleday[1] has been as kind as any dear old friend
could be, and all on your account, my dear Henry. I
am quite charmed with the frank politeness and ever
active kindness of those we have met. . . .

It has been a source of no small gratification to
find our names so well known, and so respected by the
men of science. I need no other introductions, and
this I have been repeatedly told by those I have met
with. One gentleman, Professor Hopkins, of Cambridge, who was with us at the Dean's, and who spoke
highly of you, said that we really emulated the Greg-
orys of Scotland, and that it was truly delightful to see
four brothers all devoting themselves to science. . . .

What shall I say of this wonderful London ! At
first I could not take in the impression of its vastness.
But day by day, as I have driven from place to place,
it has grown upon me, until now I feel truly overwhelmed with the thought of its immensity. And yet
it is a cleaner and more quiet place than either of our
great cities. With all the amazing activity exhibited
in its thoroughfares, there is less noise and less of the
feverish driving than you witness with us. People
give more time to recreation and do not work so fast
as we do. The English character is altogether quieter
than ours. . . .

GLASGOW, July 19, 1849.

. . . I had the good luck to meet, in Johnston's
shop in Edinburgh, with Hugh Miller, who inquired
very kindly after you. He is much such a man as I
expected to see from your description. Just now he
is bringing out a little work designed as an answer to
the geological part of the " Vestiges," which, as I suppose you know, is now universally accredited to the
pen of Robert Chambers. . . .

Of all the places we have seen, Edinburgh is certainly the most picturesque and beautiful. The eye

[1] Edward Doubleday, English naturalist, 1810–1849.

could hardly tire of the grand scene before us, as we gazed from our window in Prince's Street over the deep and narrow valley of the Prince's garden, to the Castle, crowning with its irregular massive walls and battlements the lofty, blackened crag, and the towering walls of the strange edifices, which extend themselves thence towards the Old City, descending into the dark, narrow avenues of the Cowgate and Cannongate, until they are closed by the old, gray towers of Holyrood. . . .

We are both much pleased with the Scotch.

. . . My dear brothers, I could throw my arms around you in the fervour and fulness of my heart's love for you. God bless you. Be careful of your precious health. I trust dear Robert will use the season wisely for recreation, and that James will do likewise. I will collect all the information I can for them on chemical apparatus, etc., when I get back here and to London. . . .

LONDON, August 9, 1849.

. . . By the papers I see that great preparations are making for the Birmingham meeting, which promises to be an unusually large and spirited one. . . .

Mr. Clarke [the Rev. James Freeman Clarke] is now here, and will not leave for the Continent, I believe, until next week. . . . We shall regret to part with him, for we have really enjoyed his society since he came to London. But his plan of travel and his objects are so different from ours that our union would only incommode and obstruct both parties. We all went together last night to Astley's.

I may mention, as a good token in regard to my health, that in crossing Waterloo Bridge I was weighed by one of the convenient machines stationed there, and I came up to 145 pounds! My throat only occasionally gives me any annoyance, and then it is but slight. I expect confidently to go home enjoying better health than I have had for several years, but my throat will still require care.

HEIDELBERG, August 19, 1849.

. . . I hourly wish to communicate to you fully
all the pleasing impressions I receive in my travels
through this most delightful region, so beautiful by
nature and exquisite cultivation, and so rich in monu-
ments of the past.

Professor and Mrs. Bischoff[1] were affectionately
pressing in their entreaties that we would remain
longer in Bonn. Von Dechen was absent; Von Buch
had lately been at Bonn to attend a meeting of the
Naturforscher, at which Bischoff presided, but had left
for Berlin before we got to Bonn. Robert and James
need not be ashamed of their laboratory arrangements,
compared with those of Bischoff, or indeed any others
I have seen. Bischoff and Noeggerath repeated several times, with marked admiration, the fact that there
were four brothers of us all engaged in science. I
find that on the Continent the title of Professor is
one of the most valuable I could bear, and that being
known as an American is much in my favour. The
number of the English we meet in all the boats and
hotels is really amazing, and with them is no small
sprinkling of our own countrymen, none of whom, however, have thus far proved specially attractive. . . .

We spent the late afternoon yesterday in rambling
over the heights, which are occupied by the ruins of
the castle, and by its lovely parks and gardens, and
enjoying the superb views, afforded from those lofty
terraces, of the city, river, neighbouring mountains,
and the far-stretching Valley of the Rhine, walled
in on the horizon by the blue heights of the Vosges
in France. Nothing of the kind could exceed the
beauty of the cultivated plain and the mountain slope,
called the Bergstrasse, between Frankfort and this
place. Indeed, throughout all the Valley of the
Rhine and its tributaries, we have had but a succession of pictures, rich with cultivation and abounding

[1] Gustav Bischoff, Professor of Geology at Bonn.

in views combining all the elements of picturesque beauty.

But in this lovely land where the landscape is so smiling, there remain social features which the feeling traveller is called upon hourly to deplore. The people, kind-hearted and simple-minded as I think they are, and intelligent, as they certainly prove themselves, are sadly pressed down by their political institutions, and so strongly have the cords of power, aided by old prejudices, been woven about their limbs, that I fear a long time must elapse before they can place themselves in that erect and fearless attitude for which of late, many have been earnestly but blindly struggling. Nothing I have seen on this side the Atlantic has impressed me so painfully as the continual display of military force we meet with in our travels. All the towns are crowded with troops, chiefly Prussian. Frankfort is at this time occupied by Austrian, Prussian and Bavarian battalions. From every height on the Rhine the ramparts, bristling with cannon and resounding with the rattling drum, frown down upon the peaceful villages, and intimate to the traveller the fears of the rulers and the terrible scenes which are likely to result when the antagonizing elements are brought into actual conflict. Oh, how happy should we be in America, in that security and sanctity of personal rights and free progress which we enjoy !

We are now emerging from the region of almost unmixed Romanism into the land of Protestants. I am not sure that we shall find any great improvement of morals or of social comforts. . . .

We had much rain between Coblentz and Mayence, but were able to keep on deck and see every important site as we passed. The Old Slates, which are so largely exposed from time to time in the lofty hills on either side, reminded me continually of the aspect of our Matinal slate, as exhibited in the valley of Pennsylvania and Virginia, where it is most largely developed, and is barren of fossils. In this long section the dips, with one or two exceptions, are to S. E., but I discovered an alternation of steeper and gentler dips in that direction, such as I have marked in our folded rocks, and I have no doubt that the whole of this wide slaty belt consists of such folded masses. How curious that here, as with us, these and the other Silurians have a general N. E. and S. W. strike. . . .

I will try to make one or more good sections in the Jura, and as many in the Alps. . . .

TO MRS. JAMES SAVAGE.

GENEVA, September 7, 1849.

. . . I need not say, dear mother, that in all our journeyings and enjoyings we have wished that you were with us, for who could feel more deeply than you the happiness of communing with the beautiful Alpine flowers and the clear rushing streams, or the majestic solitudes where snowy Alps sit girdled by the clouds, or fold their glacier drapery around green valleys musical with tinkling bells or the soft voice of the rude Alpine horn. You will smile at the poetic vein into which my pen is falling, but no one better understands the enthusiasm which such scenes can awaken, and had you been with us I am sure you would say that the highest efforts of the descriptive muse must fail to paint the sublime and lovely scenes through which we have been travelling. Since Emma's last letter we have ascended the Valley of the Rhone to Martigny, have crossed the celebrated pass of the Tête Noir, and have sojourned for a day or two at Chamounix, where from the chamber window we commanded a superb view of Mont Blanc. The sky was clear all the time, and we saw the snowy slopes of this vast pile successively in the dazzling brightness of sunshine, in the exquisite rose hues of the evening, and in the soft phosphorescence of the moonlight. What pictures there and elsewhere in the Alps have been engraved upon our hearts! . . .

BIRMINGHAM, September 14.

We have been all the morning at the meeting of the Association, and are going by and by to the great dinner, where I suppose there will be much amusement in the way of speaking after the cloth is removed, and when I suppose I shall be compelled to show my Yankee "gift of the gab." We are having a very pleasant time here. The scientific gentlemen are very kind and complimentary, and Lady Lyell, Miss Phillips and others will help to make E. at home.

On our return to London, we shall see Mr. Kenyon [1] and other friends, and will not again ramble from the great metropolis, except on a short excursion to Oxford and Cambridge. Professors Buckland and Sedgwick, who are here, are very desirous of our making such a visit. . . .

TO HIS BROTHERS.

LONDON, September 21, 1849.

I have now for the first time, leisure sufficient for an account of the delightful meeting at Birmingham. By the last steamer I wrote a hasty line the day after I reached Birmingham, and before I knew much of the affairs of the Association. From the humble but comfortable quarters in which we had placed ourselves, we were soon transferred to the keeping of the city, and were placed in very elegant apartments in the superb edifice of the Grammar School, where most of the sections held their meetings. Here the kindness of Mr. Gifford, the principal, and his wife made us very comfortable. For this very pleasant and complimentary change we are no doubt indebted to the friendly suggestion of Phillips, Lyell and Horner, all of whom have been cordially kind in their attentions to us. Miss Phillips was much with E., and Mrs.

[1] John Kenyon, English poet, 1784–1856.

Lyell and Miss Horner displayed much interest in having her comfortable, and contributing to her pleasure.

No one could have been more warmly and heartily welcomed than I was, not merely by those who personally knew me, but by the scientific men generally, with the greater number of whom I soon became acquainted,—Darwin, Ansted, Ramsay, Mallet, Oldham, Griffiths and, above all, Murchison, Sedgwick and Phillips among the geologists, taking me cordially by the hand. Phillips, Murchison, and De la Beche were throughout generously kind to me, and Lyell and Horner scarcely less so. The chemists were no less hospitable,—Percy, Playfair, Hunt, Stenhouse, Warington, etc., all paid me kind attentions. In the physical section I was rarely able to be present, yet I esteem myself happy in having made the acquaintance of Brewster, Robinson, Adams and Faraday. But let me say a word of my own doings.

On Friday, the day after our arrival (which I regret we deferred so late), I made my début, as I mentioned formerly, in some remarks connected with Murchison's paper on gold veins. On that night another opportunity of a rather different kind was afforded me of speaking. This was in reply to a toast of Murchison, in which he referred to the corresponding members, naming you in terms of the strongest eulogy, and calling upon me, as Phillips had previously arranged. I made quite a respectable speech, which was often and loudly applauded, and at the close I was honoured by many flattering congratulations from De la Beche, Saboni, Dr. Robinson, the president, Phillips and others. This dinner was truly a grand affair. More than seven hundred were seated in a hall said to be the most spacious and elegant of the kind anywhere in Britain. You may imagine how my heart beat to hear your name so honoured, and to have our labours so warmly eulogized. I sat between Phillips and De la Beche, and near the president.

Forchhammer and Schroeter, of Jena, were also there, but had nothing to say. . . .

" Mallet," above referred to, was the distinguished English engineer, whose son, J. W. Mallet, afterwards for many years Professor of Chemistry at the University of Virginia, was also present at this dinner, and has described Mr. Rogers's appearance on this occasion : [1] —

" Although I was but a boy at the time," says Professor Mallet, " attending the meeting with my father, I recollect most distinctly the marked impression made upon the large assembly by Professor Rogers's speech, and the enthusiasm it kindled. It came late in the evening, after much, perhaps most, of the matter appropriate to the occasion had been already utilized by others ; yet it was clearly *the* success of the banquet. Americans were less known in England than they have since become, and the slight foreign flavour which accompanied a speech excellent in itself, and fluently delivered in the mother tongue, added to the piquancy and effect."

Mr. Rogers's letter continues : —

On Saturday the members occupied themselves with the various delightful excursions which had been so well planned for them. To Dudley, first to the remarkable ten-yard coal here on end, and then through the caves, or underground quarries, of enormous extent in the limestone, and which Lord Dudley had caused to be superbly illuminated. There in the cavern, while the blue and red lights were glowing in the distance, Murchison delivered a geological speech to some thousands. After escaping unhurt from the crowd and fumigation of the caverns, we passed with

[1] See an Address delivered before the Alumni of the University of Virginia, by William Cabell Rives, June 27, 1883.

the great procession to the base and sides of the Wren's Nest. There Murchison gave another geological harangue in which he again complimented us warmly by name, and called upon me, as a present witness to his Silurian researches. He was followed by Wilberforce the Bishop of Oxford, a truly eloquent speaker, and then I was compelled to mount the stump by a call from Murchison and from all around. . . . After a pleasant collation in Dudley, and sundry amusing adventures, we returned in one of the beautiful canal boats, at eight miles the hour, and were glad to get to bed and forget the pleasures and honours of the day.

On Monday I was chiefly active in the chemical section, sharing in several interesting discussions, for which, luckily, I had facts of interest to state. I gave as one, an account of the gaseous ingredients of our thermal and other springs, in connection with a paper on the nitrogen of springs, read by West, and I communicated in some detail the mode and result of our researches on the solvent action of carbonic acid, water, etc.

On Tuesday I made a communication on the geology of Virginia, specially referring to the features of our great faults. I did not occupy more than an hour, but Murchison, Lyell and De la Beche occupied even a longer time in expressing their sense of the importance of our joint labours. Indeed, they laid on the compliments so thick that I could hardly stand up under them. But it was a real triumph and joy to hear them successively declare that our development of the great law of flexures was one of the grandest contributions to geology ever made, and to find that they gave us the entire and exclusive credit of having thus furnished a clue to the most difficult problems in European geology. This really made me happy and proud, and I only wished, my dear Henry, that you could have been present to share in the enjoyment. You cannot imagine the degree of kindness with which inquiries were continually made after you.

Murchison and De la Beche, Saboni, Sedgwick, Pentland and Darwin are a few of those who repeatedly asked about you, and spoke of the pleasure your visit had given them. I should have named Brewster among the first. He said he had received great happiness from your society. What a charming man is this venerable Scotch philosopher! I could almost have knelt down to ask his scientific benediction. . . .

Wheatstone has marvellous ingenuity. He showed me his exquisite apparatus for making visible all the conditions and combinations of waves, plane, circular, elliptical, and indeed, of all possible forms. It is an admirable thing for the lecture-room, and I intend purchasing one, although it will cost ten pounds. . . .

In the Physical section, Robinson gave an interesting popular account of the late performances of Lord Rosse's telescope, which was perhaps the most attractive thing done at the meeting. Mallet's report on the statical and dynamic laws of earthquakes was able. . . .

WILLIAM TO HENRY.

LONDON, October 5, 1849.

. . . Yesterday we dined at Playfair's, and had a pleasant meeting with Wheatstone, Lancaster, etc.; to-day I go to dine at Miller's (of King's College), where I shall meet many of the chemists, among them Andrews of Belfast, and probably Magnus.[1] . . .

Since my last to you we have made a short visit to Oxford, indeed this was the cause of my not writing by the last steamer. We were delighted with the quiet beauty of the college grounds, and I felt the conservative spirit of the place sinking into my heart. But how shocked was I to find that the chemistry and botany of the great university was exhausted upon about ten students! Ackland, the anatomist, as well as good Dr. Bliss, Mr. Savage's friend, treated us with

[1] Heinrich Gustav Magnus, Professor of Chemistry and Physics, Berlin.

great attention. We are proposing going to Cambridge to-morrow, and tarrying there until Monday morning. There I hope to see Sedgwick, Hopkins, and perhaps other acquaintances.

After all, our scientific opportunities at home are nearly if not quite as good as they have here. The men of science are poorly paid and work hard, and then they have as a class an inferior social position.

Professor Rogers returned to the University of Virginia in October. Henry was in Boston, and the correspondence of the brothers was resumed.

HENRY TO WILLIAM.

BOSTON, November 14, 1849.

I thank you for your very kind letter of the 11th, and for your sincerely affectionate words. These are ever to me a source of cheerfulness and consolation, and they seem at this time of double value, coming when my spirit is oppressed with an unwonted sense of loneliness and of life's disappointments. In all hours of trial, in all time of need, your love has given me strength. The faith that some turn of fortune may bring me again to live, as in earlier blessed days, with you and our generous and gentle Robert has for a long while past been to me the one calm star of hope that, when all other beacons have gone out, has never once grown dim. Daily do I take counsel with my heart that it may keep itself worthy of a companionship out of which, if pure, it will derive a peace such as is not in store for it from any other earthly source. That Heaven may shed upon you both, my dear brothers, its sweetest blessings is my never ceasing prayer.

I rejoice to learn that your classes are so large. Yours even much surpasses my anticipations, and as for Robert's, it quite amazes me. . . .

They have filled the chair of Engineering at the Lawrence Scientific School a few weeks ago. Lieu-

tenant Eustis, a former colleague of William Henry
Wright, under Colonel Thayer in the construction of
the fortress in Boston Harbor, is the professor; he has
been of late an assistant professor at West Point.
Military engineering is hardly wanted in this community, and something more should be given in the Scientific School of the applications of physical science,
than even civil engineering. . . .

The "Warren Club," now called the "Thursday
Evening Club," has begun its meetings.

The Club here referred to, has long been one of the
best features of Boston life. It meets at the houses of
members on the first and third Thursday evenings of
every month from December to April. It is composed of gentlemen of literary and scientific tastes or
acquirements, and embraces in its membership professors, authors, scientific men, and leaders in affairs.
Literary and scientific essays constitute the chief interest of the meetings, although the social element is
not neglected. The club was founded by Dr. John C.
Warren, and named in his honor. He was succeeded
in the presidency by Edward Everett. On the death
of his son, Dr. J. M. Warren, who followed Mr.
Everett, Mr. William B. Rogers became its president.

WILLIAM TO HENRY.

UNIVERSITY OF VIRGINIA, December 16, 1849.

. . . What a scene is this our law-makers at Washington are presenting! Surely the people will punish the factionists for the danger which their passion
and party feeling are threatening to the country ! . . .

There is great excitement growing up in the South,
and I fear there will be great passion thrown into the
debates of the coming Congress by both sides. But as
yet I have no fear of the integrity of the Union.

BOSTON, December 22, 1849.

. . . I had the pleasure of making a few very agreeable acquaintances when in Providence, among whom I deem Dr. Wayland[1] a valuable accession to my list. I stayed this time, as before, with Zachariah Allen, a very enlightened manufacturer and a trustee of Brown University. Dr. Wayland dined with me the first day, and next day (yesterday), I dined at his house with Professor Caswell. Wayland is intent upon some valuable and important collegiate reforms, and his views are shared by Allen and a majority of the trustees. They contemplate an entire reorganization of their college, introducing much more science and practical instruction, less Greek, etc., and adopting some of your system. Wayland is tired of the old monastic system, and is wishing to see the colleges more like our ideal School of Arts, if they cannot be true universities. I have nowhere found a more enlightened and independent thinker than Wayland. He has great native strength which has enabled him to get himself free from many early trammels. You would be greatly interested in his views.

I think the time is nearly at hand for an important revolution in this whole matter of collegiate education. The old institutions with their vast funds, educating youth at enormous expense, yet fitting them for nothing truly useful or calculated to advance the age, must soon meet the rivalry of institutions which will embody modern ideas.

Wayland much wishes a copy of your exposition of the system, etc., at the University, Memorial to the Legislature, and any documents or notes of your own having a bearing on the subject. He has had a copy and lent it to some of his trustees, and it may not suffice for his wants just now, therefore send him another. I wish you and I could together put our

---

[1] President of Brown University.

thoughts on paper, — we need not just now print, — on this whole subject of the sort of collegiate institution which would best suit the true wants (I do not mean the conservative wishes) of the United States, or rather of New England, where we might show what departments of human knowledge in especial should be taught, and next, how taught. We should find most willing readers in Wayland and Allen and their friends. Now, or soon, I conceive to be the fitting time.

Dr. Wayland and Mr. Allen visited the University of Virginia in 1850, and were the guests of Mr. and Mrs. Rogers. Dr. Wayland afterwards published a Report which " is said to have marked an era in the history of collegiate education in America." [1]

WILLIAM TO HENRY.

UNIVERSITY OF VIRGINIA, January 13, 1850.

. . . Have you seen Henfrey's " Outlines of Structural and Physiological Botany " ? It is an admirably compact little work, posting up the subject to the latest microscopic researches. Is it not odd that comparative anatomy here succeeds without owning or using even so much as a pocket microscope? . . .

The proposition is again before the legislature in Richmond to appoint an agricultural chemist and mineralogist for the State, to make analyses of soils, etc., and deliver lectures in the counties as well as make annual reports to the government. Some of the folks in these parts have wonderful faith in agricultural chemistry, believing that if they once know the composition of their soils, they are sure to be able to make their land and themselves rich. Liebig with much good has done some harm. The agricultu-

[1] *Thomas Jefferson and the University of Virginia*, by H. B. Adams; *U. S. Bureau of Education: Circulars of Information, No.* 1, 1888, p. 131.

ral problem, so far from being solved, is only beginning to be properly investigated. Is it not true that
the problem combines all the difficulty of the most
complex chemical, with the most obscure physiological
questions? Is it not as difficult, or more difficult
than the medical problem? . . .

HENRY TO WILLIAM.

BOSTON, March, 1850.

. . . I am also busy as Chairman of a Committee for
ventilating the Natural History Society's rooms. . . .
For a man of any brains whatever, Boston has no
peace or quiet, all is restless excitement and unpro-
ductive change of thought and of pursuit. The over-
working of the brain here without the fruits of
intellectual labour is appalling to a mind of contem-
plative tendencies. Often do I envy you and Robert
your calmer studious atmosphere. . . .

WILLIAM TO HENRY.

UNIVERSITY OF VIRGINIA, April 18, 1850.

. . . Dr. Wayland and Mr. Allen arrived on Tuesday
afternoon and remained with us until Wednesday
night. Dr. Wayland attended all the morning lectures on Wednesday, as did Mr. Allen also, and both
expressed themselves as greatly pleased with our system. They appear quite determined to adopt our
more liberal features in their new scheme. They
spent their time chiefly here and at Robert's, and were
evidently much gratified by the welcome we gave
them. The members of the faculty called upon them,
and were much struck by the intelligence and large
views of Dr. W. On the whole I am satisfied that
our guests have carried away with them much encouragement for their plan of reform, as well as valuable guides in conducting them. Robert and I had
a great deal of pleasant talk with both gentlemen,
especially with Dr. Wayland, and were charmed by

his liberal and expansive spirit, as well as his remarkable clearness of head. He spoke frequently of you
and always with much commendation.[1] . . .

Some days ago I received a letter from Mr. Joseph
Cabell written informally in behalf of the directors of
the James River and Kanawha Company, requesting
me to make a geological examination of the mountain
belt in the Allegheny from near the Sweet Springs
across to the north of Greensboro, etc., with a view to
decide upon the feasibility of placing there large
feeders for the canal, which is designed to pass
through that belt. You know this is Mr. C.'s hobby,
and he urges me strongly to undertake the work next
summer.

TO HUGH MILLER.

UNIVERSITY OF VIRGINIA, May 6, 1850.
To HUGH MILLER, ESQ. :
My dear Sir, — My friend Professor Hitchcock
hopes to meet with you while in Scotland, and as I
have already had that good fortune, I am proud of
the opportunity of giving him a line of introduction
to you. His name is, I am sure, well known to you
in connection with American geology. Our New Red
sandstone has borrowed from his able researches an
interest somewhat akin to that which your eloquent
revelations have imparted to the Old Red of Scotland.
I do not doubt that the author of "Footprints" will
find in the explorer of "Bird Tracks" a congenial
mind.

With many thanks for the pleasure I have had in
reading your last work, and with the kindest wishes,
I remain,
Very truly yours,
WILLIAM B. ROGERS.

[1] Reference is made to this visit of the authorities of Brown University in *A Memoir of the Life and Labors of Francis Wayland,
D. D. and LL. D.,* by his sons, Francis and H. L. Wayland, pp. 92
and 93, N. Y., 1867.

TO HIS BROTHER HENRY.

UNIVERSITY OF VIRGINIA, May 12, 1850.

. . . Professor Froebel[1] stayed with me the two days of his sojourn here. He won the sympathy and regard of all of us. How much he has lived in a short life, and how truly does he deserve respect and honour for the spirit in which he has devoted himself to a good cause. He impressed us as a high-aiming, earnest, single-hearted man. Robert and I, you may be sure, did all we could to make him happy while here, and I gave him such directions as might aid him in his present inquiries. . . .

The following letter gives glimpses of Newport life and of Henry Clay : —

TO HIS BROTHER HENRY.

NEWPORT, August 12, 1850.

. . . Every spot in and about Newport is crammed with visitors, for the most part very transient ones. We have been here only nine days and feel like old residents. Mr. Clay is at our hotel — much observed, but trying to keep quiet. Henry Tuckerman, of New York, whom I meet daily, has made many kind inquiries after you. The Nortons have a cottage near us, and the two Miss Guilds are now there. The Wormleys and Bruens have cottages hard by, and many other Boston folks whom you would doubtless know, but I do not. . . .

Clay holds a levée every day for an hour or two from twelve o'clock, and they say on these occasions takes the opportunity of kissing all the good-looking girls that present themselves. I believe a majority of his visitors are women. . . . I have seen no men of science amid the crowd.

[1] Julius Froebel, a German traveller, nephew of the founder of the kindergarten system; in search of lands in the United States suitable for German emigrants.

Yesterday afternoon Emma and I had a delightful ramble along the cliffs, gathering seaweed, of which the variety here is truly wonderful. . . . What superb sunsets are visible here. I have never seen finer, even in Virginia. . . .

The following are comments on features of New England geology: —

TO HIS BROTHER HENRY.

UNIVERSITY OF VIRGINIA, January 5, 1851.

. . . The impressions from Greenfield are unquestionably *Lycopodites uncifolius*, or a form generally the same. I am not yet prepared to say whether these impressions are all of one fern or belong to two. But some of them I cannot distinguish from Lindley's and Hutton's figures and descriptions of *Lyc. unc.*, which occurs in the Yorkshire Oölite, and with more delicate foliage in Chesterfield coal rocks. Take the largest-leafed specimens from Chesterfield, and the smallest from Springfield, and there is the closest resemblance. The fossils left me by Werth are truly superb. They are *Pecopteris*, etc., bearing a strong family resemblance to those of the Jura in Sternberg, and Oölite in Lindley and Hutton, but excepting a magnificent frond of *Pecopteris Whitbyensis* (the English fossil), a foot square, they will require new names. When you are next in Boston I will get you to make a short communication on these subjects to the Natural History Society.

UNIVERSITY OF VIRGINIA, February 24, 1851.

. . . While I was in Richmond the Governor expressed to me a strong desire to have a beginning made in the publication of my final Report. He has very just notions as to the scale on which it ought to be done, and says that he will be glad, in his next annual message, to bring before the Legislature any scheme I may suggest for engraving and publishing, and for revising the work in various districts of the State. He is now employing a draftsman to compile the materials of a better state map from the numerous surveys of railroads, turnpikes and other improvements. This is a proper beginning.

We passed a little more than three days in Richmond, and were very kindly entertained at Mr. Brown's. The Reform Convention is in session, and has entered on the discussion of the basis of representation which is hereafter to be established. All west of the Blue Ridge urge the white basis as indispensable. The eastern members insist on what they call the mixed basis, in which every five blacks are equivalent to two white men. It is difficult to see how the parties can make any compromise, and it is apprehended by some that the Convention will adjourn without settling the matter. There is a large mass of mediocrity in this body, but I believe a good deal of practical sense and much of a reforming spirit. . . .

Have I told you before of the excitement which Johnson created at Raleigh by a lecture before the Legislature, in which he extolled the value of the coal fields and other mineral resources of that State? The Legislature, on the strength of these representations I suppose, has organized a geological, botanical, etc., survey, appropriating $5,000 per annum for the purpose. He computes the number of cubic yards of coal at 365,000,000! by taking the distance between the two most remote parts where coal has been found and multiplying this by the breadth of the sandstone belt, counting the coal as continuous and four feet in thickness! Is not this a bold stroke? The only distinct fossil I have yet made out in this region is *Equisetum columnare*, one of the characteristic forms in Chesterfield. I have no doubt that these rocks are of about the same age. . . .

In a former letter you spoke of some saurian remains found in the Mesozoic of Pennsylvania, now in

Leidy's hands. The little conical curved tooth which I found some years ago in the sandstone of Chesterfield was at the time broken in the attempt to take it out. I have the small fragments. Perhaps a section under the microscope would give useful information. I remember that I thought it most like a tooth in Brongniart, from the Lias.

UNIVERSITY OF VIRGINIA, March 8, 1851.

I am now holding my intermediate examination. We have been seven hours in the lecture-room, and some of the slow ones have so much work remaining that I fear I shall not be released for an hour or two longer. . . .

Have you seen Maury's paper on the subject of Winds, recently published as an appendix to the Washington Observations? He has snatched at Faraday's discovery of the magnetism of oxygen to make it the basis of a wild dream as to the cause of spiral storms or currents of the air. I cannot imagine why he has published anything so unripe as this. . . .

UNIVERSITY OF VIRGINIA, June 2, 1851.

. . . What you say of the Canadian fossils is very remarkable. Surely we have not yet reached the lowest horizon of life. I cannot believe that it began in forms so developed. . . .

UNIVERSITY OF VIRGINIA, June 23, 1851.

. . . Whatever may be the age of the limestone at Burlington, Vt., which in my notes I describe as looking like a Levant rock, I cannot believe that the Berkshire limestone is of that age. Indeed, I am sure that the two are in entirely different belts. That of the Winooski is a prolongation of the belt near Whitehall, which, as you know, is much to the west of the trend of the Berkshire belt. The latter is in a line with the limestone of Rutland in Vermont, which lies immediately at the western base of the Green Mountains.

I feel with you, my dear Henry, the importance of our being able to renew our attention systematically to the comparison of our Palæozoic formations in order to secure justice to our previous labours, and to make our nomenclature acceptable. . . .

FROM HIS BROTHER HENRY.

BOSTON, March 13, 1851.

. . . Will the Smithsonian Institute do anything truly useful through the telegraph in studying the laws of our weather ? What a noble field, what a chance for some one placed, we will say, in Philadelphia or New York, at one of the great ganglia of these nervous chords, to work out, day by day, the wide oscillations of weather and all the atmospheric conditions, to have a newspaper containing only the telegraphic news, and a department devoted to weather, with stereotyped map of the United States and Canada, on which the distribution of the various winds, etc., say at noon, for each day, might in four hours' time be given to the public. This will be done, I prophesy, in less than seven years. . . .

TO HIS BROTHER HENRY.

SUNNY HILL, September 16, 1851. '

. . . I believe the new Harvard professors of Latin, rhetoric and chemistry have entered upon their duties. From James [1] I learn that the students are greatly pleased, because, for the first time, they are shown some chemical experiments. Last year they committed the chemistry to memory ! . . .

UNIVERSITY OF VIRGINIA, October 26, 1851.

. . . How I long, my dear brother, for a daily communion with you. I always catch from you fresh spirit for research, and it seems to me that we are both greatly benefited by the stimulus of thought which each of us can best apply to the other. . . .

[1] James Savage, Jr.

UNIVERSITY OF VIRGINIA, November 6, 1851.

. . . I have just been contriving a little instrument which, with a single mirror, gives the effect of Wheatstone's stereoscope. By and by I will send you an account of it, as I think it is new and curious. . . .

UNIVERSITY OF VIRGINIA, November 17, 1851.

. . . I believe I mentioned in my last that Hackley of Columbia College, N. Y., paid us a visit some time ago. He mentioned to me that Renwick would soon vacate his place, and he made some remarks that looked as if he had been thinking of me for the situation. The institution is magnificently endowed, and there is talk of an enlarged plan. At present the professors are better paid than anywhere else north of the Potomac, and according to his account, have light duties. If you have a chance in New York, make some inquiry about this. . . .

I am beginning to make arrangements for the Smithsonian lectures. I shall take with me some simple means of exhibiting the prominent properties of all the constituents of the air. Robert and I have constructed a very nice instrument for endosmose, and one for burning a jet of atmospheric air in hydrogen. . . .

UNIVERSITY OF VIRGINIA, December 26, 1851.

. . . I feel quite troubled on account of your perplexity in regard to help in your survey, and most earnestly do I wish that I could point to a suitable assistant. You will find it next to impossible, I think, to find any one person uniting all the qualifications you desire. But I would, at any rate, not seek for such abroad. . . . I do not know anything personally of Mr. Brush,[1] but I have seen some chemical analyses of his in the " Journal of Science." In the number

---

[1] George J. Brush, formerly Professor of Mineralogy and afterwards Director of the Sheffield Scientific School of Yale University.

for November, 1850, is a good paper on American spodumene by " George J. Brush, of Yale University." This, I suppose, is the same person. In previous volumes he has published analyses of albite, etc. He is no doubt fully acquainted with chemistry, general and analytical, as well as with mineralogy and goniometry, and has, I presume, had the Yale training in geology. I suppose you especially need just now one who has skill in geological drawing and such knowledge of structure as to be able to put together the materials of the summer's work. . . .

You ask what is thought of Kossuth's cause in Virginia. I hear but little of it. But our neighbours at the University are disposed to depreciate him, and are entirely opposed to his advanced policy. Indeed, this seems to be the prevailing opinion throughout the State. The Whig papers are decided in denouncing any departure from the neutral policy of our government; and the Democratic papers, although they express a stronger sympathy with Kossuth's objects, agree with the others in sustaining the necessity of a neutral course. I have no idea that he will obtain any action from the government or from the people which will compromise this country in European troubles. Still, I think his presence in Washington will create a powerful impression. How can it be otherwise? Is he not a sublime man, one whose faculties are equal to the sublimest mission that mortal ever undertook? His presence will do our country good, and not harm, as some apprehend. But the interests of liberty will be best advanced, I think, by an adherence on our part to the neutral policy. By and by when we are stronger, and when the masses of Europe are better prepared for a permanent change, and therefore stronger for the contest, our intervention joined with that of England will suffice almost peacefully to secure the right.

What a curse to France is hero worship. How artfully does the usurper in his proclamation carry his

countrymen back to the institutions of government
planned by the first consul. But can it be that the
great empire of France will tolerate the usurpation?
The army in Paris may for a time repress the public
indignation. But must it not at last hurl the usurper
from the presidency? I am most impatient to hear
the course and result of the election. . . .

UNIVERSITY OF VIRGINIA, January 6, 1852.

. . . I observe that Dr. Kane, of the Arctic exploration, is lecturing in the Smithsonian upon the history
of their voyage and the Arctic phenomena, and I am
glad he succeeds so well, for I have much respect for
his manliness and generosity of character. . . .

As far as I can learn there is here far less sympathy with Kossuth's cause, and more decided opposition to his proposed national action than in the Middle
or Western States. This is greatly due to the prejudice
created by the prominence of the abolitionists in New
York in doing him honour, but it is also the natural
result of that conservatism which of late has become
the strong feeling of the politicians of the South, a
feeling which could not fail to spring up in antagonism to the aggressive philanthropy of other parts of
the Union. The result shows how deeply these feelings operate, since from the excitable character of the
South, and its great admiration for eloquence and
chivalrous daring, Kossuth is a person for whom,
under other circumstances, an unbounded enthusiasm
would be aroused. As it is, I cannot imagine how
any one who reads his speeches can fail to do reverence in his heart to the truthful and magnetic soul
that pours out its prayer for sympathy, and pleads for
the brotherhood of nations in language so touching and
sublime. How I wish to see and hear him. Perhaps
in Washington we may enjoy that opportunity. . . .

Early in January Mr. and Mrs. Rogers went to
Washington, where Mr. Rogers gave before the Smith-

sonian Institution a course of four lectures on " Phases
of the Atmosphere."

TO HIS BROTHER HENRY.

UNIVERSITY OF VIRGINIA, March 5, 1852.

. . . I have come to just the same conclusion as you
in regard to Espy's[1] labours. Some weeks ago I received a letter from Mr. Stanton, of the House of
Representatives, desiring my opinion of his reports
as to their practical and theoretical value, and before
replying I had to look them over with some care. It
gave me real pleasure to be able to say to Mr. Stanton
that they contained a large amount of meteorological
data skilfully tabulated so as to present to the eye a
number of important partial generalizations ; that I
believed the dynamical theory proposed by Mr. Espy
brought to light a cause of atmospheric disturbances
never proposed before, and which probably had an
important agency in their production ; that his views
were thoroughly philosophical, and that whatever variety of opinion might exist as to his theory as compared with others, Mr. Espy deserved great credit for
the researches which he had embodied in the Reports
and other works, which were a really precious contribution to meteorology. I really think that Espy has
shown more power of philosophical analysis than
either Redfield or Reid. It is surely a higher aim,
that of demonstrating the great dynamic cause of
storms, etc., from preëstablished physical principles,
than merely to determine the lesser inductions regarding them, such as their rotary direction, etc. I think
with you that Espy's views must be taken along with
the rotary doctrine, or perhaps it may be found to
explain the rotation. It is a very difficult subject,
but hereafter I am determined to speak out in behalf
of Espy's merits as a thinker and investigator. I hope
they may continue him in his present place. The
question was to be brought up, and on this account
Mr. Stanton wrote me. . . .

[1] James P. Espy, author of *Philosophy of Storms*, etc.

UNIVERSITY OF VIRGINIA, March 14, 1852.
. . . We have seen a notice of a meeting of some scientific men at Albany, connected with the organization of a university there, but have learned none of the details. Agassiz, Peirce, Gould, Hall, Porter and others were there, and were spoken of as intending to take part in its organization. . . .

Indications now appear in the correspondence of the brothers that James was in failing health. On April 1, 1852, William wrote to Henry concerning him, but expressed no special anxiety, although he recommended that James be urged to take an ocean voyage. A month later a change for the worse had occurred, and the brothers William, Henry and Robert began to feel the gravest apprehensions.

It was soon discovered that Professor James Rogers was suffering from Bright's disease; and he died on June 12, 1852, in the fifty-first year of his age.

WILLIAM TO HENRY.

UNIVERSITY OF VIRGINIA, June 20, 1852.
. . . The day after receiving the sad news from you and Robert, I wrote, as well as I could, to Rachel, and intended writing to you, but I had not the power to do it. My mind for weeks past had accustomed itself to the contemplation of the sad result which has occurred, and the news of our dear James's departure, terrible as it was, was less overwhelming to me than I could have supposed it would be. But I feel that my heart can never forget this sorrow. In active occupation with books, and with preparations for the closing session, I endeavour to withdraw my thoughts from the sad theme. . . . But do not think, my dear Henry, that I give way to sorrow, or that I do not

James F. Rogers

feel in all their force the views of affectionate duty suggested in yours and Robert's letters. . . .

Those who have followed the history of the four brothers thus far will perhaps have been sufficiently apprised of the career of the eldest, James, who was now deceased; but the following brief summary of the facts already recorded may be given here.

James Blythe Rogers, the eldest of the four brothers, was born in Philadelphia, on February 11, 1802. He was educated in Baltimore, Md., and at William and Mary College in Virginia. He studied medicine, and received the degree of M. D. in Baltimore in 1822. After practising medicine for a time in Harford County, Maryland, he was chemist to a firm of manufacturing chemists in Baltimore, and subsequently lecturer on chemistry in Washington Medical college, Baltimore. He was later professor of chemistry for four years in the Cincinnati College, and also served as an assistant to his brother William, then State Geologist of Virginia, upon the geological survey of that State. In 1840 he became a permanent resident of Philadelphia, serving as Professor of Chemistry, successively, in the Philadelphia Medical Institute, the Franklin Institute, and the University of Pennsylvania. The last-mentioned position he held at the time of his death. He left a widow, two sons, and one daughter. A "Memoir of the Life and Character of James B. Rogers, M. D.," by Joseph Carson, M. D., was published in Philadelphia in 1852. A good account of his life and works is also to be found in a pamphlet entitled, "The Brothers Rogers," by W. S. W. Ruschenberger, M. D., Philadelphia, 1885.

The vacancy caused in the faculty of the University of Pennsylvania by the death of Professor James

Rogers was filled in August by the appointment of his brother, Robert,[1] who resigned his position in the University of Virginia to accept the vacant chair in Philadelphia.

To the professorship resigned by Robert was appointed Professor J. Lawrence Smith, a chemist of distinction, who brought to the University, as assistants in his private researches, Mr. George J. Brush, now Director of the Sheffield Scientific School of Yale University, and Mr. Ogden W. Rood, now Professor of Physics in Columbia College, New York.

WILLIAM TO HIS BROTHER HENRY.

UNIVERSITY OF VIRGINIA, October 24, 1852.

. . . Dr. Smith has not yet got fully under way with his duties. His assistant arrived some days ago. He and the Dr. and his wife are still staying with us, but will probably, to-morrow, remove to their own quarters. Young Brush is a zealous mineralogist of the Yale school, and seems to be familiar with all parts of chemical analysis. He talks a great deal and very admiringly of young Silliman and Dana, and I find that he supposes New Haven to be the great centre of American science. Dr. Smith is evidently much attached to the same persons and locality. . . . I think he is an independent man, and I see that he is ambitious to advance himself by actual research. He will, I am sure, be open, fair, and direct in all his scientific dealings. . . . He has yet to learn that with large classes, in our system, he will be compelled, or at least expected to devote just as much time to teaching as Robert was accustomed to give, and that he cannot have much leisure for his own researches. I am doing what I can to direct him rightly in his plans. . . .

[1] Robert E. Rogers was already a member of the Academy of Sciences, and the Franklin Institute, of Pennsylvania.

It grieves me to hear of the failure of that good cheerful, faithful friend, our gray horse. How strangely thoughtless are many persons of this most precious of servants ! . . .

I am truly concerned on account of Horner's precarious health. He is a conscientious, good man, simple-hearted and faithful to his duties. It will be much easier to find a more brilliant lecturer than it will be to find as honest and true a man.

Our classes here have now mounted to about 390, so that we are quite certain of passing the 400. . . .

The year 1852 was marked by a recurrence of the cholera.

FROM PROFESSOR S. F. BAIRD TO MRS. ROGERS AT SUNNY HILL.

CARLISLE, July 23, 1852.

MY DEAR MRS. ROGERS, — I write to you for the sake of greater certainty in sending my letter to the Professor. . . . My object is to know from him his views as to the propriety of postponing the Cleveland meeting of the Association in case the cholera should increase to any extent. There have already been several deaths there, and no decided abatement as yet. I have written to the committee at Cleveland, for its opinion, but in the mean time would like the Professor's views.

Even if the real danger of cholera be slight, yet the apprehension may keep away some of the best members. A political meeting to be held at Columbus on the 22d of August has been postponed on this account. . . .

WILLIAM TO HIS BROTHER HENRY.

UNIVERSITY OF VIRGINIA, November 28, 1852.

. . . You will see in Saboni's address a reference to quite an important discovery of Stokes,[1] the mathe-

---
[1] Sir George G. Stokes.

matician of Cambridge. He finds that the invisible
rays beyond the violet *are converted into blue light*
by transmission through a *compound* solution of sulphate of quinine. Have you not noticed the peculiar
blue colour of the upper film of this solution viewed
in certain directions? I have been to-day examining
the alcoholic solution of chlorophyll formed by adding
this liquid to the bruised leaves of our common running box. When you look obliquely down upon it in
certain lights, the liquid, although of a clear and intense green, appears reddish brown and opaque, and
in almost every light the upper film appears of this
colour. This is another case of the *alteration of the
refrangibility of the rays* by the medium, according
to Stokes. I find the red and the yellow colouring
matter of the autumnal leaves to be so far quite un-
altered. The delicacy of the former as a test for
alkalies is, I think, very remarkable, and the reaction
is beautiful. I will send you some to try. . . .

FROM HIS BROTHER HENRY.

BOSTON, December 16, 1852.

. . . Have you read in the "Journal of the Geological Society" the controversy between Sedgwick and
Murchison, touching Silurian and Cambrian? I think
our friend Sedgwick has all the philosophy and the
justice on his side, yet, through our fault of procrasti-
nation in publishing, he has allowed Murchison to
encroach on his whole ground, and to secure a sort of
title by mere priority of occupancy of what is not his.
As we must commit ourselves to one side or the other,
if we use the European equivalent nomenclature at
all, we ought now to study the whole matter and make
up our decision. I wish much to learn your views.
Sedgwick's beautiful classification and nomenclature
of the British rocks is infinitely better in harmony
with our American Palæozoic Geology than Murchison's. He calls all the Palæozoic *one system*, and

terminates the Cambrian with the Caradoc, just where
we would draw our strongest equivalent line, being at
the top of our Matinal shales.

Sedgwick's Cambrian series takes in then our
Primal, Auroral and Matinal series; the Silurian,
etc., — he insists on restricting it, — our Levant, Sur-
gent, Scalent and Pre-meridian; the Devonian, our
Meridian, Post-meridian, Cadent, Vergent and Po-
nent.[1] Certainly on this side the Atlantic the formations approximately equivalent to the Cambrian and
Silurian are as much separated by their fossils as are
the Silurian from the Devonian, either in Europe or
here. But all this geographical nomenclature will
pass away in time. The ablest geologists are feeling
doubts of the identification of strata, across wide
spaces, by fossils.

WILLIAM TO HENRY.

UNIVERSITY OF VIRGINIA, December 25, 1852.

I cannot let the mail set off on its journey northward without committing to it a word of Christmas
greeting. My heart longs more than I can express for
the coming time when we may all spend together, as
in our childhood, these festival days, and when we
shall always be so near as not to feel the sense of separation. How much of true happiness is yet in store
for us, my dear brother, when we shall thus be re-
united. The sad thought of dear James's absence from
among us is the only shadow in this happy prospec-
tive. . . .

From what I hear, I suppose that Columbia College
may, erelong, be extended upon the plane of a great
university. Merely collegiate establishments do not
prosper in any of our large cities.

The reference here made to Columbia College was
due to the fact that Professor Rogers had lately
received from Dr. King, then President of Columbia,

[1] For a note on this nomenclature, see Appendix to vol. ii.

a circular letter relating to a proposed extension of that college upon university lines.

UNIVERSITY OF VIRGINIA, January 7, 1853.

... When you have time read a paper in the December number of "Philosophical Magazine Supplement," by Helmholtz, on the "Theory of Compound Colors." It is the continuation of a critical review of Brewster's analysis of the spectrum. Helmholtz proves beyond question that the reduction of the colours to the three, blue, yellow, and red, cannot be maintained. In a word, he points out the fallacies in Brewster's observations. But strangest of all, he shows that blue and yellow, when pure and of proper intensity, form not green but white.

I send you the means of making this experiment at once. Take a small slip of thin clear glass like a

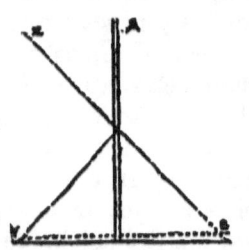

microscope slide. Hold it erect upon the flat surface of black paper or the cover of a book, place the blue paper behind it at B, and the yellow in front at Y, then look obliquely through the glass, and by a little trial of position, you will see the yellow superposed on the blue to form a pale white spot. Looking more steeply, and thereby getting a fainter blue and more intense yellow, the spot appears palish yellow. But in no case do the two tints, when superposed, produce any shade of green. This, I think, a capital *new fact.* The green formed by the mixture of the yellow and blue pigments is due to light transmitted from some little depth.

Have you tried Stokes's experiment with the solution of sulphate quinine? — remember to add a few drops of SO_3, and make the solution very dilute.

Until I found the effect of the SO_3, I could not get any striking phenomenon. . . .

UNIVERSITY OF VIRGINIA, January 18, 1853.

. . . I regret very much that last summer I was not able to pause in New York to see one of the working engines of Ericsson's new construction. How absurd the little *caloric engine!* But is not his a superb triumph? and yet how simple and entirely known the principle. I am waiting impatiently to have the details of the engine, for in this consists, I think, all the intellectual merit of the triumph.

RICHMOND, February 16, 1853.

. . . My lectures have been marvellously successful. I have had all the best intelligence and refinement of Richmond to hear me, and such has been the interest taken in the lectures that after the first, which was a full hour, the throng has been so great that half an hour before the appointed time of beginning, the room has been completely packed with people, and it has been necessary to stop the sale of tickets and close the doors. I have never seen so interested an audience, and I have been really touched to see how universally my old friends and acquaintances here have turned out to bid me welcome. Even old Mrs. Wickham, Mrs. Bruce, old Judge Robertson, and such have come forward to greet me. . . . Until now the lectures at the Athenæum here have failed to pay expenses, and this year they had barely paid for the gas and the servant. . . .

UNIVERSITY OF VIRGINIA, March 5, 1853.

. . . I find that I am in bad luck in regard to my matters of original thought, for in a recent number of "Poggendorff," just received, I see a long article on *irradiation*, coming very close to my results and explanations, although these, you know, have been familiar to me for the last ten years at least. So much for tardiness and timidity in putting into print. I have been teaching these matters in my lectures here for at least ten years. I want you to make a sketch in pencil of the appearance of a star or distant lamp, 1st for each eye separately, and 2d as seen when both are open. There is a remarkable difference in the appearance as perceived by different persons, and even by the right and left eyes of the same individual. I wish to collect a considerable number of specimens.

I think this spoke-like irradiation is produced by the influence of certain rays from the edge of the iris, which is thicker and wider than the pupil, and therefore makes the rays stretch farther over the retina. In this and some other points I am not anticipated by the German.

CHAPTER VII.

1853–1859.

Removal to Boston. — Final Effort and Failure to secure Publication of Geological Report. — An Address at Williams College. — Henry's Marriage. — William's Investigations on Binocular Vision, Sonorous Flames, Ozone, etc. — Ill-health. — Lectures in the Lowell Institute. — Removal of Henry and his Family to Scotland. — William again visits Europe. — Dublin Meeting of the British Association. — A Serious Accident. — Kind Friends in Norwich. — Politics. — Henry appointed Regius Professor of Natural History and Geology in the University of Glasgow. — Elected a Fellow of the Royal Society. — Illness of Theodore Parker.

FOR several years Mr. Rogers had greatly desired to be relieved of the duties of teaching in order to gain more time for original work. He had also ever since boyhood cherished the hope of working some day side by side with his brother Henry. Working on year after year in a university which was somewhat remote and apart, he had come to yearn for the stimulus of town-life and a more scientific atmosphere. He was now nearing his fiftieth year. His brother Robert had left him to fill an important professorship in Philadelphia; family affairs in Boston made his residence there desirable; but above all the earnest wish to complete and publish his final Report on the Geological Survey of Virginia, already too often postponed and too long delayed, finally induced him to resign in the spring of 1853 the professorship which he had now held for eighteen years, and to join his brother Henry in Boston. This important step was not taken without many forebodings. From the income of his professorship, which had been lucrative, he had by economy accumulated enough to yield a moderate income ; but for the rest he proposed to depend chiefly upon the somewhat precarious proceeds of lectures and expert work. The future, therefore, was by no means unclouded, and he was fully alive to the danger of renouncing an assured professorship for prospects so uncertain. Mr. and Mrs. Rogers left the University of Virginia with regret, and with the utmost respect and affection for that noble institution. As long as he lived Mr. Rogers cherished, as one of his most enduring and precious memories, the recollection of the years which he had spent there ; and when in the next decade it devolved upon him to found and organize the Massachusetts Institute of Technology in Boston, the model which he always had in mind was the University of Virginia.

In a letter dated June 29, 1853, Mr. Rogers writes to his brother Henry: " My successor is young Mr. Smith, the mathematical tutor, and a favorite pupil of mine."

TO HIS BROTHER ROBERT.

BOSTON, November 30, 1853.

· . . . Our course of lectures was opened night before last by an address from Mr. Winthrop. The first of Professor Chase's lectures on Applied Chemistry will be given next Tuesday. After his series has been completed, there may be others before I come on, that is, if I am to precede Henry. . . .

On Tuesday evening, besides hearing a part of Winthrop's lecture, I dropped in to a meeting of the

Academy, where for an hour I listened to Peirce. Yesterday evening Mr. Savage entertained "the Club" [1]
at No. 1,[2] when he took occasion to introduce me specially to all the old gentlemen present, among them
Mr. J. A. Lowell, Josiah Quincy, etc. I had a very
pleasant time, and from Mr. Lowell's amiable bearing
towards me, I begin to have some hopes of a course
in a year or two.

Early in January, 1854, Mr. and Mrs. Rogers went
to Richmond for the purpose of making one more
attempt to secure from the legislature the means of
publishing the final Report of the Geological Survey
of Virginia.

TO HIS BROTHER HENRY.

RICHMOND, February 11, 1854.

I know not why I have so long delayed writing to
you, unless it has been my daily expectation of hearing
something of importance to tell you in regard to the
Survey. Yet such has been the tardiness of the legislature and the crowding of small bills on the Senate,
that the matter remains as at the beginning of the
week. The bill asks for $24,000, leaving the special
apportionment for revision and publication in my
hands. The control of the fiscal part of the Survey is
placed jointly in the hands of the secretary of the Commonwealth (Wythe Mumford) and me, and the selection of assistants is given to me alone. My salary is
marked at $1,200, the others to be fixed by me and the
secretary. No time is appointed for the completion of
the work. Had I known more of the temper of the
Senate before drawing up the bill, I should have asked
for $30,000, and put my own compensation at least at
$1,500. But any amendment will now add greatly to
the uncertainty of getting the bill through, and I think
I shall not urge it, unless I find the temper of the two
houses more friendly than it is likely to be. In the

[1] The Wednesday Evening Club.
[2] Temple Place.

Senate the measure will, I think, meet no serious
opposition, but in the Lower House it may give rise
to a contest. Probably I may be called on to give
one or two lectures to the legislature to explain the
subject.

My numerous friends in Richmond seem all to be
much interested in having the measure passed, and
they do what they can to help it through. If it can
be sent down from the Senate early in the week, I
think it is likely to be carried through the Lower
House successfully.

I am utterly tired of waiting upon the movements
of the legislature. The lobby working, of which I
see a good deal and hear more, is as repugnant to my
taste as to my sense of right, and I avoid even the
colour of it. . . .

We have been staying since Tuesday at my friend
Myers's,[1] at the head of Government Street, near the
Powhatan House, where we have every comfort and
even luxury. . . .

RICHMOND, February 19, 1854.

My presence here for ten days past has been indispensable, for such has been the pressure of local bills,
even in the Senate, that without my daily reminding
my friends of the geological bill, it would not have
been brought up out of place as it has been this morning.
I went over to the Capitol about noon, and as I entered the senate lobby, heard my friend Ambler making a very earnest speech in behalf of the bill. He was
followed by a Williamsburg man, who had, I fear,
been prompted to opposition by Saunders, and who,
speaking ignorantly, made an appeal which I feared
would defeat the measure; but the vote was trium-
phant, being 35 to 7, the number 26 being necessary
to pass the bill. It was at once taken over to the
other House, where, having precedence, it will probably be called up in a few days. I now hope to have

[1] Gustavus Myers, Esq.

the matter finally disposed of by the close of this
week.   But in the Lower House the fate of any measure is not to be calculated. . . . My chief fear is that
some amendment, prescribing the time or otherwise
crippling the work, will be attempted.   This I am resolved to resist, even to the entire defeat of the bill.
I will let you know in a day or two what is likely to
be done, or has been done, in the premises. . . .

I am glad you have Lesquereux [1] with you in Boston.   How I wish I could see his drawings and gathering of fossils !

On Friday I had a very pleasant excursion with my
friend Giles among the quarries on the other side of
the river, extending some five miles up.   They have
been opened somewhat extensively by the Danville
R. R., and display very finely the great system of
joints in the granitic rock of the belt.   Have also
been prowling about in the ravines, a mile or two
below the city, where I have found grand exposures
of the Infusory. . . .

In spite of all the efforts of Mr. Rogers and his
numerous friends in the legislature and in Richmond,
the bill failed to pass the House, and on March 8,
with Mrs. Rogers, he left for Boston.   Three months
had been spent in Richmond in a futile endeavor to
secure provision for the Report, which Mr. Rogers
so ardently desired to finish.   The blow was a heavy
one, but he bore it philosophically and, pausing in
Washington on his way northward, wrote the following letter to the librarian of the state library in
Richmond, Va.: —

WASHINGTON, March 9, 1854.

. . . The hurry of preparation yesterday left me no
time for making out the list of books which I promised
to send you.   I subjoin a list of such as now occur

[1] Leo Lesquereux, Paleontologist and Botanist, 1806–1889.

to me, all of them of standard value in their way. It will give me pleasure at any time when in Richmond or the Northern cities to aid you in the enlargement of the state library.

Whewell's Philosophy of the Inductive Sciences; Whewell's History of the Inductive Sciences; Principles of Mechanism, by Professor Willis; Grant's History of Physical Astronomy; Keith Johnston's Physical Atlas (edition now in press much improved); Beckman's History of Inventions (new edition, by Francis & Griffith); Knapp's Technology, English edition; Reid on Ventilation; Gwilt's Encyclopædia of Architecture; Pouillet's Éléments de Physique, etc. (last edition); Cours Élémentaire de Paléontologie et Géologie, par A. d'Orbigny; Géologie Appliqué aux Arts et l'Agriculture, D'Orbigny et Gente; Mantell's Medals of Creation; Mantell's Wonders of Geology; Mantell's Petrifactions and their Teachings; De la Beche's Geological Observer; D'Archiac's Histoire de Géologie; Dana's Mineralogy, 8vo, last edition; Gray and Torrey's Genera of North American Plants (in process); Gray's Botanical Text-Book; Iconographic Encyclopædia. [The copy of the letter ends abruptly here.]

This list, doubtless written from memory, is of considerable value as an indication of the quality of Mr. Rogers's reading and its broad and philosophical tendency.

In March, 1854, Professor Henry D. Rogers was married in Boston to Miss Eliza S. Lincoln, a half-sister of his brother William's wife. He continued to reside in Boston until his removal to Scotland.

Mr. Rogers's interest in the American Association for the Advancement of Science continued unabated.

W. B. ROGERS TO DALLAS BACHE.

Boston, April 2, 1854.

. . . I think that, excepting one or two points, the constitution of our Association is well adapted to its objects, and that what is needed is not so much a change in its provisions as a better knowledge among the members of what these provisions are, and a more careful adherence to them. I believe, however, that in some respects our organic laws may be improved, and I would here point out certain amendments which might be usefully introduced. . . .

[The *First* and *Second* amendments refer to the election of officers, of members, etc.]

Third. Although there are, doubtless, cases in which the advice or warning of the Association might exert a salutary effect on public or even private enterprises connected with science, yet as there must always be some danger of giving a mistaken direction to this influence, it would seem to be safest and wisest to abstain entirely from the consideration of topics not originating in or strictly belonging to the business of the Society. I would, therefore, propose that the Association adopt a rule, as part of its organic laws, precluding all action in the way of recommendation or otherwise, either of instruments, books, institutions, researches, or other scientific, public or private enterprises. . . .

TO HIS BROTHER HENRY.

Sunny Hill, August 18, 1854.

. . . But what sad news to us is that of the death of our dear good friend McIlvaine! No one out of our immediate family circle could be more regretted, for no one else has been more truly beloved. My heart aches to think that he will no more greet us with that cordial pressure and that gentle kindness and true-hearted sympathy which had so endeared him to us all. I little dreamed a few weeks ago, when E. and I enjoyed the treat of our short visit to them at " Greenbank," that I should see him no more. . . .

FROM ROBERT TO HIS BROTHERS.

PHILADELPHIA, Friday, September 29, 1854.

In thinking over the beautiful experiments and the explanations William gave me of the strange movements originating out of Foucault's experiments, I was led the other day to try one which I would like William to repeat.

It appears to me to embrace the phenomena in a single form, and exhibit the forces quite clearly to the eye.

Simply hang a pretty large ball to a cord five or six feet long, twist it tightly, and in this state start it into a wide vibration. So soon as the ball acquires a little speed in the untwisting of the cord it will deviate from its original line of vibration, and will even go beyond a quarter of a circle in this deviation, — almost a half circle, — and then when the cord returns again in its twist, the ball rotates oppositely, and the deviation in the vibration becomes apparent in the opposite direction. What is pretty, too, is, just when the ball reaches the highest point of its vibration on each side, that the point at which it is suspended is twitched to one side, exhibiting the force which produces the deviation. . . .

In April, 1855, Mr. Rogers received and accepted an invitation from James Orton, President of the Lyceum of Natural History of Williams College, to address that body in aid of its building fund. A contemporary circular (issued December 1, 1854) bears the name of S. W. Bowles as secretary. The address was given on August 14, 1855, as will later appear.

During the summer Professor Henry Rogers, leaving his family in Massachusetts, visited Europe in

order to prepare for the publication by the Blackwoods
of Edinburgh of his " Final Report on the Pennsyl.
vania Geological Survey."

TO HIS BROTHER HENRY IN EDINBURGH.

SUNNY HILL, August 12, 1855.

MY DEAR HENRY, . . . E. and I leave early
to-morrow morning for Worcester, and then go to
Pittsfield and North Adams and to Williamstown,
which, if possible, I must reach before Tuesday morning, as on that morning at nine o'clock I give my
address. I am glad now that I took the trouble to
write it, so I am quite free from that kind of anxiety
which precedes extempore efforts. On Wednesday I
must try to get over to Providence, but shall not reach
there in time for the organization [1] at 10 A. M., which
I rather regret. . . .

The President, after removing Reeder,[2] seems determined upon giving Kansas in charge to some one who
is pledged in favour of the Kansas and Nebraska bill.
It is, I think, quite doubtful as yet which party is to
have the ascendant in the Territory. The pro-slavery
men are violent and unscrupulous, and the others
appear to be timid. I fear that the contest will be
marked by bloodshed. . . .

Dr. Warren has just published his " History of the
Elm on the Common," and sent us each a copy of the
book.

. . . The publication which I think is most demanded, and especially of us, is a manual or text-
book of American Geology. This would be salable
for college uses and that extensively, at the same time
that it would be very acceptable to men of science
here and abroad. It is, I think, the only mode in
which our nomenclature and dynamics and other

[1] Of the meeting of the Association for the Advancement of Science.

[2] Governor of Kansas.

views, either common to us or severally entertained, can be most satisfactorily and generally impressed. . . .

My address at Williams College is, I suppose, passing through the press. When published I will forward you a few copies, though it is not likely to have any interest for friends abroad. I take occasion in it to protest against the mystical notions now in vogue with some of the naturalists as to vital forces, ascribing the development of each organism to a kind of plastic idea, about as rational as the Archæus which Van Helmont made to preside as an intelligent spirit over each function.

Mr. and Mrs. Ticknor have been with us for two days, and appeared to enjoy the visit very much. They made kind inquiries for you. The growth of the new Boston public library is far more rapid than I anticipated. It already numbers 25,000 volumes, and in the course of another year will contain a very complete collection of works on Physics, Chemistry, etc., a matter of no small interest to us.

You will perhaps see by the papers that a great party is now organizing under the name of Republican, the uniting principle being opposition to the extension of slavery, either by state or federal government. This is likely to unite a large body of the Whigs, Freesoilers and liberal Democrats, and will probably carry the state election. Richard Dana is one of the leaders. . . .

I have been lately applied to to visit the North Carolina coal region by the friend of Mr. Frothingham, who talked of this matter last spring. If the parties will agree to my terms and time, I shall probably go to the South soon after returning to Boston. . . .

Little Edith[1] continues to improve. She knows my whistle, even in a distant part of the house, and has become quite familiar with my watch and eyeglass and my old straw hat.

[1] His brother Henry's child.

I have been delighted with the first volume of Brewster's Life of Newton, which I have just finished. It contains much wise criticism and many passages of warming eloquence.

The Williamstown address was delivered on the twentieth anniversary of the foundation of the Lyceum of Natural History of Williams College and on the day of the dedication of Jackson Hall, a new museum of natural history.

This address contains many characteristic passages, and as it is the only one which Mr. Rogers ever wrote out in full or for publication, no apology is needed for making the following lengthy extracts: —

"In the midst of scenery whose picturesque beauties are but the varied repetition of the landscape which in another region for so many years spread its quickening charms around me, I have the privilege of renewing, though but for an hour, that living intercourse of speech which in the lecture-room every enthusiastic teacher so much enjoys, and which for a large part of my life has been an almost daily recurring pleasure.

"The college bell that for nearly twenty years summoned me at this hour to my pleasant morning task seems even now with its inspiring music to fill the air around me. Let me then feel as if I were but obeying its customary call, and look upon you, young gentlemen of the Lyceum, as familiar lecture-room friends, that my heart unrepressed may take its share in whatever I may say to quicken your love of natural science, or to raise your thoughts to the contemplation of the grandeur and harmony of the universe. . . .

"As the relationship and interdependence among the different departments of natural science, although recognized in principle, is often practically overlooked or disregarded, I have thought that I might not unprofitably employ the present occasion in illustrating

its importance, and in urging upon the young votaries
of science whom I address the enlarged and catholic
spirit of study and research which, in the present advanced state of science, is as necessary to eminent
success in any one department as it is essential to
form the character of the philosophical naturalist. . . .

" Honour to the memory of the illustrious Swede,[1]
whose vast and accurate knowledge in each of the
great realms of Nature afforded the materials for a
systematic structure of the whole of natural science,
— whose comprehensive genius planned, and whose
unfaltering zeal built up and completed its sublime
proportions.   And honour, too, to the courageous,
indefatigable men who, catching from his lips or his
writings the inspiration of the true naturalist, left the
calm retreats of study and the enjoyments of society,
to brave the toils and perils of distant and inhospitable lands, in quest of new products of nature, or fresh
materials for investigation.   What isle so remote,
what mountain so rugged or lofty, as not to have been
the scene of their explorations?   What sea so wide or
continent so vast as to have been left untraversed by
these enthusiastic adventurers in behalf of science and
humanity?

" To the American naturalist there is a romantic
charm connected with the honoured names of such men
as Kalm and Catesby.   How pleasantly do they suggest the wooded mountains, the wide savannahs, the
far-descending rivers, and the lakes gleaming in sylvan
solitudes, where these earnest lovers of nature gathered the treasures of a new flora, or listened in happy
surprise to the musical rhapsody of some bird unknown
to them before.   Who that has wandered in early
summer along the slopes of the Blue Ridge or the
Alleghany, or the moist hillsides of New England,
where the openings in the forest and the rocky glens,
musical with tinkling streams, are suffused with the
delicate blush of our mountain laurel; who that has
entered sanctuaries like these has not in his heart

[1] Linnæus.

pronounced with loving reverence the name of Kalm, to whom this beautiful plant was so well dedicated? What naturalist, on a summer evening, while the moon shines doubtfully athwart the almost unmoving boughs, can listen to the wood-notes wild of the mocking-bird without recurring to the memory of that early lover of American birds, the gentle, enthusiastic Catesby? . . .

" In the state of development which they have now reached, each of the great departments of natural history is brought into close connection with the purely physical sciences; each has borrowed from them valuable methods and instruments of research, and each invokes the aid of physical laws and forces as part of the machinery by which the phases and activities of organic beings are to be explained. The moment we pass from the purely statical view of living creatures, and regard their structure, the functions of their several organs, their growth and all the complex conditions which mark them as living organisms, we are compelled to wide inquiries respecting the physical properties and transmutations of the matter of which they are composed.

" To illustrate this necessary use of the facts and principles of physics in the larger generalizations of the naturalist, let me, in the first place, refer to the long mooted question of the distinction between the animal and vegetable kingdoms.

" Linnæus attempted to define the three great departments of material nature by saying that ' stones grow; vegetables grow and live; animals grow, live and feel,' — thus making the capacity to feel, the distinctive mark between the vegetable and the animal organization. But while, among the higher animal tribes, this attribute is obvious and undoubted, it cannot be affirmed of various others on any better authority than would justify our ascribing it to the leaves of the sensitive plant, which shrink from our rude touch, or to the petals of the numerous tribes of flowers that open to the genial sunshine, and fold themselves together at the approach of night.

"Again, it has been maintained as a just distinction between animals and plants, that the former have the power of motion, while the latter are fixed. But the microscope and chemistry have combined to show that this means of discrimination is unavailing. For they have proved that the motile tissues in animals are composed of the same substance which botanists have recognized as existing in the cells of all plants, and that this substance is as actively motile in the plant as in the animal.[1] And they have further shown that in whatever quarter of the growing plant the vital transformations are most rapid, there we are sure to find this material in the largest proportion.

"Among the thread-like, confervoid forms which teem in our fresh-water lakes, as well as in the ocean, there is a large tribe which appears scarcely ever to be quiescent. Their slender, jointed filaments may be observed waving incessantly backwards and forwards, while their broken fragments, whose marvellously rapid growth can be seen as we are gazing on them through the microscope, keep up their mysterious alternating movements like the regular oscillations of the beam of a balance.

"Some of the plants allied to these, at particular periods of their growth, liberate from their bursting cells myriads of moving objects, each furnished with its little living oars (cilia). These for a time float and swim actively through the water, but presently, in the process of their development, they become stationary, germinate, and expand into forms of vegetation identical with that from which they have originated. Others again, furnished with like instruments of locomotion, may be observed, singly or in clusters, revolving with quick movements through the fluid, and filling their brief plant-lives with restless, animal-like activity.

[1] It is interesting to note that this address was published thirteen years before Professor Huxley's lecture *On the Physical Basis of Life.*

"But lately it was maintained that cellulose, the chief constituent of woody fibre, a substance nearly identical with starch, as well as starch itself, belonged distinctively to the vegetable world, and hence a simple chemical test for these substances was regarded as a certain means of making the required discrimination. But the rapid progress of research has proved the inaccuracy of this criterion and, strange to say, has detected the hard material of vegetable cell and woody fibre in the bodies of many mollusks; and stranger still, has discovered both it and starch forming part of the structure of the human brain.

"Nor is there better reason for assuming the presence of the green colouring matter chlorophyl as distinctive of plants, for but lately the microscopic chemist has proved that it is this very substance that gives colour to the fresh-water polyp whose wonderful power of reparation and growth early claimed for it the name of Hydra; and that the same pigment imparts the green tint to many other undoubtedly animal organisms.

"Thus all these means of discrimination fail. How, then, shall we trace the boundary between the vegetable and the animal world? If such a line is to be drawn at all, it will most probably be determined by the opposite relations of the two to the atmosphere. The beautiful antagonism of actions, by which the chemical changes wrought in this medium by one great division of living nature are reversed by the other, would in this case become the test, and thus a *chemical examination* of the air or aerated water in which the doubtful being dwells would be our best guide in deciding upon its animal or vegetable character. . . .

"But it may be said that this question remains yet undecided, or it may not unphilosophically be maintained that the distinction sought for has no real existence, and that *there are living forms which are both vegetable and animal in their nature.* This may be, and I think probably is true. But it must not therefore be concluded that these united inquiries of the naturalist and chemist have taught us no interesting truths. Let him who questions the value of such investigations consult the records of the discoveries in Natural History for the last thirty years; let him follow the successive steps by which the intimate structure of organized materials has been analyzed, mark how with the improving power of the microscope, *nebulæ of the organic world* have one after another been resolved, and as he views the teeming realms of life, which have been made to disclose their vital adaptations, he cannot fail to recognize in them the stellar regions of the naturalist, not less wonderful in the harmonious play of matter and of forces than are the tracts of ether bright with countless worlds. . . .

"The living being, to whatever race it may belong, and however constant for a time may seem its structure and materials, is in reality but an aggregate of ever-shifting particles, a form continually wasting by the loss of parts on the one hand, and as incessantly replenished by the stream of nutrient matter which is appropriated into its living structure on the other.

"It has perhaps its most striking counterpart, among the phenomena of inanimate nature, in that fleecy cloud which meteorologists describe as apparently resting on the summit of a mountain, while the moist wind in which it had its origin, and of which it is in truth a part, is driving furiously on, making each watery particle visible as it passes the cold mountain-top, and *building thus an enduring form from materials ever flitting and successive.*

"What dream of hoary alchemist bending over his crucible in long-deferred but still unwearied hope, or seeking with rapt eyes to read the mystic messages of the stars which are to guide to the golden transmutation, what migrations of being imagined by oriental seers, is stranger or more sublime than these cyclical transformations and phases revealed by science in the familiar materials around us?

"Look upon yonder landscape, clothed with living verdure,—the grass which, inwrought with variegated flowers, overspreads lawns and valleys and rounded hillsides; the forest that, with interlacing boughs and leaves, shelters the mountain slopes, or arrays its vast battalions on the plain and by the river side, or plants its stately sentinels in the rocky defiles, — what are these but fabrics lately wrought by Nature's vital chemistry from the invisible and inconstant air? The very particles which now glow in the yellow and purple blossoms of the meadow, or that paint the refreshing green that overspreads the whole, have been gathered from the same great, ever-moving aerial sea, — perchance from the south wind that bore its genial warmth and moisture from tropical climes, or from the northwester that came fresh from the realms of frost, breathing of snowy mountains and ice-imprisoned seas.

"Look again upon the living theatre of the earth, and, waving the wand of the systematic naturalist, marshal the procession of the myriad things that creep and swim and fly, or move with rapid bound or stately step, filling the earth and sea and air with life and music. See the harmonious play of forces which weaves the structure of the most complicate and most simple of their forms, drawing materials from the same great aerial store, not for the most part directly, as in the case of plants, but mediately through the already elaborated products of vegetable activity. Guided by the same chemical and physical laws, see by what beautiful adjustments the one great department of living Nature continually restores to the atmosphere the ingredients which the other has withdrawn; thus preserving its composition unchanged, and maintaining in happy equipoise the balance of organic life.

" Let it not be said that these grand inductions are the work of mechanical, chemical and philosophical inquiries, and are foreign to the classifications and theories of the naturalist. They are among those large truths which, being the joint result of research in all departments of physical science, are the common property of all; as the wide prospect of plain, and valley, and river, and ocean, beheld from some lofty mountain-top, greets the traveller equally, from whatever realm he may have approached, and by whatever path he may have commenced his ascent. Indeed, to carry on this comparison, may it not be said, that in ascending to such general views, all paths converge into one, which, like the Alpine roadways of modern engineering, winding from spur to spur, command successively every quarter of the horizon of knowledge, until at length the whole circle of physical relationships is brought into a single view.

" Nor can the naturalist rest satisfied with the mere phenomena of these alternately vital and purely physical phases of the atmosphere. He studies the chemical and mechanical conditions under which they take place, and endeavours, by the rules of inductive science, to learn something of the peculiar forces by which they are controlled. . . .

" Looking thus at arrangements or organization as determining the properties of bodies, who can fail to admire the sublime simplicity of the mechanism through which the Infinite Father fills all Nature with variety and beauty? . . .

" There is a peculiarity belonging to vital forces, as manifested even in the lowest organizations, which the naturalist marks with special interest, and which must ever shape the laws or generalizations he may form in regard to the agencies of life. It is that wonderful cycle of development and decay which presents itself in the simple isolated cell of the microscopic fungus, as in the form of the marvellous microcosm, man.

"That all living forms, in their first visible beginnings, are but a single cell of almost infinitesimal size, modern observations have concurred to demonstrate. Yet, when we follow their vital history, behold by what diverging lines their development proceeds, and at what various stages in different living forms it terminates! We have before us two living cells. Let us watch their growth, and mark in each case toward what form of organization it steadily proceeds, to find at length the consummation of its development. The *one*, by a simple process of division, gives origin successively to innumerable separate cells, repeating the original form, but attaining no higher development; and thus it covers the bare rock with a film of living green, or spreads its thin, crimson veil over the glittering Alpine snows. The *other*, seemingly identical with this, begins its career in the same way; but the resulting cells adhere, the development goes on according to a more complex plan forming the tissues of the embryo plant, and in due time, lo! from the germinating acorn we see arise the stately leaf-crowned oak.

"In vain do we seek to explain this marvellous progress and determinateness of growth, infinitely various when we compare the different living tribes, and yet immutable in regard to each, by referring them to any known chemical and mechanical laws. Rather should we regard them as the characteristic manifestations of other and quite different forces, with which each elementary form of organization is appropriately endowed, — vital forces, that operate by laws far more various and complex than are displayed in the changes of inorganic bodies. Yet it is important to remember that these vital forces, as they construct the living architecture of animal or plant, are ever accompanied by chemical and mechanical effects; and that, indeed, a sound induction not only recognizes them as belonging to the series of truly physical agencies, but views them as the dynamic resultants due to the combined action of particles organically grouped.

"In avoiding what I deem the error of ascribing the laws of living nature to the purely chemical and mechanical activities of matter, let us take care that we do not lose ourselves in that mysticism which imputes intelligence and prescience to embryonic cells and organs, which with Aristotle looks upon the internal essence of plants as a 'plastic soul,' or with Van Helmont enthrones in each organ an Archæus, a living spirit, to superintend its growth and direct it in the performance of its specific tasks, — or which with some eminent modern naturalists represents the vital forces (to quote the words of the most distinguished of them) as 'an idea which guides the whole process,' as 'an essence which precedes and shapes the external existence, as intentions precede and determine acts.' [1]

"Humbly yet firmly in the name of inductive philosophy would I protest against such theories, however distinguished the authority which sustains them. If, because there is manifested in the development of each living form a specific end and a fixed plan of progress, we are to assign to each a special plastic idea or guiding spirit, have we not, in fact, restored the beautiful but dreamy mythology which peopled all nature with tutelary divinities, with naiads and dryads and spirits of the air and sea, and of the moon and sun and stars? For what realm of material being fails to give us evidence of a fixed plan, and progress towards a determinate end?

"How beautiful the cyclical succession of spring, summer, autumn and winter on our earth, with their varied yet regulated alternation of day and night! How perfectly fulfilled the plan of circulation which carries the air in moving columns or in vast eddies over and around the globe, lifts the invisible moisture from the sea, pours it in genial rains upon the land,

[1] Professor Braun's " Das Individuum der Pflanze," etc., translated by C. F. Stone, *Silliman's Journal*, May, 1855.

then conducts it in countless rills into the river channels, and to complete the round of its beneficent activity again restores it to the sea !

"But shall we therefore claim for the earth a special tutelary spirit, a self-directing intelligence that
Æolus-like sends forth the winds on errands to the
four quarters of the globe, — that spins it on its axis,
poises that axis in the precise angle at which it is inclined, and wheels the revolving sphere in its grand
annual path around the heavens? Again, how perfect
the adjustment of forces and motions which carries
each planet of our system in its great elliptic road
around the sun, varying every instant in the speed
and direction of its progress, and yet with unerring
certainty fulfilling the plan of its orbital revolution;
and how marvellously combined the mutual activities
of these spheres, developing by slowly progressive
change the cyclical phases of the system, and yet
securing this 'sublime pendulum of eternity' within
safe limits in its oscillations. And must we, as we
view these marks of profound purpose, these develop-
ments of plan, ask for each revolving world a presiding spirit, an idea in action; or shall we not rather in
these and all the other phenomena of nature, living as
well as inorganic, recognize the infinite Deity operating through the medium of mechanical, chemical,
and vital forces, and with unerring wisdom adjusting
them in ceaseless and harmonious activity to his own
beneficent ends?

"In what I have now presented I have proposed to
illustrate and to urge the importance of connecting
with the special study of any one or more departments
of natural history, a liberal knowledge of the various
collateral branches of physical science. But I would
not be understood as failing in earnest reverence for
the labours of even the humblest collector of the objects of natural history, much less for those of the
systematic naturalist, who devotes to them a closer
examination, and classifies them according to estab-

lished methods. To the former the world is indebted in a large measure for the materials out of which the science has been constructed, — the museums and cabinets which are indispensable for wide comparisons and effective research. . . .

" If, then, we cannot doubt the practical benefits to science and the still nobler spiritual utilities of these systematic collections of natural objects, these beautiful epitomes of the vast volume of mineral and organic nature, with what cordial gratulations should we welcome every effort to establish them, and with what hearty thanks should we refer to the noble liberality of those who devote either time or means to their promotion. . . .

" The love of nature is spontaneous in every human soul. Ingenuous children, if left to the guidance of their instinct for knowledge, early display the curious observation, the spirit of experiment, the disposition to compare object with object, which form the characteristics of the naturalist and physical philosopher. And they unite with these in a large degree the æsthetic element of the love of the beautiful, whether in color, or form, or sound, or motion. It is not then from the rareness of an inherent love for such pursuits that we find so few persons who, after reaching maturity, feel a strong impulse to the cultivation of the natural sciences.

" The studies of the school, occupying the child with widely different though indispensable tasks, have until within a few years failed to provide the young mind thirsting for a knowledge of nature with any opportunity of useful communion with her works. But thanks to the wiser views of our contemporaries, the doors of the academy and the high school are thrown open to admit the odorous breath of flowers and the melody of birds, and the free air and sunshine of the teeming, vocal, beautiful world, and it is found that the clear, refreshing atmosphere, instead of dwarfing the plants of classical and mathematical learning, only nourishes them to a healthier and more vigorous development. . . .

"Surely conquests such as these are better worthy the ambition of educated men, and should command a higher meed of fame than all the triumphs of valour and endurance that were ever blazoned on the torn banner of a hundred martial fields. And surely, gentlemen, to come nearer home, should any of us extend our peaceful march of scientific inquiry beyond the latitude of 49° on the one hand, or, taking to the water, invade the coral isles of the Pacific, or possess ourselves of Mexican territories of science, or carry our bloodless arms into the tempting Archipelago, which, as a chain of pearls, stretches to unite our northern and southern continents on the Atlantic side, our additions to the area of truth would be an annexation [1] approved and honoured by all parties. . . .

"But it is not through the allurements of ambition, even of that noble kind which aims at enlarging the boundaries of knowledge, that the cultivators of natural science are led to the purest enjoyment and the truest success in their pursuits. A higher, more spiritual sensibility must nourish their enthusiasm. The love of truth for its own sake, the power of deriving exquisite satisfaction, not only from the discovery of new relations among objects, but from contemplating them in the light of known facts as subordinated to harmonies and laws; a loving appreciation of beauty in external characters, and of that subtler beauty of structure and affinities, akin to the most delicate perceptions of the artist and poet, but which discloses itself only to the penetrating eye of the naturalist, — such are some of the impulses and tastes that qualify us for enjoying the pursuits of natural history, and for giving them their highest usefulness.

"In speaking of the delights of knowledge as compared with other pleasures, Lord Bacon has eloquently said: 'In all other pleasures there is satiety, but of

[1] An allusion to the politics of the time, — the annexation of Texas.

knowledge there is no satiety, but satisfaction and
appetite are perpetually interchangeable.' Surely of
no kind of knowledge can this be more truly said than
of that which unfolds to us the characters, structure
and mutual dependences of the endless variety of organic and inorganic objects with which natural science
has to deal.

" And it should be remembered that this pure and
ever-recurring satisfaction is not merely the privilege
of the few who possess great collections of specimens,
libraries for reference, and all the refined means for
observation and research, but is accessible to the humblest observer who pursues his inquiries in the ardent,
truth-loving spirit of the genuine naturalist. It needs
but to stir the waters of the great teeming tropical sea
to make them give forth their latent rays, whether
in the silvery flashes marking the wake of some huge
ocean steamer, or in the drops of liquid light that
fall from the lifted oar; whether in the long line
of flame that reveals the breaker's advancing crest, or
in the luminous footprints left by the traveller on the
moistened beach.

" It was once the fashion with poets to decry the
growth of positive science as unfriendly to poetical
and spiritual conceptions of the material world, and
to lament, although we may trust only for the verse's
sake, ' the lovely views ' which have been forced to
' yield their place to ' what they please to call ' cold
material laws.' But, thanks to a juster knowledge of
the spirit, objects and results of physical inquiries,
now generally diffused among scholars, such complaints are no longer likely to find sympathy with
them. From the known laws of the intellect, what
more certain conclusion can be drawn, than that
thought becomes exalted and suggestion quickened in
proportion as they embrace a wider and more varied
field of objects and relations? Who that, gazing on
the vault of the sky, thinks of the innumerable multitude of worlds which the sure demonstrations of

astronomy there point out to him, — measures in imagination their dimensions and the vast distances which separate them, — follows the planets in their stately march, and watches the whole solar system, as like a majestic fleet of argosies it moves sublimely on its voyage of circumnavigation among the stars, — and while witnessing in thought this grandest of nature's spectacles, reflects on the profound adjustment of forces and motions by which these results are secured, — who thus looking and reflecting can see in the material laws which control and harmonize this universe, aught lower or less spiritual than the thought of Infinite Wisdom and the handiwork of Infinite Power? Surely such a meditative gazer on the skies must feel in his soul the inspiration of a far nobler poetry than ever charmed the reveries of him

> " ' To whose passive ken
> Those mighty spheres that gem infinity
> Are only specks of tinsel fixed in heaven
> To light the midnights of his native town.' "

" And what is true of astronomy is not less true of even the obscurest walks of natural history. For it is less in the magnitude and distance of objects than in their mutual activities, their harmonious arrangements, and their adaptations to wise and beneficent ends, that material phenomena become imbued with a spiritual and poetical significance. Let us then rejoice that in our scientific communings with living and inanimate things we are not only able to catch sweet notes from Apollo's lyre, but to gather into our souls the deeper harmonies which are felt to be the echoes of voices from the skies; let us indeed believe that

> " ' Nature hath her hoarded poetry
> And her hidden spells, and he
> Who is familiar with her mysteries is even as one
> Who by some secret charm of soul or eye
> In every clime beneath the smiling sun
> Sees where the springs of living waters lie.' "

SUNNY HILL, October 9, 1855.

There are now four organized political parties in Massachusetts, viz.: Democrats, Whigs, Americans and Republicans. The last is a fusion of all, which holds the non-extension of slavery by the National Government as its polar principle, and proposes to ignore all differences on other points. Its candidate is Rockwell, the former United States Senator, a leading Whig, but now disowned by the Whigs proper. The latter have had a meeting, at which George Hillard made quite an effective speech. My impression is that the *Republicans* will succeed.

The Natural History Society, I am told, think of sending their working-man, Samuels, to California, to collect birds and other objects for the museum. . . .

I have never seen Eliza in better health, and the dear little Edith grows more winning daily. As I look at her gentle, thoughtful face, the traces of her father impress me with a tenderness that brings moisture to my eyes.

In the autumn of 1855 overtures were made to Henry concerning the professorship in the University of Glasgow, to which he was later appointed.

MR. ROGERS TO HIS BROTHER HENRY.

BOSTON, November 20, 1855.

The Academy is yet quite asleep. Wyman is making good experiments on the impressions made by raindrops on firmly prepared clay. Some of the slabs thus marked are very instructive. In connection with this, I have been computing the terminal velocities of drops, ranging from 1-10 to 1-2000 inch in diameter, using one of Hutton's formulæ of resistance. I hope to get up an arrangement for determining the weight, and then the actual diameters of raindrops of various sizes.[1] . . .

You will see in "Silliman" that my inquiries on binocular vision have extended. There will be one more section after that in the January number, which I have just sent to New Haven. When completed, I want some of those who have studied the matter in Scotland or England to go over the observations critically, for I believe they will find much that is new and important in them. I have just hit on a beautiful geometrical law for certain cases. The binocular resultants of a right line and circular arc are always a conic section. I will send you the drawings and explanation, which, perhaps, you may show to some friend in Edinburgh, and have inserted in the "Quarterly Journal."

I shall keep on with the gathering of materials for our geological text-book, for I am satisfied that there is nothing we could do that would tell better in every way. . . .

Did you see one of Professor Connell's pretty hygrometers? . . . God bless and keep you, my own dear brother. Day and night my thoughts are with you ; I form many a fancy picture of you and the circle around you. My heart warms to the good friends that have cheered you by their welcome in kind Scotland. . . .

TO HIS BROTHER ROBERT.

Boston, November 21, 1855.

. . . On Monday night next I give the first of my two lectures in the Tremont Temple.[2] I understand all the tickets of the course, about twenty-five hundred, have been taken. Last Monday there must have been at least that many persons present to hear a lecture from an eminent pulpit orator and lecturer,

[1] *Boston Society of Natural History*, vol. v. pp. 266, 282.
[2] Lectures before the Mercantile Library Association.

Starr King. His subject was " Substance and Show."
I shall talk of Physical Forces. . . .

Only think, Judge Cushing has commenced printing his book,[1] having made quite a favourable arrangement with Little & Brown. He appears quite revived
by the thought of having finished his ten years' task,
which few of us thought he would live to finish. . . .

How is our dear little friend Beppo? Poor little
fellow. E. and I can hardly believe that he is no
longer accompanied by the beautiful, loving Zeo.[2] His
image rises always in thinking of the dear home in
Girard Street. . . .

TO HIS BROTHER HENRY.

BOSTON, November 30, 1855.

. . . On Monday night I gave my first lecture in
the Tremont Temple. It was a rainy night, but still
there were about two thousand persons present. I
found it an easier matter than I anticipated to keep
up the interest of this crowd, although the subject was
not of the showy kind. From indications at the time
and what I have since heard, I believe I was quite
successful. But how *very elementary* all such lectures
must be to be at all intelligible! On Wednesday next
I give a lecture at Lawrence on Geology. . . .

BOSTON, December 4, 1855.

. . . I have this morning closed and directed your
box, and put it in the hands of the expressman. . . .
Longfellow's last poem, Rush on the Voice, and other
books will remind you of home, but perhaps not so
much as the copies of my lecture at Williams College,
of which I wish you to present one to Brewster, one
to Balfour; make what other distribution you please.
I should like to know what the naturalists say of my
criticism of the German notion of living forms as determined by ideas, so largely dwelt on by Braun, and

[1] *Cushing's Parliamentary Law*, by Judge L. S. Cushing.
[2] Two dogs, Beppo and Zeo.

so much favoured by Burnett and Agassiz. Some of my friends here have spoken well of the literary execution of the lecture.

Hayes has received the Report of the Torbane Mine trial. The substance of it is, I believe, published in the "Journal of the Microscopical Society," along with Quckett's detailed observations and beautiful plates.

I read eagerly the numbers of the "Edinburgh New Philosophical Journal," as they come out. The October number is now before me. It is interesting to see in such papers as those of Harkness, of Cork, the recognition of the principle of folded structure, which we knew and applied so extensively twenty years ago. There is an odd awkwardness in the descriptions given by Harkness in the article on Cleavage which surprises me. You will see that the whole of the paper might, with greater clearness, be given in one third the space. How different are your descriptions of structural features. Indeed, my dear Henry, I think that even in our old annual reports the kind of description is far more precise and picture-like than what we meet with in geological writings generally. But think what a training we had in the study of Appalachian structure! . . .

I am expecting criticisms and objections[1] from Brewster, and still more from Wheatstone, but I am ready for them. I shall send along with the MSS. some cards of figures in ink, to illustrate my experiments by the use of the common stereoscope. . . .

I have no higher objective than 1-4 inch. My microscope is of the make of Smith & Beck, recommended by Morris. It is the next to their largest size. I should like to have an objective of greater power. Indeed, I believe their present 1-4 inch is much greater. But I have no money as yet for such a luxury. Before you are leaving I may write again on the subject. . . .

[1] On his *Observations on Binocular Vision.*

BOSTON, Christmas Morning, 1855.

The ground is white with snow and sleet, and the icy shower is rattling against my windows as I sit down to speak a loving word to my dear brother across the sea. There is an influence coming from early association which fills this holiday season with tender recollections of the past, and with kind as well as wise resolves for the future. With what an earnest solicitude for your happiness does my heart now warm towards you, my dear brother, and with what true joy do I dwell on your improved health and the prospect of future cheerful labour and mutual helpfulness for us all. A thousand wishes crowd to be expressed, but I can only say, God bless you, my own dear brother! and beg you to take as the type of my present thoughts the happy affection of our boyhood which, ever dwelling on and around us, overflowed our breasts in this festive season, making our home, even shadowed by poverty, a place full of earth's truest, sweetest happiness. The long interval of years has not dimmed the images of parental goodness or of loving brotherhood. To-day we may open the casket in which they are kept within our heart of hearts, and have sweet pleasure in dwelling on the dear memory of those who have left them to us. . . .

BOSTON, March 11, 1856.

. . . I am glad you saw Brush and were able to do him service. He has talent, and will, I am sure, come home well skilled in all branches of practical chemistry, as well as much else. . . .

In a letter from Robert a few days ago, I learned that he had been superintending some attempts to blow up the ice in the Delaware, opposite the city, using some of his Bunsen cells, and igniting by wires extended from the wharf. The effect was insignificant. . . . Tell me in your next what sort of an audience you had at the Royal Institution. What is

Faraday about just now? and Wheatstone? Tyndall
seems to be taking a leading part at the Royal Institution. He has fine talents, and I hope he is a good
fellow; but where is there another Faraday!

Boston, March 25, 1856.

I shall look impatiently for the March number
of the "Philosophical Journal." Surely Sir David
Brewster will read what I have written before criticising. If what you say of his comments be true, he
has entirely misconceived me. But I can readily set
him right. He is, I know, very irritable and tena-
cious, and I should dislike controversy with him.
Besides, I have a true veneration for his services as a
man of science. . . .

Gardner, of Edinburgh, mentions you in very complimentary terms. What a lovable old man is this
Patriarch of the Faculty ! . . .

TO JAMES SAVAGE, JR. (TRAVELLING IN EUROPE).

Philadelphia, April 21, 1856.

My dear Jim, — E. and I have for nearly a week
been enjoying the milder climate of this pleasant city,
and the true home comforts of Girard Street, where
my dyspeptic ailments have been almost dispersed by
the skill of my brother Robert. I was far from well,
but in a few days I hope to bound whistling up the
stairs at No. 1 Temple Place.

Will you let me, ignorant as I am of things European, offer you advice? From your last letter I
infer that your desire to see more of the Continent
may detain you from England until it will be too
late to make a satisfactory visit to the Blessed Island,
as your father calls it. After all, my dear James, it
is from the Fatherland (i. e., the mother country) that
we must continue to draw the most valuable helps in
our social and practical life, and the most reliable
guidance in politics and philosophy.

As a Bostonian you will be pleased to learn that the fire-alarm system has just been introduced here, and will soon be put in operation also in New York.

Population is flowing into Kansas rapidly from the free States; more slowly, but yet I fear too actively, from the region of slavery. I have no fear that the latter will succeed in establishing its institutions in the new country, but I dread the general effect of the fratricidal conflicts that seem to be impending. I am, however, of those who think that our Union is too strongly framed in constitutional right and bolted together by mutual interest, to be severed by even such a shock as this.

We have not forgotten that this is our dear Jamie's birthday. We shall drink your health at dinner in bumpers of foaming ale.

God bless you, my dear fellow, and send you back to us as good a boy as you were on leaving.

TO HIS BROTHER HENRY.

BOSTON, April 29, 1856.

. . . Can you learn from Gregory or James Forbes whether any definite law has yet been made out in England or Scotland in regard to the meteoric conditions proper to the greater or less abundance of ozone? Thus far I have found it always abundant upon the setting in of a wind from any quarter between W. and N., and quite *absent* in those from between E. and S. I will tabulate the results by coördinates and send them to you.[1] . . .

Robert has been made Dean of the Faculty by the unanimous wish of Carson and the rest of his colleagues. The office will give him but little trouble and will add something to his income. It did my heart good to see how universally he is beloved and respected in Philadelphia. . . .

[1] See *Boston Society of Natural History*, vol. v. p. 32; also *Silliman's Journal*, vol. xxii. p. 141, 1858.

SUNNY HILL, July 6, 1856.

. . . I believe I mentioned in a former letter having met in Washington with Blodgett and Newberry. Leidy is active in the description of fossils from the West, and indeed from all quarters. . . . Wyman, I believe, is working systematically at the lower reptilians, *Menopoma*, etc., expecting to bring out his results in the " Smithsonian Contributions." . . . Poor Sumner's strength appears to be seriously broken, and it is doubtful if he will be able to resume his seat this session. The effect can hardly be due to the physical hurt he sustained, but must be owing to the great perturbation of his nervous system.

The Report of the Kansas investigating committee confirms the very worst reports we had of the border outrages. It has not yet been acted on in Congress.

Appearances indicate that most of the Whigs of the Northern and Eastern States will favour the Frémont ticket, as the only means of preventing the triumph of the slave power. Indeed, under present circumstances, I do not see why they should hesitate to do so. The Boston Whig committee in their late meeting avoided any committal of the party in this matter, and this, I believe, is Hillard's counsel just now. But they will be obliged, individually, if not as a party, to act decidedly in so momentous an alternative. . . . I am glad to hear that you are to have the benefit of a trip to Arran, and other excursions, and that you may probably go to the Continent to meet Desor.[1] . . .

BOSTON, August 12, 1856.

. . . As all the *Paradoxides* are confined to the very lowest Silurian of Murchison, or the Primordial division of the Bohemian rocks according to Barrande, we shall probably have to place the slates of Quincy and Braintree very near the base of the Palæozoic series, at least as low, I presume, as the Potsdam, or our Primal rocks. . . .

[1] P. J. Edouard Desor, Swiss geologist.

Nothing of consequence is doing in the societies. The Natural History meetings, of which I attended the last, are fuller and more interesting than formerly, chiefly on account of Agassiz's presence.

TO HIS BROTHER ROBERT.

BOSTON, August 13, 1856.

I write a hurried line to say that I have lately been much interested in a discovery I have developed of old Silurian fossils in some of the altered slates almost adjoining the sienite of Quincy, and that, feeling myself in pretty good plight, I intend taking them to Albany, where they will excite great interest. This is the most curious and important discovery ever made in the geology of this region. . . .

TO JOSEPH L. BATES.

LUNENBURG, September 5, 1856.

SIR, — Your communication inviting me in behalf of the Massachusetts Charitable Mechanic Association to act as one of the judges of stoves, etc., reached me yesterday. In reply, I have to say that my strong interest in the progress of applied science, and therefore in the general objects of your exhibition, will not suffer me to withhold any small help it may be in my power to give in the particular department to which you refer. At the same time I wish you to understand that my attention to this important branch of mechanical invention has been too slight to familiarize me with the details of construction, and that I must look to the practical knowledge of others to assist me in my decisions. . . .

TO HIS BROTHER HENRY.

SUNNY HILL, September 9, 1856.

. . . Robert and Fanny, who have been with us since our return, are still here, and we are enjoying pleasant idleness. . . . Should you see our dear old friend Sedgwick before leaving, assure him of my kindest remembrances, and of the true admiration with which I regard, not only his great scientific labours, but the manliness with which he has battled for his rights and for the truth. . . .

I fear that yet graver troubles are arising in consequence of the wicked tyranny of the administration in regard to Kansas. The Fillmore Whigs, led by Winthrop, Everett and Hillard, are, I think, only encouraging the aggravation and outrage of the slave power. Whether Buchanan or Frémont be chosen, there will be immense excitement. In the latter event some, or perhaps all, the slave States will make a feint of resistance and disunion, but I do not believe they will carry out their threats. How changed is the ground of contest within a few years! Formerly the doctrine of Frémont to let slavery alone where already established, and to make no more slave States north of the compromise line, was considered good conservative doctrine, even in the South. Now it is denounced as abolitionism, and the Southern demagogues have advanced to the position of claiming that all new territory shall be open to slavery, and worse than this, shall be given up to it. But I believe the storm will blow over, and leave us in a really better condition. . . .

The great mechanical exhibition in Quincy and Faneuil Halls opens to-morrow, and perhaps Robert will accompany me to Boston to take a look at it. . . .

During the winter of 1856–57 Mr. Rogers was in feeble health, and passed some weeks in Philadelphia, under his physician's care. He was able, however, to give a course of lectures in the Lowell Institute on the Elementary Laws of Physics.

In the spring of 1857 Professor Henry Rogers visited Boston, and on his return to Scotland took with him his wife and daughter Edith. They resided for a time in Edinburgh, while he superintended the pub-

lication of his Pennsylvania Report. Mr. Rogers
was still in delicate health, and in July determined to
try the effect of an ocean voyage and a short visit to
Great Britain.

TO HIS BROTHER HENRY.

LUNENBURG, July 13, 1857.

. . . I am seriously thinking of a short visit to
England, especially for the advantage of the voyage
to and fro. For although I believe I shall gradually
get well even as I am now living on, I think I might
in a great degree shake off my feebleness with all its
disabilities by the sea air and the pleasant excitement
and variety of a month or two spent in England, Scotland and Ireland. By the steamer of next week I
will write you what I decide upon in this matter. . . .

I have been studying up the subject of magnetism,
especially terrestrial, in connection with Saboni's admirable memoir and map, and I have had occasion
to remark a very gross and wholesale plagiarism of
Noad in the second volume of his work on electricity
and magnetism, now in course of publication. I have
written a short notice of it, exposing this unacknow-
ledged transfer of more than forty pages from Brewster's "Magnetism."

TO HIS WIFE.

LONDON, HANOVER SQUARE, August 12, 1857.

. . . We encountered head-winds nearly all the
way to the northwest coast of Ireland, but for the last
two days we have had the luxury of a calm sea, and
an atmosphere exquisitely balmy, and clear enough to
afford me the precious opportunity of seeing in detail
the picturesque and lovely features of the Irish coast.
We ran so near the shore of Antrim as to be able to
study the wonders of the Giant's Causeway, and to
see on the gentle seaward slopes of the mountains the
hamlets and villages scattered amid the enamelled
verdure which clothed the hills and valleys and crept

far down the slopes and into the crevices of the rocky
cliffs washed by the breakers of the Atlantic. . . .
Each new beauty that opened as we moved from headland to headland, catching now views of the misty
mountains, now of the far-receding rocks, made me
lament afresh that you and dear Jamie were not with
me, to help me to be happy by sharing in my delight.

We anchored in the Mersey at four A. M. on Monday, but we were not relieved by the custom house in-
spector until nearly ten. As I was escorting one of the
ladies up the pier, whom should I see among the ex-
pectant crowd but Henry, who had come to receive
me. . . .

13th.

. . . In the afternoon went with Henry to Kew
Gardens. Failed to find Sir William Hooker, but
left my letters and packet from Gray. Walked about
the enchanting grounds, more beautiful than when
you were here, and returned late in the evening by
omnibus.

14th. Henry has gone by special invitation to
breakfast with the Duke and Duchess of Argyll.
The Chair in Glasgow is vacant, and he will probably
apply for it.

. . . You may say to the servants that I have often
thought of them, and to Mary I thought the mountains of Donegal as beautiful as any I ever saw.

BOWDIN, NEAR MANCHESTER,
Tuesday Morning, August 18.

Finding London nearly deserted by our scientific
friends, we made a visit with our good friend Morris
on Saturday to Sydenham Palace, and took the cars
next morning for Manchester; thence to this beautiful
spot a few miles beyond, where we find, in a country
inn, comfortable lodgings, and have easy access to the
Art Exhibition by frequent trains. . . .

Yesterday was mostly spent in the Art Exhibition,

Manchester, where with some thousands of others, mostly well-dressed people, I went, book in hand, through the early ages of Art, beginning with Cimabue and Giotto, as far as to the period succeeding Raphael.

This carried me over about one half the southern wall of one of the three great divisions of the edifice. A glance further on showed a glorious gathering from Titian, Velasquez, Murillo and on the opposite wall an immense wealth of Dutch and Flemish works. Of course, I shall only look at a few, but I perceive that the relish for this enjoyment has become keen, and if I were strong and had more time, I should regard some weeks' study of this unrivalled collection as time well applied.

LLANDUDNO, Thursday.

Here I am for the second day at one of the most lovely spots on the Welsh coast, in the curve of the beautiful bay that lies between the Great and Little Orme's Head, and only four miles from Conway. . . .

This afternoon, on a little pony, I ascended the lofty hill which forms the crown of Orme's Head, and thence I looked down upon the sea and out into the hazy space, where sea and sky could not be separated, and where the very ships and boats seemed rather suspended mysteriously in the haze than floating on the water. Here are some seeds of wall flowers from the top of one of the Conway towers, to which I clambered by a ladder, thinking you would prize this little token.

My last letter was mailed at Llandudno, the day before my trip through North Wales. This journey carried me through Conway, thence up the beautiful vale of Llanrwst, in which I passed several striking waterfalls, and had a succession of exquisite views, combining richly cultivated hillsides and valleys with grand masses of mountain and rock, alternately clothed with forests and with blooming heather which overspread the cliffs like a velvet mantle. . . .

As to my health, I think I can say it is improving. I have gained two or three pounds, but my sleep is rarely good. I slept little during the voyage, and not well since, but I think I shall improve in this particular, and that will be the signal for a rapid recruiting, so you must expect to hear the most cheering accounts from me. . . .

DUBLIN, September 3, 1857.

. . . Since coming here, on Wednesday, I have been in a perpetual whirl of business and amusement, if you may so term the crowded receptions at the castle and the Provost's house, and the various smaller entertainments.

. . . The meeting [of the British Association] is quite as full as that of Birmingham, although in the geological section the absence of the most prominent men, Lyell and Murchison, has been much felt.

September 4.

I am before breakfast snatching a few minutes to close this letter, as we are to leave in less than an hour on an excursion to Parsonstown to see Lord Rosse's telescope. We shall remain there until to-morrow afternoon. . . . Yesterday, at noon, the imposing ceremonies of conferring honorary degrees took place in the grand old college chapel. A number of the members of the Association were thus complimented. Among them brother Henry and Foucault, who is also present.

. . . Henry received several days ago the announcement of his having been appointed to the Chair in the University of Glasgow, so that altogether the present is a season of very just elation with him. He has had even greater success than I imagined in making powerful friends in Scotland and England, to whose influence with the Lord Advocate he owes his very complimentary appointment.

Last evening we dined at Malahide Castle, the residence of Lord Talbot de Malahide. It is about nine miles from the city, surrounded with lawns and parks and noble clumps and avenues of old trees. The building is mostly of the date of Henry II., a grand old castle, and it was not a little impressive to be received within these ancient walls, which had never ceased to be inhabited by the Talbots for the last seven hundred years.

The superb dining-hall was hung with paintings of the illustrious ancestry, and over our heads, from the lofty rafters of the ceiling, were hanging many an ancient banner, the history of which I longed to learn. How I wished you could see this fine specimen of the ancient times so nobly preserved, and enjoy, as I have done, the elegant and quiet hospitality of Lord and Lady Talbot.

On Monday morning we shall set off by rail for Antrim Castle, the abode of Lord Massereene. He very cordially urged me and Henry to pay him a visit, and from his house to make our tour to the Giant's Causeway, which we can accomplish in less than a day. We shall then go to Glen View House, where our friend Mr. Ogilby will make us acquainted with some of our cousins through the father's side. . . .

DUBLIN, Saturday, September 5, 1857.

On Thursday morning at ten o'clock, we joined the party of the Association going to visit Lord Rosse. As we approached Parsonstown in a long procession of jaunting-cars and carriages, carrying us from the terminus, some six miles across the country, our progress was cheered by crowds of smiling peasantry gathered at numerous points along the road. At Parsonstown most of the party stopped to take their lodgings with the kind inhabitants, while those of us who were to be the special guests at the Castle went on, through the beautiful avenue and under the noble Gothic gateway that led into the grassy lawn in front of this castellated mansion. Eighteen of us were provided with pleasant chambers in this hospitable home. Among the number were Foucault, the Abbé Moigno, Abbadie, Daubeny, Gassiot, the Schlagen-weits, Lord and Lady Massereene, etc. All the party, amounting to about one hundred and eighty, were feasted most luxuriously in the ample dining-hall, and were entertained in the beautiful drawing-rooms and libraries. The workshop, laboratory and grinding-rooms were thrown open for our inspection.

Lady Rosse showed us a large number of photo-graphs of her own execution, and acted the amiable and kind hostess to perfection.

Before taking our leave on Friday, we had a sump-tuous lunch, or rather dinner, at the close of which Dr. Daubeny proposed a vote of thanks to our excel-lent entertainers, which, at his request, I seconded with a short speech. This was so well received that the reporters present, who had not expected anything of the kind, and had taken no notes, bored me after-wards for a copy of my remarks, which, of course, I could not give except in a very general way. . . .

ANTRIM CASTLE, Thursday, September 10, 1857.

In this seat of beauty and refined hospitality we have been passing the hours most pleasantly since Monday evening, when we arrived a little before din-ner. Lady Massereene was detained in Dublin a day later, but we spent Tuesday in walking and driving over the wonderfully beautiful domains of his lord-ship, embracing a great extent of park and lawn, bor-dering on the northeastern side of Lough Neagh, the largest of the Irish lakes. This being my first oppor-tunity of seeing thoroughly the luxurious improve-ments of an aristocratic seat, I have, as you may have supposed, found great enjoyment in my walks and drives. The castle, modelled originally after a French château, is surrounded in great part by the most exquisite gardens I have ever seen, separated by huge walls of trimmed thorn and linden and other

plants. Numerous avenues through the neighbouring
wood, converging at various points, offered pleasant
vistas, at one time, of the lake and Thane's Castle
beyond, at another of a distant round tower, with its
conical cap, the mystery of Irish antiquaries; here
the village spire, there the strange terraced moat, at
the angle of the castle surmounted by the flag; at
the end of another avenue, the mimic waterfall.
Fuchsias, trained like vines to the castle walls, blend
with ivy and our Virginia creeper. The climate is so
balmy that the tenderest flowers flourish out-of-doors,
and such a bright verdure overspreads the lawn, even
at this season, as has no counterpart with us except
in the first week of the most genial spring. I can give
you no details of park, grove and stream, and all the
other beauties that have made this spot so charming
to me. The general appearance of the castle itself
you see in the little engraving which I send. Yesterday, Henry and I made a visit to the Giant's Causeway. . . .

Lady Massereene likes a house full of guests, and
beside ourselves has now some eight others, among
them two pleasant young ladies, the Misses Forbes,
from Scotland, and a young Irish girl from Dublin,
all, of course, refined and cultivated. The eldest
child, Dorcas, is a beautiful shy girl of about fifteen,
the next a bright boy of thirteen, and all have the
simplest and most cordial manners imaginable. We
breakfast at nine and a half, lunch at two, and dine
at six and a half, then we have chat and music, and
an amusing game, in which all can join, called
" races." . . .

GLENNOCK COTTAGE, NEAR NEWTON STEWART,
COUNTY TYRONE, September 15, 1857.

I am now seated in the neat parlour of Mr. John
Rogers, a distant relative of my father, and as I look
out through the spacious bow-window over the verdant slope on which his hospitable cottage stands, I

see, beyond the old stone bridge that spans the Strule-
water, the neat village of Newton Stewart, nestling at
the base of Betsey Bell, one of the loveliest hills I
have yet seen, even in this land of verdant beauty.
Betsey Bell on one side, and Mary Gray on the other,
rising from the fertile valley, watered by the winding
and romantic Strule, recall to me the song I heard my
mother sing when I was on her knee, and speak to
me of many a legend which I heard in my earliest
childhood.[1]

After leaving Antrim Castle, where Henry separated from me the day before, I took the cars for
Londonderry, and thence was driven in a jaunting-car
to Glenview, the residence of my hospitable friend,
William Ogilby. He has very large landed possessions, and lives in great elegance, as well as comfort,
on the slope of Dunellen, amid the long-swelling hills
of Tyrone, and in view of the nearer peaks of the wild
heathery mountains of Donegal. His wife, a niece
of Lord Abercorn, and relative of Lord Aberdeen, is
a gentle lady of refined manners but simple home
tastes, devoting herself chiefly to her children, two
beautiful rosy boys and as many girls. . . .

5 P. M. I have been rambling up the beautiful valley, partly by railroad and partly in a car, and am
seated in the hotel of Omagh, waiting for the return
train to Newton Stewart. I have seen Edergole, the
large tract, or township, I may call it, which once belonged to our family, and have trod the ground which
my father's feet pressed in his childhood. It is one
of the loveliest spots of this exquisitely beautiful
country, — gently rolling hills covered with grass and
grain, adorned with clustering trees and uncut hedge-
rows, and watered by a stream that winds alternately

---

[1] *Bessie Bell and Mary Gray*, an old Scotch ballad,

> "Sing Bessie Bell an' Mary Gray,
> They were twa bonnie lassies,
> They biggit a bower on yon burn-brae,
> An' theekit it o'er wi' rashes."

between rocky banks and emerald meadows. My heart has been full, and I have above all thanked God for America, and felt with yet stronger force the sentiment which has continually presented itself since I have been abroad, that my dear western home deserves to be more loved than even the heartiest American loves it. Ireland is, indeed, a land of extraordinary natural beauty and has an elysian climate, but long, long will it be ere its people will have that general culture and personal independence which make the glory of New England. And this is no less true of parts of Wales and Scotland, and in a degree, I think, of England.

To-morrow I go southwards to Enniskillen, where I shall perhaps visit Florence Court, Lord Enniskillen's beautiful residence, thence to Galway and to Killarney, and lastly to Cork, where I expect letters to be forwarded to me from Edinburgh and London. . . .

As I am improving in health, I am inclined to stay two or three weeks longer than I at first proposed, and may not leave until the last of October. A week ago I weighed 136 pounds, which is four or five more than when I left home. . . .

To-day has been a day of sad feeling with me. To see old homesteads and what was once a beautiful realm of social and family joy abandoned fills my heart with sorrow ; — and yet why did I expect aught else ? Certainly I had no reason to look for another result. Yet I have performed a pious duty, and I shall soon banish the sadness that has accompanied it. . . .

On October 1, 1857, Mr. Rogers very narrowly escaped death in a peculiar accident while travelling. The following letters tell the story, but Mr. Rogers makes as light as possible of what was really a most serious affair : —

TO HIS WIFE.

SWAN INN, NORWICH, ENGLAND,
Monday, October 4, 1857.

I am seated in a cosy room in this most comfortable inn, thankful to God that I am so well as to be able with ease to write to you. On my way hither on Friday night I was injured by a large stone thrown into the car, while we were moving at a high speed; and I am compelled to remain here some days to recruit. The stone (a piece of flint) struck me in the centre of the left cheek, producing a large wound, but luckily did not pass entirely through, and caused a small fracture both of the lower and upper jaw. I have had but little fever, and the doctor thinks the wound is doing well, and that the broken bones will not be long in uniting. We were twelve miles from Norwich when the injury was done, but I preferred continuing my journey to this place, in spite of the great pain and loss of blood. It was well I did so, as I have fallen into kind hands, and am provided with every comfort and attendance that could be desired. The principal people of the city have offered their services, and have shown their sympathy in a variety of grateful ways. I may be detained here until the end of the week, or even longer, but I am in hopes of being able to pursue my journey to London by Friday. How little we know of our future! When I last wrote you, the day before leaving Manchester, I was exulting in my improved health. At that time I had not decided on coming this way, which I was led to do by a kind acquaintance telling me that I should certainly find Sedgwick here. I therefore agreed to make this digression, and was much pleased on the way by my view of the cathedral of Peterborough, and of the far grander one of Ely. It was about two hours after I had enjoyed the ancient wonders of this structure and the superb restorations that I received the terrible blow from which I am now suffering. . . .

I believe my injury is already noised in the papers, although on that night and the following day I enjoined upon the police and reporters not to mention my name, as I feared that the exaggerated news might reach Edinburgh and America before I could write. ... Rest assured that I have been frank with you as to the nature and extent of the injuries. They are severe, but not at all serious. The wound in the face will, I trust, not leave much of a scar, and the slight fracture will doubtless soon be healed. . . .

TO HIS BROTHER HENRY.

NORWICH, Saturday Morning, October 2, 1857.

. . . It grieves me to have such a letter to write. But I made good escape with my life, for an inch or two higher would have brought the jagged missile upon my temple. . . . I find that Sedgwick left Norwich three days ago. . . .

. . . The doctor does not apprehend any serious delay in the healing. I have had very kind visits from the mayor, and sheriff, and other gentlemen of Norwich, as well as from Mr. Gurney, the M. P. for this county. The people of the house are extremely attentive, and make me quite comfortable.

TO HIS WIFE.

NORWICH, Thursday, October 7, 8 P. M.

. . . The wound on my face is so much closed that I am able now to assure you that my beauty will not be much marred by it. The swelling slowly subsides, but still gives me an aldermanic look on one side. As to the progress that the broken bones are making in healing their differences I cannot so certainly speak, but they *are* making progress, and in two or three days more I hope I shall be able to venture into the open air.

Thus far I have alternated between my chamber and sitting-room, in both of which I have had a very lonesome time, as you may suppose. I contrive various illusions as a substitute for society, such as having two chairs beside my own, at the round table where I now write, and placing you in one and Jamie or Robert in the other, and then talking in whispers for all three in earnest; this has been quite a comfort to me. Of course I see the papers, and besides have some books from the library, for I am rather lionized in Norwich. . . .

TO HIS BROTHER HENRY.

NORWICH, Friday, 8 P. M., October 8, 1857.

. . . They tell amusing stories here of Sedgwick's preaching, which is full of geology and natural science in general, and digressive to an extraordinary degree. He errs evidently in making his sermons much too long, although I find the substance of them much approved of by the more intelligent hearers. . . .

TO HIS WIFE.

EDINBURGH, October 16, 1857.

In my anxiety that you should hear of my injury first from me, I last week wrote several letters to you, one of which to go by the line from Southampton. I continued to do well at the inn, under the watchful care of the nurse and my kind, sympathizing doctor,[1] and on Saturday he insisted on removing me to his own house. There I remained in delightful quarters for three or four days, walking a little and riding out with him, until I thought I could venture to make the journey hither, which I did without hurt the day before yesterday.

Never was a stranger more kindly and generously treated than was I by these noble people of Norwich. After all his laborious care of me at the inn, and afterwards, my good doctor positively refused to accept a fee. Other friends gathered about me, and before I had left Norwich I had grown to love the city and

[1] Mr. William Firth, surgeon.

people as if it had long been my home. By the
kindness of Mr. Stark, Mr. Fitch, the Mayor, Mr.
Gurney, M. P., and others, I saw nearly all the points
of interest in and about this fine old city without
weariness and with great enjoyment. . . .

This afternoon I walked, in company with Henry,
Robert Chambers and Mr. Cross, son of the noted
electrician, to the celebrated Craiglieth quarries, about
a mile beyond the wonderful ravine of the Dean
Bridge, which you no doubt remember. Here we
looked down into the vast excavation which was once
filled with the material out of which the whole of the
new city has been constructed, — a warm gray sandstone belonging to the coal measures. From this
high bank we had a superb view of the city, flanked
by the Castle and Calton Hill, and backed on one
hand by the darkly shaded crags and Arthur's Seat,
and on the other by the softer hazy undulations of the
Pentland Hills.

I am getting a frock coat made by Henry's learned
tailor, John Anderson, who has found time to drink
deep of philosophy while struggling to support life by
his handicraft. I have spent two very pleasant evenings at Robert Chambers's, and the last time I enjoyed
the sweet music of the girls singing together, and Mr.
and Mrs. Chambers afterwards, with piano and flute.
Meanwhile, the third daughter, the genius and beauty
of the family, sketched as by magic very good like-
nesses of both Henry and myself. This evening we go
to Professor Maclaren's at Morningside, where his
newly built library is to be inaugurated by a merry
party, with some dancing on the part of the young
folk. . . . You will see from this that my remaining
discomforts of face and jaws do not preclude me from
some social enjoyment. Of course I cannot go to
dinner parties, and at these more informal affairs I
keep very quiet.

Yesterday I rode out to the botanic gardens, where
Balfour very kindly showed me through the various

treasures of which he has charge, almost rivalling the
richness of Kew. I have received very kind letters
of inquiry from my cousin John Rogers and from
other friends in Ireland and England since my accident, and have had a pleasant correspondence with
those dear Norwich friends, who have written to know
of my progress. . . .

. . . You cannot imagine a more lovely child than our
dear little Edith. She is much in the garden with
her kind young nurse, and has the most perfect health.
Her faculties are opening rapidly; she talks in her
own sweet dialect very fluently. Of course she and
her uncle William are the best of friends.

. . . I have just received a very kind letter from
the Provost of Trinity College, Dublin, inquiring anxiously about my recovery. . . .

Love to James and father and kind remembrances
to Dottie and Jimmie.[1] Please enclose the note to
Mr. John A. Lowell, or, if you think better, ask father to give the message orally. Kind regards to the
Ticknors.

EDINBURGH, November 6, 1857.

. . . My stay has given me the opportunity, especially during the last ten days, of making many very
agreeable friends, and seeing something of the working of the University, which I visited on Monday. I
have had very pleasant interviews with Forbes, Gregory, and others who have the lead in science here, and
I have received invitations for next week to dinners
and other parties, which I shall not be here to attend.
To-morrow we dine with Professor James Forbes, and
Dr. Gregory pressed me to remain next week and
dine with him. I spent a very pleasant evening on
Wednesday at Lord Murray's, and shall be this evening at George Combe's. So you see that Edinburgh,
at first so dull, is beginning to present great social
attractions. . . .

1 A maid and man servant.

12 A GEORGE STREET, HANOVER SQUARE,
LONDON, November 15, 1857.

. . . I came up from Edinburgh on Monday night, having paused in Liverpool to secure a berth by the steamer of the 21st, — the *America*. My good friends the Edwardses had a snug chamber ready for me, and when Henry joins me in a day or two we shall have between us a nice little sitting-room. On Tuesday I made a visit to father's friend, good old Mr. Hunter, who was glad to see me and made many inquiries about father and his work. He is very hale-looking, and says his health is good. As he and his daughter pressed me to take family dinner with them, it being late when I called, I gladly did so, and stayed until after tea chatting with them and young Mr. Hunter, now about being admitted to the Bar.

TO HIS BROTHER ROBERT.

LONDON, November 11, 1857.

. . . The best inductive coils made here by Ladd give a spark not exceeding 4½ inches, and cost twelve guineas. Forbes, of Edinburgh, has requested me to order from Ritchie [1] one of his best apparatus. . . . Henry, who has gone over to Glasgow for a day or two, will be here by the close of the week to look after his engraver. He is pressing forward his work with all energy. . . .

TO HIS WIFE.

LONDON, November 20, 1857.

. . . I have now been nearly two weeks in this vast wilderness of men, and am beginning to enjoy some of its noble opportunities for scientific intercourse.

On Wednesday I had a delightful dinner with the Geological Club from 5.30 to 8, when we proceeded to the meeting. There, after a paper by Phillips, we had a long abstract on American Geology from good old Dr. Bigsby, which called up Henry and myself as

---

[1] E. S. Ritchie, electrical inventor and constructor of physical apparatus, Boston.

well as Murchison and others, making the meeting a very animated and interesting one.   Last night I had the honor of dining with the Royal Society Club, and then of attending a meeting in the fine apartments of Burlington House.   General Sabine read a valuable paper on Terrestrial Magnetism, on which by invitation I made a few remarks.   I meet with a very kind welcome from all my old scientific friends, and have made a number of valuable new acquaintances.   It was Professor Miller's kindness that procured me an invitation yesterday.   I forgot to insert in order, that before attending the Royal Society I spent half an hour with the Chemical, in a neighbouring room, where the president, Professor Playfair, called upon me to give an account of my ozone observations and other matters. These were very kindly received.   Since being here I have seen a good deal of Morris, Rupert Jones, Murchison, Bigsby, Tyndall, Wheatstone, Faraday, Gassiot and others, and were you here and we could remain for some months, I could profit by and enjoy greatly these interviews. . . .

We are to take tea at Leonard Horner's on Monday night, when this kind old friend will have several knights of the hammer to meet us. The Lyells I shall not see, as they are not to return until next month. To-morrow morning I breakfast with Dr. Carpenter ; on Monday I lunch at Hammersmith with good Mr. Wheatstone, on Wednesday dine with Gassiot, and thus I am likely to have my time filled up with pleasant social and scientific engagements.

Will you please say to Mr. Ritchie that I have seen Ladd's coil in action, the best in England, and it can scarcely yield four inches of spark.   I hope he will be able to fill Forbes's order promptly.

If I can find time I must run up to Oxford to see the registering apparatus in the Observatory, and to meet Phillips and his sister.   Henry's continued stay has brought him into the most favourable notice, so that now honours of all kinds are in his path.   Erelong he will be made a member of the Royal Society, and other learned bodies are seeking to enroll his name on their list. There is any amount of confusion as to the personality of the two of us.

Mr. Rogers reached home on December 14, 1857.

TO HIS BROTHER ROBERT.

BOSTON, February 8, 1858.

. . . The steamer of yesterday has brought me a letter from Henry. He is working from nine A. M. to nine P. M., as he has been, through the season. I trust the Legislature [of Pennsylvania] will be satisfied with waiting a little longer for the second volume. The whole work will be most superb, far finer than anything of the kind published on this side the Atlantic.

TO HIS BROTHER HENRY.

BOSTON, February 8, 1858.

. . . The Lecompton Constitution, the work of a faction organized by Missouri votes, has been actually commended to Congress by Buchanan in a message full of sophistry and disingenuous statements, and will probably command a majority of the Senate. A motion is to-day to be considered in the lower house for referring it to a special committee with instructions to inquire into the facts, and we are expecting to hear of scenes of stormy debate and violent personalities. There can, however, be no question that Kansas will come in when admitted as a free State, however the weakness of the President and the madness of the Southern fire-eaters may delay the result. I see with sorrow and indignation that Senator Mason contemplates some general provision for bringing new States into the Union by *pairs*, so as to maintain the present balance between slave and free States!! But this *cannot be done*.

Your friend, old Mr. Quincy, attained his 86th birthday last Friday.

BOSTON, March 9, 1858.

. . . Here but little is doing beyond the usual slow movement of some of the surveys. Dale Owen has, I learn, published a second Report, but I cannot get it. Hall is, I believe, bringing out another volume. The most striking news in geology, however, is contained in a letter from Swallow [1] to Dana, in the March number of " Silliman," in which he states that he has found quite a large number of undoubted *Permian* shells, etc., above the Coal measures in Kansas. He claims thus to have established a Permian group of deposits in that region. . . .

I am now surrounded by books and documents on Terrestrial Magnetism, in which I have become more interested than I had ever been before. Some weeks ago I took up inadvertently some experiments on sonorous flames, which have occupied Tyndall and others of late, and hitting upon a number of curious and new results, I have been anxious to complete my little piece of research. I am now resuming these magnetic studies, and am desirous of drawing up a pretty full paper on the subject, but shall not be in time for your April number.[2]

I am sorry to hear such news of good Professor Gregory's health. His kindness and simple love of truth greatly interested me. . . .

Theodore Parker, whom I saw a few days ago, asks very earnestly about you. Last Sunday I heard a superb sermon from him. He is quite himself again. . . .

My health has been on the whole much better than a year ago, though my old troubles do not suffer me to forget them. . . .

[1] Professor G. C. Swallow, State Geologist of Missouri.

[2] *The Edinburgh Philosophical Journal*, of which Henry was one of the editors.

BOSTON, March 9, 1858.

. . . Among my curious new experiments on flame are the following : —

1. I simply vibrate the jet-pipe within the tube, and the silent flame becomes at once sonorous.

2. When the flame refuses to sing by other modes of excitement, I cause it at once to commence its song by sending a properly graduated current of air up the tube.

3. With a small mechanism, constructed for the purpose, I cause the jet-pipe, with its flame, to revolve rapidly in the tube. When silent, the flame, of course, presents the appearance of a hollow cylinder of light, but as soon as it begins to sing, the upper edge becomes serrated, like a crown wheel, and at length almost completely divided into narrow separate columns arranged in circular order, thus giving us a very beautiful proof of the *intermitting combustion* of the singing flame.

NEW HAVEN, March 17, 1858.

I thank you most warmly for the photograph of your trilobite. It is exceedingly fine. Your photo-lithographic illustrations of the subject will make a beautiful suite ; the effect is so good that they almost bring the old world back again. I should like much to make room for your paper in our next, and regret to say that our printers reported to me two days since that I already had the number more than full. . . . I wish you would send a note on the Virginia and North Carolina, etc., rocks, containing the views in your letter. . . . You have the whole subject at your fingers' ends, and can balance rightly the pros and cons, and a notice from you would, therefore, be of great value. . . .

I am glad to know that you have recovered (for so I learn) from the terrible accident that befell you in England. . . .

Blake is at No. 4 St. Mark's Place, New York city. Brush is here working in the mineral way. He has made out a part of the agalmatolite of China to be massive pyrophyllite, as Malmstedt had done. He sends his kind regards.

FROM J. G. GASSIOT.[1]

CLAPHAM COMMON, April 16, 1858.

I forward per post half a dozen copies of the abstract of my paper, which you may present to any of your friends who take an interest in this research.

I have also desired Mr. Casella to send you a tube. . . .

Private. Your brother was among the fifteen selected yesterday by the Council of the Royal Society. Do not take any notice of this; you will hear of it in due course.

TO J. G. GASSIOT.

BOSTON, July 2, 1858.

On coming to town yesterday I was delighted to find the box from Mr. Casella, and proceeded with all care to unwrap its precious contents. The tube was in perfect condition, and last night I had the pleasure of trying it with a coil machine, which Mr. Ritchie had just finished for one of our Southern universities. The effects were wonderfully beautiful. I shall make further experiments with it in the various ways indicated by you, and shall give my scientific friends the pleasure of witnessing these novel phenomena. Let me thank you, my dear Sir, for the trouble you have taken to send me this instrument, and for the instruction and pleasure I am deriving from it. May I ask you, when you meet Mr. Casella, to return my acknowledgments for his care in transmitting the tube, as well as for the printed circular which he enclosed.

---

[1] English physicist and investigator in electricity.

I have read with interest your account of Ritchie's induction apparatus in the "Philosophical Magazine" just received, and knowing that it would gratify him, have sent it to him for perusal. The coil used last night is of the same power as yours, and would no doubt by urging yield a spark much beyond 12 inches. I observe that Ruhmkorff has recently improved his apparatus so as to obtain from it a spark nearly as long as that from Ritchie's coil. But I do not understand his need of using 25 cells for the purpose.

I have just completed a description of curious experiments upon the *rings* formed by gases and liquids under certain conditions of intermittent discharge, and the like phenomena, from bursting and exploding bubbles.[1] Hereafter I may trouble you with some of the details which have been quite interesting to me.

Have you tried Quet's curious experiment on the decomposition of carburetted hydrogen gas by the induction current? The separation of the carbon *at the poles only* is very interesting.

We are greatly disappointed at receiving no news of the Atlantic cable, and have come to the unwelcome conclusion that the attempt has failed. But nevertheless I have strong confidence in its ultimate success.

I am glad to find that Moigno, in the "Cosmos," stands up manfully for Wheatstone's claims in the great invention of the telegraph.

Professor Henry Rogers now paid a brief visit to America in order to attend to matters connected with his Geological Survey of Pennsylvania.

---

[1] "In this paper Professor Rogers anticipated some of the later results of Helmholtz and Sir William Thomson." — J. P. Cooke, *Proc. Am. Acad.* vol. xviii. p. 426.

MR. ROGERS TO HIS BROTHER ROBERT.

SUNNY HILL, Saturday, July 11, 1858.

. . . To-morrow I return to Boston, where I shall remain to see Henry off. I shall feel very sad at parting with him, perhaps for some years, but I believe we shall all be the happier in being no longer anxious for his health, and in the enjoyment of his success abroad. . . .

I send you a copy of my little paper on sonorous flames, as printed in "Silliman."

Henry has recently been elected a fellow of the Royal Society. I do not know that it has been publicly announced, but I have the news in a letter from General Portlock, the geologist, who is a member. . . .

TO HIS BROTHER HENRY.

SUNNY HILL, August 10, 1858.

. . . After reading the exciting narrative of the dangers and difficulties of the earlier trial, I had almost despaired of the laying of the cable this season, and such seems to have been the prevailing impression until the receipt of the startling news of the arrival of the *Niagara* at Trinity Bay, and of the success of the experiment. I recollect no event since the news of peace in 1814, of which I have a vague but glad impression, which has been received with such an acclamation of delight throughout the land. Certainly none has given so unanimous a joy. As might be expected, those immediately instrumental in carrying out the attempt receive an extravagant share of laudation. But the scientific labours which have culminated in this dazzling result will soon become more generally known and fairly appreciated, and I trust that Wheatstone and his British colleagues will reap their full share of the honours of this grand achievement. To Wheatstone certainly belongs the credit of framing a plan com-

plete in nearly all respects for a submarine telegraph
many years before any attempt had been made to lay
one. When with him last autumn I had the pleasure
of seeing his original drawings and plans, which, if
capitalists had favoured, would have secured for him
an acknowledged priority in this great application.
But thus it is often with the most inventive genius,
which passes too rapidly from one creation to another
to secure to itself the honour or profit of its intellectual
labours. . . .

TO JAMES SAVAGE, JR., AT HIS FARM IN ASHLAND, MASS.

SUNNY HILL, Thursday Morning, September, 1858.

Taking pity on your loneliness this morning, I send
you through this stormy air a short missive telling of
our continued thought of you, and giving you the
latest news of our wire.

As the winds were mustering for this great equi-
noctial review all day yesterday, we had good opportunity for our experiment.[1] The kite soars superbly
with all the string and an equal length of wire, and
has force enough for twice as much. We obtained
many pleasant and some rather severe shocks, of which
the women-folks had a share. When you come up
next month we shall have a still finer display in one
of our steady nor'westers.

The peach-trees this morning are surging to and
fro like a stormy sea, and I suppose have been
stripped of most of their fruit, but the storm has
not allowed me yet to make personal inspection. As
usual the house has let in the driving rain at certain
points, and we are entertained by the musical reso-
nance of sundry tubs and buckets made vocal by
descending drops. . . .

Our games of football were of the feeblest after
your departure. But E. and the two Fannys performed surprisingly in an impromptu way when left

[1] Franklin's famous experiment.

to their own wild wills. Robert and I have been
contriving optical whirligigs when not employed in
dragging down the thunder.

Now, my dear Jim, you must forthwith respond to
this bagatelle, and tell us all about your doings and
musings in calm or storm.

E. and the rest send love.

TO HIS BROTHER HENRY.

SUNNY HILL, September 21, 1858.

. . . Donati's comet is now a fine object in the
evening as seen from our hill.

FROM HIS BROTHER HENRY.

BURLEY WOOD, NEAR LEEDS, October 1, 1858.

. . . The meeting of the Association here closed on
Wednesday, and yesterday (Thursday) the members
dispersed on several pleasant excursions.

I made a communication upon the late researches
of Meek and Hayden, and others, stating the evidence
for and against their Permian in Kansas. The general impression of the geologists is that the so-called
Permian may be intermediate between the Coal measures and Permian of Europe, and Emmons's facts do
not convince them that the Carolina beds are genuine
Permian. Do send me an original communication on
your more recently found Richmond coal fossils for
the January number of the "Philosophical Journal,"
and let Silliman copy it.

I am staying with a Mr. Firth, a wealthy merchant
of Leeds, who has grown rich in the American trade.
He and his family have treated me with the genuine
English hospitality, and you know what that means.

TO HIS BROTHER HENRY.

SUNNY HILL, October 3, 1858.

. . . We have had many fine opportunities for ob-
serving the comet for the last two weeks. Two nights

ago we were favoured by that perfectly clear state of the air which marks a cool October night, and I sat watching the superb train for upwards of an hour, until, in fact, the bright nucleus had sunk below the horizon, leaving the train still distinctly visible through the crystalline atmosphere. The fluctuations in the extent and shape of the train early struck my attention, — at one moment we see it suddenly contract in length or in both dimensions, the next instant it flashes out to more than double magnitude. In these strange movements the light frequently spreads out fitfully on the lower or concave side of the train, greatly increasing its breadth for some distance, and then as suddenly contracts with a much narrower band.

As seen on the night of the 2d of October, it had the aspect, when largest, of a magnificent eagle-feather, having a gracefully curving outline above, but a less regular and defined limit beneath, reaching, with its faintly vanishing end, through a superb ascending arc to near the end of the tail of the Great Bear.

1 TEMPLE PLACE, October 19, 1858.

Wyman told me yesterday of his intention to go to the La Plata with Bennett Forbes, who is taking one of his own ships to that region on some commercial enterprise. Wyman's health has again become very feeble, which forms his chief inducement for this voyage, but he will make it profitable in the way of palæontology and natural history. He is studying Darwin, etc., by way of preparation. . . .

How much pleasure, my dear Henry, you have given me by your frequent letters. Do, I beg of you, continue to write thus often, and I will engage to send you a line weekly as you request. I do not permit myself to dwell on your removal to a distant land, or I should sometimes grow very sad. But this active interchange will seem to keep us linked as we have ever been in thought as well as affection. . . .

BOSTON, November 2, 1858.

. . . Since coming to town I have been much occupied in getting up preparations for my Lowell course.[1] As I shall make it somewhat experimental, and as the material at the Institute proves to be very meagre, I have to spend much time in contriving, and either constructing or getting Ritchie to make, means of illustration. Besides which I have many plain diagrams to draw on cloth. . . .

The "Philadelphia Magazine" republished from "Silliman's" some months ago Le Conte's paper on the sonorous jet, with his speculation about the *cohesion of the gas* in a flame. I think he ought to have published my criticism on the same, of which I sent him a copy, and which you have so recently republished in your last "Journal."

I thank you, my dear Henry, for the interesting address of Professor Owen, which treats a variety of topics with great ability. I confess, however, to some surprise at the readiness with which he adopts Faraday's dreamy notions about gravitation. To me it seems as if many of those who are discussing this question of the conservation of force are plunging into the fog of mysticism. I like Grove's phrase, "correlation of forces," better. Faraday would incline, I believe, to go back behind inertia to find some power in matter to produce it, and yet what is matter but localized inertia? Are we not in danger soon of passing into modes of discussion which will be but a modern phasis of the old mysticism? . . .

BOSTON, November 17, 1858.

. . . Whitcomb[2] tells me that the number of names recorded since yesterday betokens a pretty full at-

---

[1] In 1858–59 Mr. Rogers gave before the Lowell Institute a course of lectures on "Water and Air in their Mechanical, Chemical, and Vital Relations."

[2] Janitor of the Lowell Institute.

394 FIRST YEARS IN BOSTON. [1858.

tendance. . . . I want to study Owen's address with
more care than I have given it. Parts quite astonished, and I must say disappointed me. There is a
good deal of preaching in it, and what seems to me
unsound philosophy. There is nothing new here except that Mr. Everett has agreed to supply to the
" New York Ledger" (circulation over 100,000) an
article every week on some general topic, and has received the consideration $10,000, to be appropriated
to the purchasing of Mt. Vernon.

I have been able to repeat Savart's experiment of
musical jets of water with great success. The tones
are loud and exquisitely smooth and swelling. I have
also prepared for my first lecture a cylinder of oil suspended in alco-water, like the sphere of my former
experiment. The experiment is on a far larger scale
than anything described by Plateau. . . .

BOSTON, November 29, 1858.

. . . I was unable to write by the last steamer, as my
first lecture demanded my thoughts and time. It went
off well, although the extreme inclemency of the night
made the audience less than I could have wished. . . .
In a late number of the " Edinburgh Review " I find a
capital article on the stereoscope, in which Sir David
is properly handled, and Wheatstone's claims are fully
vindicated. I am sure it is from the pen of Carpenter. Besides the physiological views, which are his,
I see he alludes to the photograph of my trilobite, of
which I gave him a copy, pointing out the curious
optical effect of a change from convex to concave relief. . . . I gave Mr. Appleton your message, which
pleased him. He asked most kindly after you. I cannot tell you, my dear brother, how continually I miss
your society. There is no one else in this world with
whom I can exchange thoughts and share the process
of philosophic meditation but with you. . . .

WEDNESDAY MORNING, December 10, 1858.

. . . E. has kept her letter open for a short appendix from me, as my preparations for last night's experimental lecture deprived me of the opportunity of writing yesterday. I am now treating of the mechanical properties of the atmosphere, and have found the preparation of experiments, with the imperfect means at command, very hard work. In spite of a rainy sky, and " Piccolomini " and Bayard Taylor to boot, I had quite a good attendance, and indeed throughout my numbers have kept up, and the class has shown strong interest in the lectures.

I went after the lecture last night to the Academy meeting, held at Judge Shaw's, the first I have attended for a long time. There were some fifty present, and among them Peirce and Agassiz, who also made their first appearance after a long interval. . . .

How my heart leaped up on hearing by Eliza's letter that the Book [1] was finished, the *Magnum Opus* which embodies so much physical toil and so much brain-work. But think, my dear brother, what a reward you have in the memory of generations.

The President's message is of great length, and advocates many measures, such as the acquisition of Cuba, which will startle foreign powers, and excite great opposition at home. He has become a shameless champion of the slave interest.

BOSTON, January 11, 1859.

. . . Lord and Lady Radstock are still here, and likely to remain several weeks. We have seen her frequently, and think her a most charming person. I have not succeeded in meeting him as often as I desired, but we hope to have him to dine with us next week. He is much with the Ticknors, and seems to have been busy in studying the schools and charitable institutions. . . .

[1] Professor Henry Rogers's *Report on the Geological Survey of Pennsylvania.*

You will be pained to hear that Theodore Parker is now prostrated by a bleeding at the lungs, and will, as soon as he is able, go to the south of Europe. His ardour has placed him in this peril. For while quite an invalid he prepared for the Fraternity lectures two elaborate discourses lately, on Washington and John Adams, the last of which he read only a week ago to a great crowd at the Music Hall. They were masterly specimens of discriminating and manly criticism. But the effort has brought on this very serious attack. So great is the interest felt by thousands in his safety that a bulletin is hung up at his door twice every day to inform friends of his condition. I have anxiously read them for two days. They report that he is comfortable, but requires absolute quiet and rest. I have therefore not ventured to ring the bell. My heart is really sad when I think of the possibly permanent injury he has sustained. For the more I have seen of him, the more I have learned to reverence his character and admire his ability and multifarious knowledge.

BOSTON, February 4, 1859.

. . . I think I mentioned in my last that the trustees of Frank Gray have lately conveyed $50,000 to the use of the Agassiz Museum, the interest being devoted to the maintenance and extension of the collection. In addition to this, efforts are now making to secure from the State an appropriation of $100,000 for the erection of a large building to receive the collection, and for salaries for curators in the several departments.

Theodore Parker went to New York yesterday, and will sail in a few days in the British steamer *Karnac* for St. Thomas and other points in the West Indies. He is accompanied by his wife, Miss Stevenson, and Dr. and Mrs. Howe. I saw him about two weeks ago for a few minutes, and found him looking better than I had expected, and evidently quite hopeful of a recovery.

I have never known an instance in which so true a concern and sympathy moved so many hearts. In my interview he spoke most affectionately of you, and he refers to you again in touching language in a little pencil note which he left for me before his departure. I cannot but have a strong hope that his life may be prolonged many years, and that he may be able with the pen, if not with the voice, to resume his place among the noblest of the champions of humanity. There is no one here to fill his place. He expects, after pausing awhile in the West Indies, to go to Europe, and does not count, under the most favourable conditions, on coming home in less than eighteen months. He spoke of the pleasure he should have in meeting with you. I cannot help feeling sad as I think of his danger, and yet he has already done nobly more than a man's work. In less than two weeks I shall go to Virginia where, I am sorry to say, I committed myself to giving two or three lectures.

FROM THEODORE PARKER.

BOSTON, February 1, 1859.

MY DEAR PROFESSOR ROGERS, — I return Mr. Owen's remarkable pamphlet. What an instructive thing it is! I should have been surprised that it could all have come from one man if I had not known yourself and your brother, who in such matters taught me the *nil admirari*. I shall buy it when I get to London. *When I get to London!* I hope it does not sound presumptuous to say so! Yet I know how uncertain my life is.

Allow me to thank you for the instruction I have received from you, and for the many friendly and noble words you have spoken to me. My acquaintance with you began with your brother, and I feel gratitude to you both. For you both turn your deep, wide science into Humanity. I have found you both

always on the side of mankind and felt strengthened
and encouraged by your example.

Please remember me kindly to your wife and brother, and believe me,

Faithfully yours,

THEODORE PARKER.

My wife and Miss Stevenson join in kindly greet-
ings.

APPENDIX.

APPENDIX A. (Page 240.)

REPORT FROM THE COMMITTEE OF SCHOOLS AND COL-
LEGES [OF THE LEGISLATURE OF VIRGINIA] AGAINST
THE EXPEDIENCY OF WITHDRAWING THE FIFTEEN
THOUSAND DOLLARS ANNUITY FROM THE UNIVERSITY
[OF VIRGINIA].

1845.

Doc. No. 41.

(*Prepared by* W. B. ROGERS, *Chairman of the Faculty.*)

THE Committee of Schools and Colleges have considered,
according to order, the expediency of repealing the law
allowing an annuity of fifteen thousand dollars from the
Literary fund to the University of Virginia; and have
come to the following resolution : —

Resolved, That it is inexpedient to repeal the said Law.

The Committee of Schools and Colleges having, as directed
by a resolution of the house of delegates, passed on the 22d
day of December, 1844, carefully investigated the past
history and present condition and influences of the University of Virginia, with the view of forming their opinion
upon the question of " repealing the Act of Assembly grant-
ing an annuity of $15,000 " to that institution, beg leave
to report the following facts and considerations as the result
of their inquiries : —

On reverting to the known intentions of the illustrious founder of the University, and his distinguished colabourers, and of the legislatures by whose enlightened liberality it was set in operation, we recognize as the leading object of its establishment the institution of a higher and more thorough system of intellectual training than had yet been attempted either in our own or any of the sister States, and through this means the introduction of a better intellectual culture in our colleges, academies and elementary schools.

In the period of twenty years, which comprises the as yet brief history of the University, it would be unreasonable to expect more than a very partial attainment of all the salutary objects which inspired the hopes of its founders. The great literary institutions of the Old World, which now exercise so benign an influence on the progress of letters and of general education, have gathered their strength to do good by the slow growth of successive ages; and although in our own time and country more speedy effects are to be anticipated, because wiser and more practical methods of culture are adopted, the extensive diffusion of these good influences through the public mind is necessarily a *gradual*, though a continually progressive operation.

That the University has been successful in establishing within our borders a higher and more thorough system of scientific and literary training than had previously been accessible anywhere in the United States, is, we think, admitted by all who are familiar with its course of studies, and with the influences these have exerted through its well-trained alumni on the methods and aims of academic teaching in many sections of the State. In proof of this, referring in the first place simply to the training of its own students in literature and science, whether professionally or with general objects, we would call attention to the extent and thoroughness of the instruction which it offers, and to the system of intellectual culture it adopts. . . .

SYSTEM OF INTELLECTUAL CULTURE.

On comparing the system of intellectual culture adopted in this institution with that in use in the higher seminaries of learning in other States, we remark two distinctive features which from their influence upon the interests of education, may be deemed worthy of especial note. The *first* is the privilege allowed to students of selecting such studies as have a more immediate reference to the pursuits in which they design afterwards to engage, and the *second*, the practice of combining to an unusual extent, oral instruction in the form of lectures, with the use of text-books.

It should here be added that many years before the establishment of the University, the privilege of an election of studies was allowed at William and Mary. Within her venerable precincts liberal methods of instruction found a home long before they were adopted by the thronged and applauded colleges of New England; and in her halls were delivered by Bishop Madison the first regular courses of lectures on physical science and political economy, ever given in the United States.

Election of Studies. The former of these peculiarities of system originating in a wise regard to the practical wants of society, has been found well adapted to the genius of our country, and at the same time eminently favourable to that thoroughness of knowledge which in a just plan of education is even more important than variety of attainment. In virtue of this system the student preparing for divinity, law or medicine is enabled to secure substantial attainments in ethics, metaphysics and political economy, or in chemistry and general physics; the young engineer, in mathematics, mechanics and geology; and the incipient teacher, in the languages, mathematics, *belles-lettres* and such other portions of knowledge as will accomplish him for his intended pursuits; while in neither case is he

required to spend his resources and his time in the acquire-
ment of branches which are but slightly related to the
objects he has in view.

Nor does the privilege thus granted often lead, on the
part of those who aim at a general education, to a neglect
of the more indispensable branches of study, since custom
has established a particular order of studies to which, with
some modifications, the great majority conform. Besides,
all are aware that, although a separate diploma is conferred
in each department, nothing short of a full and thorough
course in all the academic schools can prepare the student
for the highest honours to which he may aspire.

It is not unworthy of remark that the advantages of such
an election of studies, clearly evinced in the experience of
the University, have been substantially recognized of late
by the adoption at Harvard, and we believe other prominent institutions abroad, of a similar feature, to replace the
Procrustes system hitherto in general use. But we may
be allowed to add that, while engrafting upon their old
established methods this liberal improvement, they have
allowed much latitude of election even to their candidates
for the higher honours, and, thus departing from the stern
requisitions of our University, have held out inducements to
the student to choose his studies rather in accordance with
his fancy or love of ease, than with the claims of a rigorous
mental discipline and a more profound and thorough schol-
arship.

Instruction by Lectures along with Text-Books. Adverting now to the other distinctive feature in the system
of the University, the extensive use of lectures as a means
of training and instruction, we would in the first place call
attention to the fact that distinguished scholars abroad
agree in regarding this mode of teaching as the most
valuable improvement in the plan of university instruction
witnessed in modern times, and that they ascribe to its
inciting influences, both upon teachers and their pupils,

much of that marvellous advancement in letters and science which has made so many of the seats of learning of the Old World the renowned centres of a knowledge no less beneficent than bright.

The advantages of an extensive use of this method in association with text-books, as compared with the old and still very usual practice of exclusive text-book study and recitation, although as yet but imperfectly recognized in many of the colleges in this country, must, we think, become apparent from considering, first, the greater impressiveness of knowledge orally conveyed, and secondly, the more wholesome discipline of the faculties which such a method renders habitual.

Respecting the former of these considerations it may be enough to add that this greater force and permanency of the impressions made upon the mind by the teachings of the lecturer, proceeding from a very simple law of our mental organization, is exemplified by the familiar experience of all, as well in the lessons imparted to infancy by maternal lips as in the oral instructions descending from the forum, the pulpit and the bar. In proof of the prevailing conviction on this subject in Europe as well as at home, reference might be made to the eagerness with which crowds of all classes of society gather around the desk of the distinguished expounder of philosophy, science or taste, and the earnest activity of thought with which they analyze and assimilate the knowledge he imparts. Indeed, so highly is this method of teaching valued at the present day, that, while it has been made a prominent feature in the system of all the most active and successful institutions of learning in the Old World, and has been legitimately applied as a most efficient mean of popular instruction by the learned and wise, it has not unfrequently been spuriously employed to deceive the simple and to tax the purses and the credulity of the uninformed.

In judging of its good influences we should bear in mind

that they show themselves as much in the increased viva-
city, clearness and originality of thought excited in the
teacher as in the quickened apprehension and sharpened
criticism of those whom he instructs, and that thus by a
reactive sympathy of thought the one becomes better qualified to teach, and the other more ready fully to appropriate
the lessons he receives. It is true that, unaided by the
systematic study of well-selected books, mere lectures alone
would prove but an ineffective means of thorough collegiate
instruction. But when united with the daily or occasional
study of a text-book, they conduce, as we think, to a more
wholesome discipline of the faculties than any other collegiate system could.

On comparing this union of the two means of instruction,
that of the lecture-room and the closet, as in use at the
University, with the almost exclusive system of text-book
teaching, which characterizes the method of a large number of our colleges, it will readily appear that from the
very nature of the two methods, they must exert entirely
different influences in the mental training of the pupil.

Experience has amply shown that a large proportion of
the students at academies and higher institutions, where
book lessons are confided in too much, fall into a mechanical routine of unreflecting labour, and, discovering that it
is easier to remember words than to analyze and compare
ideas, cease to apply the higher faculties of thought to the
subject of their studies. And even where this worst of all
the abuses of scholastic training does not follow, we but too
generally find them resting with implicit confidence on the
reasonings, and resorting to the very language, of their
book, without so much as daring to frame for themselves
other arguments or illustrations, or even imagining that
such are to be discovered. Thus habitually leaning upon
the thoughts, and repeating the words of others, accustomed
to be satisfied with whatever stands *in verbis magistri,*
their powers of thought are but imperfectly developed,

and whatever of invention they may have had is enfeebled or paralyzed by disuse. Inured to influences such as these, and scarcely permitted to walk alone, how little is the mind prepared for that vigorous and independent exercise of its powers demanded in the pursuits of life, and how utterly unfit for the hardy achievements of original and inventive genius!

Glancing now at the other, and as we believe far better method of instruction, we discern a different order of effects. Here the pupil accustomed in the lectures of his teacher to hear doubtful questions discussed, and to see new proofs and illustrations given of established truths, catches the enthusiasm of critical or inventive thought, and learns to reason and to demonstrate for himself. Taught by his own efforts rightly to value the systems of philosophy and science, and the productions of taste, which have been wrought out by the master-minds of our race, he acquires a deep reverence for their authority, because it is the authority of truth. But along with this modest deference to the oracles of knowledge, he cherishes that manly self-dependence of thought which springs from the conscious vigour due to the free training of his faculties; and when he quits the halls of his *alma mater*, he carries with him the spirit of an intellectual freeman beneath the bright insignia of his first literary achievement.

HONOURARY DEGREES NOT GRANTED AT THE UNIVERSITY.

While referring to those features in the organization of the University which distinguish it from most of the leading institutions in this country, and which are regarded by its friends as among its highest merits, it is appropriate to state that by an express law its authorities are forbidden to grant honourary degrees, and that accordingly no diploma of compliment has ever yet received its imprimatur. In most other colleges and universities, as is well known, such honours are extended not only to those who have earned some reputation in divinity, medicine or law, or even in the uncongenial pursuits of party politics, but are accorded, as of course, in the case of Master of Arts, after the interval of a few years, to all who have taken their first academical degree. Rejecting a system so little friendly to true literary advancement, the legislators of the University have, we think, wisely made their highest academic honour, that of Master of Arts of the University of Virginia, the genuine test of diligent and successful literary training, and, disdaining such literary almsgiving, have firmly barred the door against the demands of spurious merit and noisy popularity. . . .

ALLEGED EXTRAVAGANT INCOMES OF THE PROFESSORS.

Among the complaints made against the University, we sometimes hear it urged that the incomes of the professors are extravagantly large, and that a regard to republican moderation as well as a cheapening of the expenses of instruction require them to be reduced. In the last four sessions, including the one now in progress, the average income of all the professors has been very nearly as follows : —

In the session of 1841–42	$2,300
of 1842–43	2,250
of 1843–44	2,150
of 1844–45	2,350

It thus appears that the average for the whole period of four sessions may be set down at $2,300 for each professor. That this sum exceeds the income of the professors in a number of our literary institutions, is undoubtedly true. But it is equally certain that it does not surpass, and in many instances falls short of that of the teachers generally in seminaries of distinguished literary rank. Thus the receipts of those professors who are steadily employed in a full course of duty in Cambridge, in Columbia

College New York, at West Point, in the collegiate department of the University of Pennsylvania, of several of those in Princeton, in the University of South Carolina, and several other institutions in the Southern States, are as great and in many instances greater than are received by the professors of our University. And it should be borne in mind that the comparative cheapness of the means of living and of the prevailing habits of society has the effect of bringing the smaller emoluments of the teachers in many of the New England and Western colleges more nearly to an equality with the receipts of those elsewhere who are more liberally paid.

It should also be remarked that in many of our institutions the numerous tutors who share the inferior duties of the professors, and thus greatly lighten their toils, divide the emoluments of the department, and thus very properly reduce the incomes of the principal instructors in a ratio somewhat corresponding to the diminution of their labours. At our University, on the contrary, the tasks of tutor and professor fall upon the same individual; and those who are familiar with the daily routine of instruction, especially in some of its schools, well know the unceasing drudgery it involves. Comparing the emoluments at Cambridge and most other prominent institutions with those at the University, as bestowed upon each leading department or school, it will be found that, for the amount of laborious teaching they perform, the professors at the University are less liberally rewarded than their brethren at any of the institutions in view. In a word, the full circle of instruction in any one school or department is really obtained at much less cost at the University than by their complex system it can be with them.

But we turn to another view of the question, comporting, we think, better with right conceptions of the high interests it involves. The qualifications which fit a professor for the duties of any chair at a distinguished seat of science and

letters are such as are won only by long years of studious
labour, and of abstinence from pleasing relaxations of
society. They are the mingled fruits of genius and perseverance, matured often at the cost of health and generally
by the sacrifice of many a plan of easy self-advancement.
They are the gathered treasures wrought with anxious toil
from amid the deep labyrinths of thought to be sent abroad
with the impress of truth as a precious part of the intellectual currency of the world.

Are qualifications thus rare, difficult of attainment, and
valuable in application, to be estimated as but of little
price? Compared with the easy training which prepares
men for the ordinary vocations of life, they are surely
worthy of at least an equal remuneration. Besides, we
should remember the toil and confinement of the professor,
as well in his closet as in the presence of his class, in forming our estimate of the value of his services. Yet with all
his hard-earned acquirements in science and letters, and
his daily exhausting labours of instruction and discipline,
his emoluments at the University, thus alleged to be extravagant, will scarcely vie with those of the middle class of
lawyers, physicians and merchants in any of the thriving
communities of our country.

The cultivators of letters and science, eminently social
in their activity, and especially so in modern times, naturally seek the incentives and rewards of their efforts in
the wide circle of emulous spirits gathered in the larger
cities. Nor can we expect that small pecuniary inducements will suffice to tempt the really worthy of their number to exchange such congenial scenes for the isolation of a
professor's chair, even though it be one in our honoured
University. Even the more liberal compensation formerly
given has proved, as is well known, insufficient in some
instances to secure the services of distinguished scholars
invited to its halls, and has not prevented the resignation
of many professors who had for a time filled its stations

with undenied success. To stint their emoluments then
would be at once to exclude from its chairs the command-
ing abilities and attainments necessary to accomplish the
high ends for which it was established, to paralyze the
living spirit of its organization, and to degrade this noble
institution into a cumbrous machine for class-book recitations and superficial, though, it might be, plausible, academic routine.

ENDOWMENT OF THE UNIVERSITY AS COMPARED WITH
OTHER INSTITUTIONS OF LIKE RANK.

In claiming from the Commonwealth a continuance of
the pecuniary help heretofore accorded to her, the University only asks, in behalf of the great interests of education,
for that just and reasonable support which is essential to
the discharge of her peculiar functions in the intellectual
training of the youth of the State. If this higher and
more thorough training be really as important to the welfare and honour of the community as the wise and patriotic
of our own and other countries have uniformly maintained,
then Virginia cannot, without grave injury to her interests
and her reputation, dispense with such an institution as her
University. It only remains to be considered at what rate,
compared with other communities, she purchases these
precious advantages. On this point we do not hesitate to
say that, adverting to the great comprehensiveness of the
scheme of actual instruction in the University, and comparing her income with that of other prominent institutions
sustained either by public liberality or private munificence,
her annuity of $15,000 cannot be regarded as more than a
merely moderate endowment.

The most richly endowed universities of this country
cannot be compared in their resources with the long-estab-
lished institutions of Europe. Cambridge and Oxford in
England, and the University of Edinburgh in Scotland, are
possessed of incomes the accumulated growth of ages,

which vie with the revenues of some of the most opulent States of the Union, and which far exceed the aggregate income of all the universities and colleges in our land. Many of the German universities have resources almost equally extensive, and there is probably not one of them of reputation whose means do not exceed that of any university or college in the United States. In most of them the professors and other officers, forming a very numerous corps, receive their salaries directly from the government, and are regarded as a part of the official organization of the State.

Referring to the institutions of our own State, we find William and Mary and Washington colleges each provided with a permanent fund yielding an income, which, considering the scale of operations in the two cases, is as large, if not larger, than that of the University. The University of South Carolina, endowed by the State, and formerly entitled to an annuity of about $12,000, is, we believe, at present receiving the same or a greater sum from the public treasury. Two of the collegiate institutions in Louisiana have been sustained by an annuity of $15,000 each, and the University of Alabama is supported, we believe, by a still ampler contribution; while several of the institutions of the Northwestern States, richly provided for by grants of land, are beginning to receive or are already enjoying valuable and daily augmenting resources. The permanent income of Columbia College, New York, is, we understand, but little, if at all, inferior to that of our University; while the revenue of Harvard, the institution most justly compared with ours, is not much short of $60,000.

With these facts in view, the annuity of $15,000, instead of appearing wastefully large, cannot fail to be regarded as but a very moderate contribution in behalf of the high literary interests devolved upon the University. Indeed, considering the expansive scheme of its instructions, and the substantial literary merits which have given it so distinguished a place among the higher seminaries of our country, this annual provision might justly be viewed as a comparatively meagre endowment, which, though large enough perhaps for the present literary wants of our community, may hereafter be augmented with great benefit to the Commonwealth.

It may perhaps be objected that, as the fixed revenue of Harvard, and some other institutions above mentioned, is derived from the munificence of individual benefactors, and therefore makes no call upon the treasury of the State, it is unfair to adduce the example of these seats of learning in support of the claims of the University. But our argument, of course, supposes that an institution such as the university is demanded by the highest interests as well as the reputation of the Commonwealth, and we have referred to these other distinguished seminaries only for the purpose of showing at what general cost such an institution can be maintained.

At the establishment of the University, the hope was no doubt indulged that sooner or later it also would become an object of private benefaction; but we have not the slightest ground for supposing that in the patriotic aspirations of its founders these private endowments, should they accrue, were ever looked to as a means of withdrawing the University from legislative control, by dispensing with the annual bounty of the State. It would on some accounts certainly be desirable, were our University, like Harvard and several others, sustained entirely or in great part by funds derived from the munificence of individuals. But it should not be forgotten that, while by this means the public would be relieved from the annual contribution now required, the general interests of the community, as affected by the operations of the institution, would be either wholly neglected or but partially secured. The entire government and organization devolving upon self-elective boards of trustees, irresponsible to the State, would of necessity be exposed to the narrowing influences springing from the predilections and prejudices of religious sects and classes of society; and the University, by an easy transition losing the liberal features of a school suited equally to all, would become the property and the spoiled favourite of a particular denomination or rank.

APPENDIX B. (Page 249.)

(Page 249.)

STUDENT RIOTS IN THE UNIVERSITY OF VIRGINIA.

A Circular Letter prepared and issued by W. B. ROGERS, Chairman
of the Faculty.

UNIVERSITY OF VIRGINIA, April 29, 1845.

SIR, — The Faculty of the University of Virginia, complying with the recommendation of the Board of Visitors,
and urged by a sense of duty to the parents and guardians
of the youth committed to their care, beg leave to present a
brief history of the disorders which for some time disturbed
the peace, and if not arrested would have endangered the
safety of the University. They hope thereby to disabuse
the public mind of any false impressions produced by
erroneous statements propagated through the public prints
or otherwise.

The session for the first months was peaceful, and a large
proportion of the students evinced a laudable diligence in
their studies. The few cases of discipline which occurred,
requiring the serious action of the Faculty, were violations
of the law prohibiting the use of intoxicating liquors; and
in these the penalty imposed was indulgently remitted in
consideration of pledges given by the offenders, and a large
number of other students, to abstain from intoxicating
drinks throughout the session.

Early in the winter, a number of students organized
themselves into a company, and, furnishing themselves with
horns and various instruments with which to produce loud
and discordant noises, and wholly or in part disguised,
paraded the lawn and other parts of the precincts, at a late

hour of the night, disturbing the peace and good order of the University.

These parades occurred at irregular intervals of about a fortnight, but, however pernicious in their effects on the discipline and character of the University, were not attended by any outrages on the private dwellings or the public property. And the combination, now ascertained to have comprised a number of otherwise exemplary students, is said to have been informally dissolved before the first occasion of outrage committed. This occasion was the 24th of February, when the suspension of three students for disorderly conduct at one of the hotels was immediately followed by a parade at night of a like band, but more noisy and more numerous, attended by attacks on the dwelling of the Chairman and the hotel referred to, in the course of which a door and windows were broken.

An interval of some three weeks occurred, during which there was no disturbance; but from this time forth, screening themselves from detection by perfect disguise, and combining in larger numbers, with multiplied means of annoyance, one or more bands at short intervals of time disturbed late at night the peace of the University, superadding to other annoyances violence done to private dwellings and public property.

To show the spirit of insubordination and violence which, advancing step by step, at last exhibited itself in nightly riot and outrage, it may be enough to mention some of the more violent acts of the last few weeks.

On one occasion, stones and other small missiles were thrown against the parlour windows of a professor's dwelling while ladies were sitting in the room. On another occasion, persons wearing the usual disguise, and employing for the purpose of annoyance, besides pistol firing, the implements of the organized band of disturbers, galloped through the alleys and arcades of the University on horses, two of which had been obtained by breaking open, at a late hour of the night, the stable of the Proctor. On the Sabbath, the 13th of April, in the open day, and in the immediate vicinity of the University buildings, two persons, of whom one had lately withdrawn from the Institution, and the other was a student, engaged in a horse race, at which their friends attended and betted on the result. It need scarcely be added that the names of the chief offenders having come to the knowledge of the Faculty, the one who was amenable to our laws was immediately dismissed from the Institution. On Monday, and again on Wednesday night, the band of disturbers repeated their acts of insubordination and outrage ; on both occasions, the dwellings of several Professors were attacked, and in the latter case more violently, the windows of two of the houses being broken, and the doors of these and others struck. The nights of Thursday, Friday and Saturday were marked by more unrestrained outrages, in which, in addition to the attacks made on the dwellings of some of the Professors, by striking and breaking windows and door panels, as before, two doors of the Rotunda were forced, some of its windows broken, and the door of a lecture-room burst open.

During Friday and Saturday, the 18th and 19th, efforts were made to engage the body of the students to discountenance these outrages, and by expressing their disapprobation, to aid in arresting them : but these efforts were totally unsuccessful. They were met by indifference on the part of some ; others who had themselves been implicated in the disturbances made by the first band, or had friends implicated, unhesitatingly refused, on this account, to join in any expression of disapprobation, however mild, of the later outrages ; and those who were more or less concerned in these outrages, it was well understood, went so far as to threaten with personal injury any of their fellow-students who should venture to attend a meeting to condemn these acts of violence. Even a simple resolution not to continue the riotous proceedings found no adequate support, and the comparatively small number who were anxious to restore good order were compelled to yield to circumstances which they could not control.

As early as Friday, the 18th, the Faculty sent for the Executive Committee of the Board of Visitors, that they might avail themselves of their counsel. On Saturday it was ascertained that the immediate attendance of the Executive Committee could not be had, and the lectures were suspended for the day, to afford the Faculty an opportunity to deliberate on the measures to be taken. From the steadily increasing violence of the outrages committed; from the utter rejection of all efforts of the well-disposed students to stay the disorders; and from the unconcealed design on the part of the rioters to compel a premature close of the session, by continuing the riots, and by carrying their violence even to greater lengths, the Faculty were satisfied beyond a question that no reasonable hope remained of putting an end, by other means, to the existing disturbances, and therefore determined, after taking the advice of eminent counsel, to place the public property under the protection of the Civil Authority. This course was sustained and approved by the two members of the Executive Committee who reached the University on Monday.

On this day the Justices with a Jury convened at the University to inquire into the riots of which it was the scene, and under their authority the Sheriff of the County placed a guard of armed citizens at the Rotunda during that and the following night. On Monday morning, in anticipation of the meeting of the Justices, and in conformity with an express enactment, notice was given by the Proctor to a number of students who, there was reason to believe, were themselves concerned in the disturbances, or could give information of their authors, that they would be summoned to appear before the court as witnesses.

Whereupon a large body of the students assembled on Monday morning, and adopted resolutions in which they plainly avowed their determination *to evade the Civil Authority or resist it as far as possible.* These resolutions they handed by a committee to the Chairman to lay before the Faculty. Being without signatures, the resolutions were returned, and shortly after the assemblage of students from which they apparently emanated, dispersed without again presenting them; and before the assembling of the Justices, nearly all of these students left the precincts in order to evade the civil process, remaining absent during the time the Justices were in session, although many of them returned at night.

At a later hour on Monday, and when the Justices were hourly expected to convene, an attempt was made by some gentlemen of Charlottesville and the neighbourhood, without any communication with the Faculty, to effect an arrangement by which the interposition of the Civil Authority should be prevented; and with this view a meeting of students, amounting according to the highest estimate to some seventy in number, was held at 10 o'clock, A. M., and another at 4 o'clock, P. M. No resolutions adopted under such circumstances and with the number present, could have afforded any guaranty of the safety of the public property and the peace of the University: much less could they secure the removal from the Institution of those who had so flagrantly violated its laws and the laws of the land. But none were formally communicated to the Justices, and, although induced by the representations made to them to defer their meeting until the afternoon, they found no good reason to believe that their interposition was in any degree less necessary than when it was called for. On the same night, a meeting of students was held and a pledge signed by a considerable number to withdraw from the University. To this course, a part were moved most probably by the conviction to which they were brought that the Civil

Authority would render necessary their removal from the University, and they were glad to make this cover to their retreat. Others, it is believed, acted partly from the persuasion of those who were themselves committed, and partly under a feeling of irritation produced by the disappointment of the hopes they had been led to entertain of preventing the interposition of the Civil Authority. This pledge, inconsiderately made, had the effect of carrying away a number who would otherwise have gladly remained.

The Board of Visitors having assembled on Wednesday, the 23d, continued their session through the following day. After a full inquiry into the history of the riots and previous disturbances, they adopted the subjoined resolutions, intended to mark their entire concurrence in the measures adopted by the Faculty.

"*Resolved*, That it be recommended to the Faculty through their Chairman forthwith to address to the parents and guardians of the students of the University, a circular letter setting forth a brief statement of events connected with the recent disturbances; of the withdrawal of the Civil Authority from the precincts; of the meeting and adjournment of the Visitors, and of the resumption of the lectures and exercises of the Institution.

"*Resolved*, That it be recommended to the Faculty, in case of the recurrence of scenes similar to those which have recently disturbed the peace and good order of the University, to endeavour through their Chairman to concert such measures as may be deemed prudent to secure the prompt and efficient aid of the Civil Authority in preserving the peace and protecting the property of the University."

The action of the Civil Authority in ordering a guard to be stationed at the Rotunda, having been followed by an immediate cessation of the riots, and the disturbers of the peace having left the precincts, the continuance of the guard was no longer deemed necessary by the Justices, and it was accordingly withdrawn after the second night. The lectures were regularly resumed on Friday the 25th, and it is expected that the parents and guardians of such students as have left the University without having participated in the disturbances or other acts of insubordination, and without evading the Civil process, will cause them to return, should it be their wish that they shall do so, at the earliest practicable day.

By order of the Faculty,

WM. B. ROGERS, *Ch'm.*

A PLAN FOR A POLYTECHNIC SCHOOL IN BOSTON.

1846.

A SCHOOL of practical science completely organized should, I conceive, embrace full courses of instruction in all the principles of physical truth having direct relation to the art of constructing machinery, the application of motive power, manufactures, mechanical and chemical, the art of engraving with electrotype and photography, mineral exploration and mining, chemical analysis, engineering, locomotion and agriculture. It would require two departments.

First, one in which by courses of lectures, amply illustrated, a broad and solid foundation should be laid in general physics, including especially the mechanics of solids, liquids and airs, and the laws of heat, electricity, magnetism and light, and in the chemistry of the more important inorganic and organic principles. Without a sufficient groundwork of this kind in general physical laws, it is obvious that the details of applied science would have but little attraction, and being but vaguely apprehended would convey very little valuable instruction. This department would, I think, give employment to two instructors, dividing the various topics between them as might be found convenient, and perhaps at the same time lecturing on some of the applied branches, as portions of the chemical arts, the strength of materials, motive powers, the steam engine, or any of the practical subjects capable of being taught in lectures with the aid of experiments, models and diagrams.

The other, and entirely practical department, would

embrace instruction in chemical manipulation and the analysis of chemical products, ores, metals and other materials used in the arts, as well as of soils and manures. *Second,* — A course of practical, elementary mathematics, and *Third,* — full instruction in drawing and modelling. This branch should also include special courses of teaching in architecture, engineering and the various branches of the arts not treated of in the first department. This second division of the school besides employing two or three tutors, or sub-professors, to give personal instruction in the laboratory, workshop or room for drawing, might yearly invite the aid of eminent practical men to give courses of lectures on the various branches of applied science not otherwise provided for, or it might engage the services of such permanently for the more important subjects after a trial of the practical benefits of their collaboration. A scheme of this kind begun with two professors in the scientific department and two subordinate instructors in the other, under the direction of the former, would, I am certain, prove so signally successful as ultimately to require its expansion into a polytechnic college on the most ample scale, in which, along with all the subjects above referred to, would be embraced full courses in elementary mathematics and instruction, perhaps, in the French and German languages. In a word, I doubt not that such a nucleus-school would, with the growth of this active and knowledge-seeking community, finally expand into a great institution comprehending the whole field of physical science and the arts with the auxiliary branches of the mathematics and modern languages, and would soon overtop the universities of the land in the accuracy and the extent of its teachings in all branches of positive knowledge.

According to my present notions of expediency and usefulness, the two professors in the scientific, or more properly the mixed department, should so frame their general courses of lectures as to make them acceptable

and useful to the public at large, and thus furnish annual
courses on general physics, chemistry and geology, which
might draw all the lovers of knowledge of both sexes to
the halls of the Institute, whether they proposed or not,
continuing their studies in the other and directly practical
branches of the Institution.   This, of course, should be, as
it very well could be, done without any sacrifice of the
exactness of scientific or practical demonstration to mere
popular effect.   We know how successful have been the
courses in the Royal Institute of London, where Brandt,
Faraday and Wheatstone have for years been the chief
instructors of practical science.   The school in Boston, too,
might well adopt the valuable practice of the Royal Institute of having stated lectures for diffusing a knowledge of
important new inventions in the arts, and discourses in
physical science.   By so doing besides the general benefit
of an early communication of valuable truths, often so
important to practical men, there would arise the special
advantage to the Institute itself of a reputation for being
foremost in the appreciation and promulgation of such useful knowledge, and this would give it a strong claim upon
the respect and affection of the public.[1]

The true and only practicable object of a polytechnic
school is, as I conceive, the teaching, not of the minute
details and manipulations of the arts, which can be done
only in the workshop, but the inculcation of those scientific
principles which form the basis and explanation of them,
and along with this a full and methodical review of all
their leading processes and operations in connection with
physical laws.   When thus instructed in applied science,
the mechanician, chemist, manufacturer or engineer clearly
comprehends the agencies of the materials and instruments
with which he works, and is, therefore, saved from the

---

[1] The six paragraphs (and one sentence) next following have already been given on pp. 260–262, but are here introduced in their
proper connection.

disasters of blind experiment, is guided securely because understandingly in a profitable routine, and is directed in the contrivance of new and more efficient combinations. We cannot but believe that, with a proper training in science, the host of unprofitable inventors, living within the last half century, would have contributed innumerable valuable aids to human industry, and advanced the arts to a far higher stage of improvement than they have yet attained. Of this no stronger argument could be asked than a glance at the encumbered cases of the Patent Office in Washington.

Indeed, the unexampled progress, both here and in Europe, of every branch of the arts for the last fifty years is but the result of that general diffusion of a better knowledge of physical laws which has flowed from the researches and teachings of men specially devoted to natural science; bearing in mind too, how few of the almost countless products of ingenuity, even in these times, are of real and permanent value and how immense the number of utterly barren inventions, the laboured contrivances of acute but undirected or misguided mind.

Among practical pursuits there are, perhaps, none whose dependence upon the determination of physical science is more generally recognized than those of the machinist, the engineer and the architect. Yet even in these professions, while all admit that many of the details are but immediate applications of the leading laws of mechanical philosophy, how few have formed a just conception of the variety and extent of science they involve.

In the first place, the materials used in construction must be studied in their more important chemical and mechanical relations. Rules must be applied for computing the strength of beams and columns of timber and metal of various shapes and dimensions, and placed in various attitudes within buildings or machinery, and these cannot be safely used without a knowledge of the experimental data and mechanical principles from which they have been deduced. So likewise in resolving the often recurring problem of the distribution of forces to the several parts of a structure as dependent on the arrangement of the parts and the position of the load, or other pressure, the necessity for scientific principles is immediate and unavoidable. Of the durability of the materials employed in masonry, it is evident that no confident judgment can be formed without a knowledge of their composition and of the chemical action to which they are liable from air, water and thermal changes. The machinist should understand all the principles of equilibrium and of the composition of forces; in other words, the general doctrines of statics and dynamics, those of friction and resisting forces generally, the mode of operation of the various motive powers of which his machines are to be, as it were, conductors, and the methods of computing the relation between the force applied and the useful effect obtained, or in other words the economical value of the combination.

The engineer of roads and canals with ample knowledge in all these particulars should further have a good acquaintance with the mineral and geological character of the region in which he operates, should know when to interpret the appearances on the surface either as an encouragement or warning in directing his locations; should be prepared to judge of the value of the rocky materials he encounters in building an embankment, and should be qualified to form an estimate of the relative advantages of different districts as influenced by the extent and nature of these mineral products.

Instruction in all these and other kindred particulars, essential as it is to the fullest success in the pursuits referred to, involves, it will be seen, no insignificant acquaintance with some of the leading branches of mechanical and even geological and chemical science.

If we turn now to the manufacturing arts, we shall find

an equal and, in many cases, even more urgent demand for scientific guidance.[1] Beginning with those connected with metallurgy, we see in the various processes by which iron, copper, lead, zinc, silver and other metals are obtained from their ores the most direct application of chemical and mechanical science. The form and materials of the furnace, the character of the fuel and flame, the preparatory processes of roasting, or washing, the due modification of the procedures according to the nature and proportion of the foreign substances present, with numerous other practical details in the various stages of the operation, are only intelligible through the medium of scientific principles, and are most likely to be successfully pursued, or improved, when these principles are clearly understood and habitually recurred to. So also in the fabrication of steel and the mixed metals, such as brass, bronze and tinned iron, and in casting, rolling, wire drawing and other mechanical and chemical processes of the same kind, the truths of science have many important applications, and are capable of affording suggestions of high utility. In gilding, plating and the processes of electrotype, in engraving in all its branches, including lithography, zincography and the various departments of photographic art, we see the most varied agencies of physical laws, involving the mechanical properties of materials, their relations to solvents, and the powers of heat and light. In the fabrication of pottery and porcelain in all the varieties, and in the colouring and painting of both these classes of products, every step is but an application of some well-known scientific principle.

Of the refining of sugar and the manufacturing of alum, copperas, white lead, bleaching salts, the acids, and a hundred other important chemical products, it is needless to say more than that the processes they involve are but the vast practical enlargement of the common experiments

---

[1] See p. 262. The letter there begun is here continued.

of the laboratory and lecture-room. The production of illuminating gas from coal, fats or rosin, and the processes for its purification, the manufacture of stearine, wood vinegar, and all the whole variety of soaps, the purification of oils, the making of cements and varnishes, the arts of tanning, bleaching, dyeing and calico printing, with a hundred others extensively practised at the present day, are either the direct results of modern scientific research, or are largely indebted to it for those experiments in mechanical and chemical details which have bestowed on many of them a more than hundred-fold productiveness. So clearly indeed has the importance of a scientific guidance been proved in some of these arts, that we now in many cases see them claiming the superintendence of skilful chemists to direct their daily operations, and I need not add that the fruits of this happy union of science and art are nowhere better exemplified than in the dyeing and printing works for which Lowell has been so celebrated.

In the various forms of mechanism devoted to spinning and weaving in all their branches, in mill work of almost endless variety, in the steam engine, as applied to stationary or locomotive uses, in water wheels, turbines, propellers and the innumerable forms of hydraulic and hydro-pneumatic machinery, we have almost numberless applications of the laws of mechanics, which those only who clearly understand can guide or improve to the best advantage.

In the business of mining in all departments, including that of exploration on the surface and by borings, every important step calls for the suggestions of geology, chemistry and mechanical science.

To close this long but still incomplete catalogue of illustrations, we may safely affirm that there is no branch of practical industry, whether in the arts of construction, manufactures or agriculture, which is not capable of being better practised, and even of being improved in its processes, through the knowledge of its connections with physical truths and laws, and therefore we would add that there is no class of operatives to whom the teaching of science may not become of direct and substantial utility and material usefulness. It would, I think, be especially adapted to fulfil another, and in some respects a higher purpose by leading the thoughts of the practical student into those wide and elevated regions of reflection to which the study of Nature's laws never fails to conduct the mind. Thus linking the daily details of his profession with the grander physical agencies around him, and with much of what is agreeable and ennobling in the contemplation of external things, it would insensibly elevate and refine his character and contribute to the cheerfulness as it aided the efficiency of his labours. In this respect it is, I think, demonstrated that physical studies are better capable of being useful to the operative classes than the study of literature or morals, because their truths are more readily and eagerly seized upon by such minds and form the strong staple of practical usefulness thus firmly infixed. It is easy to extend the golden chain of relations until these may embrace every realm of nature and of thought.

A polytechnic school, therefore, duly organized, has in view an object of the utmost practical value, and one which in such a community as that of Boston could not fail of being realized in the amplest degree.